An Exhibition of Malice

Emily L. Finch

This is a work of fiction. However, in order to set it in the mid-Victorian period, efforts were made to include historical figures, events and places where possible. As such, the characters of Inspector Whicher, Angela Burdett-Coutts, Mrs. Brown, Dr. Skey, and Mr. Crabb-Robinson, though their roles within the story, including any dialog, while entirely fictional, are based on their real life counterparts. Several other historical figures are referenced without appearing in the story. All other names and characters are products of the author's imagination. Any resemblance to actual persons, living or dead, is purely coincidental.

Copyright © 2024 Emily L. Finch

All rights reserved.

No part of this book may be reproduced or used in any manner without written permission of the copyright owner except for the use of quotations in a book review.

First paperback edition September 2024

Book cover design by Bespoke Book Covers

ISBN: 978-1-7377372-4-7

www.emilylfinch.com

ONE

London. April 1862.

    Samantha Kingston was beginning to think no part of London was safe for her. As she ran past marble pillars and priceless oil paintings, she threw a glance over her shoulder. The corridor was empty, but she could just make out a shadow at the far end, growing larger as the sound of footsteps grew louder.

    Samantha turned left and was dismayed to find that she'd come to a dead end. There was a door to her left and two to her right, but across from her was only a narrow hall table supporting a blue porcelain vase overflowing with flowers. She tried the handle of the door on the left and found it locked. The footsteps drew nearer and her panic increased as she ran to the first of the doors on the right. To her relief, the knob turned easily, and the door swung inward. She slipped through it, closing it softly behind her.

    The room within was unoccupied. A trio of tall, narrow windows on the wall opposite her let in a scant amount of moonlight, casting most of the room in shadow, but she could make out a desk, a globe, and a couple of chairs. A study, then. She felt a brief qualm at entering so personal a space without her host's permission, but that was quickly forgotten when, putting an ear to a crack in the doorframe, she heard the footsteps louder than ever. Straightening, she ran to the desk, but one glance at the space beneath told her she would never fit, not in her flounced evening gown with   flowers in her hair. In a moment of desperation, she yanked at the heavy, tapestry-like curtains that bordered the windows behind the desk and flung them around herself, backing into the wall and tilting her crinoline to a flatter angle just as the doorknob jiggled.

Samantha held her breath. She heard the door swing open, then a click as it shut, followed by another, deeper click and she realized, with horror, that she was locked inside with her pursuer. The footsteps crossed the room and stopped just behind the desk. She knew a moment of fear as she anticipated the curtains being thrown back, and she tensed.

The curtains remained untouched. Instead, she could hear shuffling paper and the opening and closing of drawers. Releasing a barely audible breath, Samantha reconsidered the last ten minutes.

She and her friend Madge—Lady Bradwell—were attending a concert at the home of a Mr. Ponsonby. Samantha had been surprised when Madge accepted the invitation on their behalf, as Mr. Ponsonby was a wealthy manufacturer, not a member of the peerage or even the gentry. After the aversion Madge had displayed that winter to Sir Rupert, who possessed a similar background, even before he was revealed to be a traitor to the crown, Samantha thought it odd that she would willingly subject herself to similar company.

She had done it for Samantha's sake, it seemed. Madge explained that she wanted to give Samantha the chance to ease her way back into Society. This would be her first Season since coming into her inheritance. It would also be the first time many in Society would see her since her aunt and uncle were murdered by her childhood friend who was then murdered himself. Madge felt that an event hosted by a man on the fringes of Society would be a perfect opportunity to go out and be seen without the pressure of meeting every notable in town.

It had been a good plan. However, as they had attended several supper parties, a card party and two plays since arriving in London a little over a week ago, Samantha had already attracted half a dozen would-be suitors. Somehow, they had all learned she would be at the concert this evening and were all in attendance.

Ten minutes ago, during an intermission in the program, she had seen Mr. Mason, by far the most persistent of the would-be suitors, headed her way. He seemed to take it for granted that she would see his admittedly handsome face as fair compensation for the loss of autonomy she would experience were she to acquiesce to his dreams of giving him her fortune in marriage. Hoping to avoid another tedious conversation, Samantha had slipped out one of the back doors and found herself in a deserted corridor. When she heard footsteps behind her, she thought Mr. Mason had followed her. Afraid that he might have come to steal a kiss or attempt to compromise her and force the issue, she had panicked and run. Now it seemed her assumption was wrong.

Her next thought as to who might be in the study with her was her host for the evening, Mr. Ponsonby. It did seem odd that he should have chosen the middle of a concert to attend to matters of business, but it was his study. Yet, as the minutes dragged on, she began to suspect she was wrong again. The shuffling of papers had not given way to the scratching of a quill. Rather, it sounded as though every drawer in the desk had been opened and shut, as if the person were looking for something.

Samantha's leg had begun to cramp. She tried to ignore it, but she could tell that, if she did not stretch it, the cramp would soon become unbearable. Careful to move as little as possible, she shifted her weight to her left leg and wiggled her right. She would have sworn the sound of her skirts brushing against the curtains was imperceptible and yet, suddenly, the movement at the desk ceased. Samantha froze.

A moment later, the curtains were flung back. She had just enough time to register by the dim light of the single gas lamp when the man stepped forward that he was too broad-shouldered to be the lanky Mr. Ponsonby. Flinging her hand out reflexively, she felt her palm connect with his nose. The man stumbled back, and she took the opportunity to dart past him towards the door.

"Samantha, wait!"

There was only one man who called her by her Christian name. Samantha let out a sigh of relief as she stopped and turned back. It had been almost four months since she'd seen him last but, even with shadows obscuring part of his face and his hand covering his nose, she could see that it was, unmistakably, Wyatt.

Samantha had met V.T. Wyatt, hobbyist private investigator and younger son of a viscount, while she was hiding on the streets of London, a suspect in the murders of her aunt and uncle. Not knowing who she was, he had hired her to work as an informant in a robbery he was investigating. She soon realized that the men involved in the robbery were the same ones she believed responsible for the murders of her aunt and uncle. Though she hadn't immediately trusted Wyatt with this information, it hadn't been long before they were working together to discover the truth.

The truth was, to Samantha's shock and horror, that the murderer had been Charles, her uncle's son by his first marriage and her only childhood friend. After Charles was shot to death in front of her on the way to his trial, Samantha had retreated to the country with Wyatt's cousin, Madge, while Wyatt remained in London to deal with the fallout. They hadn't seen each other for three months after that—hadn't even written to each other—yet when he arrived at Madge's estate that December, it felt as though no time had passed.

Though Samantha had felt herself drawn to Wyatt, she had no

idea how he felt until the night of the Winter Ball when, finding themselves alone in the library, they had given in to the impulse of the moment and kissed. Looking back, Samantha couldn't be sure if she or Wyatt had moved first, but it hardly mattered. Neither of them had stopped it. At least, not until Wyatt proposed and everything fell apart.

Even now, the memory of that blissful, passionate kiss was overshadowed by the conversation that had followed. She'd spoken harshly, overwhelmed with self-recrimination for damaging one of the few reliable friendships in her life and with frustration with him for not understanding her fears about marriage. Then, when they finally took the time to talk through their differences, he revealed that he had lied to her—had hidden the truth about the investigation into Charles' death. Though he'd done it to protect her, both the fact that he considered that a justifiable reason to lie and the reason he thought she needed protecting—that he thought she couldn't handle the truth—only served to validate her response to his proposal.

He had apologized and he said he would never lie to her again, no matter the reason, but the trust between them had been damaged. They both knew it. But Wyatt had persisted. He'd asked for the chance to prove she could trust him—that a marriage between them was possible—and she, clinging to a hope that felt as fragile as the trust he'd broken, had granted it.

Then, before she could learn how he intended to earn her trust, the world had come crashing down around them. Annie, a girl who had helped Samantha when she was alone on the streets, had turned up at Madge's London home brutally beaten. She had brought with her the ominous news that Skinny Jim, the notorious criminal who ran much of the city's underworld and whom Samantha had the misfortune to meet and work for while in disguise during her time on the streets, had figured out her real identity.

In a strange mirror of the events of last summer, Samantha had retreated to the country with Madge (and Annie) while Wyatt stayed in the city to see if he could learn what Skinny Jim's plans were. This time, however, Wyatt wrote to Samantha. The letters had been shorter than she would have liked and less frequent, too, but they had been something. Still, it had been four months since they had seen each other last. Four months since he'd essentially asked for the chance to win her over and then all but disappeared from her life. She didn't know how to react to seeing him now, unexpectedly alone.

"What are you doing here?" Wyatt asked, his voice slightly muffled behind his hand.

"I could ask you the same," Samantha said, barely keeping the irritation from her voice. After four months apart, that was how he chose to greet her?

He seemed to realize how his words had sounded.

"That's fair," he said apologetically. Then he winced. "I think you broke my nose."

"I didn't hit you that hard."

Wyatt pulled his hand away, and Samantha gasped when she saw blood staining it.

"I think you underestimate yourself," he said with a wry smile. "Though it is a comfort to know you can defend yourself when called upon."

"I had no intention—" Samantha began, stepping forward and reaching out towards him. When he caught her eye, she dropped her hand. "*Is* it broken?"

"No," he assured her, reaching into his evening jacket and pulling out a handkerchief "At least, I don't think so." He grinned as he held the handkerchief to his nose, tilting his head back.

"I didn't know you were at the concert," she said. "I didn't even know you were in town."

"I came late," he said, speaking to the ceiling. "I sat in the back.

And I just arrived in the city yesterday. I was planning to come by Grosvenor Square tomorrow after the boat race."

"Why not today?" Samantha asked. She hated the vulnerability in her voice, but she needed to know.

Wyatt glanced down at her. "Trust me when I say I wanted to come straight away, but unfortunately, I had business in the morning, and I knew you and Madge were receiving callers this afternoon. I didn't want our first meeting in months to be so public."

Samantha felt her spirits lift, and she smiled. "Well, it's certainly not public."

Wyatt chuckled. Then he removed the handkerchief, twitching his nose a few times before wadding up the cloth and shoving it in his pocket. He met her gaze, his eyes searching hers. They were standing so close now that she could see every fleck of gold in the deep brown of his irises reflected in the lamplight. Her breath hitched as he reached up to tuck a stray curl behind her ear, his fingers brushing her skin.

"I've missed you," he murmured, his gaze traveling over her face.

"I've missed you, too," Samantha said.

Perhaps it wasn't wise to admit it with her feelings for him so unsettled, but it was true. She had missed him. Wyatt's lips curved into a smile, and he took a step closer, narrowing the gap between them. Samantha felt a thrill of anticipation, but the logical part of her mind rose up to remind her there was a reason she had turned down his proposal, even if she couldn't quite recall it in that moment.

"You didn't answer my question," she said in a faint, breathy voice quite unlike her own.

"Didn't I?"

Wyatt's voice was deeper than usual as his fingers trailed down her arm. Samantha closed her eyes and drew in a deep breath, refocusing on her surroundings.

"What are you doing in here?" she asked, her voice back to normal as she opened her eyes.

He froze and seemed to pull himself together with an effort, looking around them as though just remembering where they were. His fingers left her arm, and he dragged a hand over his face.

"Right, yes. I'm supposed to be looking for something." He shot her a disarming grin. "If you hadn't distracted me by nearly breaking my nose, I might have found it by now."

"What are you looking for?"

"A blueprint." He turned slowly, running his fingers through his hair as he surveyed the room. "I couldn't begin to tell you what it's for. Some piece of machinery. But I know the name that should be on it—Leclerc."

"Why do you think it's here?" she asked, also surveying the room.

"I don't have time to explain it all now," Wyatt said, "though I will later, if you like. Suffice it to say, Mr. Ponsonby stole it."

Samantha nodded, having anticipated something of the sort. After all, Wyatt had snuck into the man's study. But he was right, they had been in this room for too long as it was. The second half of the concert would be starting soon, if it hadn't already.

"How big is it?" she asked.

"I'm not sure, but it's likely to be hidden, possibly folded up. It's not in the desk. I even found a hidden compartment, but it was empty."

"You take the bookcase on that side," Samantha said, pointing behind him. "I'll take the other side."

Moving swiftly and silently, they searched the shelves, lifting out books, leafing through them, and replacing them. On the bottom shelf of the second bookcase, Samantha tried to pull out a thin blue volume, but it wouldn't budge. Moving her fingers down the spine, she wiggled the book and found that it shifted back, into the wall. She pushed, and a soft thunk came from below. She looked down to see that a panel that had seemed merely decorative had popped open, revealing a small recess.

"Brilliant," Wyatt said from behind her.

She turned to him with a triumphant grin, and he smiled back. They bent down, and Wyatt reached inside, lifting out a long roll of paper.

"Is that it?" she asked as he unrolled it, revealing a faded blueprint for some type of mechanical device.

"No," he said slowly, "and that's odd."

Samantha peered into the recess and saw half a dozen similar rolls of paper. She pulled out a second one and had started to unroll it when she heard footsteps coming down the corridor. Her gaze shot to the door, and she heard Wyatt curse under his breath.

"Quick!" he hissed.

He jumped to his feet, snapping the panel shut as he did so and reached out a hand. Samantha took it and he pulled her up. Together, they ran to the windows, Wyatt turning down the gas lamp as he passed it. Standing with their backs to the moonlit exterior, they pulled the curtains shut around them.

As Samantha pressed herself against the cool glass, panting, she heard the jiggle of the doorknob. Her heartbeat quickened and she fought to quiet her breathing. A strong hand enveloped hers and she turned her head to see Wyatt. He gave her a reassuring nod and squeezed her hand. She nodded back, her stomach twisting in knots.

The door opened, and Mr. Ponsonby's voice, thin and reedy, became audible.

"...didn't remember locking it," he was saying. "My apologies."

"Unnecessary, I assure you," another, deeper voice replied.

Wyatt's eyebrows rose and he mouthed, "My brother."

Samantha felt a little of her apprehension leave her. From everything Wyatt had told her, his brother was deeply concerned with the honor of the family name. If she and Wyatt were discovered now, they could at least count on his brother to cover it up.

"After all the fuss you've made," Wyatt's brother continued, "a locked door is the least inconvenience."

"It was never my intention to be an inconvenience," Mr. Ponsonby said, and Samantha could not tell if he was sincere or not. "If you'll give me a moment. I have it on the desk here."

He shuffled some papers around, and Samantha held her breath, squeezing her eyes shut and gripping Wyatt's hand in an effort to stay perfectly still.

"There you are," Mr. Ponsonby said. "Let me know if you need anything else, and I'll be more than happy to provide it."

"With sufficient incentive?" Wyatt's brother asked with a heavy note of sarcasm. "You won't find me so accommodating in future, I assure you. This exhibition is a serious endeavor, not a tool for your political advancement."

He had to be referring to the International Exhibition. A continuation of the Great Exhibition of the previous decade, it had been a pet project of Prince Albert's before his death that winter. It was set to begin in a few weeks and was one of the main topics of conversation at every gathering. Though, in what way Mr. Ponsonby might be using it for his advancement or why Wyatt's brother was involved was a mystery.

"I understand."

He didn't sound cowed. If anything, Mr. Ponsonby sounded amused.

"We're done here," said Wyatt's brother.

She heard him stride away towards the door. After a moment, Mr. Ponsonby followed. The sound of footsteps receded as the two gentlemen made their way out to the corridor.

"Well, I hope you—"

The rest of Mr. Ponsonby's sentence was cut off as the door

closed behind them.

Samantha let out a long breath. "That was close."

"Too close," Wyatt said, shaking his head.

"What was that about?"

"I have no idea."

"Will you ask your brother?"

"I suppose I'll have to."

At his shuttered expression, Samantha hesitated before asking, "Do you think he knows about the theft?"

Wyatt released her hand to pull back the curtains.

"No," he said. "If he did, he wouldn't be here. Tom is rigidly upstanding. He wouldn't taint himself by association with a thief."

As they returned to the bookcase, Samantha unrolled the blueprint she had been examining before they were interrupted.

"This one says the inventor was Harold Miller," she said, tilting the paper so Wyatt could see the detailed drawing of the inner workings of a machine with wheels and levers. "Did Mr. Ponsonby steal all of these?"

"I don't know," Wyatt said. He pressed the blue book and the lower panel popped open once more. "Leclerc is the one who asked for my help. He didn't mention any others."

They unrolled three more blueprints before they found the one Wyatt had been seeking. The name Victor Leclerc was printed in small letters in the bottom right corner.

"Should we put the rest back?" Samantha asked, looking at the small pile of scrolls between them with uncertainty.

"I can't know that he stole them," Wyatt said. "It's likely, with them all hidden here together, but he may well have purchased one or more of them."

It seemed wrong to replace the probably stolen documents in their secret hideaway, but Samantha conceded that Wyatt was right. After all, he only had Mr. Leclerc's word that his own blueprint had been stolen, and while Samantha wanted to ask his reasons for trusting the man, there wasn't time. The concert would have resumed by now and Madge would be wondering where she was.

When all the blueprints had been safely hidden away and the panel shut, Wyatt went to check that the corridor was empty, and Samantha pulled the curtains shut again, leaving them as Mr. Ponsonby had last seen them.

"It's clear," Wyatt whispered, gesturing for her to join him. They exited the room, and he closed the door softly behind him. Then he turned to her. "Go back by way of the retiring room. If anyone has remarked your absence, it will seem as though you've been there the whole time. I'm going to hand this to my man. He's waiting outside."

"Will you return to the concert?" Samantha asked.

"Would you like me to?"

His tone was casual, but she sensed that the question was anything but. He searched her face, and she met his gaze, noting the vulnerability behind his deep brown eyes that she suspected was reflected in her own.

"Yes," she said.

A smile lit his face. "Then I will."

The pianist was partway through *La Marche des Scythes* when Samantha entered the back of the drawing room a few minutes later. Five rows of chairs with a center aisle faced away from her towards the piano. The music was so loud that no one noted her arrival, and she was able to slip into her seat beside Madge near the end of the third row.

"Are you alright?" Madge asked, leaning over to speak into Samantha's ear.

Samantha nodded. When Madge narrowed her eyes, unconvinced, Samantha mouthed the word, "Later", and Madge nodded, sitting back in her seat. The pianist continued to assault their ears. Royer may have been a talented composer, Samantha thought, but his works were perhaps better suited for a larger concert hall than this small drawing room.

Looking down the row, Samantha spotted Wyatt's brother, Lord Boxley. As it was every time she saw him, his clothing was immaculate, perfectly tailored and cleanly pressed. His hair, which was darker than Wyatt's, was slicked down with not a strand out of place, and his mustache was precisely shaped with the ends at a slight curl. He held himself with a rigidity not often seen in his brother, yet it was still clear at a glance that they were related.

He was sitting with some of the single gentlemen, having apparently come alone. That wasn't unusual. She knew he had been married a few years past, but since his wife died less than a year after they were married, he had shown no interest in securing another Lady Boxley. Samantha wondered if Wyatt knew why that was. It seemed strange, considering that the late Lady Boxley had not left her husband with any heirs. With all that Wyatt's brother seemed to care for the honor and legacy of the family, he did not seem to be doing his part to maintain it. Had he loved his wife so much that he couldn't bear to be with another woman? She wouldn't have thought him the passionate type from the little she'd seen of him, but one never knew.

It was ten minutes before Wyatt appeared. Samantha was careful not to turn her head after she spotted him out of the corner of her eye. Having decided for whatever reason to play the pieces out of their original order, the pianist was in the middle of *Le Vertigo*. It was unfortunate that Wyatt moved to take his seat during one of its pauses, causing several heads to swing round to look at him. Though she kept her face firmly forward, Samantha could still see some of those around her throwing glances her way as they turned back around. She pretended not to notice as they whispered behind their hands.

When the concert was over, some people stayed in their seats, turning to talk to their neighbors, while the rest of the crowd slowly filtered down the rows towards the back of the room. Samantha tried to spot Wyatt without seeming to do so, but her efforts were hampered by Mr. Ponsonby, who appeared suddenly in front of her. His thick grey hair had been carefully styled with pomade so that not even a curl of his side whiskers was out of place. He was of average height, but his lanky form made him seem taller, even as he bowed over Madge's hand.

"Lady Bradwell," he said. "It was such an honor to have you here this evening."

"Yes, well," Madge said, extracting her hand from his, "I do enjoy music. Your selection was certainly invigorating."

"Might I perhaps have the honor of your presence repeated then, my lady? And that of your charming friend, Miss Kingston?"

He twisted slightly to give Samantha a half-bow.

"Oh, I never commit to anything this early in the Season, Mr. Ponsonby," Madge said, "but one never knows."

Their host seemed content with this non-answer. He bowed and left them to speak with Wyatt's brother, one of the only other persons of rank in the room. To Samantha's disappointment, Mr. Ponsonby's place was filled almost immediately by Mr. Mason and another would-be suitor, Mr. Ramsey. Both men were in their early thirties with dark hair. Mr. Mason might have been the better looking of the two if not for the over-eager, almost desperately happy expression he seemed to adopt whenever Samantha was around. Mr. Ramsey had a mustache that connected to his side whiskers in a way she did not quite like, but his confident air and good sense of humor almost distracted her from it.

"Did you enjoy the concert, Miss Kingston?" Mr. Mason asked, fixing his attention on Samantha to the exclusion Madge.

"The pianist was very talented," Samantha said diplomatically.

"Indeed," said Mr. Mason. "Most talented."

"Have your ears recovered yet?" Mr. Ramsey asked.

"Mine haven't," Madge muttered, and Samantha laughed.

"Do you like...Roy...er..." Mr. Mason squinted as he searched his memory for the composer's name.

"Almost there," Mr. Ramsey said with a sardonic half-smile, "but I believe it's pronounced Roy-ay."

"I prefer Beethoven," Samantha said as Mr. Mason blinked in confusion. "Though I suppose, as Royer composed mostly for the harpsichord, it is perhaps not fair to judge his works by how they sound on the piano."

Madge, who had stopped paying attention to the exchange, suddenly reached out an arm and snagged Wyatt as he was passing.

"There you are, my dear," she said, drawing him into their circle so that he was standing between her and Samantha. "How dare you arrive in town without telling me. How long have you been here?"

"Not long," he assured her. "I was planning to stop by tomorrow after the race to pay my respects." He turned to address the rest of the group. "Good evening, Miss Kingston, Mr. Ramsey, Mr. Mason."

"No point in coming tomorrow," Madge said, ignoring everyone else's attempts to respond to Wyatt. "And you ought to have known that. Bradwell will either be out celebrating or drowning his sorrows all afternoon, and he'd been devastated to miss your call."

As much as Madge's husband liked Wyatt, Samantha doubted he had any strong feelings one way or the other about seeing him. She guessed that Madge was making a point to remind people of Wyatt's ties to the whole household so that it would seem less singular when he came to visit.

Unfortunately, though Samantha and Wyatt had been able to hide the truth of her time on the streets from the public in general and Society in particular, doing so had necessitated the creation of the lie that she had spent the summer living under Wyatt's roof. Madge had joined in the deception by pretending to have been chaperoning them all along, but it was still quite scandalous for a single young lady to live in the home of a single gentleman, even if it was ostensibly for her protection and done under proper chaperonage. For the sake of Samantha's reputation, it was imperative, therefore, that they quash the growing rumors that their relationship had been anything other than perfectly respectable in that time.

"Well, I would hate to disappoint Bradwell," Wyatt said, and Samantha caught a hint of laughter in his eyes, though his tone was serious.

"You can come by the next day," Madge said. "I'll be certain we aren't out. Unless, Samantha, dear, do you have any plans the day after tomorrow?"

"As it happens, I do," Samantha said. "I was planning to visit Miss Coutts with Lady Stuart-Lane."

"How foolish of me to have forgotten," Madge said. "Still, I suppose you can see Wyatt some other time."

"Yes, though I'm sorry I'll miss you," Samantha said, dipping her head to acknowledge Wyatt.

Before Wyatt could respond in kind, Mr. Mason interrupted.

"Will you be at the Carrolton's card party on Saturday?" he asked.

"We will," Madge answered for Samantha. "And you may continue to impress Miss Kingston with your conversational skills then. For now, Lord Bradwell is expecting us home. Good evening to you all."

"I'll escort you to your carriage," Wyatt said.

Samantha suppressed a smile at Mr. Mason's look of affront as Madge steered her away. Mr. Ramsey merely looked thoughtful.

"A little heavy-handed, I think," Wyatt said in a low voice as he walked behind them.

"Nonsense," Madge said. "If anything, I undersold it. One should never overestimate the intelligence of these young men about town. Especially ones so foolish as to have wasted whatever meager inheritance they had to begin with."

"Fortune hunters?" Samantha pretended shock. "You mean they aren't dangling after me for my charm and vivacity?"

"She did say they were fools," Wyatt said in a tone that made Samantha's stomach swoop.

"Did you talk to your brother?" she asked to distract herself.

"I didn't get the chance," Wyatt said. "Ponsonby tried to draw him into discussion, and he couldn't escape fast enough. I'll try to catch him at the club in a day or two. I don't want to put his guard up, which it definitely would be if I made a point to seek him out."

"What's this about?" Madge asked as a servant handed over her wrap.

Wyatt and Samantha exchanged glances, and Madge frowned.

"Is it Skinny Jim?" she asked. "You had better not be hiding something from me. He sent that poor girl to my house, so I'm involved whether you like it or not."

"It isn't Skinny Jim," Samantha said. "It's just something Wyatt's been asked to investigate. I was helping him with it."

"Is that where you were during the intermission?" Madge raised her eyebrows, then lowered them as she narrowed her eyes. "You two should be more careful. I'm sure I wasn't the only one who noticed your absence—and if anyone saw that Wyatt was missing, too... Are you trying to undo all the work we've done to preserve your reputation?"

"Of course not," Samantha said. "It was pure coincidence."

"Hmm." Madge sounded unconvinced. "Do let me know of any other coincidences that occur, so I can prepare for the consequences."

Samantha shot Wyatt an exasperated look, but he just grinned and shrugged his shoulders.

"Thank you for your help," she muttered.

"Anytime," he said.

TWO

There was something soothing about the process of shaving that had always appealed to Wyatt. The soft schick of the razor against his skin, the plop of shaving cream dropping into the cloudy water, and the ting of metal on porcelain as he tapped the razor against the side of the bowl created a perfect accompaniment to thought. The morning after his raid on Lucas Ponsonby's study, he had much to think about.

He hadn't been eager to take on the task when George approached him for help. George Canard was a reporter for *The London Inquirer* and, though Wyatt considered him a friend, he didn't entirely trust him.

"There's almost no risk to you," George had said when he showed up at Wyatt's home the day he arrived back in London. "Ponsonby is hosting a concert at his house, so you wouldn't even have to break in."

"I don't even know this Mr. Leclerc," Wyatt had said. "What made you think I'd do it? Especially since, last we spoke, you insisted that I owed you an explanation about Miss Kingston's past before you'd help me again. Wouldn't this rather put *you* back in *my* debt?"

George had snorted at this. "Not hardly. The secrets you're

hiding about Miss Kingston are worth infinitely more than a simple job like this. As for why you'll do it, is justice not a good enough reason?"

He had proceeded to explain how his friend Victor Leclerc, a struggling inventor, had tried to sell an idea for a machine part to several manufacturers, including Mr. Ponsonby. Ponsonby had appeared interested, even offering to fund his patent, and asked to borrow Leclerc's blueprint to show his engineers. Later, he'd told Leclerc he had decided not to buy the invention, but when Leclerc asked for the blueprint back, Ponsonby claimed he had already returned it. Then he'd begun production on a part exactly like the one Leclerc had invented.

"He's completely shameless," George had said. "He said he had witnesses, all his own people, of course, who would swear he was telling the truth about returning the blueprint."

"Why can't you help?" Wyatt asked. "Threaten to drag Ponsonby's name through the mud in that paper of yours if he doesn't give the blueprint back."

"Much as I would love to do that, my editor wouldn't let me. Ponsonby's got the resources to sue the paper for libel and, without proof, he'd win."

In the end, Wyatt had agreed to look for the blueprint. It was a relatively low risk for him, after all, and it would be good to have George owe him something. Besides, if the story was true and he was successful, he would be glad to right a wrong.

As he had half expected to find nothing, it was an unpleasant shock to discover not only Mr. Leclerc's blueprint, but several others as well. He wondered if they had all been stolen and, if so, what he ought to do about it.

The door opened, and Wyatt's valet entered. Through the small mirror that hung above the wash basin, Wyatt could see the man drop a sheaf of papers onto the bed before moving to the wardrobe.

"Morning, Durand. How did they turn out?" Wyatt asked, dragging the razor down his jawline.

"You'll have to let me know," Durand said over his shoulder. "You didn't give me much, but I did my best."

"I only saw them for a minute. I'm lucky I remembered as much as I did."

"Do you want me to track down the names you gave me?"

Wyatt tapped his razor against the edge of the basin, then rinsed it and set it aside. He grabbed the clean towel Durand had set out earlier and dried his face before answering.

"That might be a good idea," he said. "Harold Miller could be difficult. There are bound to be dozens of those. But Franz Leipzig should be easy enough. Are you sure you're up for it?"

Durand was no ordinary valet. Shorter than Wyatt but with the physique of a boxer, he would have stood out among the ranks of poker-stiff gentlemen's gentlemen even without his dark hair and bronzed skin that spoke to his decidedly un-English origins. In their first encounter on the streets of Paris, when Durand had saved Wyatt from muggers, Wyatt had been impressed with his ability to keep a cool head. When he later learned that Durand was looking to leave the city, he'd offered him a job, nominally as a replacement for his most recent valet, but practically as an assistant/bodyguard as the need arose.

"*Monsieur* Wyatt," Durand said. "I am the one who suggested it. Naturally I am 'up for it.'"

"I was only asking because I know it will be a lot of work," Wyatt said. "I don't mind looking into it myself. I have the time."

Durand smirked. "No, *monsieur*, I have the time. Your ironing does not take my whole day. Whereas you will be occupied trying to win over your Miss Kingston before someone else snatches her away."

Wyatt groaned. "I regret telling you about her. And for the last time, no one else is going to snatch her away. The problem is that she doesn't want to get married at all."

"That is just something a woman says when she doesn't want to hurt your pride. She is kind, yes, but still a liar."

Wyatt didn't bother to correct him. Durand had said much the same thing the night Samantha had rejected Wyatt's proposal almost four months ago. Wyatt had still been angry at the time, hurt by her bleak assessment of his character as much as by her rejection. Even then, however, he had known Durand was wrong. Samantha was not a liar. It was her brutal honesty that was the problem.

Wyatt had come to regret that disastrous proposal. There was so much he should have said differently, so much he would say differently, if she gave him the chance to try again. He hoped she would, but he wasn't sanguine. He knew she liked him and even that she found him attractive. She had been an eager participant in the kiss they had shared. She had even agreed to let him court her —to attempt to win her trust. Yet, he understood better her qualms about marriage and he feared that, even if she came to trust him, she might not love him enough to take that leap.

They had exchanged a few letters in their months apart. These had been agreeable, amusing letters, but contained little substance. He knew he was as much at fault as she in that respect, but he found written communication between them unsatisfying. He needed to see her face, to catch her eye across a crowded room as they shared a private joke. He needed to see that arch look she wore when she was teasing him. Simply put, he needed her, and banal letters about day-to-day goings-on were a poor substitute.

"I've laid out your blue checked trousers, *monsieur*," Durand said. "Will you be wanting the blue waistcoat as well?"

"Why not?" Wyatt said, happy for the change of subject. "I'm sure I won't be the most ridiculously dressed. At last year's boat race, Freddy Wigeon was blue head to toe. He even managed to dye a straw hat to match. You know, I hate to say anything to

Oxford's credit, but at least that dark blue is subtle."

Durand chuckled. Wyatt walked to the bed and, ignoring the trousers, picked up the sheaf of papers Durand had left there earlier and began to leaf through it.

"These are good Durand, especially given my poor descriptions: 'A sort of water wheel with semi-circular pails attached.' That's exactly what you've drawn here. Much better than the blobs I would have made."

"Thank you, *monsieur*."

"Put them in my study for now. I may have a use for them later. And order a cab. I should be ready shortly."

"Very good, *monsieur*."

After Durand left, Wyatt finished dressing and headed downstairs, picking up the bag that held Mr. Leclerc's blueprint as he left his room.

When he entered the dining room, Mrs. Hexam, his housekeeper, was setting out his breakfast at one end of the long table.

"Good morning, sir," she said, her back to him as she adjusted the table linens. "I know you're ready to be on your way, so I had Mrs. Plummet fix you something quick. And I've brought you a coffee."

"Thank you, Mrs. H. It smells delicious."

He slid into his seat and reached for the flaky, buttery sausage roll that was his cook's specialty. As he took a bite, Mrs. Hexam gasped.

"What's that?"

He looked up to see her pointing at his nose. He reached up and touched it, wincing as it was still tender where Samantha had hit him. He'd forgotten about the bruise. Durand hadn't mentioned it, which was odd, because he had gotten plenty of amusement the night before when he learned how Wyatt acquired it.

"It's nothing," he said, taking another bite in hopes that his housekeeper would take the hint and leave the room.

"It doesn't look like nothing," she insisted with the same tenacity she'd employed as his nanny whenever he tried to hide his misdeeds from her. "Did you get in a fight? Was it one of your *investigations?*"

She pronounced the last word like a distasteful epithet, lowering her voice as though afraid someone might hear. Wyatt couldn't help but smile. Swallowing, he said, "I was not in a fight. If you must know, it was a lady who did it." He amused himself watching the play of emotions across her face—shock, confusion, horror, suspicion—before adding, "Miss Kingston hit me."

"She didn't. Not that sweet young lady."

"I assure you she did. In her defense, she thought I was someone else."

"Were you someone else?" Mrs. Hexam asked, narrowing her eyes.

It hadn't been possible to hide from her the fact of his occasional transformation into Archie Kennedy—the alter ego he and his friend Bingo had invented in their school days and which he still assumed from time to time. Mrs. Hexam knew far too many of his secrets.

"I was not," he said. "I startled her, and she didn't see me at first. That is all."

"Hmm."

Wyatt was saved further interrogation by the appearance of Durand.

"The cab has arrived, *monsieur*," he said. "Would you like me to ask him to wait?"

"No need." Wyatt grabbed the cup of coffee and drank it down, coughing as the hot liquid burned his throat. Then he pushed his chair back and stood. "Thank you, Mrs. H. My compliments to Mrs. Plummet if you don't mind." He picked up the sausage roll and saluted her with it before hurrying out the door.

After giving Leclerc's address to the cabbie, Wyatt climbed into the black hansom and leaned back against the upholstered cushion. He wished he hadn't mentioned Samantha to Mrs. Hexam. She would be sure to task him about the incident later. She had grown attached to his house guest last summer and made no secret of her desire that Wyatt marry Samantha. Comments about the need for a mistress to better run his household had grown more frequent and more pointed since Samantha's stay with him and were now paired with questions about whether he'd heard from Miss Kingston and what Miss Kingston was up to. As though he didn't wonder that enough on his own.

Mr. Leclerc was surprised and pleased at the return of his property. He informed Wyatt of his plan to confront Ponsonby with the reclaimed blueprint and demand compensation from the sales of the part Ponsonby had already manufactured. Wyatt tried to convince him to wait, explaining that he may not be the only one Ponsonby had stolen from and that it might be better to know what they were up against before proceeding. Leclerc didn't know a Harold Miller or Franz Leipzig, but he did agree to wait a few weeks, provided Wyatt kept him informed of his progress.

Wyatt got back in the hansom and took it to the Thames, where traffic slowed to a crawl. After ten minutes with almost no movement, Wyatt decided he'd do better to walk the rest of the way. The riverside was packed with race-goers but, as they were all headed in more or less the same direction, it wasn't hard to navigate the crowd. As he drew nearer the river, he glimpsed a familiar thin face under a shaggy head of blond hair standing off to one side. Wyatt ducked his head, hoping to avoid notice, but a moment later, he felt an elbow jab his side and the voice of one of Skinny Jim's lackeys, an Irishman whose name Wyatt had never learned, spoke.

"So you're back, are ya?" Wyatt glanced over in time to see the Irishman flash him a cheeky grin before continuing. "About time, I'd say. I'd've bet good money on your coming same time as Miss Kingston, and she's been here more than a week. Maybe you don't care about her as much as he thought you did."

Wyatt ground his teeth to keep from responding, aware he was being goaded. If he'd thought his coming earlier would have helped, he would have. But Samantha didn't live with him. It wasn't as though he could guard her day and night. Madge was aware of the danger and had engaged a capable footman as bodyguard, putting all her staff on alert.

"Mind you, she took her sweet time. We were starting to worry she might've been scared away for good, and that wouldn't do. Not to say he couldn't find a way around it, but this is definitely easier."

Wyatt stopped in his tracks, causing the man behind him to run into him. The Irishman stopped, too, his grin back as the traffic flowed around them.

"What does he want?" Wyatt growled. "Enough with the threats. Just say it."

"So you do care about her. Good to know. Good to know." He laughed when Wyatt scowled at him. "As for what he wants...he'll be in touch."

Then, before Wyatt could say anything else, the Irishman melted into the crowd and disappeared. Wyatt pulled off his hat and ran his hands through his hair as he let out a breath of frustration. He'd been expecting another message from Skinny Jim, but this one was as cryptic as the last. "Skinny Jim sends his greetings" and now, "He'll be in touch." He'd shown that he knew who Samantha was and how to find her, but he still hadn't shown what he meant to do with the information. He was playing with them—showing them that he had all the power—and there was nothing they could do about it.

When Wyatt reached Hammersmith, it was just past eleven o'clock. It didn't take long for him to spot his friend Bingo, Lord Aston, leaning against a tree by the bank, drinking a pint of ale, his auburn hair and effortless good looks setting him apart from the crowd around him. Bingo smiled when he spotted Wyatt and stood straight, but as Wyatt drew closer, his eyes widened.

"What happened to your face?" Bingo asked, pointing to Wyatt's nose.

Wyatt sighed, resigned to explaining the story again. By the time he finished, Bingo was doubled over laughing.

"Where are Fenton and Carstairs?" Wyatt asked, rolling his eyes at Bingo's reaction.

Bingo gestured behind Wyatt, still laughing. Lord Fenton and Henry Carstairs, two of their old school friends, were queued in front of one of the food vendors who had set up along the banks of the Thames for the race. They waved when they saw Wyatt.

"I won't say anything," Bingo said when he'd gotten ahold of himself. "I'm sure Mrs. Hexam had plenty to say already."

"And Durand."

Bingo grinned. "Exactly. But know I'm thinking quite a lot about this extraordinary situation you got yourself into."

"That is clear enough."

"Why are you so late?" Bingo asked, smothering his grin. "Fenton and Carstairs were here half an hour ago. We'd almost given you up."

"I had business in Soho," Wyatt explained.

"On Boat Race Day? Who does business on Boat Race Day?"

Wyatt gestured to the dozen or so food stalls before them.

"Fair point," Bingo said. "But no right-thinking university man ought to. It's a holiday. Take a break for once, Val."

Val was Bingo's nickname for Wyatt from their school days.

Short for Valentino, it was one of Bingo's many joking attempts to guess Wyatt's given name. As terrible as it was, nothing could be worse than Wyatt's actual name, so he'd let it stand.

"Your life is a holiday, Bingo," Wyatt said.

"Isn't it just?"

A darkness passed over Bingo's brow as he took a swig from the pint in his hand. Wyatt had noticed a restlessness and a discontent in his friend of late but, as it was clear Bingo didn't want to talk about it, Wyatt didn't press. By the time Carstairs and Fenton joined them, Bingo's carefree manner had returned. After a round of greetings, they pushed their way through the crowds to board the steamer *Citizen J* that was docked nearby.

Once on board, Bingo was in his element, shouting greetings to everyone he knew, which was most of the passengers. By the time they'd jostled their way to the edge of the deck, it was a quarter to twelve. In the distance, Wyatt could see the long narrow boats—one with rowers in dark blue, the other with rowers in light blue. There were other steamers on the river, all filled to capacity. Up on the banks, above the crowds, those wealthy enough to do so had rented out rooms and houses and stood on the balconies looking out at the river. Samantha would be up there somewhere with the Bradwells. It seemed as though the whole of London had turned up for the race. There must have been thousands, possibly tens of thousands of people there, and the noise was deafening.

At eight minutes to twelve, a loud crack sounded across the water, and the race began. Cambridge started out strong, but Oxford soon pulled ahead.

"Come on Cantabs," Bingo shouted to the Cambridge rowers. "Row!"

His words were all but drowned out in the cacophony.

The boats drew near the warehouse district and passed between the steamers. Oxford slipped through easily but, as the

Cambridge crew attempted to edge ahead, the steamers began to pull in front of them. Wyatt and Bingo watched in horror as their own boat, *Citizen J*, floated forward and cut off the Cambridge rowers. Bingo actually turned around as though to give the captain a piece of his mind, but the boat moved and Cambridge was able to get through. The damage was done, however, and by the time the crews reached Hammersmith Bridge, Oxford led by more than three lengths.

"Unbelievable!" shouted Carstairs. "Ruddy cheating, that was!"

A massive crowd covered every inch of Hammersmith Bridge, spilling up into the crossbeams. Along the shore, people surged forward to watch the rowers draw near, sending several of those in the front tumbling into the river.

Wyatt cheered until he was hoarse, though he and the others knew it was no use. It was rare that a race was not determined by the halfway point, and the gap between the boats seemed only to be growing.

"I can't believe it!" Bingo shouted as Carstairs and Fenton shook their heads. "I cannot believe it. We've lost it."

"We're still up in the totals," Wyatt reminded him. "If there's no miracle at the end and they win, it'll still be ten wins to nine."

"And a streak for Oxford," Bingo pointed out, refusing to be consoled.

By the time they reached Mortlake, it was clear that Oxford had, indeed, won. The Oxford cox was soaking wet from his dunking in the river, and all the Oxford supporters were cheering and chanting at the top of their lungs.

"Cheer up, Bingo," Carstairs said, clapping him on the back. "We'll get 'em next year. In the meantime, we can drown our sorrows. First round's on me."

When they entered the United University Club, they were met with shouts of laughter and off-key singing from the direction of the main dining room where the Oxford alumni had already begun to gather to celebrate.

"Fenton!"

Three men came striding towards them down the hall. Wyatt had to suppress a glare when he recognized them—his brother, Tom, and two of Tom's closest friends. Together, they had done their best to make his school days miserable. The speaker, Lord Norland, walked slightly ahead of the others, a grin on his face as he held out a hand to greet Fenton. He clasped Fenton's hand in his and shook it vigorously. Wyatt saw Fenton wince. Lord Norland had rowed for Cambridge, and he'd clearly kept up his training in the years since.

"I hoped I might see you," Norland said. "Are you in town for the Season or just the race?"

"The Season," Fenton said. Then he turned to indicate the rest of their party. "You remember Carstairs? And Aston and Wyatt."

Norland's gaze flicked to each of them in turn, lingering a moment longer on Wyatt, who kept his expression impassive, almost bored, though inside he was seething.

"Naturally," Norland said. "How could I forget?"

"I'm sure we all have excellent memories," Bingo said.

His tone was casual, but the stare he fixed Norland with was pointed. Wyatt appreciated his loyalty, but he didn't want to start something that would only serve to get them all kicked out of the club.

"Tom," he said before Norland could respond to Bingo's provocation, "I'm glad I caught you. I've been meaning to have a word."

If there was one thing he could count on his brother for these days, it was a strict adherence to propriety. He wouldn't want a fight any more than Wyatt did. His response was almost friendly, therefore, as he said, "Of course. Gentlemen, I'll join you in the billiard room when I'm finished. Gin and tonic if you don't mind."

"Very well," Norland said. Then he turned to Fenton. "Join us?"

"We were on our way to the card room, as it happens," Fenton said. "Next time."

"I'll hold you to it."

They parted ways. Wyatt led Tom to the smoking room, where they were able to find a couple of chairs in a quiet corner.

"Did you really want to talk?" Tom asked as he took a cigar from the table beside his chair and chopped the end off with the tiny guillotine. "Or was that an excuse to get away from Norland?"

Wyatt set his jaw but refused to rise to his brother's bait.

"I was surprised to see you at Ponsonby's the other night," he said. "I didn't know you were an admirer of Royer."

"As a matter of fact, I am."

"Did you enjoy the performance?"

Tom narrowed his eyes as he lit his cigar.

"What's this about V.T.? You don't care what I thought of the performance. What do you really want?"

"Must I want something?"

"Why else would we be here?"

Tom's stare as he took a long drag of the cigar was as much a challenge as his words. Wyatt looked away first.

"How well do you know Ponsonby?" he asked.

"Why do you ask?"

"Curiosity."

"Oh, no." Tom leaned back and shook his head. "You've never been just curious about anything. If you're asking questions, there's a reason, and ten to one, the answer spells disaster. What's wrong with Ponsonby?"

"How well do you know him?" Wyatt repeated.

Tom puffed his cigar twice before answering. "Not well. We've met a handful of times. He's an exhibitor in Agricultural and

Horticultural Machines and Implements, for which I'm on the committee. One of the primary exhibitors. He's been dragging his feet on submitting his registrations. When he invited me to the concert, I hadn't planned to accept until he said he would hand over his papers when I came."

"He blackmailed you?" Wyatt asked in surprise.

"Hardly. He was aware how important his machines were to the exhibit as a whole and that we would accommodate him to a certain degree, but I could have found another way to force his hand. However, it would have taken more time and effort than I was willing to expend. And really, attending a single concert wasn't such a hardship."

"It didn't rankle to be seen as a prop to impress his friends?"

Tom shrugged, looking bored. "Not especially."

Wyatt couldn't resist needling him.

"Doesn't it violate some sense of the honor due the title to use it in such a grubby exchange?"

He expected Tom to take offense, so he was surprised when his brother actually snorted in response.

"What do you know of the honor due the title?" he asked.

"Only what you've drilled into my head these past few years."

Tom fixed Wyatt with a penetrating look.

"You're avoiding my question," he said. "What's wrong with Ponsonby?"

"Why does it matter to you? You said yourself you hardly know him."

"It matters because he is part of the Exhibition. It was Prince Albert's passion, and ever since his death, it's become a sort of memorial to His Highness. If there are problems with Ponsonby, there are problems with the Exhibition, and problems with the Exhibition will reflect on the prince's memory as much as they will on the nation. The eyes of the world are on us." He kneaded his forehead. "The Exhibition has enough problems as it is. If we could only rely on the attendance of Her Majesty the Queen at the opening, that might make up for some of the difficulties we have had, but that seems unlikely."

"Even as important as it was to the prince?" Wyatt asked.

"One would think that would sway her, but she seems resolute in her continued refusals to attend any official event since his passing. Then, of course, there are the expected difficulties with scheduling and the logistics of coordinating with so many foreign governments. And on top of that, we've had numerous complaints about the structure itself. I'll grant that it isn't as elegant as the Crystal Palace was, but it was designed to be easier to maintain as a permanent structure. So, I'll ask again, what's wrong with Ponsonby?"

"He's a thief," Wyatt said. "I have evidence that he stole at least one idea that he proceeded to manufacture himself, and I suspect he's done it more than once."

"You have evidence?" Tom asked sharply. "What are you doing with that evidence?"

"I returned it to the original owner."

"Is he planning to bring a lawsuit against Ponsonby?"

"He's hoping to avoid that, but he's agreed to hold off on any action for now to give me time to investigate the other potential thefts."

Tom set his cigar down in the ashtray beside him and leaned forward, dropping his head into his hands.

"A thief," he said dully. "Perfect."

He was silent for a moment. Wyatt stood, preparing to leave. Then Tom sat back up.

"I can work with this," he said. "Don't tell anyone else what you know and keep me informed as you go. I'll speak with some of the others on the committee. We might be able to clean this up before anyone learns of it."

"I'm not going to help you cover up a crime," Wyatt said,

annoyed at Tom's presumption.

"Don't act like you've never done it before. And you won't be helping me. You'll be helping Britain. I've told you what's at stake here."

Wyatt wanted to scoff, but he hadn't needed Tom to explain the importance of the Exhibition's success. People were still talking about the first exhibition eleven years later.

"I'll see what I can do," he said, not keen to commit himself to anything yet.

Tom nodded and picked up his cigar, taking Wyatt's assistance as inevitable. Then he said abruptly, "Mother has been asking about you."

Wyatt's jaw tightened as the familiar sense of displeasure that accompanied thoughts of his mother settled over him. "Has she?"

"Yes. She's wondering why you haven't been to visit her yet. She's here for the Season."

"I know."

Tom puffed on his cigar and threw a look of annoyance Wyatt's way.

"You know, seeing how busy I am, you could manage to help out with Mother from time to time."

"Help with what? She's not as enfeebled as she likes everyone to believe, and I won't pretend otherwise. I don't know why you do."

The atmosphere instantly cooled. Tom's face was blank as he snuffed out his cigar and got to his feet.

"I should be going," he said. "Norland and Timmons will be waiting. Call on Mother. It's the least you can do."

He left before Wyatt could think of a reply, not that he had anything further to say. Conversations with his brother always seemed to go this way—trading barbs until one of them hit too close to the mark. Wyatt may have landed the final blow, but he felt anything but victorious. They had come closer than ever to talking about something that mattered, but as usual, a wall had come between them. It didn't used to be that way. They'd been friends as small children, but somewhere along the way, the wall had grown up, and now there was too much resentment and animosity for either of them to want to tear it down.

When Wyatt joined his friends in the card room, they were seated around one of the small round tables, the only inhabitants of the room apart from a waiter. Carstairs was laughing heartily at something while Bingo glared at him. Wyatt felt himself relax, happy for the distraction from his conversation with his brother.

"Be kind to old Bingo," Fenton said, hiding a smile behind his glass. "He bet Smithy his prize pointer that Cambridge would take it."

"You didn't." Wyatt was half exasperated, half amused.

"Did you see Oxford's crew?" Bingo asked. "It seemed a sure thing. Besides, if you'd heard what he was saying—"

"He was winding you up," Wyatt said, pulling back the empty chair and sitting down. Fenton slid a glass of whiskey across the table to him and he nodded his thanks. "Everyone knows you're an easy mark when provoked."

"Do they?" Bingo's tone was disinterested. He took a swig from his glass. "I didn't realize my proclivities were a subject of such interest."

Wyatt and Fenton exchanged looks. Fenton raised his eyebrows.

"They are when they make other people money," he said.

"You speak as though I always lose. I'd wager my wins are higher, if only slightly."

"I'd take that wager," Carstairs said with a grin.

Bingo shrugged. "What fun is life without a little risk?"

"Here, here." Carstairs raised his glass.

Wyatt stayed silent. He used to find Bingo's extravagant betting amusing, but lately his friend had become more and more reckless. Bingo refused to see it and Wyatt wasn't interested in reviving that argument now.

"You call it fun," Fenton said, leaning back in his chair. "I call it courting disaster."

"It's no wonder no one invites you round for cards anymore," said Bingo. "You and Wyatt ought to form your own club for you and all the other sticks in the mud."

He finished his drink in one gulp and signaled for the waiter to bring him another.

Fenton chuckled. "I suppose that was a bit harsh. After all, you can certainly afford to lose if you like. I was only considering it from my perspective. I've my mother and two younger sisters to support, not to mention the title and estates."

"I don't think anyone envies you that," Carstairs said, taking the glass the waiter handed him. "I thank the Lord every day he made me a second son."

"I'm sure your mother and sisters do the same," Wyatt said.

Carstairs guffawed. "To be sure, they do. My brother, too. He's always saying I'd have bungled the whole thing if I'd been in charge."

"I'd say you're both fortunate," said Bingo, swaying slightly. "You and Fenton. You know where you stand—that's what I'd say."

Wyatt looked at Bingo sharply. The glass the waiter had brought him was half empty already. Wyatt wondered how many Bingo had drunk while he was with his brother.

"Me?" Bingo continued, "I don't know where I stand. In fact," he paused and snickered to himself. "I don't stand, I sit. Right where my governor puts me."

"Can't be easy," said Carstairs.

"Oh, but it is," Bingo said. "It's always easy. Easiest job in the world. No need to bother my head about a thing."

Wyatt took a sip of his own drink and contemplated his friend over the rim of his glass. He had no doubt that Bingo would regret being so open about his feelings the minute he sobered up. His relationship with his father was one he rarely discussed, even with Wyatt. He would hate to learn he'd spoken about it with anyone else.

"As amusing as it is to wallow here with you all," Wyatt said, standing, "I think I might go home after all. What about you, Bingo? You wouldn't mind taking me back in your carriage, would you?"

Bingo looked at him and frowned. He wasn't so far gone that he couldn't tell what Wyatt was doing, but he may have been drunk enough not to care anymore. After a moment's hesitation, he shrugged.

"May as well," he said. "Got to write home about the dog, haven't I? Can't have Smithy saying I don't pay up."

In the carriage, Bingo slumped back against the cushions.

"You're lucky, too, you know," he said. "Your governor wasn't so bad when he was alive, was he? And now you've got Tom, and I'm not saying he isn't a bit of a rotten egg, but he can't tell you what to do, can he? You've gone your own way."

Wyatt didn't consider himself particularly lucky. His father, with whom he had gotten along decently well—better than Tom had, anyway—had died not long after his sister, Helena, leaving Wyatt at the mercy of a brother who'd always been more of a rival and a manipulative, vindictive mother. Only an unexpected inheritance from an aunt he barely remembered had given him the freedom to step away from them both.

"And now you've got Miss Kingston," Bingo said.

"I haven't got Miss Kingston," Wyatt objected.

Bingo waved his hand vaguely. "You will. And she understands you. I didn't even know that was possible."

Wyatt snorted. "Didn't you?"

"I didn't mean understanding you was impossible. I meant, having that sort of understanding with a woman." He frowned and picked at a loose thread on the cushion. "I've dreaded the sort of Society marriage I'm destined for, but I've taken it as inevitable. My parents manage it well enough and I figured I would, too. Now? Seeing you two? Knowing it can be more than tolerable?"

He snapped the thread off and twisted it around his fingers.

"You're talking as though you have no choice in the matter," Wyatt said, watching Bingo's unusually somber countenance.

"I suppose I do, to an extent." He continued to look grim, then he turned to Wyatt and forced a smile. "You're right, of course. It's only the drink talking. You know I get melancholy when I've overindulged. It was bound to happen on Boat Race Day. Good you got me out of there. The last thing anyone needed was me bringing them down with a whole dining room of Oxonians waiting to do just that."

With that, he closed his eyes and pretended to sleep, precluding further conversation. Wyatt let him take the out.

THREE

On the Monday following the boat race, Samantha and Eden drove to Highgate in Eden's carriage. They had been invited to tea at the home of Miss Angela Burdett-Coutts, the well-known philanthropist. Samantha had met Miss Coutts that February when Madge, following through on her promise to help Samantha decide how to use her inheritance, had invited her to Derbyshire. Like Samantha, Miss Coutts was an heiress in her own right, though her fortune was considerably larger. Since inheriting, she had spent a great portion of her wealth on a variety of charitable concerns.

During their initial meeting, something of Samantha's passion when she spoke of the plight of young women on the street—though she had been careful not to explain how intimately she understood it—seemed to have impressed Miss Coutts. She invited Samantha to call on her in London, which Samantha did almost as soon as she arrived.

Though she was earnest in her desire to use her fortune for the good of others, a part of Samantha was able to recognize that some of the urgency she felt was driven by a need for control. She had spent most of her life being passed from one guardian to another with no say in where she went or how she lived. And, while she had loved her grandfather, those few years of happiness with him were overshadowed by the years that followed under the tyranny of her uncle.

Now, her uncle was dead, and she was in full possession of her fortune, but she still felt trapped. She still wasn't free. The lies she had told, which Wyatt and Madge had been complicit in, were designed to protect her, yet the threat of exposure loomed over her, particularly now that Skinny Jim had learned who she was. She had to be careful with what she said, where she went and whom she spoke to.

Her money, however, was hers to do with as she pleased, and she was determined to use it well. The tea today was the first step. Miss Coutts had invited a handful of friends and acquaintances who worked with and supported various charitable institutions in the city. Samantha was hoping to make helpful connections, or at least to be inspired. She wanted to be an active part of whatever good she was able to do, but she had no idea how.

Eden, the widowed Lady Stuart-Lane, had met Samantha at Madge's house party back in December. Despite their short acquaintance, they had become close friends, exchanging daily letters when Eden returned to Cornwall to care for her young son and her late husband's estate. Samantha had made few friends in her life, and friendship with a woman near her own age was a new and precious experience, so she was both surprised and delighted when Eden had offered to come to the tea to support her.

As Eden's carriage rolled to a stop in front of Holly Lodge, Miss Coutts' stately Highgate mansion, a footman jumped down from his perch on the back. He began to walk slowly along the gravel drive, scrutinizing their surroundings, looking for signs that they had been followed. After the attack on Annie, Samantha and Wyatt had been forced to reveal the truth of Samantha's time on the streets and her relationship with Skinny Jim to Madge and her husband. It had been a relief, really, not to lie anymore to the woman who had risked her reputation for Samantha's sake and treated her like family. Afterwards, Samantha had decided to let Eden and Wyatt's friend, Lord Aston, in on the secret as well. They had proved themselves trustworthy friends and Samantha had not liked lying to them.

The footman walked back to the carriage and, after fiddling with the release, unfolded the steps. He held out a hand to Eden, who took it and stepped lightly down. Samantha was less graceful in her descent, but she doubted she could ever match Eden in that respect. As Samantha's feet hit the gravel, the front door opened, and the butler stood ready to welcome them inside.

It was a small party, as Miss Coutts had promised. Apart from their hostess, Samantha counted two ladies and four gentlemen. At Samantha's and Eden's entrance, the gentlemen rose to their feet, and Miss Coutts came to join them.

At first glance, there was nothing particularly out of the ordinary about Angela Burdett-Coutts. With her narrow face and long, thin nose, she could appear severe, harsh even. And yet, in her eyes was spark that had drawn Samantha in from the moment Madge introduced them.

"Miss Kingston. I'm so glad you could make it," she said, taking Samantha's hands in hers and pressing them.

"As am I," Samantha said. "May I present my friend, Lady Stuart-Lane? Eden, this is the estimable Miss Coutts."

"It is a pleasure to meet you," Eden said, smiling at Miss Coutts. "Samantha has told me so much about you. I have been quite looking forward to this afternoon."

"You are too kind."

Miss Coutts took Samantha's arm and began to lead her and Eden around the room. She introduced them first to her companion and former governess, Mrs. Brown. Next came the elderly Mr. Crabb-Robinson, who bowed gallantly over their hands. Then Mr. Murphy, a middle-aged man with a bristle-brush mustache, who explained that he worked with the London Ragged School Union, a charity that set up schools for impoverished children around the city.

Leaving Mr. Murphy, they came to a woman of indeterminate age dressed in striped pink silk with matching pink roses adorning her blonde curls.

"May I present Mrs. Heywood," Miss Coutts said, "one of the London stage's brightest stars."

"Former stars," Mrs. Heywood corrected cheerily in a heavy Cockney accent.

"True stars never fade," intoned the young man beside her, adjusting his glasses as he watched her with an almost slavish adoration.

"Really, Mr. Curtis," Mrs. Heywood said with a trilling laugh. "You are too much." She turned to Samantha and Eden. "Mr. Curtis is a dramatist. He's composing a play for me. Well, not for me personally, but for my theatre."

"It opens next month," added Mr. Curtis.

"Mrs. Heywood helped me organize a benefit for the veterans of the Crimean War last year," Miss Coutts explained.

Mrs. Heywood became solemn as she nodded. "There is still so much to be done, but I think we were able to ease some suffering."

"We certainly have much work ahead of us," Miss Coutts agreed. Then she guided Samantha and Eden over to the final member of the party, a gentleman of about forty with neatly curled dark hair. "Lastly, Lady Stuart-Lane, Miss Kingston, meet Mr. Spenser. Mr. Spenser is a banker, a generous supporter of many fine institutions, and a good friend."

Mr. Spenser inclined his head. "It is a pleasure to meet you both. Miss Coutts speaks very highly of you, Miss Kingston, and I confess I have been curious to meet you."

"Curious on Miss Coutts' recommendation or because of my infamous circumstances?" Samantha asked, emboldened by the relaxed atmosphere to be more blunt than usual.

Mr. Spenser's lips curved in an appreciate smile. "I won't pretend to be above morbid curiosity, Miss Kingston, but you may be certain that most of my interest stems from Miss Coutts' description of you and your interest in finding good use for what you have been given."

"That is certainly my hope," Samantha said.

"Now that we are all assembled," said Miss Coutts, "I will have Hallifax bring in the tea. Please, sit wherever you like. As you all know, we do not stand on ceremony here."

The guests availed themselves of the comfortable furniture. Samantha and Eden were joined on the sofa by the colorful Mrs. Heywood.

"Did you really run from the peelers—the police, I mean?" Mrs. Heywood asked, leaning in so that her question could be heard over the babble of talk.

"Yes," Samantha answered, wondering if she would ever be allowed a conversation that did not involve her adventures of the previous summer.

"How thrilling." Mrs. Heywood's eyes sparked with interest. "Not that I doubt it was terrifying as well, but what an adventure! It reminds me of a play I was in once. I was the victim and it was such a laugh running shrieking across the stage."

Samantha could only blink at her, unsure whether to be offended at the lady's casual dismissal of her traumatic experience or relieved to find at least one person who didn't respond to it with either pity or horror. Mrs. Heywood didn't seem to notice her discomfort, however, and barreled on.

"Of course, it's less fun once you've done it six nights a week, twice on Saturdays for I don't know how many months, but it was still one of the more enjoyable plays I was in."

"Do you miss acting?" Eden asked with polite interest.

"At times, but I'll tell you what I don't miss, and that's all the scrimping and scrounging and the worrying that some young thing'd come along and take my spot. No, I was glad an' all when Mr. Heywood come along and offered to take me away."

"How does he feel about your running a theatre now?" Samantha asked.

Mrs. Heywood chuckled. "I do wonder sometimes what he'd think. He's been dead these three years now, and I only opened the theatre last year."

"Oh, I'm so sorry," Samantha said.

"No need to worry. You weren't to know." She lowered her voice further and glanced around before adding, "Truth be told, though I am sad as he was quite good to me, I've had great fun as a widow."

She straightened as the butler entered and began passing out the tea things.

It was an afternoon unlike any Samantha had experienced. Miss Coutts had assembled an eclectic group, but they nevertheless seemed to get along perfectly well. Conversation flowed freely and easily, centered, as it was, primarily on the various charitable causes in which the guests participated.

"But it isn't only the problem of money, Mrs. Heywood." Mr. Murphy set his teacup down to address the former actress. "The Ragged Schools rely heavily on volunteer teachers, especially female teachers, and we are forever struggling to fill those positions."

"It sounds like a problem of money to me," Mrs. Heywood replied. "If you had more money, you could pay the teachers, and you wouldn't be relying on them volunteers."

Mr. Murphy shook his head. "It's not as simple as that. We have over two hundred Sunday schools, and almost two hundred night and day schools. If we diverted donations to wages, we'd have to close half the schools."

"What do you use the money for, if not for wages?" Samantha asked.

Mr. Murphy turned to her, his expression eager. "The children who come to us do not come solely for education, Miss Kingston, though teaching them a trade is one of our primary aims. We also try our best to provide them with food, shelter, clothing and whatever else they need. Many of the children have been abandoned by their families, some by illness or death, some by neglect. You would be appalled to see the circumstances in which they live and the trials they must experience, young as they are. We aim to be a source of comfort for them, and to give them hope for a better future."

Samantha had seen at least some of the trials experienced by children of the street and had, indeed, been appalled. She was glad to know the schools were doing what they could, but even with two hundred of them, it was not enough.

"A noble goal," Eden said.

"That is kind of you to say, my lady, but we are merely trying to provide basic human rights to a populace that has been neglected for far too long."

There was a general murmur of assent.

"It's an embarrassment." The elderly Mr. Crabb-Robinson, who sat in an armchair by the fire, spoke in a quavering voice. "Such poverty at the heart of the great British Empire."

Samantha had always been proud to be British, but living on the streets, coming face to face with the realities of starvation and deprivation and what it drove people to had forced her to confront the irony of an empire that spanned the globe but couldn't manage to take care of its own people.

"More than an embarrassment," said Mr. Spenser from his seat by the window. "It's shameful. Particularly for a nation that boasts a head of state who is also head of the church. Is not charity the duty of every Christian?"

"Very true," Samantha said. It was shameful, and she was happy to hear that fact acknowledged aloud. She dipped her head to Mr. Spenser and he nodded back.

"As a clergyman myself, I cannot disagree," Mr. Murphy said. "Sadly, I find many of my parishioners prefer to think charity the sole purview of the church and that their part in it ends with their tithes."

"Well, the church ought to be doing its bit," Mr. Crabb-Robinson argued. "It's certainly rich enough."

"And it would, were it run by angels, rather than men," Mr. Murphy said with a sad smile. "As it is, not all of the funds end up where they ought but, even if they did, the church has more responsibilities than charity. And, as the Scriptures tell us, ' Pure religion and undefiled before God and the Father is this, to visit the fatherless and widows in their affliction, and to keep himself unspotted from the world.' We must all take responsibility for our own faith and, in so doing, for the needy among us."

"Well said." Mr. Spenser raised his teacup in salute to Mr. Murphy.

"Do you work with the Ragged Schools, too, Mr. Spenser?" Samantha asked. "Or some other charitable institution?"

"I support the schools and a handful of other organizations," he said. "However, my primary interest is in industrial progress." He set down his cup and began to gesticulate as he spoke, his eyes alight with passion. "We are living through a period unique to any other in history. Only think: The railway system is younger than I am and already it has completely changed our way of life. Now we have steam-powered factories that make goods faster and cheaper than ever before. I wouldn't be surprised if, in another decade or two, it were possible for even the poorest among us to afford not only what they need, but what they want as well."

"That is a beautiful hope," Miss Coutts said, "but we cannot look so much to the future that we neglect those who are suffering presently."

"Naturally," Mr. Spenser said. "Yet, if we do not invest in that future now, it may never happen."

"Did Miss Coutts tell you about the work she did with Mr. Dickens?" Mr. Crabb-Robinson's less-than-subtle attempt to steer the conversation away from conflict was directed at Samantha. "They were great friends, you know."

"So I heard," Samantha said.

"Yes," said Miss Coutts, her narrow face appearing more angular as she pursed her lips. "That was before he treated his wife in that unforgiveable manner."

An uncomfortable silence descended, and Samantha was sure they were all considering the rumors that had spread about the Dickenses. They had separated three or four years back, and though Mr. Dickens had shared his abbreviated version of events in his magazine, naturally Mrs. Dickens had not been given the same opportunity. The Dickens marriage was one of those horrific examples that solidified Samantha in her fears of marriage. Mrs. Dickens now lived on her own, kept apart from most of her children as well as her husband. It had been said by some that Mr. Dickens complained it was her fault they'd had so many children, costing him dearly. He had also, it was said, complained to friends that she was a bad mother, and may even have attempted to have her institutionalized.

"Urania Cottage," Miss Coutts said. "That is what it was called. A home for fallen young women of the working classes. For all his faults, I will not deny that Mr. Dickens was a dedicated partner in the venture. It was my idea to form the institution, and I provided the funds, but he did much of the work. Once convinced of its merits, he was quite dedicated to the cause."

"It is a shame it no longer exists," Mr. Spenser said.

"Does it not?" Samantha asked, surprised.

"Unfortunately, no," said Miss Coutts.

It was a shame, Samantha thought. There were so many women who could benefit from such a place.

"Miss Coutts told us you are searching for a cause," Mr. Spenser said, eyeing her keenly. "Though I am, as I said, primarily interested in creating a brighter future, I am not unmoved by the plight of today's suffering. If you are interested in joining me, I would be willing to inquire into the work needed to restart such a venture. It is a worthy cause."

Samantha considered the idea. As Mr. Spenser had said, this was, in theory, precisely what she wanted and why she had come to tea. She was searching for an opportunity to use her fortune to help others, and here was just such a one. Yet, she had intended to ease her way in—to start by funding already existing projects while learning about the work involved. She was a novice after all, completely inexperienced, particularly when compared with some of the other people there that evening. Would she be able to be an effective partner?

"It is a good cause," she agreed. "I don't have any objection to learning more about the work involved, though I do think we should see if we work well together before we go further."

Mr. Spenser smiled. "I appreciate your caution."

They arranged to meet at Mr. Spenser's place of business in a few days to discuss the details, and general conversation renewed. Samantha felt a growing sense of camaraderie with the others in the room. She was one of them now—a philanthropist. Or she very soon would be.

Before returning to Madge's home on Grosvenor Square where Samantha had once again been staying, she and Eden stopped by Madame Foussard's dress shop. Eden wanted to add a few items to her order. There wasn't room for the carriage in front of the shop, so they were forced to park farther down the road and walk. Matthew, Eden's footman, accompanied them.

Madame was as talkative as ever, so it was almost an hour later when they were able to leave. Despite having gone in with no intention of buying anything, Samantha had somehow been persuaded to add an extra chemise and two petticoats to her own order. She no longer wondered how Madame had risen to become one of the most successful dressmakers in the city.

As she and Eden walked back to the carriage, arm in arm, Samantha felt a prickle of awareness on the back of her neck. She turned to look behind them, but in a street full of people, no one stood out to her apart from Matthew, who looked at her quizzically. Facing forward once more, Samantha quickened her pace.

"What's wrong?" Eden asked. "Is someone following us?"

"I don't know."

Samantha glanced back again. Stepping around a young couple who had stopped in front of a shop window, a tall man with sun-darkened skin and thick forearms strode towards her. His eyes met hers and he scowled, but he didn't look away.

"Yes," she amended, lowering her voice as she turned back to Eden. "I think so."

Eden tensed beside her and began to walk faster. Samantha copied her, glancing back to confirm that the man had also picked up speed, not letting them out of his sight.

"Matthew," Eden began, her voice pinched in fear.

"I've seen him," Matthew said. "Get to the carriage, my lady. He won't do anything where he can be seen, and I'll make sure he doesn't follow you."

He sounded calm as he spoke, as though defending his mistress from hulking men stalking her and her friend through the streets was something he did every day. Samantha found herself comforted by his confidence, even though she wasn't certain it was earned.

When they reached the carriage, Samantha wrenched open the

door and ushered Eden in before her. As she stepped inside, she turned back to see Matthew standing like a sentinel ten paces away, facing down the stranger. They were exchanging words and, though the stranger seemed to be speaking to Matthew, his gaze remained fixed on Samantha. She couldn't read what emotion lay in his eyes, but the threat was clear enough in his posture.

To Samantha's surprise, the stranger turned and left. Matthew waited a moment before returning to them.

"What did he say?" Samantha asked when he opened the door.

"He said he's got a message for you," Matthew said, looking up at her curiously.

"What message?" Samantha couldn't keep the alarm from her voice.

"He wouldn't tell me, but he said he'd find a way to deliver it one way or another."

Samantha and Eden exchanged horrified looks.

"Thank you, Matthew," Eden said when he did not leave. "You may go."

The footman bowed and shut the door. They felt the carriage shift as he climbed up to his post on the back. Eden tapped the ceiling, signaling to the driver that they were ready to leave.

"What do you think he meant?" she asked as they swayed with the motion of the carriage as it set off.

"I hate to think," Samantha said. "He must have been sent by Skinny Jim, and if he intends to deliver a message like he did when he sent Annie...but whom would he send?"

"Would he attack you, do you think?"

"I don't know." Samantha was beginning to hate how often she'd uttered that phrase lately. "I don't know what he wants from me. But since he hurt Annie before, I'm more worried it will be you he attacks next. Or Madge. Or Wyatt."

Eden leaned across the carriage and squeezed Samantha's hand.

"Don't worry about me," she said. "I am taking every precaution. I do think you should talk to Wyatt, though. He might have an idea of what to do."

"We will see him at the ball tomorrow night. I'll talk to him then."

Eden nodded and leaned back against her seat. Samantha's gaze drifted to the window as she wondered for the hundredth time how her life had become so complicated.

FOUR

Samantha had never felt completely at home in the ballrooms of London. When her uncle was alive, his suffocating presence had loomed over every event. She had felt his eyes follow her, waiting for her to make a mistake and assuring himself that she danced only with those of whom he approved. She had been unable to make any real friends, aware he would force her to cut off any acquaintance that did not further his ambitions and certain she would not like anyone he did.

Now that he was dead, her ball experience was not much improved. Instead of one pair of eyes, she felt dozens. They followed her every move, waiting for her to make a mistake to confirm their suspicions about her character. This was the first ball of the Season, which had officially begun with the Oxford and Cambridge Boat Race and, while she hoped the novelty of her appearance would eventually wear off, she was not sure how long she could last before it did. She hated that everywhere she walked, heads turned and people whispered behind their hands.

Madge ignored it all, and Samantha strove to emulate her, but she found it difficult, especially when some people made no effort to hide their disdain. If they regarded her with such suspicion merely because of her innocent association with an infamous murder, Samantha hated to think how they would react to knowing what she had done to survive on the streets.

Across the room, she spotted Wyatt talking with his friend Mr. Carstairs. He caught her eye, and the corner of his mouth curved up in a subtle smile, but he did not move to join her. She assumed he did not want to draw attention to them by being the first to greet her, but she wished he would anyway. Instead, it was Lord Aston who approached her, looking dashing as ever, with his auburn curls and radiant smile.

"Lady B, Miss Kingston, how wonderful to see you again. May I say how delightful you both look this evening."

"You may," Madge said. "You may also comment on my gown, which Bradwell had the poor manners not to notice."

"It's new, is it? Yes, of course, I see that it is. It complements your complexion beautifully, my lady. I am sure his lordship noticed that extra shine in your eyes, even if he did not recognize the cause."

"I am sure he did not, but it is kind of you to say so. I hope you will keep this talent for pretty compliments when you are married. Your wife will be the envy of all. I assume you are here to ask Samantha to dance?"

"If your ladyship will consent to be parted from her."

"I daresay she will be happy to be rid of me, will you not, my dear?"

"Never," Samantha said, still smiling at the easy banter between the two of them. She turned to Lord Aston. "I accept your implied invitation, my lord."

As was often the case, the first dance was a country dance. Samantha supposed it was meant to encourage the guests to intermingle, but with so many people arriving fashionably late, it hardly achieved its purpose. Following the patterns of the dance, she joined hands briefly with Mr. Mason, Mr. Ramsey and Lord Norland before returning to Lord Aston.

"How are you readjusting to city life?" he asked as they took their places as the new lead couple. "Do you find it as exciting as when you were last here, or has the pace settled?"

He looked at her pointedly so that she knew he was really asking about Skinny Jim and his threats. She wished she could reassure him on that front, but the encounter with the man outside Madame Foussard's was still fresh on her mind.

"It's as exciting as ever," she said. "Perhaps more so, though I do not know for certain."

Bingo's expression darkened, and his scowl was all the fiercer for being so rarely seen on his cheerful countenance.

"I wish you had accepted my invitation to visit my cousins in Avignon," he said. "The French countryside is so far from exciting as to be utterly dull."

"I'm not sure I would have enjoyed that," Samantha said, amused in spite of herself at the strangeness of the double meaning of their conversation. "I dislike being bored. Besides, I imagine that London would be just as exciting whenever I returned, and I don't wish to stay away forever."

Lord Aston grunted but did not disagree with her conclusion. After a moment, he changed the subject.

"My father has arrived in town," he said. "He's not here tonight, but he'll want to meet you."

At Madge's house party that winter, Lord Aston had asked her to pretend to court him in the upcoming Season to mollify his father with regard to his marriage. When she told him she was loath to lie about another aspect of her life, he had countered by saying she need not lie at all, only dance with him an extra time or two every ball and accompany him to the occasional theatrical performance. They would do so as friends, and if anyone drew other conclusions (which of course they would), it would be their own fault for buying into Society's notions that men and women who spent any time together must necessarily be romantically involved. When put in that light, Samantha had agreed. It was such notions, after all, that had led to half the complications in her relationship with Wyatt. People ought to learn not to assume.

"Is there anything I should know before I meet your father?" she asked.

"If you are hoping to charm him, you may as well abandon the notion. Anyone less capable of being charmed I have yet to find. I'm not sure I've ever seen him smile. But I wouldn't let that worry you. All he will care to know is your pedigree, which is excellent, and that you have proper respect for the title and what your duty to it would be, if we were to marry."

"If you do this again next Season," Samantha said as they joined hands and promenaded, "you ought to choose someone with a host of siblings. That would reassure him along those lines, for she'd be bound to produce a brood of her own, wouldn't she?"

"Heaven forfend. A whole brood?" He shuddered.

They separated again. When they came back together, Lord Aston's smile had returned.

"Have you seen Wyatt since he returned to town?" he asked. "Apart from tonight, I mean."

"Yes," Samantha said. "We met at a concert at Mr. Ponsonby's."

She was careful in her response. Lord Aston knew a great deal more about the relationship between her and Wyatt than most people. He knew Wyatt had proposed, for one, and he seemed invested in promoting Wyatt's good qualities to her whether she asked to hear about them or not. She was happy for Wyatt that he had so loyal a friend but, much as she liked Lord Aston, that loyalty made her cautious to share too much with him.

"Who is Mr. Ponsonby?" Lord Aston asked.

"I don't really know him, and I don't think Madge does either, but she accepted a host of invitations to small events as soon as we got here to ease me back into Society."

"What was Wyatt doing there?"

Samantha could tell by his tone that he thought Wyatt had met her there by design. She was quick to disabuse him of the notion.

"He was working," she said. "If you're curious about the details, you should ask him."

The dance took them apart again. They came back together for the final movements and then the song ended and the dance broke apart. Lord Aston held out his arm and escorted her off the dance floor.

"I told him about our scheme," he said, leaning down to speak in her ear.

"What scheme?" she asked, noticing as she did, a small circle of ladies watching them intently.

"This one," he said, acknowledging the ladies with a nod of his head. "Our plan to appear madly in love."

A surprised laugh passed Samantha's lips before she clamped them shut. She looked up at Lord Aston, who was watching her with amusement, and narrowed her eyes.

"That was never the plan," she said.

"No," he agreed. "But it's what I told Wyatt at first. I wanted to see how he'd respond."

Because she could tell that Lord Aston wanted her to ask what Wyatt had said, she kept her response to a hum of polite interest, though inside she was burning with curiosity.

"You are no fun," he huffed after a moment. "Very well, I shall tell you though you did not ask."

Something in her expression when she looked up at him must have betrayed her eagerness because his face broke into a wicked smile and he said, "On second thought, never mind. I don't wish to bore you."

At her indignant glare, he laughed.

"That's better," he said. "I don't know what it is with you two. You're both so stubborn. Naturally, he was upset when I told him, though he made a valiant effort to appear unaffected. It was amusing to watch him struggle to hide the murder in his eyes before I clarified our plans. Now that he knows I won't be fawning over you, he thinks it a very good idea indeed."

"Does he?" Samantha asked, surprised. "Why?"

"He thinks it might deter some of your would-be suitors if it appears you've already chosen a favorite."

"Perhaps," Samantha said doubtfully. "Or it might spur some of them to be more desperate. It's a lot of money to give up on."

They were unable to speak further as Samantha was approached by a group of gentlemen hoping for the chance to add themselves to her dance card. Lord Aston stayed by her side while they requested their dances, then left when Madge appeared. Samantha was sorry to see him go. She enjoyed their talks.

The next hour passed quickly. Samantha danced every dance. There was a time when she would have been thrilled to do so, for she loved to dance. However, she wanted to talk to Wyatt about the man who had followed her out of Madame Foussard's, and dancing so much meant she never had a chance to do so. Nor did her dance partners make the experience enjoyable, either. Mr. Mason was already half drunk and kept missing his steps. Mr. Thurow and Lord Norland droned on without giving her space to think, much less respond. She would not have minded so much had they not also been so loud that their voices drowned out the sound of the music. It was a relief, therefore, when the orchestra played a mazurka or a polka and the dancing was too fast to allow space for conversation.

Lord Godwin, whom she had met at Madge's house party that winter, tried to reserve the supper dance, but she had promised it to Lord Aston, so he took the dance before it—a waltz. When he came to claim his dance, she was talking to Mr. Thurow and Lord Norland. They had been listing the reasons they were prime candidates for marriage—most of which seemed to be less actual reasons than the names of their illustrious acquaintances—and had been speaking over each other for five minutes. She was, therefore, happier than she might otherwise have been to accept Lord Godwin's hand.

"If you'll excuse us, gentlemen," he said, bowing to the others, whom he had cut off mid-speech. "Miss Kingston and I have much to catch up on."

"Do we?" Samantha asked with a spark of irritation when they were out of earshot. "Or was that a subtle way of asserting your advantage over them? An advantage you imagine you have because you spent a few weeks in my company some months ago."

"Would you rather they think they have a chance?" Lord Godwin asked.

"I suppose not, but I'd hate for you to leave with the notion that you do, either."

Lord Godwin smirked. "You certainly don't mince words, Miss Kingston. Is Wyatt really so wonderful that you won't even consider anyone else? Or are you holding out for a bigger prize? You and Aston looked quite intimate."

Samantha stiffened as he placed his hand on her waist. "Tell me, Lord Godwin, for I am curious. What would you say to persuade me to consider you?"

"I wouldn't say anything. But," he added, his tone laced with suggestion, "I would show you, if you let me."

Samantha felt a wave a nausea at his implication. Then the music started, and he led her across the floor, spinning past the other couples.

"You aren't the first man to try that," she said, proud that she had kept her composure. "Though I will give you some credit for asking."

"I won't be the last, either. You know they won't rest until you've made your choice. Perhaps not until you've walked down the aisle."

"Or until they realize their efforts are fruitless."

When Lord Godwin smirked again, she frowned.

"Do you disagree?" she asked.

"I think you are being naively optimistic."

"Do you intend to be as persistent as you imply your fellows will be?"

"Not beyond reason. I have my pride. You should prepare yourself, however. There are others willing to sacrifice a lot more than pride for the chance at a fortune such as yours."

"I suppose I should be thankful that you, at least, are not maintaining the pretense that my popularity is driven by anything more than my purse."

He could not fail to hear the bite in her tone. He looked down at her and smiled.

"I would not do you the disservice of pretending it is not a significant factor, but I know I am not the only man to notice the packaging of that purse. You have a very pleasing figure, Miss Kingston, and your eyes have a sultriness to them that could make a man—"

His speech was interrupted by a hiss of pain as she stamped on his foot.

"How clumsy of me," she said without a hint of regret. "Perhaps we ought to end this dance early. You will no doubt wish to rest your foot before asking another lady."

"No doubt," he said, eyeing her shrewdly. "Very well. Where may I escort you?"

She would rather he didn't escort her anywhere, but she had no wish to make more of a scene, so she said, "You may take me to Lord Aston. He and I have the next dance."

After handing her over, Lord Godwin departed with an ironic

bow. Samantha was pleased to note the slight limp that he made an effort to disguise as he walked away from them.

"Another disappointed suitor?" Lord Aston asked.

"I would say, rather, another unsuccessful fortune hunter," Samantha said.

"It will slow down," Lord Aston assured her. "Not this Season, perhaps, but in a few years, if you remain unmarried, they will begin to understand your resolve."

"Lord Godwin said such thoughts were naively optimistic."

Lord Aston frowned at the other man's retreating back.

"I wouldn't listen to him if I were you. It's in his interest to make you despair. He knows it's the only way you'd ever consider him."

"If he thinks anything would make me consider him, it is he who is naively optimistic."

Lord Aston chuckled. Then he held out an arm and suggested they take a turn about the room.

The stress of the evening had left Samantha with little appetite for supper, so she and Lord Aston returned to the ballroom before many of their acquaintances. He left her by the wall as he went to get them drinks and it was then, in the quiet of the sparsely populated room as the musicians took their break, that Wyatt found her.

"You look beautiful," he said, his gaze raking her from head to toe.

"Thank you," she said, feeling heat rise to her cheeks.

It was strange to hear him compliment her so openly, but not unwelcome. She would have liked to see what else he might say but, as this might be their only chance to speak tonight, she chose to focus on what was most important first.

"One of Skinny Jim's men found me outside the dressmaker's yesterday," she said.

Wyatt's look of dismay was soon replaced by a frown which

grew more pronounced as she proceeded to describe the encounter.

"He said he plans to seek you out again?" he asked when she had finished. "Without a bodyguard, I presume."

"I suppose he might talk to me if I had a guard," Samantha said. "He made it clear that he won't give the message to anyone but me, though."

"He won't have the chance to talk to you," Wyatt said. "I'll make sure he doesn't get near you."

Though Samantha felt a thrill at his defense of her, she couldn't help but notice that he had, once again, made a decision for her.

"He *may* have the chance," she said, pointedly. "We've been wondering what Skinny Jim's aim was in sending me his greetings through Annie. How will we know if we don't listen to the message? And if his man is willing to tell me while I have a bodyguard, it's better than waiting for him to spring out at me when I least expect it."

Wyatt ran a hand through his hair. "I don't like it."

"I don't, either, but without knowing what he wants, we are stuck in limbo."

"Then I'll find out," Wyatt said. "I ran into one of his men before the boat race. He said Skinny Jim would be in touch. I'll ask him what he wants from you."

"You 'ran into' one of his men?" Samantha asked. "Was he following you?"

"Probably." Wyatt shrugged. "It was the same man who followed me around the last time I was in London."

A wave of guilt crashed over Samantha. Wyatt never would have been involved with Skinny Jim if not for her.

"Samantha." Wyatt tipped her chin up, forcing her to meet his eyes. "It's not your fault. We've talked about this before. I'm the one that pushed you into meeting him. At the same time, if you'd never met him, we might never have connected his men to Charles and learned who the real killer was."

Samantha turned away, and he dropped his hand. She hated how much she missed the contact.

"You wouldn't be involved with any of it if not for me," she said. "Neither would Madge. I didn't just tie you to him, but to Charles and my aunt and uncle and me and the whole scandal."

"If you think I regret any of it for a moment, you are much mistaken."

The fierceness in his voice made her turn back to him in surprise. He was watching her with an intensity that made her stomach flip.

"I'd do it again, if I had the choice," he said. "No matter what happens between us, I'd do it again because you needed help, and I'll always help you if I can."

"I hope you aren't trying to cut me out, Val," Lord Aston said, his cheerful voice jarring as he appeared suddenly beside them. He handed Samantha a cold glass of lemonade. "I'm having a hard enough time as it is fixing my interest with Miss Kingston. Don't want you poaching her."

He laughed at his own joke, but Samantha and Wyatt didn't join in. Samantha couldn't decide if she was glad Lord Aston had interrupted what had become a dangerously personal conversation, or if she wished him gone.

"'No man is offended by another man's admiration of the woman he loves'," Wyatt said.

"Says who?" Lord Aston said. "And why shouldn't I be offended?"

"Says Jane Austen."

Samantha thought his words had sounded familiar. She turned to Wyatt in surprise. "You read it!"

Lord Aston looked between the two of them, bemused. "What am I missing? Read what?"

"*Northanger Abbey*," Samantha said. "He was quoting it just now."

She had recommended the book to Wyatt in one of her letters that winter as it was one of her favorites, but she had not expected him to read it. While she was pleased to learn he had, she wondered if she ought to read any significance into the fact that he had left off the end of the quotation, the crucial part of that particular line. *It is the woman only who can make it a torment.*

"I did read it," Wyatt said.

"And?"

He smiled. "And I liked it much more than I expected."

"Considering that your expectations cannot have been very high, that does not tell me much."

"On the contrary. I knew any recommendation of yours must have some merit. What I did not expect was to laugh aloud, which I did at several points, nor to want quite so much to thrash a fictional character."

Samantha laughed. "You must mean John Thorpe. He is supremely unlikeable, but I still find him amusing."

"Is this a novel?" Lord Aston asked. "I didn't know you read novels, Val."

"'The person, be it gentleman or lady, who has not pleasure in a good novel, must be intolerably stupid'," Samantha said, then added hurriedly. "That is also a quote, my lord. From the same novel."

"I don't know whether to feel more or less offense that you chose another's words rather than your own to insult me."

"There is no need to feel either, my lord, as it was Mr. Wyatt's reading habits we were discussing. Are you saying *you* do not enjoy novels?"

"I wouldn't dream of saying as much now."

"Which is your favorite?" she pressed.

"I think I recall reading *Tom Jones* in school. It wasn't half bad, though I hope you won't expect me to quote from it."

"'It is as possible for a man to know something without having been at school, as it is to have been at school and to know nothing'," Wyatt said.

"Is that from *Tom Jones*?" Lord Aston laughed. "Well done. I suppose I did set you up for that."

"Beautifully."

"I concede. I beg you will both end this pointless quotation game, for you know I can contribute nothing to it, and I don't have a mind to be lectured to all night."

"I beg your pardon, my lord," Samantha said, dipping into a mocking curtsey. "You have been much put upon."

"Speaking of which." Lord Aston looked around to see that no one was nearby and lowered his voice. "Has Harold Lennon come up to scratch yet?"

Samantha shook her head, wishing Wyatt wasn't there to hear, as Mr. Lennon was another would-be suitor. However, Wyatt said, "Lennon? Don't you mean Will Lennon?"

"No, I mean Harold. Will's younger brother."

Wyatt scoffed. "You can't be serious. He's a boy. Last I heard he was up at Oxford."

"He just came down."

Well, if they were going to discuss her suitors, perhaps it was better that it happened now, with Lord Aston present to add some levity to the conversation.

"He may be young," she said dryly, "but he is practical. He told me that he abhors the army and is too adventurous for the church but that he thinks the life of a country gentleman would suit him."

"He told you that?" Wyatt asked with incredulity. "Did he also indicate which part of the country would suit him?"

Samantha nodded. "An estate in Somersetshire. Or possibly a castle in Scotland. He would leave the exact location up to his *beloved* wife."

"Naturally."

"He is more pleasant to look at than Mr. Panzer, who assured me only yesterday that his two previous wives, both of whom passed on immediately after bearing him a child, were much less robust than I, so I need not fear I would meet the same fate."

Wyatt's eyebrows rose, and Lord Aston hid a laugh behind his hand.

"Of course, neither of them can compare to Lord Aston."

She placed a hand on his arm, and he patted it distractedly.

"Yes, but you didn't answer my question. Has Lennon come up to scratch?"

"If you mean, has he proposed—no, he has not. I believe he intends to orchestrate some semblance of a romance, and we have not yet had the time for him to do it properly."

"Well, let me know when he does."

She tilted her head as she looked up at him in confusion. "In what way does it concern you, my lord? Surely you cannot think I will say yes?"

"I don't think *that* is his concern," Wyatt said.

"Then what...? Oh." Samantha sighed. "Please tell me I am not the subject of your latest scheme to waste your family fortune."

Lord Aston's grin was unapologetic. "It's only a small bet. They're running odds at White's on how many proposals you'll receive before the Season is over."

She gaped at him and looked to Wyatt, who nodded.

"I probably shouldn't have told you," Lord Aston said, "but it hardly seemed fair, knowing you as I do, that you should be in the dark."

"I'm glad you told me," she said, fighting back her growing indignation.

"You're not the only one," he assured her. "There are odds laid on the fates of many of the ladies each Season."

"I cannot say that makes me feel any better. It is bad enough that we are paraded out each spring for the highest bidder like cattle without also being bet on like horses."

"That may be an apt analogy," Lord Aston said, "and I don't wish to detract from your point, but don't forget that I am viewed mainly as the prize of a hunt to be caught and displayed by the victor for all to see."

"Better to be a deer, able to run, than a cow driven to the slaughter."

"Touché, Miss Kingston," Lord Aston said. He flourished his hand as he gave a mock bow. "I concede."

"Is it not considered cheating for you to encourage me to welcome more proposals?" Samantha asked.

"It's a bet among friends," Lord Aston said. "Cheating is assumed."

"In which case, do you plan to propose yourself?"

She saw him glance at Wyatt, who was watching him with the enigmatic expression she found so frustrating. "I may, though I will have to take care when I do so. There is another wager going that I am not meant to know about concerning my own chances with 'the latest heiress.' I've been attempting to place a bet by proxy before the odds shorten."

"I shall await your proposal with bated breath, my lord."

Lord Aston's eyes twinkled with amusement. Then, looking over her shoulder, he said, "As I have already had my two dances with you, Miss Kingston, I'm afraid your rescue must come from another quarter."

Samantha turned to see Mr. Panzer making his way towards her with determination.

"Oh dear," she intoned.

"Are you already engaged for the next dance?" Wyatt asked.

"I'm afraid not."

"Then, may I have the honor?"

She turned back to see a smile playing around his lips as he held out a hand.

"You may."

Before they departed for the dance floor, Lord Aston caught Wyatt's arm, and she heard him mutter, "If you wish to dispel the gossip, you had better not look at Miss Kingston like that. I'll swear you'll undo all my efforts this last week in one evening."

FIVE

Dancing with Samantha was at once the best and the worst part of Wyatt's evening. It was the best because having her near—having an excuse to hold her in his arms as the waltz required—was what he'd been wanting from the moment he saw her enter the ballroom. It was the worst because he was so focused on Bingo's parting words, so afraid to give those watching the wrong idea about his relationship with Samantha, that he was unable to enjoy the experience fully.

When the dance was over, Wyatt escorted Samantha to Madge, who informed them both that she was tired and ready to go home. Wyatt immediately offered to go with the two of them to get their carriage. After what Samantha had told him about the man who followed her outside the dressmaker's, he didn't want to take any risks with her safety. To his surprise, neither woman objected, leading him to wonder if Samantha was more worried than she let on.

Wyatt took Madge's arm and Samantha followed. A few people noticed them leaving, but Madge put on a good show of looking unwell, leaning heavily on Wyatt's arm so that his accompanying them did not appear suspect.

"You might want to rein in the dramatics," Wyatt said in a low voice as they passed through the door to the hall. "People will begin to think you're deathly ill, and you'll have a host of well-wishers descend on you tomorrow."

"So much the better," Madge said. "If there are more people calling to see me, there won't be space for those calling to see Samantha. And before you accuse me of heartlessness, I can assure you she would feel the same."

"I would," Samantha agreed, entering the hall behind them. "I hope that is what happens. I'm already dreading morning calls tomorrow."

"You could always catch whatever has made Madge so ill," Wyatt said.

He looked back in time to see her mouth turn up in a half-smile at his suggestion.

"As appealing as that sounds," she said, "I can't very well be ill for the rest of the Season. I knew what lay in store for me when I returned to the city."

The butler stood waiting near the door. Wyatt asked him to have Madge's carriage sent for. He nodded in acknowledgement and disappeared down the hall.

"Oh! I almost forgot," Madge said. "I left something in the retiring room. I'll be back in a moment."

"What did you leave?" Samantha asked, but Madge just waved her hand as she hurried away.

"I suppose she's done pretending to be ill," Wyatt said, watching his cousin almost sprint down the hall before she turned the corner.

As Samantha chuckled, Wyatt was struck by the realization that they had been left alone.

"Samantha..."

He wasn't sure what he was going to say. He hadn't thought it through, but it didn't matter, because he didn't get the chance. A door to their right opened and Percival Mason stumbled out.

"Miss Kingsley!" he said, his words slightly slurred, as he caught sight of Samantha. "Fancy meeting you here."

"Mr. Mason." Samantha dipped her head in acknowledgement, graciously overlooking the way he had botched her name. She shot Wyatt an amused half-smile, though. He returned it, but his attention was mostly focused on the inebriated Mason, who did not seem to have noticed Wyatt's presence.

"Glad I caught you," Mason continued. He sauntered towards Samantha, knocking into the hall table and upsetting a bowl of calling cards. "Been meaning to have...to have a word."

"Now may not be the best time," Samantha said, watching him warily. "We were just leaving."

"Good plan." Mason bent down and attempted to scoop up the fallen cards. They watched as he swiped uselessly at the floor, spreading, rather than gathering, the pile. "Should have left an hour ago. Thought I could turn my luck. Didn't work." He straightened and kicked at the cards before stepping over them with dubious grace.

"Would you like us to call for your carriage?" Samantha asked.

Mason shook his head. "Haven't got it anymore, have I? Lost it. But you..." He looked between them, appearing baffled by Wyatt's presence beside her. Then he shook his head as if to clear it, pointed a finger at Samantha and narrowed his eyes. "Thought I had more time, but this'll have to do."

He dropped to his knees so precipitately that Wyatt thought for a moment he had collapsed in a faint. Then he held a hand out to Samantha and spoke in a theatrical, singsong way.

"Miss Kingsley...Kensington...Ken...Miss Kinkleton, would you do me the pleasure of my hand in marriage?"

Wyatt couldn't help himself. He snorted out a laugh before he could turn away to hide his face. Samantha's mouth hung open in disbelief. When he caught her eye, a flush of pink tinged her cheeks, and she looked away. Wyatt wasn't sure what she was embarrassed about. It was Mason who looked the fool. Even now, he blinked up at her, his brows furrowed in confusion.

"What was that?" he asked.

"I didn't say anything," she said. "But my answer is no."

"No?"

Mason stood up and stumbled towards her. Before he reached her, Wyatt had him by the collar.

"Let us call you a cab," he said.

He pinned Mason's arms to his sides and marched him out the front door. There was always a cab or two nearby when a ball was in progress. Signaling to the nearest one, Wyatt waited for the driver to pull up beside them and practically shoved Mason inside. Though he protested Wyatt's rough handling, Mason was self-possessed enough to call out his address to the cabbie and was soon on his way.

"I'll have to tell Lord Aston the good news," Samantha said as the cab disappeared down the road. "There's another proposal to add to the total."

Though her tone was light, her stiffness of manner that told Wyatt she was less sanguine than she appeared.

"If you like, I could place a bet on your behalf," Wyatt said, hoping to cheer her up. "Then you could at least profit from your misery."

Her reluctant grin warmed his soul. He put a hand on her back to escort her inside but froze when a voice spoke from the shadows.

"Sam."

Samantha's only response was a sharp intake of breath. Wyatt slid his hand to her waist and moved to the side, blocking her from view as a man stepped out of the shadow of a nearby streetlamp.

He was taller than Wyatt, with a heavy brow that obscured his eyes so that they appeared as black holes beneath it. In his long grey coat, he blended him into the darkness behind him. When he spoke, his gravelly voice was barely above a whisper, but in that nearly empty street, they heard every word.

"That's what you called yourself, wasn't it? Sam?"

Beneath Wyatt's fingers, he could feel Samantha tremble.

"Do you have a message?" Wyatt snapped.

"For her, yes."

Samantha took a shaky breath and made to step around Wyatt.

"Wait," he said, tightening his grip on her waist.

She gave him a small smile. "It's alright, Wyatt. We talked about this. I want answers and so do you. This is how we get them."

He let his hand fall as she stepped forward, but she reached back and caught it, holding it tight.

"What is the message?" she asked, her voice firm.

"He wants you to meet him," the man said. "Down at his pub. He'll tell you the rest then."

"You've got to be joking," Wyatt said.

"You should know, he doesn't like to be crossed," the man said, unmoved by Wyatt's outburst. "He'll be expecting you."

Then, as suddenly as he had appeared, he stepped back into the shadows and vanished.

A moment later, the front door opened, and Madge came out, wrapped in her shawl and carrying Samantha's under her arm.

"There you are," she said with a hint of exasperation. "I came back, and the butler was there but had no idea where you'd gone. I went all the way to the ballroom searching for you. What are you doing out here?"

"We were helping Mr. Mason to a cab," Wyatt said, peering in the direction Skinny Jim's man had disappeared, trying to catch a glimpse of him.

A clatter of wheels announced the arrival of Madge's carriage.

"I don't see why you didn't come back in afterwards," Madge

said. "Samantha, you must be freezing."

She handed Samantha her shawl and gave Wyatt a disapproving frown.

"We'll explain in the carriage," Wyatt said as Madge's footman jumped down and opened the door.

"In the carriage?" Madge sounded bemused. "Are you coming with us? Why?"

"We'll explain in the carriage," Samantha repeated, ushering Madge in ahead of her.

As soon as the footman closed the door behind Wyatt, Madge burst out, "Alright, what is going on?"

She looked from Wyatt, who sat across from her, to Samantha on the seat beside her. It was Samantha who spoke.

"One of Skinny Jim's men had a message for me."

"Just now?" Madge's jaw dropped, and she spun around to look through the back window. "Here?"

"Yes," Samantha said. "Skinny Jim wants me to meet him at his pub. Apparently, he'll tell me what it is he wants from me there."

Madge turned back so quickly Wyatt was surprised she didn't crick her neck. She fixed Samantha with a penetrative stare.

"You told him no, of course," she said, both questioning and demanding.

Though Wyatt knew Samantha hadn't said anything one way or the other, he watched her for her reaction. He was curious as to whether she was considering answering Skinny Jim's summons. It would be dangerously foolhardy and, while he knew Samantha was no fool, he feared that her guilt and anxiety over the situation might make her reckless.

He needn't have worried. Samantha looked from Madge's concerned face to his own and narrowed her eyes.

"Do you both think so poorly of me that you imagine I wouldn't recognize the imprudence of such an action?" she said. "And no, I did not tell him 'no' because I have no wish to face

Skinny Jim's retaliation before we've had time to consider our options."

Wyatt wished she had not so correctly interpreted his expression. She was right to be irritated with him. He ought to have had more faith in her. Instead, he had given her more reason to distrust him.

"I'm sorry, my dear," Madge said. "You are probably in the right. Refusing may well have been as rash as going along with his demands."

"I'm sorry, too," Wyatt said, though he knew how paltry an apology it was.

"Thank you," Samantha said. Her demeanor, however, made him think he was not forgiven yet.

"You should be extra vigilant," Wyatt said. "Both of you. I know Samantha has been traveling with extra protection, but I don't think you should be walking out alone either, Madge."

"Will you be applying the same advice to yourself?" Madge asked. "You are in as much in danger as either of us."

"I'll be careful."

"That isn't what she asked," Samantha said.

Her tone was firm—fierce, even—but as she stared him down, her gaze softened. She sounded almost pleading as she added, "Wyatt?"

"I'll take Durand with me," he said.

She smiled. "Thank you."

The next morning, Wyatt found himself on Throgmorton Street in the City standing in front of Carpenter's Hall, home to The Worshipful Company of Carpenters. It was a large building, not unlike the clubs he was familiar with on the Pall Mall, with Corinthian columns and a row of tall, arched openings at street level.

Durand had tracked down Franz Leipzig, one of the inventors

whose blueprint Wyatt had found in Mr. Ponsonby's possession. He was a member of the company of carpenters and, when Durand asked him to meet with Wyatt, he'd suggested the hall as a meeting place. Wyatt had never been inside a livery company hall before, and he was glad for the excuse to sate his curiosity.

The clop of horse's hooves over cobblestone drew Wyatt's attention to the departing carriage behind him as Durand came to join him, having just paid the driver.

"He's still following us," his valet said, knocking a clod of dirt from his shoes.

He didn't so much as nod his head in the direction of the man tailing them, but Wyatt was all too aware of the man's presence.

"I know," he said.

"You're going to let him?" Durand sounded incredulous.

"For now, yes. As long as he doesn't do anything else, there isn't much I can do."

Durand looked unconvinced, but after rolling his eyes and muttering "*les Anglais*," he followed Wyatt inside.

When he had given his name to the attendant, Wyatt, along with his valet, was directed to the elegant reception room. He didn't have long to wait before a bald man with a thick blond mustache and narrow, pointed goatee entered, his gaze sweeping the room. When he saw Durand, recognition lit his eyes, and he came to join them.

"Monsieur Durand," he said in lightly accented English. "Good morning. And this must be your employer, Mr. Wyatt."

Wyatt took the hand the man held out and shook it. "I am. Thank you for meeting me, Mr. Leipzig."

"I'll admit, I was curious," Mr. Leipzig said, gesturing to a set of chairs clustered around one of the windows that faced the street. "I cannot think how I came to be of interest to a private inquiry agent. Monsieur Durand made it sound as though it would be worth my while, however."

"That depends," Wyatt said. "Do you know Mr. Lucas Ponsonby?"

Mr. Leipzig stiffened, and his manner became wary.

"The manufacturer?" he asked.

"Yes."

"I know him."

Wyatt nodded. Despite Durand's confidence that he had found the right man, Wyatt was glad for his suspicions to be confirmed.

"Did he steal a blueprint from you?" Wyatt asked.

His bluntness was instantly rewarded by the look of shock that overtook Mr. Leipzig's face. The shock gave way to a frown of displeasure before he settled on resignation.

"In a sense, yes," Mr. Leipzig said. "In another sense, no. I gave it to him of my own free will. We were in the process of drawing up an agreement with regards to an invention of mine. He was going to manufacture it for me. He even offered to fund the patent, which I couldn't afford on my own. He said his lawyers needed the blueprint to complete the paperwork. He had been entirely trustworthy up to the point. I had no reason to doubt him. Then, once he had the blueprint, he said he had changed his mind about the agreement. When I asked for it to be returned, he claimed he had already done so. When I insisted that he had not, he called me a liar and refused me access to his place of business."

"Why did you not go to the police?"

"I tried, but it was his word against mine. He is a prosperous businessman, and I am a lowly carpenter, and a foreigner at that. You can imagine whom the police believed."

Wyatt nodded. "Have you tried any other means of retrieving it?"

"What other means would those be?" Mr. Leipzig looked exasperated. "I haven't the money to take him on in a court battle, nor to hire a private inquiry agent. I have all but given it up for lost.

How did you come to learn of my misfortunes?"

"As it happens, you are not the only man Mr. Ponsonby has defrauded in this way."

"Not the only fool, you mean. That is some comfort, I suppose. Were you hired by this other man?"

"Something like that. I found your name and another in connection to the theft I was investigating. You were the easier to track down. I wasn't certain if you and he were victims as well, or if you had consented to the use of your blueprints."

"Now you know I did not consent, what will you do?" Mr. Leipzig asked, watching Wyatt with a mixture of curiosity and hope. "Will you be able to return my property to me?"

"I will see what I can do," Wyatt said, careful not to commit himself. "You may be sure that I will keep you abreast of any developments."

"Thank you." Mr. Leipzig let out a sigh. "I wish you luck. Mr. Ponsonby is not accustomed to giving up what he wants. I hope you may have more success than I did. If there is nothing else, I will bid you good day. You may leave a note for me at the hall if there are any developments."

He escorted them out before going back inside. When the door had closed behind him, Wyatt turned to his valet.

"It seems Mr. Ponsonby is as devious as I feared," he said.

"I suppose if a scheme works once, it is only natural to try it again," Durand said.

"It would have been a lot simpler if I'd known about the rest of them before I broke into his study. Or perhaps I ought to have taken all the blueprints, anyway."

"I think you made the right choice, *monsieur*. If you had been wrong, and the other blueprints had been acquired legally, you would have been the one guilty of theft."

"Yet now I will have to risk another break-in and this time without an invitation."

"Why?" Durand asked, eyeing him with a genuine curiosity. "You have done the job that was asked of you and answered the questions you had after. You do not owe these other men anything. You do not even know them."

Wyatt pulled off his hat and began to turn it idly in his hands. His valet made a valid point. He had agreed to retrieve the blueprint for Mr. Leclerc as a favor to George, and he had succeeded. What Leclerc chose to do from this point shouldn't be his concern. Not only did he not know the other inventors, he didn't know Ponsonby. He had no personal reason to be involved. He couldn't even claim to do it for the challenge, because he already knew where the blueprints were, and it was hardly the first time he'd broken into a house the size of Ponsonby's.

Yet, when he considered abandoning the case, the injustice of it did not sit well with him.

As if Durand could sense where his thoughts were going, he said, "This Ponsonby is not the only thief in London. The city is full of men like him, and it always will be. That is the way of the world."

His attitude was not too dissimilar from what Wyatt's had been a year ago. Most of the investigative work he had done had been for his own amusement or to help a friend, motivated by his interest in solving puzzles and testing his intellect. The series of robberies he had been investigating when he met Samantha had intrigued him because he sensed a pattern in them that had been overlooked. Even his offer to help Samantha had been driven more by his curiosity about her than his altruism.

Wyatt didn't know when his attitude had begun to shift—it must have come on gradually. What he did know was that he was no longer content to stand by when he had the power to effect change.

"You are right that there will always be men like Ponsonby," Wyatt said, replacing his hat on his head and signaling for a cab.

"Like him and worse. Stopping him won't do much good, but it will do some. And I would like to do some good."

A cab pulled up, and Wyatt told the driver to take them to Boodles, one of the gentleman's clubs he frequented. It was an open cab, so conversation on the way to the club would have been impossible without shouting over the clattering of horses' hooves and carriage wheels against stone, the calls of the costermongers and the general chatter of Londoners going about their business. As they rode, Durand cast him frequent contemplative glances. Wyatt knew he was considering his response—he always had an opinion of Wyatt's actions—so he wasn't surprised when Durand opened his mouth to speak the moment the cab dropped them off on St. James Street. He was surprised by his words, however.

"I'll do it," Durand said.

"Do what?" Wyatt asked.

"I'll get the blueprints from Ponsonby."

"What? Why? I didn't ask you to. In fact, I said I would do it."

Durand shrugged. "Yes, but if you are caught, there will be trouble."

"There'd be almost as much trouble if you were caught," Wyatt pointed out. "You are in my employ. People would assume I sent you."

"I won't be caught," Durand said with maddening self-assurance.

"Neither would I."

"But you have been," Durand said in a matter-of-fact tone. "In the same study. By a woman, no less."

Wyatt wasn't sure which part of Durand's statement annoyed him more—the dismissive way he referred to Samantha or the inaccuracy of it.

"She didn't catch me," he said. "She was hiding, and I..." He shook his head, refusing to let himself be drawn into an argument. "Why are you volunteering to do something you were trying to talk me out of not half an hour ago?"

Durand shrugged again. Wyatt had noticed it was a favorite gesture of his.

"I like you," he said. "That is rare for me. You trusted me. That is also rare. If it matters to you to stop this man, I will help you, even if I think it is a fool's errand."

For a moment, Wyatt was speechless. He had known Durand was grateful for the work he had given him and for the opportunity to escape Paris, but he'd always assumed his valet merely tolerated him. That little speech had been akin to a declaration of undying loyalty from the normally sardonic Durand.

"Very well," Wyatt said finally. "If you want to be the one to break into Ponsonby's study, go ahead."

SIX

A week later, the snap of fabric woke Samantha as Alice, her maid, yanked open the curtains, letting in a stream of pale, early morning sunlight. Squeezing her eyes shut, Samantha groaned and rolled over, pulling the bedcovers over her head. A moment later, these were mercilessly pulled off of her.

"You told me to wake you early," Alice said far too cheerily in response to Samantha's wordless grumble. "'No matter what', you said."

"I know," Samantha croaked. With an effort, she pushed herself into a sitting position, yawned and stretched. She hadn't batted an eye when Mr. Spenser suggested meeting at half past eight in the morning to go look at a property he had found that he thought might work for a women's refuge. She wanted to make a good impression on him, after all, and suggesting that they postpone because she would be at a ball the night before had seemed frivolous.

There was a light tap on the door, and Annie entered. Her blonde hair, much lighter now that it was no longer covered in dirt as it had been for most of the time Samantha knew her on the streets, was caught up in a white cap. Her bright eyes alit on Samantha, and she made a brief, slightly wobbly curtsey, pinching the edges of her apron-clad black dress as she held it out from her body.

"You left your brush again," Alice said when Annie had straightened. She pointed to the fireplace. A long-handled metal brush lay propped against the mantle.

"Beg pardon, miss," Annie said.

"Don't let it happen again," said Alice. "That sort of thing could get you sacked some places."

Annie nodded meekly, but Samantha saw her roll her eyes as Alice turned back to the wardrobe. Samantha bit back a smile. Though she knew Alice was right to warn Annie to be more careful, especially in the event that she left them at some point for another household, she still found Annie's irreverence amusing.

"How are you, Annie?" Samantha asked.

Annie looked from Samantha to Alice and back.

"Am I allowed to answer that?" she asked, dropping the somewhat affected tones she had adopted moments before.

"Of course," Samantha said.

"Only, and no offence meant, your ladyship, seeing as how it's you as got me this job and I am that grateful, but I ain't never had so many rules in all my life. I can't remember more'n half of 'em even with Mrs. Meadows reminding me every time she sees me."

Samantha had given up trying to explain to Annie that she was not a titled lady. She could only say so many times that, yes, she was a lady in breeding but not in title and ought not be addressed as such before it began to sound nonsensical even to her ears.

"There are a lot of rules," she agreed. "But how do you get on? I know you didn't like Derbyshire, but now we're back in London, have things improved? Are you treated well?"

"I get on alright with most. There's some as look down their noses at me. The boy what cleans the boots said as he'd put me in my place, but I knocked his tooth out, and he don't bother me no more."

Samantha let out a laugh, before schooling her features. "You shouldn't get into fights, Annie."

Annie shrugged. "So says Mrs. Meadows. Another of them rules. But I ain't never stood no guff, and I don't plan to start now. Anyway, once you and Mr. Wyatt are set up, and I'm with you, I won't see that little tick the boots boy no more."

"Mr. Wyatt and I?" Samantha asked, looking to Alice for explanation. "What do you mean once we're set up?"

"Hitched, you know. Married. That's why Mrs. Meadow's training me, ain't it? I know I'm not meant to stay with Lady Bradwell, and you did bring me back to London with you."

"I didn't intend to bring you back to London," Samantha said, a little taken aback to hear Annie's assumptions. "I wanted you to stay safely in Derbyshire, but the housekeeper said you were insistent on coming back. She thought you were homesick."

"I was a bit, I suppose. Never been out of the city before, and I can't say I liked the country much. Not to say it ain't alright for some, but it was too quiet to my mind. And you had to walk for miles to get anywhere interesting. Not to mention I couldn't understand what anyone was saying. It's like they wasn't even speaking English. Anyway, I thought I might as well be here as not, not knowing when you was planning to get hitched."

"I'm not sure why you thought Mr. Wyatt and I were getting married," Samantha said, sure that Alice would have told her if the servants were gossiping about her, "but we're not."

Annie's brow furrowed. "But he's the one you went to when you was in trouble, ain't he? And he's always hanging round. He wrote you letters when we was in the country. One of the maids there saw them."

"She did?" Samantha asked, disconcerted.

"Ain't he asked you yet?"

Samantha glanced at Alice, who had been quietly folding linens on the edge of the bed. She had finally told her about Wyatt's proposal and the subsequent conversations and, though Alice understood Samantha's hesitations, Samantha did not get the feeling she wholly sympathized with them.

"He...may have," Samantha said. "Though that isn't something I would like you to repeat."

"Why? Is it a secret?"

"It is. We aren't engaged."

Annie's eyebrows rose. "You don't like him then?"

"No, I do like him."

"You like someone else better?"

"No, I don't. I don't...I don't intend to marry him or anyone else."

Annie's brow furrowed. "Why?"

Not wishing to delve into her reasoning at that moment, Samantha simply said, "I have money."

Annie laughed. "You had money before. I know the quality of them petticoats what you sold to Joe. He didn't give you close to half what I'm sure he sold 'em for."

In the first weeks of her time living on the streets, Samantha had been forced to sell most of her undergarments to afford food and rent on the small lodging she shared with Annie and four other girls. While her dress was one she had purchased from a secondhand shop not long before her aunt and uncle were murdered, her undergarments had been much finer. Still, she felt a need to explain herself.

"That wasn't my money," Samantha said. "It was my uncle's. And if I hadn't inherited what I did from my grandfather, I'd have needed to marry for security. Now, I don't."

"Never been married myself," Annie said, "but I can't say as I blame you for not wanting to be. From what I've seen, a husband's more trouble than he's worth. Out the pubs half the night, spending all the money on drink, throwing his wife around when he's angry and filling her up with babies when he's not. And that's when he's got a job, which sometimes he hasn't. My cousin says I'll feel differently when I've got a sweetheart, but I told her that won't never happen. I'd sleep in the gutters first."

Samantha remembered all too well sleepless nights in the tenement housing she shared with Annie, being kept awake by loud arguments between couples and the screams of the women. The comparison made her uncomfortable, too, because, however much she might fear the loss of control that came with marriage, she knew Wyatt would never treat her violently.

"If you won't marry Mr. Wyatt, what'll you do?" Annie asked. "Get your own place?"

"Eventually, yes, though I can't do that yet without causing a stir. Madge—Lady Bradwell—thinks it's best if I spend this Season showing Society how ladylike and ordinary I am to stop all the rumors."

"And then you'll get your own place."

"Yes." Samantha smiled. "And I will take you on as a housemaid, if you like."

"If you can learn to do as you're told," Alice said, looking sternly at Annie. "You can't expect Miss Kingston to protect you if you keep hitting boots boys."

Annie huffed indignantly. "I don't expect no one to protect me."

"I'm sure you will do quite well," Samantha said. "I don't wish to keep you from your duties any longer, though. You may go."

Tapping the long-handled brush against the hearth to remove some of the soot, Annie curtseyed again and left the room. Alice brought Samantha's petticoats to her and began to help her dress.

"Are you dissatisfied with Annie?" Samantha asked.

"I know you owe her a debt," Alice said, lifting the first petticoat over Samantha's head, "but she is causing disruptions in the servant's hall."

"How so?"

"In some ways, merely by being there. They were all around when she turned up this winter, bloodied and bruised and insisting on seeing you. It caused no end of speculation." Alice reached for the second petticoat and shook it out. "Then you disappeared with her to the country and returned in the spring saying she was a housemaid. No doubt they heard all about the trouble she was in Derbyshire from the staff there and wondered why she'd been kept on." She went to the wardrobe to retrieve a blue pinstriped dress and began to help Samantha into it. "Then, there's her way of speaking, and not only the language she uses, but the disrespect she shows to the upper servants. In any other household, she would have been sacked weeks ago."

Samantha grimaced. "I know it's a strange situation, but I couldn't think what else to do for her. After all, it is my fault that she was attacked, and if I sent her back on the streets, who's to say that it wouldn't happen again?"

"It wasn't your fault, miss," Alice said, looking up at her from where she was adjusting Samantha's skirts. "You can't hold yourself responsible for someone else's actions."

"Can't I?" Samantha sounded defeated even to her own ears. "Even when those actions were clearly a message for me?"

"Even then. How could you have known he would do such a thing?"

Samantha knew Alice was trying to console her, but no words could erase the facts.

"It still never would have happened if not for me," she said.

"It never would have happened if not for him," Alice said stubbornly. "And it won't happen again because of you—because you took her in when she needed protection."

"I thought you disapproved of her being here."

Alice took her time before answering, busying herself in searching Samantha's wardrobe for her boots.

"Of her being a servant, perhaps," she said when she returned with the correct pair. "And I think she ought to have stayed in Derbyshire, but I don't disapprove of you taking her in."

Alice may have been Samantha's servant, rather than her peer, but she had known her longer than anyone else, and it was a comfort to have her support.

"Thank you," Samantha said.

If Alice found it strange to be thanked for her approval of her mistress's actions, she didn't show it. She merely nodded and finished fastening the tiny row of buttons that secured Samantha's boots.

For the twin purposes of chaperonage and moral support, Eden had offered to accompany Samantha on her errand that morning. Samantha picked her up in Madge's carriage, and together they went to fetch Mr. Spenser.

Samantha had been afraid the trip from Mr. Spenser's city offices to the property he had found in Hammersmith would be awkward. After all, though they had exchanged half a dozen letters discussing their ideas and she had come to like him, they had only met once in person since their initial meeting at Miss Coutts'. However, he proved an easy conversationalist.

When they had covered all the usual pleasantries, he turned to Samantha and said, "I hope you are as eager as I am to see if this property is a match for our purposes."

Samantha relaxed under his friendly gaze. "I am indeed, sir. From what you sent me, it seems almost perfect."

"That it does. Whether it lives up to it in reality is another matter."

"Have you bought a lot of property, Mr. Spenser?" Eden asked.

"Enough to know the tricks, my lady."

"Is property your primary interest?"

Mr. Spenser smiled. "Not property, my lady, but progress—the progress of this great nation through technological and scientific advancement." He sobered. "But I would never wish that progress to be made at the cost of the less fortunate among us. That is why I so appreciate finding like-minded people to work with." He nodded to Samantha. "We must all do what we can to help those who cannot help themselves."

"That is very enlightened of you," Eden said with a nod of approval. "There are many among us who would claim poverty is the effect of a lazy and unmotivated workforce, criminal by nature."

Mr. Spenser frowned. "Yes, it is a comfort to those who would not lift a finger to save a dying child to imagine that their efforts would be wasted. After all, if class is a matter of inborn moral virtue, there is no need to feel guilty overspending on fripperies while your fellow man starves to death."

Samantha appreciated the passion with which Mr. Spenser spoke. It increased her confidence in their partnership.

"That is very neatly put," she said. "Though, while I agree with you in principle, I think, perhaps, there is room for grace."

He frowned, tilting his head to one side. "Why would you say that?"

Samantha considered her words. She had been thinking of herself when she spoke and the way her understanding of poverty had changed after living with it and meeting people like Annie. She had never wholly subscribed to the tenet that the poorest among them were inherently criminal, particularly after reading Henry Mayhew's journalistic work on the subject, but she had allowed herself to see the poor as something separate from her—a people of such different lives as to be almost another species. It had been easy to do so when everyone around her did the same, and it made it simpler to disconnect from the degradation she saw from the windows of her carriage, particularly when, while under her uncle's power, she could not do much to alleviate it.

"For many," she said, "ignorance is certainly a choice, but it takes strong character to question a deeply ingrained belief, and a strong conviction to reject it."

"You may call me cynical, Miss Kingston," Mr. Spenser said with a shake of his head, "but I cannot hold such a positive view of those who would see a malnourished child and think it was living its own just reward."

"Naturally not, but I do not think many people consider the matter so consciously. Perhaps if they did, they would see the fallacy in their own logic."

"Unconscious or conscious ignorance, the result is the same—neglect."

Samantha nodded, uncomfortably aware of the truth of his statement as it applied to her past self. "You make a valid argument, sir."

"Certainly there is no one here who is so ungenerous," Eden said, ever the peacemaker. There hadn't been any danger of the argument escalating, but Samantha appreciated her friend's diplomacy none the less.

"I believe Miss Kingston said we are going to Hammersmith," Eden continued. "Is that correct?"

Mr. Spenser said it was, and they spent the rest of the drive discussing the merits of a location so removed from the center of the city.

Samantha had never been as far west as Hammersmith, but it had been in the nearby borough of Shepherd's Bush that Miss Coutts and Mr. Dickens had established Urania Cottage. From all Miss Coutts had said, it had been an ideal location—far enough from the familiarity of the women's old lives to allow them to reestablish themselves while still being within easy distance of the trains and the shops.

"To the left is the entrance to Ravenscourt Park," Mr. Spenser said, pointing out the window to a narrow green space. "It's really quite large, but it's surrounded by houses, so most of it isn't visible from the road."

"That will be nice for the women," Eden said. "There is so little green space in the East End."

"Wait until you see the house."

A minute later, they turned onto Goldhawk Road and stopped in front of a modest, two-story house with a walled front garden. With square windows and a flat, unassuming yellow brick façade, it was far from what Samantha was used to, but she knew it was more than what many of the women she hoped to bring to it could have imagined. All the houses on that side of the road were detached, and Samantha could see through the gaps between them to the farmland beyond.

"It's lovely," she said as she took Madge's footman Peter's hand and stepped down from the carriage.

She took a moment to look around as the others exited behind her and was pleasantly surprised by what she saw. The train tracks to the south were the sole blot on an otherwise beautiful—for London—landscape. It was quieter here than in the heart of the city and the air felt fresher, cleaner. She could imagine it being a haven to women who had spent their lives surrounded by the coal-black grime and tightly packed housing of the East End.

A dull thump and movement to her right drew Samantha's attention back to the carriage, and she turned in time to see a man roll out from underneath it. He wore a black cap over his dirty blond hair and his boots were caked in mud. He looked up at the house and then down the street as though taking note of the location. When he turned back, he caught Samantha's eye. The corner of his mouth lifted in a smirk that made her heart seize up with fear.

"Peter?" Samantha called over her shoulder.

"Yes, miss. I see him."

Madge had assigned Peter to her in part because of his

intimidating size. At six foot three and almost fifteen stone, he was not a typical footman, but he was an effective bodyguard. As he stepped in front of her, the blond man tipped his black cap mockingly and turned down the street, moving swiftly but steadily away. Samantha watched him go until he turned the corner and disappeared.

"Are you alright, miss?" Peter asked, turning to her now that the threat was gone.

Samantha closed her eyes and pinched the bridge of her nose.

"I'm fine," she said.

"You've no need to worry, miss. I won't let anyone come near you."

"I know." She gave him a tight smile. "Thank you."

"Is something wrong?" Mr. Spenser asked, coming to join them. He followed Peter's gaze to the end of the street.

"No, nothing is wrong," Samantha said, dropping her hand and forcing a smile. She turned and squinted up at the house. "Are you ready to show us inside?"

For the next half hour, Samantha tried to focus on the task at hand. She exclaimed over the view out the back windows and complimented Mr. Spenser on finding a house in such a perfect location. She made notes on the condition of the kitchen range, the state of the outdoor privy and the number of windows that would need replacing. Yet, the whole time, she could not stop thinking about the blond man.

She had no doubt Skinny Jim had sent him to follow her. He had made his wishes known, and he was going to intimidate her into complying. She wondered how long he would be content to merely threaten before he made good on those threats. Were she and Wyatt fooling themselves into thinking they could avoid him at all? The blond man had made particular note of the house. Once Skinny Jim learned of it, what did he plan to do with the information? She thought of Annie that Christmas, covered in blood and bruises. Was she risking condemning the women she might bring here to the same fate? Ought she to give up her plans? Or would meeting with him really be so bad?

By the time they had finished the tour and piled back into the carriage, Samantha was no closer to an answer than she had been. She wished Wyatt were there to discuss it with her, but she had no idea when she would see him next. She supposed she would just have to wait.

SEVEN

Waiting proved disastrous. The third morning after her trip to Hammersmith began, as it often did, with Samantha sitting down to breakfast with Madge and her husband, Lord Bradwell. Their breakfasts tended to be quiet affairs, with each reading through the newspapers or their correspondence, occasionally sharing snippets of information but mostly keeping to themselves. Samantha enjoyed these meals. The relaxed atmosphere was a world away from the heightened tension that had marked meals in her uncle's household wherein she tried her best not to be noticed by or made a target of her uncle's caustic temper.

That morning, Samantha was reading an article about a robbery and murder in Soho when she recognized the name of the victim: Theodore Spenser. She felt the blood drain from her face. Quickly, she re-read the article.

At half past three yesterday afternoon, the residents of Soho received a shock when the body of a man, brutally stabbed to death, was discovered in an alleyway between a chemist's and a draper's shop. The man who discovered the body, Mr. Alan White of Warwick Street, said that he was on his way home when he saw a man in a brown checked suit exiting the alleyway at undue speed.

"He gave me a queer feeling," said Mr. White. "And I was sure I saw blood on his trousers and jacket. My wife was with me, and I told her to stand back, but I had to check that alleyway. Never thought I'd see what I did, though. I won't easily forget it."

Mr. White immediately went to get the nearest constable, who alerted the detective branch of Scotland Yard. Inspector Whicher was the first detective on the scene. He declined to comment, but an unnamed source says that the victim's personal items, including watch and wallet, were missing, leading police to suspect a robbery gone wrong.

Since our report in last evening's paper, police have identified the victim as one Theodore Spenser, 48, a known philanthropist and proprietor of Spenser's Bank in the City.

The newspaper dropped from Samantha's numb hands.

"What's wrong?" Madge asked.

"It's Mr. Spenser," Samantha said. "He's dead."

"What?" Madge exclaimed.

Lord Bradwell jumped at the sound and dropped his teaspoon with a clatter.

"What's wrong?" he asked.

"Oh, Samantha, I'm so sorry," Madge said, ignoring her husband. "How did he die?"

"Who died?" Lord Bradwell asked.

"Mr. Spenser, my love," Madge explained. "The man Samantha was working with on that charitable venture."

"Ah. My condolences, Miss Kingston," Lord Bradwell said.

He picked up his spoon and resumed stirring his tea.

"Thank you," Samantha said. Then, to Madge, she added, "He was murdered."

"Murdered?" Madge said. Lord Bradwell stopped stirring his

tea. "What happened?"

Samantha read the article aloud.

"Don't know what this country's coming to," Lord Bradwell said. "Man can't get around in his own city without being set upon."

"I'm so sorry, my dear," Madge said, leaning forward to pat Samantha's hand. "Do let me know his address, and we'll send flowers and a basket to his widow. Was he married?" Samantha shook her head. "His mother then, the poor woman."

"If you don't mind," Samantha said, pushing her chair back and getting shakily to her feet, "I think I need a moment."

She hurried out of the room. In the hall, she took several deep, unsteady breaths as she fought to calm her stomach. Mr. Spenser was dead. He'd been murdered. She could not stop her mind from imagining the kind, good-hearted Mr. Spenser meeting a horrific, violent end. Nor could she stop the cold sweat that trickled down her back as she realized it was all her fault.

When she could move again, she hurried to the morning room, where she found a stack of paper and a pen. She dashed off a note to Wyatt, asking him to meet her at the National Gallery in an hour and went to find a footman. With the note dispatched, she rushed upstairs and rang for Alice to help her dress.

Pacing up and down the central hall of the National Gallery almost an hour later, Samantha barely looked at the paintings that hung around her. She had taken off her gloves and was twisting them in her hands, glancing with increasing frequency through the vestibule towards the front entrance.

"You'll stretch them beyond repair," Alice said, taking the gloves and smoothing them out.

"What if he wasn't home?" Samantha asked. "What if he didn't get my note?"

"Then we'll wait another half hour and send a note to his

clubs."

"That is a good plan," Samantha nodded. She rocked back and forth on the balls of her feet. "Though, I don't know that my nerves will stand to wait that long."

"Nor mine," Alice muttered loud enough for Samantha to overhear.

Samantha smiled. She was about to thank Alice for relieving some of the tension when she glanced to the door for the hundred and first time and saw Wyatt enter. The nervous energy she had built up over the past few minutes urged her to run to him, and it took all of her restraint to walk slowly, not drawing attention to herself.

She saw the moment he recognized her. His eyes lit up, and he hurried up the steps. They met in the middle of the vestibule. Samantha's hand reached out of its own accord and grasped his arm, needing the physical reassurance of his presence.

"What's wrong?" he asked. He stepped closer, taking her elbow as his eyes searched her face. "Your message said it was urgent. Is it Skinny Jim? You aren't hurt, are you?"

"I'm not hurt," she assured him. "It's about Mr. Spenser. He's —he's dead, Wyatt."

The first time she had said the words aloud, she had been in a state of disbelief, and they had seemed unreal. This time, she felt the weight of truth in them. She had just been talking to him three days ago, and now he was gone. Though she hadn't known him well, the suddenness and harshness of his passing hit her with an unexpected sadness.

"I'm so sorry, Samantha," Wyatt said softly.

He pulled her in and wrapped his arms around her. She leaned into his embrace, breathing in the scent of woodsmoke that clung to his coat. For a moment, she forgot where they were, reveling in the strength of his arms and the sense of comfort he gave her. Then Alice cleared her throat, and they broke apart.

"It's alright," she said, blinking against the sudden sting of tears. "It isn't as though we were close. I hardly knew him. But he was a good man, and it was so sudden."

"How did he die?"

"He was murdered. Stabbed to death in an alleyway."

Wyatt's head reared back. "What?"

Samantha took his arm and led him down the gallery. Alice fell into step behind them. Lowering her voice, Samantha said, "I didn't want to worry Madge or Lord Bradwell. That's why I asked to meet you here."

"He was murdered?"

"The newspaper says he was killed in a robbery, but I'm afraid that isn't what really happened."

Wyatt nodded to a couple passing in the opposite direction.

"You think Skinny Jim was involved," he said.

"I do."

She proceeded to explain about her visit to the house in Hammersmith with Mr. Spenser and the man who had ridden there on the back of their carriage.

"He was looking at the house," she finished by saying. "I assumed, if anything, it would be the house Skinny Jim targeted at some point, or at least that he wanted me to know he knew about it to frighten me. I was going to talk to you about it, to ask if I shouldn't go forward with the project, at least for now. I never would have imagined it would be Mr. Spenser he targeted."

The muscles in Wyatt's arm tightened under Samantha's grip, and she looked up to see him scowling, his jaw tense.

"It's certainly an escalation from what he did to Annie," he said.

They walked in silence for a minute. Samantha's mind raced as she contemplated their options. But, realistically, there was only one.

"I think we have to meet him," she said. "We have to find out what he wants."

Wyatt rubbed the back of his neck and grimaced. "I know. I hate it, but it's true. I still can't help but worry we'll be walking into a trap. I'll have to think of the best way to go about it."

"He has spent the last few weeks showing me that he can get to me whenever he likes," Samantha pointed out. "If he wanted to kill me, he could have done it by now."

"True, but killing you isn't the only harm he could do." He sighed. "I want us to go in disguise. Not to fool him, but so that no one recognizes us on the way there."

"I'll have to find a way to sneak out without anyone seeing me," Samantha said. "Alice will help, but we should probably go at night."

"Does she know about Skinny Jim?"

"She knows everything."

They stopped walking in front of a painting of a serious-looking young man in sixteenth century clothing standing at a table holding a large pair of scissors. Samantha read the placard beneath the painting. *The Tailor*, by Giovanni Battista Moroni.

"I don't recognize this," Wyatt said.

Samantha looked behind them and saw several people had come within earshot.

"It's probably new," she said. "I read that the director of the gallery was traveling to Italy this year to expand the collection. This could be one of his new acquisitions."

"I like it." Wyatt's eyes were trained on the face of the portrait's subject. "His appearance is so lifelike. It's almost as though he's in the room with us."

"And wishing us gone," she said. "He looks annoyed."

"I suppose we are interrupting his work. He seems a serious fellow, despite those comical trousers."

They walked on to the next painting and were not followed.

"When do you think we can go?" Samantha asked in a lowered voice.

"Give me a couple of days to work it all out. I want to plan our route there and back, and I'll need to get us something to wear. I'll let you know."

Samantha nodded.

"There's something else," he said.

His tone worried her. What else could there be?

"I'm telling this so you'll be on your guard. Bingo warned me about a bet in a private betting book. A bet that concerns you."

"According to him, there are a number of bets that concern me."

Samantha sounded bitter even to her own ears.

"Yes, but this one has the potential to be dangerous for you. Mr. Ramsey has bet fifty pounds he will steal a kiss from you by the end of the Season."

She gaped at him. "Fifty pounds? Is he mad?"

"Desperate, according to Bingo. I don't want you to worry—he and I will be keeping an eye on Ramsey—but I want you to be careful."

"Yes," Samantha said hollowly. "Thank you."

She felt sick. It had been bad enough to learn that men were betting on her future as though she were an entrant in the Derby, but this was much worse. Even without the bet being fulfilled, she felt violated. She remembered Mr. Ramsey. She'd danced with him on more than one occasion. He'd been friendly, funny even, with a sardonic humor. As with her other suitors, she hadn't taken him seriously, but she had actually liked him. Now, knowing what he had planned for her, she wanted to vomit.

"He's a vile, pathetic excuse for a gentleman," Wyatt said, "and if it weren't that people would ask why, I'd knock his teeth in."

A slow smile formed on her lips.

"I'd join you," she said.

"I know you would."

He rubbed his nose and her smile widened.

They walked on past half a dozen paintings. Samantha hardly noticed them, too distracted by Wyatt's presence beside her.

"It occurs to me now," Wyatt said, drawing her closer and offering her a mischievous grin, "that we find ourselves in a unique situation. There's no suitor of yours nearby to make a nuisance of himself nor any friends or family to interrupt us."

"There is Alice," Samantha said even as her pulse ticked up.

"True, but she's very politely focused on the artwork."

"Hadn't you better go?" Samantha asked, aware she was floundering for an excuse. "You said you needed to plan for our excursion."

"I can't do much now that I couldn't do this afternoon. Time with you, on the other hand, is a rare commodity. I wonder that I never considered meeting you like this before."

The way he looked at her—like she was the center of his world—made her breath catch. She found herself leaning into him, wanting everything that look promised. Then Alice coughed, and the spell was broken. Samantha shook herself mentally and responded to what he had said.

"Likely because it could have consequences if someone were to see us." She was proud of how calm and collected she sounded. "We don't need to fuel the gossip further."

She started to pull her arm away, but he laid his hand on hers.

"Samantha," he said, leaning towards her, "we've done all we can on that front. People will gossip as they like. Besides, you and Bingo are doing a fine job confusing things. I'm only asking for twenty minutes more with you. Maybe thirty."

"Twenty," Samantha said.

Wyatt's smile broadened. "Twenty, it is."

*****

As Samantha climbed out of her bedroom window two nights later, holding fast to the rope she had tied to the bedpost, she couldn't help but think of the last time she had done so. It had been almost a year since that fateful day when her aunt and uncle were shot and she had fled the house in terror of becoming the next victim. So much had changed in the meantime. Yet, as Samantha looked down to estimate her distance to the ground, some of the terror she had felt then resurged in her breast.

She was more prepared this time, she reminded herself. The rope was more secure than the trellis had been, and she'd had time to put on shoes. Too, the loose shirt and trousers Wyatt had sent her were easier to climb in than her dress had been. There was no one in the house wishing to kill her. In fact, she was only sneaking out because she knew Madge cared about her and would disapprove of her leaving.

Still, as she glanced down again, the memory of Slater, Charles' accomplice in the murders, standing below her in his long dark coat, assailed her. As clearly as she had that night, she saw his piercing blue eyes fixed on her as he raised his pistol and aimed it at her. Her heart sped up, and her fingers tightened on the rope. She closed her eyes and took several calming breaths.

Slater was dead. She'd seen him laid out on a table in the morgue after they pulled him from the Thames. Charles had killed him, as he had killed her uncle, her aunt, their housekeeper, and her cousin, Cyril. Charles was dead now, too. Though they'd never found his killer, they were fairly certain Skinny Jim had been behind his death. He'd had Charles killed to keep him from testifying about the role he had played in those deaths as well as the robberies he had forced Charles to commit. And now Samantha was going to see the man—to visit him at his pub as she had all those months ago before she really knew who he was or what he was capable of.

When Samantha's feet hit the ground, she tugged three times on the rope and watched as Alice drew it back up into the room. Alice had been less than enthusiastic about Samantha's plan to sneak out and travel through the city at night with Wyatt. She had spent all day trying to dissuade her but, in the end, she had announced that, if Samantha was going to be foolhardy, she was going to make sure she was as safe as could be. Alice had pinned Samantha's hair up under her cap so that it was much more secure than when she'd pretended to be a boy before. She had also thought to smear dirt on Samantha's face to disguise some of her femininity. She even procured the rope they'd used to lower Samantha out the window.

When the rope had disappeared completely, Alice's head popped out. It took her a moment to find Samantha in the darkness, but when their eyes met, Samantha gave her a reassuring wave before stepping through the back gate to the mews.

Keeping her head down, Samantha exited the mews and turned left along the street. Just as she had the last time she wore trousers, she felt uncomfortably exposed without the concealing protection of skirt and petticoats and she was terrified that, at any moment, someone might see through her flimsy disguise. Yet, at the same time, she felt a freedom in being a boy. Her posture relaxed and she slouched along, shoving her hands into the pockets of her rough canvas trousers.

When she left Grosvenor Square behind, she began to look out for Wyatt, ducking her head whenever someone glanced in her direction. As she passed a narrow alleyway, a hand shot out and grabbed her arm, pulling her inside.

"You could have called out," she said, placing a hand over her racing heart. "You scared me half to death."

"What would I have said?" Wyatt asked. "'Oy! Samantha!'?"

"Sam would have served the purpose."

"Very well, 'Sam'. Let me look at you."

Wyatt took a half step back, which was all he could manage in that narrow alleyway, and looked her up and down. She did the same to him, taking in his linen shirt and trousers and the ill-fitting coat with its patched elbows.

"May I?" Wyatt asked, gesturing to her shirt.

When she nodded, he tugged at the fabric, pulling it loose of her waistband so that it ballooned out more at the waist. She was intensely aware of the way his fingers brushed her sides.

He stepped back and surveyed his work. Then he frowned.

"What?" Samantha asked.

"I *might* be persuaded you were a boy from the neck down, but your face gives you away."

"I was a lot dirtier when I did this before," Samantha said. "The black eye also helped."

"Well, that isn't an option now. Here."

He scrubbed a hand over the stone wall, smearing his palm and fingers with coal dust. Then he stepped closer. Taking her chin in his hands, he began to rub the dust onto her cheeks and under her eyes. They were so close now, Samantha could feel the heat from his body. She could see the flecks of gold in his eyes and the shadow of the beard he must have grown to aid his disguise.

Without thinking, she reached up and touched his cheek, feeling the rough stubble beneath her fingers. Wyatt stilled. His eyes flicked to hers. She felt caught, yet she did not remove her hand. For several breathless moments, neither of them moved. Then, slowly, Wyatt slid his hand behind her head, his fingers cupping the nape of her neck. With his other hand, he tilted her chin up. She saw his pupils dilate and her breath hitched as he lowered his mouth to hers.

A loud crash resounded in the street beyond. The sound pulled Samantha's gaze from Wyatt's to the opening of the alleyway. She could see a man standing over the wreckage of a crate. He appeared to have dropped it while unloading a cart. A second man began chastising him for his error, and the shouting echoed down the alleyway cutting the tension of the moment.

"We should go," Wyatt said.

Samantha looked back at him in time to catch the flash of regret in his eyes before he released her and stepped back. She tried to ignore her own regret as she nodded in agreement.

"Yes," she said. "We don't want to be out all night."

It was a long walk to The Lion and Eagle, the pub from which Skinny Jim did most of his business. Samantha wished they could have taken a hackney, but it would have looked odd for a working-class man and boy, as they appeared to be, to have money to spend on a cab. They didn't talk. Wyatt was focused on watching their surroundings, looking for threats, and Samantha was struggling with the memories walking the streets at night had triggered.

When they reached Blackfriars, Samantha began to recognize the buildings they passed. The last time she had been that way, she'd been with Slater and Palmer, Skinny Jim's men. They'd been on their way to rob a house, and Skinny Jim had expected her to return with them afterwards. She hadn't. Instead, she'd gone to Wyatt. Now, Slater was dead, Palmer had been sent to Australia, and Skinny Jim knew her real name.

A boy of about twelve with a mop of untidy dark hair stepped out from a doorway in front of them. Samantha thought he might have been Chinese, but she wasn't certain. During her time on the streets, she had come to realize that London was much more diverse than the narrow world she occupied had led her to believe.

Wyatt approached the boy and muttered a few words to him. Then he flicked a coin, and the boy caught it in one hand and bit the edge. Satisfied, he nodded to Wyatt and went back inside.

"Who was that?" Samantha asked.

"Bo. He's one of my informants. If we're not back here in an hour, he'll take my card to Inspector Whicher and tell him what happened."

"Oh."

She had known they were taking a risk by agreeing to meet Skinny Jim in his territory, but hearing that Wyatt had made a contingency plan to inform Scotland Yard if it all went badly made the danger of their situation suddenly more tangible.

"We don't have to go," Wyatt said, and she realized that some of her uncomfortable epiphany must have shown in her face. "If you want, we can turn around right now."

"No." She shook her head, resolve overcoming her fear. "We need to go. It's the only way we'll get answers."

Wyatt nodded and glanced around. "If you're sure, we should hurry. I don't want to be here any longer than we have to be."

"How will Bo know when it's been an hour?" Samantha asked as they started walking again.

"I got him a cheap pocket watch yesterday. He promised not to hock it until this is over."

When they reached the river's edge, Samantha spotted the pub right away.

"There it is," she said, pointing to the swinging sign with its poorly painted lion.

As they approached it, laughter and loud conversation, muffled by the heavy wooden door and lead-lined front window, trickled out into the street. Through the window, Samantha could see some of the pub's rough clientele, warped by the glass, gathered around the small square tables that filled the main room.

"Last chance," Wyatt said.

But Samantha had already made her decision, and she wasn't about to go back on it. She walked past Wyatt to the door and pulled it open.

Her first thought as she crossed the threshold was that nothing had changed; her second, that it would have been absurd to imagine that it had. It had been less than a year, after all, since she last stepped foot inside The Lion and Eagle. And, judging by the blackmail he was holding over her head, Skinny Jim hadn't changed, so why should his pub?

The moment they walked inside, Wyatt's demeanor altered. He swaggered up to the bar and leaned on the counter as though he belonged there. When she didn't immediately follow, he looked back and jerked his head impatiently, thoroughly immersed in the role he had adopted. Considering that when they first met, he'd been disguised as Archie Kennedy, it shouldn't have been a surprise to her, but she found herself in awe of the ease with which he slipped into character.

As Samantha joined Wyatt, the barman approached. She recognized him as Daniel, the tall black man who'd run the bar when she was there in the guise of "Sam."

"We're here to see Skinny Jim," Wyatt said when Daniel asked what they wanted.

"You and everyone else," Daniel said. "You want a drink or what?"

As Wyatt ordered, Samantha's attention was drawn to the figure at the back of the room. Skinny Jim—the author of her nightmares and the source of all her ills—sat at his usual table, alone. Still the largest and most intimidating man she had ever seen, he lounged back against his chair. Yet despite his relaxed posture, he had an air of watchfulness about him. His gaze flicked from person to person, taking in his surroundings, though his stoic face betrayed none of his thoughts.

When his eyes met hers, they lingered. She forced herself not to react as his eyebrows rose a fraction of an inch. A smile that failed to add any warmth to his countenance stole across his lips, and he crooked a finger in an unmistakable beckoning gesture. Samantha's stomach twisted with a combination of fear and loathing. She put a hand on Wyatt's shoulder. When he turned to her in inquiry, she nodded her head in Skinny Jim's direction. A slight stiffening of his posture was Wyatt's only reaction before he set down his drink and followed her to the back of the pub.

Skinny Jim maintained eye contact with Samantha as she approached him. She forced herself not to look away; it felt as though doing so would be an admission of defeat. Somehow, she managed to negotiate the tables and chairs between them without tripping and stopped in front of him. He gestured for her and Wyatt to sit, which they did. Then, they waited.

Samantha had the uncanny sense that she was in the middle of a game for which she did not know the rules. Was she meant to wait for Skinny Jim to speak, as though he were royalty? If she spoke first, would it prove her contempt for the man? Or was it the one who spoke last who maintained the upper hand? Did that demonstrate control?

Beside her, Wyatt was also silent, though he radiated tension. They had agreed before coming that Samantha would take the lead in the conversation since it was she Skinny Jim had compelled to come. It had been Wyatt's suggestion, in fact, and she appreciated the trust he placed in her, as she knew it could not have been easy for him to choose to sit back.

In the end, Samantha's impatience won out over logic. She was tired of playing this man's games.

"We got your messages," she said, unable to keep the bite of bitterness from her voice.

Skinny Jim nodded slowly. Then he spoke, his voice deep and hoarse.

"Yet, you took your time in coming."

"I'm not sure why you couldn't have told me what you wanted through one of your lackeys," Samantha said, putting up a brave front but electing not to engage with him about their delay. Any excuse she could give would only make him angry. "There was no need for us to come all the way here."

"There was," he said. "I needed you to know I was serious about this business."

"What business?" Samantha asked.

"The kind between an employer and an employee."

"I'm not your employee," Samantha said, laying a hand on Wyatt's knee as he stiffened beside her.

"I don't bring people on for a job or two," Skinny Jim said, his voice deceptively nonchalant. "Once you work for me, you work for me until I say otherwise."

"I never agreed to that."

Skinny Jim's expression was flat as he said, "You came to me, *boy*. It's your own fault if you didn't learn what you were agreeing to first."

Samantha stared at him. He couldn't think she'd work for him again, could he? He knew who she was now. He had to know how absurd a suggestion that was.

"Do you really expect her to house-break for you?" Wyatt asked contemptuously. "She's not some street urchin you can order around."

Skinny Jim gave Wyatt an assessing look. Then he smiled. It did not reach his eyes.

"I wondered what it would take to make you speak, Mr. Wyatt. You really are as chivalrous as the newspapers make you seem. Or is it only my snakesman that brings it out of you?"

"She's not your anything," Wyatt snapped.

"Nor is she yours," Skinny Jim said placidly. "At least, not legally. I suppose the two of you might have a less socially acceptable arrangement."

Samantha grabbed Wyatt's arm to keep him from striking out at Skinny Jim. She was almost as angry herself, but Skinny Jim ignored her furious scowl.

"No, I don't suppose you do," he said. "Imagine what it would do to your delicate reputations if you did, and anyone found out. It would almost be as bad as if someone found out you lied about being together all summer when Sam, here, was working for me."

"No one would believe you," Samantha said, though she had gone cold with dread.

"I wouldn't say no one," Skinny Jim said with a shrug. "But it'd be hard to ignore the half dozen people who saw Lady Bradwell board a train at Hope Station while she was supposed to have been in London for over a month. Or the local curate who remembers having dinner with her more than once during that time."

The bottom dropped out of Samantha's stomach. She felt sick. When Wyatt asked Madge to come to London to act as chaperone while Samantha stayed under his roof that summer, they'd known the idea wasn't perfect. It covered the proprieties during the time of Samantha's actual visit, but, as they were pretending she'd been with him during the five weeks she'd actually been hiding on the streets, they'd had to pretend Madge had been there during that time, too.

Aiding them in their deception was the fact that most of Society had been in London for those weeks, which meant that Madge had been living in relative seclusion out in Derbyshire, playing host mainly to local dignitaries with few connections to London Society. Too, she had an impeccable reputation, and few were brave enough to gainsay her. However, if anyone took the effort to make inquiries, it wouldn't be hard to poke holes in their story, as Skinny Jim apparently already had.

"Let me understand," Wyatt said through gritted teeth. "You have no qualms about killing a man in order to get us to this meeting, but once we're here, you restrain yourself to the threat of social ruin to force Saman—Sam to work for you?"

Skinny Jim was quiet for a moment. He picked up the tankard in front of him and took a drink.

"I may not be a toff," he said, setting the tankard down, "but I know enough of them to know the power of social ruin. Some even call it social death. And the benefit of this kind of death is that the person has to live through it. To many, it's far more effective than a death threat. To me, it's far less messy."

"Then why kill Mr. Spenser at all?" Samantha said indignantly. "If you were going to threaten my reputation, why kill an innocent man?"

Skinny Jim actually laughed. "There's no such thing as an innocent man."

"He hadn't done anything to you," Samantha insisted.

"I have a job for you," Skinny Jim said. "Tonight. I wasn't planning to have you start tonight, but you already look the part."

"I don't work for you."

"You do if you want to keep your precious reputation." He smiled. "And as an extra incentive, when you finish the job, I'll tell you what you want to know about Mr. Spenser."

"What job?" Wyatt asked.

Samantha looked at him in surprise. She would have expected him to throw Skinny Jim's offer back in his face.

"An easy one," Skinny Jim said. "And one that won't bother your high and mighty conscience because it's about getting back what's already mine."

Wyatt met Samantha's gaze. "What do you want to do?"

What she wanted to do was wipe the confident smirk from Skinny Jim's face before leaving his pub and never returning. However, two things held her back. The first was the threat of exposure and not only because of the effect it would have on her own life, but because Wyatt and Madge and Madge's whole family were tied up in the deception. She didn't feel she could make a decision one way or the other without consulting at least Madge. The second thing that held her back was curiosity. Skinny Jim's offer to tell her what she wanted to know about Mr. Spenser implied there was more to the man's death than retaliation for her refusal to come to the pub. If there was more, especially if there was a chance his death was not her fault, she had to know.

"I'll do it," she said.

A series of emotions flickered across Wyatt's face. She didn't catch them all, but the one she had feared to see—disappointment —did not appear.

"I'm coming with you," he said.

"Not that I don't trust you," Skinny Jim said blandly, "but I'll be sending Kieran with you as well. You remember Kieran, Sam? He'll make sure everything is done properly."

He motioned with his hand, and Samantha turned to see the stern face of a man she could have gone a lifetime without seeing again. Heavily muscled arms strained against the fabric of his sleeves, and the tattoo of an anchor on his bicep showed faintly through. He didn't so much as glance at Samantha, showing her the same disregard he had last summer, when she'd been assigned to help him break into a house.

"You're still on for the Connor job," Skinny Jim said, addressing Kieran, "but these two are coming with you now, 'stead of Billy. Sam'll get you in."

"Yes, boss," Kieran said.

"Report back here," Skinny Jim said. Then, with a significant look at Samantha and Wyatt, he added, "All of you."

EIGHT

When they left the pub, Kieran took the lead, not even glancing behind him to ensure that Wyatt and Samantha were following. Wyatt let Samantha precede him so he could keep an eye on her without appearing to do so. He wished he could talk to her, to ask her how she was doing after that conversation with Skinny Jim, but they couldn't risk it. Nor, at the pace Kieran was going, would such a thing have been possible in that moment.

Once there were half a dozen buildings between them and the pub, their muscled escort stopped and turned to face them. Ignoring Wyatt, he fixed Samantha with a glare.

"Listen," he said, pointing a calloused finger at her. "I don't care where you disappeared to or why you're suddenly back after all this time. I don't care about you at all. But I won't have you pulling a stunt like you did last time."

Wyatt didn't know what he was referring to. Samantha had not told him much about her time on the streets, beyond what she did with Slater and Palmer. He watched her reaction, but her face gave nothing away.

"I've worked too hard to get back in his favor for you to ruin it for me," Kieran continued. "You won't mess this up for me. Nor will you." He turned his glare on Wyatt, then added, "I'll make sure this goes smoothly however I need to. Understood?"

They nodded. Though, when Kieran turned back around, Wyatt's hand went to his coat, feeling the reassuring presence of the pistol concealed within it. He would use it only as a last resort because he didn't want to bring down more of Skinny Jim's wrath, but he wasn't going to let Kieran follow through on his threats, either.

As they left the riverside, the rank smell of the Thames diminished, but its replacement was hardly an improvement. Kieran kept to the rookeries where overcrowding and poor sanitation combined to create a uniquely malodorous atmosphere.

Once, during a visit to London in the Easter holidays when he was still a student at Cambridge, Wyatt had visited the slums with a group of friends. It had been, and unfortunately still was, a popular activity among the wealthy to pay the slumlords for the chance to see how the other half lived. Wyatt still felt sick with himself for going along with it. He'd felt like such a monster as he followed his friends from room to room, peering in at the residents like they were animals in a zoo. Yet even that visit did nothing to prepare him for seeing the slums of St. Giles at night.

Everywhere he looked, Wyatt saw evidence of extreme poverty. A river of sewage ran down the center of the road. The fetid water carried discarded animal bones and refuse past soot-stained tenement houses with half-rotted window frames. People who couldn't afford even the dilapidated housing around them lined the streets, covered in threadbare rags and huddled together for warmth so that they appeared at first glance to be nothing more than large piles of dirty washing.

The three of them weren't far from the junction of the seven roads that gave Seven Dials its name when Kieran stopped. The houses around them were older than the hastily erected modern tenement housing. Wyatt guessed them to be Georgian, if not slightly earlier. Their superior construction was evident in the way they held up when compared with their modern counterparts. However, even they had not escaped the harsh reality of life in the East End. Broken roof tiles and shattered and missing windowpanes showed that their current tenants could not repair them in the way their predecessors had.

"Is this it?" Samantha asked.

Her voice was hoarse, which Wyatt supposed was meant to disguise its feminine qualities. Kieran didn't seem to suspect anything, so he hoped it was working.

"First floor," Kieran said, pointing to a window that was missing the entire top half.

Samantha looked around, clearly searching for a way to scale the flat façade.

"You should be able to get a foothold there," Wyatt said, pointing to an uneven section of brickwork. "Climb on my back and I can lift you to it."

He gave her a reassuring smile, determined not to show the way his every instinct was screaming at him to scoop her into his arms and take her as far from there as he could. He knew it would be foolish, that it would solve nothing as far as their problems with Skinny Jim went and likely make them worse. Yet, he could not suppress his desire to protect her—to shield her from the evils of the world and those who sought to take advantage of her. For now, he offered what he could—a leg up, a smile, and the willingness to do whatever it took to get her back home safely when this night was over.

"Thank you," Samantha said, and he sensed that she was referring to more than just the lift.

She squeezed his arm, then climbed onto his back. He stood up slowly and did what he could to stabilize her as she climbed to his shoulders and reached up. She braced herself against the wall and, with a surprising amount of agility, stretched her leg to the uneven bricks and pulled herself up to the ledge of the broken window. She hung, suspended by her arms, for a moment as Wyatt stood beneath her, ready to catch her if she fell. Then she swung her leg up onto the ledge and lifted herself, grabbing onto the edge of the windowpane as she stood, her feet just gripping the ledge. It wasn't until she ducked her head through the open window frame and climbed inside that Wyatt released the breath he hadn't realized he'd been holding. His muscles remained tense, however, and his heart beat loudly in his ears.

He glanced at Kieran, whose attention had shifted to the door now that Samantha had disappeared. He didn't look relieved that the plan was proceeding smoothly thus far, nor worried about what might happen. He was focused, his body tense like a relay runner waiting for the baton to be handed off to him.

When the door opened, he strode forward, almost shoving Samantha aside in his haste. For her part, Samantha looked just as eager to leave the house as he was to enter it. She jogged over to Wyatt as the door shut quietly behind Kieran, her eyes wide and her breath labored, and threw her arms around him.

Surprised, but not displeased, Wyatt wrapped his arms around her and held her tight. They weren't alone in that street, but no one had so much as batted an eye at the sight of a boy climbing into a first-story window, so he was sure no one was watching them now.

"That was awful," Samantha said after a moment, her voice muffled as she spoke into his chest.

"I'm sorry," Wyatt said, sliding one arm down to rub circles on her lower back. "I'm sorry you had to do it. I would have taken your place if I could."

"You wouldn't have fit," she said, a smile in her voice. She lifted her head to look up at him. "But I appreciate the sentiment."

In that moment, with her comfortably in his arms and despite the coal and dirt that smeared her face, he wanted nothing more than to kiss her. He resisted, however, because he doubted he could stop if he started, and they had no idea how long Kieran would be.

"What are you thinking?" Samantha asked.

Judging by her impish smile, she knew, or thought she knew, where his mind had gone.

"Guess," he said.

She flushed, and he wondered if she would be bold enough to say what she thought or if she would try to deflect.

Just then, a loud crack resounded through the street, followed by a scream of pain. Samantha startled in his arms.

"Was that a gunshot?" she asked, stepping back and looking around.

"I think so."

Wyatt glanced up and down the street but, though the handful of people he saw walking were also looking around with curiosity, no one seemed alarmed. He supposed gunshots were commonplace in a neighborhood like St. Giles.

A moment later, the door of the house in front of them opened, and Kieran came hurrying out. With his left hand, he was shoving something into his pocket and in his right, he held a pistol.

"Did you shoot someone?" Samantha asked, failing to disguise her voice in her shock.

Kieran shot her an irritated scowl.

"Keep your voice down," he hissed.

"Is he dead?" Samantha asked in a hoarse whisper. When Kieran didn't respond, she added, "We did not agree to be part of a murder."

Kieran raised an eyebrow, and Wyatt thought he might have been amused.

"You do whatever he tells you, Sam." He pulled his hand from his pocket and gestured for them to follow him.

"Did you kill him?" Wyatt asked as they fell in behind Kieran.

Skinny Jim had insisted this job wouldn't bother his "high and mighty conscience," that it was merely about getting back what was already his. Wyatt had believed him because he had practically spit out the words, as though he were furious that someone had dared to steal from him.

"He's not dead," Kieran grunted. "Though, right now he probably wishes he was."

Wyatt looked at Samantha, who appeared torn between relief and horror. Wyatt's own sentiments were in the same vein. While it was good to hear that they hadn't facilitated a murder, helping Skinny Jim to torture a rival was hardly any better. However they managed it, they had to get out from under his thumb.

As Wyatt passed a warehouse near The Lion and Eagle, a man in a dark coat and hat stepped out of the shadows beside him. Kieran and Samantha were ahead of them and didn't notice. The man lifted his cap, and Wyatt recognized the pock-marked face of Inspector Whicher.

Resolving to give Bo a bonus for following through on his promise, Wyatt shook his head.

"Not here," he said in a low voice. "Meet us by St. Bride's. We'll head there as soon as we can."

The look Whicher gave him promised retribution if Wyatt didn't make the trip worth his while, but he said nothing as he tugged his cap down and disappeared down the street. Wyatt hurried to catch up with Kieran and Samantha.

Skinny Jim was busy when they returned to the pub, so they were forced to wait at the bar until he called them back.

"Any trouble?" he asked once they were before him.

"No," Kieran said.

He reached into his pocket and drew out a small object wrapped in a handkerchief. As he dropped it into Skinny Jim's outstretched hand, Wyatt forced himself to stay silent. Much as he wanted to take the man to task for hiding the reality of what he had sent them to do, he knew it wouldn't accomplish anything. Besides, he had promised Samantha to let her take the lead in their conversations with Skinny Jim.

A glance at Samantha told Wyatt she was also fighting the urge to shout at Skinny Jim, but, when he looked up at her expectantly, all she said was, "Tell us about Mr. Spenser."

"I never met him," Skinny Jim said. "He never borrowed money from me or played at one of my establishments. But he was still a gambler of a sort, and I'm sure he made somebody angry along the way, just not me."

"Are you saying you didn't kill him?" Samantha asked. "I don't believe you."

Skinny Jim shrugged. "Believe me or not, it's true. I didn't kill him, and I didn't have him killed. Maybe he really was robbed." He leaned back in his chair. "For now, go home. When I need you again, I'll be in touch."

He turned from them, dismissing them as much by his actions as by his words, and began to talk to Kieran as though they were already gone. Wyatt bristled, but he was glad enough to be out of there not to care too much how his escape came. He and Samantha left the pub without talking to anyone, including each other. Their silence continued until they were out of sight of the river. Then, Samantha stopped.

"Do you think he was telling the truth about Mr. Spenser?" she asked. "That he didn't kill him?"

Sweat had caused the soot on her face to streak, and Wyatt could see smears where she had wiped her brow. Wisps of hair had escaped the confines of her hat and now lay plastered to her skin. Yet, the concern in her eyes shone through.

"I do," he said. "The reason we thought he killed Mr. Spenser was to send you a message. It would be counter to his purpose to then claim not to have done it."

"Do you think it really was just a robbery, then?"

"I don't know. Would you have thought it was if you weren't considering Skinny Jim?"

She threw her arms out and let them drop to her sides with a sigh. "I suppose so. I didn't know him well enough to know for certain, but I can't imagine why someone would want him dead."

"What did Skinny Jim mean when he said he was a gambler of a sort?" Wyatt asked.

"That was annoyingly cryptic, wasn't it?"

He smiled. "It would have been too much to ask for him to be straightforward with us."

Samantha squinted at the empty washing lines strung above them as though trying to remember something.

"Mr. Spenser said he liked to invest in the future," she said. "Industrial progress was a passion of his. I suppose investments are a form of gambling. Perhaps that is what Skinny Jim meant? That he might have made enemies through his investments?"

"That may be the case," Wyatt said. "Perhaps someone whose product or company he rejected sought revenge? Or he might have had a rival. He was wealthy, was he not? Who benefits by his death?"

"I don't know." Samantha looked thoughtful. "He wasn't married, and he had no children, or none that I'm aware of. It seems an awfully risky way to kill someone, though—in broad daylight where anyone might have seen it happen. And someone did see it—at least, they saw someone covered in blood hurrying away. If that was the murderer, he only just got away. If it was Mr. Spenser's heir seeking to kill him, surely poison would have been a safer way to go about it. The murder might have gone unnoticed then."

"Perhaps. It would depend on the poison."

"This is all supposing someone wanted to kill him," Samantha said. "For all we know, he may have had a wonderful relationship with his heirs." She rubbed her temples and sighed. "No, I suppose it was most likely what it seemed to be—a robbery that went wrong. Poor Mr. Spenser. He didn't deserve to die like that."

She looked dejected. Wyatt hated to see her that way.

"We should hurry," he said, seeking to distract her. "I told Inspector Whicher we'd meet him at St. Bride's as soon as we could."

"Inspector Whicher?" Samantha looked confused, then her eyes widened. "Your friend, Bo! We were gone over an hour, weren't we? And he took your card to the inspector. But, when did you tell him to meet us at St. Bride's?"

"He was near the pub when we returned. I had only a few seconds to hold him off. I don't think he was very happy with me."

She shot him a look of exasperation. "Then why didn't you tell me as soon as we left the pub? Let's go."

She brushed past him, heading up the street at a half-run. He almost laughed at the way she'd barreled ahead without even knowing where she was going when he realized that she likely knew the way better than he did. That sobered him quickly.

He'd known she had lived on the streets. The fact of those five weeks had been one of the primary reasons for the lie they constructed with Madge. Yet, though he'd had a vague idea of what she must have experienced, the reality of it had begun to catch up with him as they traversed the East End that night. The street sewers, dilapidated housing and general devastation would have been daily sights for her. The dangers he was trying to protect her from tonight had been ever-present for her then. One of those people sleeping on the street might have been Samantha if she'd been there much longer. Or her story might have had an even more tragic end.

"What's wrong?"

Wyatt hadn't realized he'd stopped walking. Samantha stood in front of him, her brow furrowed as she gazed up at him.

"Nothing, really," he said. "I just...I wish the story we made up were true—that you came to me right after your aunt and uncle were killed and never ended up on the streets. I wish you hadn't had to experience it."

She pursed her lips and nodded. "I know what you mean, and I appreciate your concern, but it wasn't all bad. Also, crucially, it was only temporary for me. There are thousands of people for whom this cruel life is an inescapable reality."

It felt to Wyatt as though, in coming with Samantha to the East End, he'd gained a unique insight into her character. Her experiences here had helped to form who she was today—a woman he had come to love more than he ever thought possible.

"You want to help them," Wyatt said as he watched her earnest expression. "I knew charity was important to you, but I think I'm beginning to understand why and perhaps just how much."

The smile that burst across her face was as bright as it was beautiful. Then, she reached up and grabbed his face, pressing her lips to his in a brief, passionate kiss, before turning and running off down the street.

"Come on!" she called over her shoulder. "We don't want to keep him waiting!"

Wyatt was still grinning when they reached St. Bride's, and if he hadn't spotted Whicher right away, he might have caught Samantha and continued where they left off. However, he had an irritated inspector to pacify, so he dropped the grin and adopted a more somber mien.

"Well?" Whicher snapped as he stepped out of the shadows of the church to join them. "I'm here now. Are you going to tell me why I've been summoned in the middle of the night for no apparent reason?"

Wyatt grimaced. He hadn't meant to abuse his...friendship? Professional partnership?...with Whicher. He really had thought they'd be back before the hour was up and that Whicher would become involved only in a worst-case scenario. While being coerced into working for the city's biggest crime lord wasn't as bad as torture or death, it wasn't great, either. But, neither was it something Whicher could help them with. At least, not until they'd had the chance to talk to Madge about it.

"I can't apologize enough," Wyatt said. "I told Bo to get you if we hadn't returned in an hour. I thought that would be plenty of time, but we were delayed, and I was unable to tell him to wait."

"Delayed doing what? And is that...Miss Kingston?" Whicher asked, narrowing his eyes as he took in Samantha's appearance.

"Good evening, Inspector," Samantha said, bending her knees slightly in an approximation of a curtsey, as though they were meeting at a social event rather than skulking beside an old church in the middle of the night. Wyatt almost laughed, but he was trying not to annoy the inspector further.

"What on earth are the two of you doing out here at this time of night?" Whicher asked.

Wyatt wasn't sure quite how to placate the inspector. He couldn't, in all honesty, say it was nothing illegal or even that no one had gotten hurt.

"Chasing wild geese, apparently," Samantha said with an impressive amount of nonchalance. "We thought we had found the answer to a mystery and it turned out not to be the case."

Whicher kneaded his temples and rubbed a hand over his mouth, looking from one of them to the other with an expression somewhere between irritation and resignation.

"I don't want to know whatever it is you're hiding," he said finally. "But get one thing straight, Wyatt. I'm not your dog to sic on whoever crosses you."

"That was never my intention, sir," Wyatt said, adding the honorific for good measure. "I only wanted the city's best detective on the case if something happened to us."

Whicher gave him a look that showed how little he thought of

Wyatt's blatant flattery before responding.

"Nevertheless, whatever foolish risks you take with your lives are none of my business. Hire a bodyguard next time. Don't come bothering me."

Wyatt had considered bringing Durand with them, but he hadn't wanted to risk Skinny Jim using him as collateral damage. He had been reasonably certain Skinny Jim wouldn't harm him or Samantha while he wanted something from them, but he'd already shown a disregard for the people around them when he attacked Annie.

"We're very sorry," Samantha said. "It won't happen again."

Whicher nodded sharply. "See that it doesn't."

By the time they reached Grosvenor Square, the first faint flushes of dawn had brushed the sky. They passed a lamplighter carrying his tall ladder on his way to douse the streetlamps.

"I'll call on you later today," Wyatt said to Samantha, aware that the scullery maid—the first of the household servants to wake—would be getting up soon. "We need to talk to Madge."

Samantha sighed heavily. "I know."

"She may be able to talk to the curate or whomever it was she dined with during the time she was supposed to have been in London."

Samantha was shaking her head before he'd finished the sentence. "No. We can't do that. I won't ask even more people to lie for me."

"Then what?"

The obvious answer was that they would have to reveal their deception before Skinny Jim could—to remove the weapon he held against them. That was why he wanted to talk to Madge. It was her reputation that was on the line, as well as his and Samantha's. She had staked her name on a lie.

Samantha rubbed a hand over her face, smearing the coal dust across her nose.

"If we tell everyone the truth, he won't be happy," she said. "He'll probably take it as us undermining him. He might retaliate."

Wyatt had considered that possibility. He wasn't sure what to do about it yet, apart from removing Samantha from London.

"We can talk about it tomorrow," he said. "Madge might have some ideas."

Samantha did not look hopeful but, as she also looked dead on her feet, she was probably too tired to think clearly, anyway.

"Very well," she said. Her mouth stretched into a yawn, and she held her hand up to hide it. "Good night."

"I think you mean good morning," Wyatt said.

She smiled. "I suppose I do. Good morning, then. I'll see you this afternoon."

She gave him a mock curtsey, pulling at the edges of her trousers as though she wore an elegant gown. Wyatt bowed in turn, flourishing his hand in an over-the-top manner to make her laugh, which she did. Then he watched her head down the mews. She waved as she passed through the gate to Madge's property. Only when it had shut behind her did he depart for his own home.

NINE

Samantha had been afraid that her trip to the East End, which had awakened so many memories, would revive her nightmares as well. Yet, possibly because she was just tired enough, she had slept peacefully and long, not waking until almost noon. She ate in her room to delay a confrontation with Madge, emerging in time to meet her downstairs before their first callers arrived.

"So, you're alive after all," Madge said as Samantha entered the drawing room. "I did wonder."

"I'm sorry," Samantha said. "I slept late."

"And ate in your room." Madge raised an eyebrow, waiting for Samantha's response.

Samantha had known there was no point trying to hide anything from Madge. It was why she had stayed in her room, after all.

"Wyatt is coming today," she said. "We have something to talk to you about."

"How intriguing. And you won't say what? No, of course not. Is it good news or bad?"

"It's bad," Samantha said.

Madge nodded as though she had expected this answer. "Very well. At least you've come down now. I was beginning to fear I'd be left to juggle your admirers all on my own."

Headley, Madge's butler, entered then and announced the first caller. For the next half hour, Samantha and Madge made polite conversation with half a dozen gentleman, among whom were Lord Norland, Mr. Panzer and Mr. Lennon. To Samantha's relief, Mr. Ramsey was not among them. She hadn't seen him since Wyatt told her of the bet he'd made to steal a kiss from her, and she wasn't yet certain how she would react when she did see him. Part of her wanted to confront him with what she knew, but she wondered if feigned ignorance would serve her better and keep him off his guard.

Conversation centered around the upcoming Great International Exhibition, the grand opening of which was only a few days away. It seemed Her Majesty was unlikely to attend, but who might represent her was hotly debated, with Mr. Panzer adamant that the Prince of Wales was the most likely candidate, a suggestion Lord Norland roundly mocked.

Samantha was relieved when Lord Aston arrived. Lord Norland and Mr. Lennon had already left, sticking closely to the proscribed fifteen minutes that calls were meant to last, but Mr. Panzer had happily ignored even the most obvious hint to leave. He sat beside her, droning on about his plans for his estate, enveloping her in the smell of stale coffee that permeated his breath.

"Miss Kingston, you are the picture of health," Lord Aston said as he bounded up to her and took her hand, pressing it to his lips. "I hope you will accept my apologies for my tardiness. Would you be mollified if I told you I was rescuing a kitten from a puddle?"

"I might if I thought it were true," Samantha said with a smile. "Though, considering that it hasn't rained in several days, I find that highly unlikely."

"It was worth a try," Lord Aston said carelessly. "In truth I—

oh, forgive me, didn't see you there, Panzer. Budge up, will you? —In truth, Miss Kingston, I lost track of the time, but I'm here now. Tell me all that I've missed."

Mr. Panzer gave an indignant squawk as Lord Aston inserted himself between him and Samantha.

"I say!" he began, but Lord Aston spoke over him.

"Has everyone been babbling about the Exhibition?" he asked.

"You could say that," Samantha said.

She was torn between amusement and a sense of obligation as a hostess to ensure that all her guests were accommodated. Although, if he had been a polite guest, Mr. Panzer would have been long gone by now.

"I've half a mind to skip the opening ceremonies," Lord Aston said. "From what I can gather, all of London plans to be there. I can't think of anything less enjoyable than being trampled by a hoard of overeager ladies and gentlemen only for the pleasure of being among the first to see Germany's biggest clock or whatever treasures await us."

"The Exhibition represents a meeting of minds from all the great nations of the—" Mr. Panzer began, but Lord Aston cut him off again.

"Stuff and nonsense," he said cheerfully. "The Exhibition is a vanity project and a futile attempt to capture lightning in a bottle—possibly literally, for all I know—by copying the success of the first exhibition."

"That is cynical of you," Samantha said, surprised to hear such a negative outlook from him.

Lord Aston gave her a wry smile. "Do you disagree?"

"Not necessarily," she said. "Though a less cynical person might say pride, rather than vanity. Britain has accomplished much in these last ten years."

"Are you a less cynical person?" Lord Aston asked, a twinkle in his eye.

"Perhaps not," she admitted with a grin. "I confess I find myself looking with a more critical eye at my country this last year."

"As one should," Lord Aston said.

"I beg your pardon," Mr. Panzer said heatedly, "but—"

"Oh, Mr. Panzer," Lord Aston said with a laudable feint of surprise. "I am sorry. I ought to have offered to help you to your feet. You will, no doubt, be wishing to leave. Forgive us for delaying you."

Mr. Panzer's sputterings were no match for Lord Aston's unheeding helpfulness and, within minutes, the old man had been escorted out the door. The reprieve was short-lived, as another two suitors arrived shortly after. Lord Aston had returned to Samantha's side by then, however, and remained there for the next quarter hour. His presence clearly irked the other men, and Samantha couldn't help but notice that he seemed to take a perverse pleasure in provoking them as much as possible.

Wyatt did not arrive until the last moment. Lord Aston was the only remaining guest and was just taking his leave of Madge when Wyatt entered the drawing room behind Headley. His gaze swept the room before landing on Samantha. His smile of recognition held a hint of mischief that led her to believe he was taking in her clean face and the dress of pale blue-checked cotton and remembering her disheveled appearance of the night before. As he came to greet her, she noticed he had shaved. He looked good, but she couldn't help but prefer him in the stubble she had run her fingers over the night before.

"Good afternoon," he said, taking her hand and kissing it. "I hope you slept well?"

"I did," she said. "And you?"

"Well enough."

"What dull conversation you two engage in," Lord Aston said, appearing at Wyatt's elbow. "It makes eavesdropping utterly pointless."

"I disagree," Madge said, coming to join them. "You have no subtlety, Aston. It is what they are not saying that interests me. What were you two doing yesterday that makes you concerned about her sleep, Wyatt?"

Lord Aston let out a guffaw, and Samantha's cheeks flushed.

"Madge!" she said.

Madge waved a hand dismissively. "You know what I meant, my dear. You sleep until past noon, then tell me you and Wyatt have bad news. Now he comes over, implying that he knows you were up late. What is this bad news?"

Samantha glanced at Lord Aston, who seemed torn between amusement and concern. She hadn't intended to make him part of this conversation, as he had not been a part of the lie Skinny Jim was blackmailing them with, but he did at least know the truth. She looked up at Wyatt, who shrugged and nodded to her, allowing her to make the decision.

"Very well," she said. "We may as well sit down, though. This may take a while."

When they were comfortable, she proceeded to summarize everything that had happened since she read of Mr. Spenser's death in the paper. She spoke quickly, glossing over the details of her and Wyatt's trip to Seven Dials and ending with their meeting with Inspector Whicher. When she finished, Madge pursed her lips and regarded her and Wyatt through narrowed eyes.

"You thought Skinny Jim killed a man because of you, and you decided to go ask him about it?" Samantha opened her mouth to respond, but Madge held up a hand. "Don't. I'm sure you have fully justified it in your minds. All I can say is that I am glad I did not know ahead of time. Good heavens, you might have been killed half a dozen times over."

"Did he say when he plans to demand your services again?" Lord Aston asked, uncharacteristically somber.

"No," Wyatt said, frowning at the floor. "Nor how often. Just that he would let us know."

"We'll have to do something to get you out from under his thumb," Madge said. "I don't suppose killing him is a viable option?"

They all stared at her in shock. She smiled wryly.

"Don't worry, I wasn't in earnest. Though, to be frank, it does seem as though his death would be a boon to the city. I don't suppose he might have been bluffing?"

"What do you mean?" Samantha asked.

"Well, did he really collect these witnesses he says he did? Or was he only saying he might?"

"I believe he already spoke with them," Wyatt said. "Or rather, had someone speak with them."

"I'd like to be certain," Madge said. "Because, if he hasn't spoken with them yet, I might be able to nip this in the bud."

Samantha shook her head. "I don't want to ask them to lie. There's been too much of that already."

"I wouldn't do that, my dear. I doubt I even could. Ask a curate of the Church of England to commit perjury? I may be eccentric, but even I'm not that far gone. No, I meant that, if he hasn't actually spoken to anyone yet, I could simply warn them against talking to him or anyone he might send."

From what she knew of Skinny Jim, Samantha thought it was unlikely his threats had been unfounded. But if Madge wanted to double-check, Samantha wasn't going to argue with her. It was Madge's secret, too, and she had a right to have a say in how it was handled.

"I assume we have at least some time before he demands our help again," Wyatt said. "He seems to enjoy dangling us along, making us sweat with anticipation."

"Then don't do it," Lord Aston said. "Why are we even talking about this? You should be leaving London. Both of you. Go somewhere he can't reach you."

"It's not that simple," Samantha said, touched by his anger on their behalf. "We'll have to come back eventually, unless we want to live in perpetual exile—which I don't. Unless we handle this now, it will always hang over us."

"And we don't have to be in London for him to reveal the truth," Wyatt pointed out.

Lord Aston walked to the window and leaned against the frame, narrowing his eyes at the street beyond.

"Seven Dials," he said. Then he turned to look at Samantha. "Did you really scale a building in Seven Dials?"

"Wyatt helped," she said, unsure by his tone how he felt about the matter.

Having Wyatt there had helped in more ways than one. Yes, he had physically lifted her, but knowing he was outside had given her courage as she snuck through that rundown building to the door. She had been struggling with the memories that running through the streets had resurrected, and breaking into a house had called up all the fear and dread that had filled her the first time she'd done it. But she'd been alone then, and she wasn't this time.

"I can't see it," Lord Aston said, tilting his head as though considering her from a new angle. "I can't picture you climbing the side of a building."

"I was dressed as a boy, if that helps," Samantha said. "I wore trousers."

Lord Aston let out a surprised laugh. "As a boy? No, I'm afraid I can't picture that, either."

"Nor should you," Madge said. "In fact, weren't you on your way out a few minutes ago? Headley! Ah, there you are. Get Lord Aston's things for him, will you? And get Mr. Wyatt's while you're at it. They are ready to depart."

"Your hospitality is, as always, unmatched, my lady," Lord Aston said, bowing over Madge's hand.

"I'd wager it is, where you're concerned," Madge said. "There aren't many who would tolerate your particular style of humor as I do, especially when combined with your manners."

As Lord Aston retorted, Samantha caught Wyatt's eye and motioned to the door. Taking the cue, Wyatt took her arm and escorted her into the hall.

"You don't think he's bluffing, do you?" she asked when they were out of earshot.

"Skinny Jim?" Wyatt said. "No, I don't. But if Madge needs to be sure..."

"I agree, but we need to think about what we will do when she is." Samantha glanced at the open door to the drawing room and lowered her voice. "I've turned it over and over in my mind, and the only solution I can come up with is revealing the truth ourselves before he can. I'll still be ruined, but it has to be better coming from us than by whatever method Skinny Jim has in mind."

"I know you're worried about Madge, but I think she will come out relatively unscathed," Wyatt said. "Her disdain for Society is widely known. It might even be seen as her idea of a joke on her peers. And you don't need to worry about me. I'll deal with whatever the consequences are. It's you I'm concerned about."

Samantha tried to appear as though her impending social ruin was of no great concern as she shrugged and said, "I shall simply have to buy a castle in the highlands as you suggested last summer."

Much as she disliked many aspects of the small part of the world in which she had lived most of her life—the hypocrisy and gossip being chief among them—she didn't wish to be ostracized from it. She felt as though, after years under her uncle's rule, she had just begun to explore and to search for her place within it. And, while she now knew the world in general to be so much bigger than the narrow confines of Society had led her to believe, she wasn't certain she fit into any other part of it better than she did the part she had been born into.

"It won't come to that," Wyatt assured her.

There was one way they could mitigate the scandal. It hung unspoken between them, and Samantha found herself grateful to Wyatt for not saying it aloud. The idea of marrying him just to save their reputations was abhorrent to her. She wouldn't do that to herself, and she wouldn't do it to him.

Wyatt was a good man. He was thoughtful, intelligent and amusing. She was coming to rely on him perhaps more than she ought, and she liked him a great deal, but she didn't love him. She wasn't even sure she knew what love was. She'd hardly seen it in her life. But she knew he deserved it, which was why she could never marry him for convenience.

Madge's and Lord Aston's voices grew louder as they approached the hall. Knowing her time alone with Wyatt was running short, Samantha asked, "Have you made any progress with the blueprints?"

Wyatt grimaced. "Not as much as I could have wished. Durand, my man, if you recall, searched Ponsonby's study hoping to recover the rest of them now that we are more certain they were stolen, but they were gone."

"Gone? Do you think Mr. Ponsonby noticed one was missing?"

"I assume so. Durand and I broke into Ponsonby's place of business a few nights ago and couldn't find them there, either, so he's hidden them well." Madge and Lord Aston entered the hall, and he leaned down to whisper the rest in her ear. "I've warned Leclerc. Ponsonby must assume he stole his blueprint back, and I don't know how he'll respond."

Samantha nodded her understanding, though she had almost missed Wyatt's words, too distracted by the sensation of his breath on her neck.

"I will admit," Wyatt said, straightening as Headley returned and handed him his hat and cane, "I have been less concerned with all of that than with keeping you safe."

"As you should be," Madge said with approval.

"As we all are," Lord Aston said. He accepted his things from the butler as well and placed his hat on his head before adding, "Do be careful, Miss Kingston. You may be a world-class burglar, but you aren't invincible."

Samantha laughed even as Madge rolled her eyes.

"Ignore Lord Aston, Headley," she said. "He is speaking nonsense as usual."

"I'm afraid I have grown somewhat deaf in my old age, my lady," Headley said. "Did his lordship speak?"

"You're a good egg, Headley," Lord Aston said, clapping the butler on the back.

"Come on, Bingo," Wyatt said, "before you say anything else we'll all regret."

Samantha chuckled as she waved farewell to the two of them. When the door had closed behind them, Madge said, "Well, it seems I have some letters to write. I shall be in the morning room."

The next day, Samantha once again found herself in a black bombazine gown, surrounded by other similarly dressed people gathered to honor the deceased. It was the first funeral that year when she felt truly sad at the death, however. She had been unable to dredge up much emotion for her aunt or uncle or even her cousin, Cyril, and she hadn't even met the prince, but Mr. Spenser was different. In spite of their short acquaintance, she had liked him. She felt her eyes well up when she entered the room where he had been laid out and saw his body, peaceful in repose.

He was surrounded by family. She was introduced to his two brothers and three sisters as well as innumerable aunts, uncles and cousins. His mother sat beside him. She was a tiny thing—stooped and frail—and the bombazine gown she wore threatened to swallow her up. She greeted the other mourners with a fractured smile. Her cold hands were smooth but brittle, and when she had finished greeting Samantha, she set them back on the edge of the bed where her son lay.

"What will happen to her?" Samantha asked Mr. Murphy as they stood in the far corner of the room. He, along with the others she had met at Miss Coutts' house with Mr. Spenser, had come to pay his respects. "Mr. Spenser said his mother lived with him."

"I believe I overheard one of her sons say Mr. Spenser left the house to her," he said. "Though, I suppose one of them will likely move in with her. Or one of the daughters. They seem a close family. I'm sure she will be well looked after."

"Such an awful way to go," said Mrs. Heywood, the retired actress, from Samantha's other side. "And so senseless. Taken out for a few bob, when he'd given a hundred times that to causes that helped those who needed it."

"It is a tragic irony," Samantha said.

And it was, if it were the truth. She could not dismiss her suspicion that it might have been more. After all, people were robbed every day, but they were rarely killed because of it. Had Mr. Spenser put up a fight? Had he refused to give up whatever he carried with him? He hardly seemed the type to risk his life over a few shillings when he could easily spare them. She wondered if his friends might have some insight.

"Are the police certain it was a robbery?" she asked.

"What do you mean?" Mr. Murphy looked surprised.

"I don't know," she said hesitantly. "It's just so strange. You don't hear about people being killed on the streets these days, at least not people like Mr. Spenser."

"Not being killed, no," Mrs. Heywood said. "But there were a lot of garrottings a few years back. The newspapers seem to think it's happening again."

Samantha had a vague recollection of her uncle ranting about garrotting—a method of robbery whereby the victims were strangled to incapacitate them while their money or jewelry was stolen. He blamed its increase on a change in criminal law.

"But Mr. Spenser wasn't garrotted," Samantha said. "He was stabbed."

"That is strange," Mrs. Heywood agreed.

They watched as Mrs. Spenser attempted to rise to greet Miss Coutts, who had just arrived. Miss Coutts waved her back, and a chair was fetched so she could sit beside her instead.

"Do you think he would have tried to fight the thief?" Samantha asked. "Could that be why he was killed?"

Mrs. Heywood snorted. "Not likely."

"Mr. Spenser was an intellectual man," Mr. Murphy said diplomatically. "He preferred his books to more strenuous activities."

"I doubt he ever threw a punch in his life," Mrs. Heywood said. "You met him. Pale as a ghost, that one. Never spent time outside if he could help it."

"In that case," Samantha said. "Why would a thief have felt the need to kill him? Surely, he would have given the man what he wanted right away."

There was silence as Mr. Murphy and Mrs. Heywood appeared to consider Samantha's words.

"What are you suggesting?" Mr. Murphy asked finally.

Samantha lowered her voice. "Is there any reason someone may have wanted him dead?"

"Do you mean murder?" Mrs. Heywood asked, a little too loudly.

Samantha waved her hands to shush her as she glanced around. Thankfully, no one seemed to have heard.

"Perhaps," she said. "I didn't know him well enough to know why anyone would kill him, but neither can I believe he was killed at random. As you said earlier, it would be senseless."

Mrs. Heywood patted her arm. "Sometimes that's the way of it, love. The good ones are taken far too soon, and the bad ones seem to go on forever."

They watched as Miss Coutts was encouraged by one of Mr. Spenser's brothers to accept a cup of tea. More visitors entered the room. Samantha saw Miss Coutts' friend Mrs. Brown among them.

"Did you know Mr. Spenser well?" Samantha asked Mrs. Heywood.

"Not particularly," she said. "He wasn't a fan of the theatre, and I could only take so much talk about the progress of the nation, but he was nice enough. Generous, too. Mr. Murphy will tell you. He was a frequent donor to the Ragged Schools."

"That he was," Mr. Murphy said. "In fact, he had promised us a sizeable donation at our last meeting, but the transaction was not finalized before his death. I've been trying to think how best to approach his heirs about the matter."

Samantha was taken aback by his...she supposed she might charitably call it boldness. Before she could consider how to respond, Mrs. Heywood beat her to it with her usual plain speaking.

"You're going to ask them for money?" Mrs. Heywood said. "Goodness, and people think *I* lack tact."

Mr. Murphy reddened. "Not now, obviously, and if it had been merely a small matter, I wouldn't trouble them, but it was a sizeable amount and, frankly, we need the money."

"We missed our chance to discuss the matter at Miss Coutts'," Samantha said, "but if you can tell me the best way to send the money, I would be happy to donate to your cause, sir. From what you said, it seems a worthy one and well-run."

The lines in Mr. Murphy's forehead smoothed. "That is most generous of you, Miss Kingston. If you will give me your direction, I will send instructions round as soon as may be."

"Excellent."

When Samantha left Mr. Spenser's home half an hour later, she was still uncertain as to the reason for his death. His family seemed genuinely bereaved and, though she did not know who inherited the bulk of his fortune, the fact that he'd left his home to his mother indicated that he had been considerate in his bequests. Was one of his brothers more desperate than he looked? Or was his death not related to inheritance at all? Could it have been a business rival, as Skinny Jim had suggested? Did he know more than he let on? Or, as seemed more likely by the moment, was she merely inventing intrigue where there was none? Perhaps something had scared the thief, and he had simply panicked. Though that seemed the logical answer, she could not quite bring herself to believe it.

TEN

Though it had been more than ten years, Samantha could still remember the excitement that had accompanied her visit to the Crystal Palace during the Great Exhibition of 1851. There had been fewer trains then, and her grandfather had not trusted them anyway, so they had come down to the city by carriage. He opened up the London house for the week, and they had visited all the sights she cared to see: the National Gallery, the Tower, Kensington Gardens, and the British Museum. Of them all, it had been the Crystal Palace—the main hall of the Great Exhibition—that impressed her the most. Almost forty meters from floor to ceiling, built of iron and glass, it had glittered in the sunlight as though it really were made of purest crystal. Artistically intricate, it had dazzled and inspired her.

It may have been that her imagination enhanced the memory of the original exhibition hall, but she felt a sense of disappointment when she stepped down from the Bradwells' carriage on Thursday morning and got her first good look at the new hall. It was certainly impressive in scale—rectangular with sides so long she could hardly see the other end of the building. A glass dome bigger than the dome of St. Paul's sat above the main entrance, and she had to squint to see it as she tilted her head up.

Yet, there was something soulless about the building. The façade was mainly brick, lined with windows, and with no ornamentation, no decoration to enliven the sandy yellow. It was surrounded by a flat expanse of dirt so similar in color to the brick, it was easy to imagine that the building had simply risen from the earth and might just as easily melt back into it.

"Ah," Madge said as she stepped down beside Samantha. "It is so often true that the original is the best. Attempts to imitate never do quite live up to what came before."

"It's an eyesore," Lord Bradwell said, tucking Madge's hand in his arm and holding out his other arm for Samantha.

"Perhaps it hides a beautiful interior," Samantha said.

"Let us hope so," Madge said. "Else I will have difficulty persuading Bradwell to stay long."

"Don't pretend to worry over me," Lord Bradwell said. "You won't stay a moment less than you wish nor a moment longer."

"True, but it is so convenient to use your desires as an excuse, my dear. It makes me appear much less mercurial."

"Don't know why you bother. Miss Kingston knows you well enough by now."

"Too well, by half." She reached across her husband to pat Samantha's arm. "I don't know how you've stood us this long."

"There is no question of my withstanding you," Samantha said. "You are both a pleasure to be around."

Samantha smiled as Lord Bradwell grunted, which she knew to mean he was touched by the sentiment.

"Thank you, my dear," Madge said. "That is kind of you to say."

The day was fair and not so cold that it was a torment to stand outside listening to the opening address given by Lord Granville, the chairman of the commissioners of the Exhibition. When the fanfare was over, the building was officially opened, and the most important visitors—foreign dignitaries, people of highest rank and the commissioners of the Exhibition—entered first. Samantha and the Bradwells allowed themselves to be drawn inside with the crowd, too caught up in the atmosphere of excited anticipation to mind the jostling.

Samantha's first impression on walking through the doors beneath the eastern dome was of color. Bright reds, blues and golds were splashed across every visible surface, decorating every wall, surrounding every window and even covering the metal arches that supported the curved roof. Nowhere was this more prevalent than in the massive ten-meter-high fountain that stood in the center of the space under the dome. It was flanked by golden lions and circles of griffins supporting bowls of cascading water with their wings. Red and gold vases filled with tropical plants surrounded it on all sides. Above the lions, red-robed women with blue-feathered wings raised their arms above their heads directing attention to the statue that balanced at the very top: George slaying the dragon. The whole space was a feast for the eyes and so wholly unexpected after the blandness of the exterior that Samantha could do nothing but gape as people moved around her.

"Now, that is beautiful," Madge said. "I believe that alone may have been worth the trip."

They watched as a couple of children broke away from their parents to run forward and splash their hands in the water of the basin before being hauled away. Then, moving slowly and craning their necks to see all around them, Samantha and the Bradwells walked around the edge of the fountain. A long nave stretched from the eastern dome to the western dome. The exposed iron arches of the ceiling were decorated with intricate designs that were echoed in the ceiling itself. Flags of the world hung from the arch supports every few feet. Below these, two stories of exposed iron trestles comprised the viewing galleries.

"The textiles are up there," Lord Bradwell said, pointing to the second level where a sign read *Woolen and Mixed Fabrics*.

The region of Derbyshire that contained Lord Bradwell's family estate was best known for textile production and had been so even before industrial mechanization had altered the process. One of his primary interests in coming to the Great Exhibition had been to see his local area's representation.

"We will get to them," Madge said. "I know how eager you are, but I don't want to miss anything along the way."

"It's almost like a cathedral," Samantha said, still looking around in awe, "with its naves and transepts and these vaulted ceilings. Yet the exposed levels are so industrial that it's more a warehouse than a house of worship."

"One could almost see it as a cathedral of industry," Madge suggested, "worshipping the gods of progress and invention."

Samantha nodded, struck not only by the aptness of this description, but by the thought of how much Mr. Spenser would have loved it.

Despite their best efforts to stay together, the crowds made it nearly impossible and, soon, Samantha found herself alone, out of sight of either of the Bradwells. She was not overly concerned. She didn't doubt they would find their way back to one another eventually. In the meantime, she was happy to have the opportunity to focus on the exhibits that interested her most.

After examining the statuary brought from Italy, viewing the famed Koh-I-Noor diamond, and listening to an orchestra play works specifically composed for the opening of the Exhibition, she moved on to the northeast transept. A gilded obelisk from Australia caught her eye. She was reading the placard beside it, which stated that it weighed one hundred tons and represented the amount of gold found in that colony in the last five years, when she heard her name being called.

She looked up to see Lord Aston, flanked on either side by his mother and father. The Marquess and Marchioness of Rotherham were exquisitely dressed, as they had been when Samantha met them a week ago at the opera. Despite Lord Aston's assurances that his father was incapable of being charmed, she had hoped to endear herself to him. She had failed, but his rude behavior towards his only son had kept her from being too unhappy about it.

"Miss Kingston," Lord Aston said, stepping forward and taking her hand. "What a delight to see you here."

He made a grimace that his parents could not see, and she repressed a smile. Then he came around beside her so that he was facing his parents and tucked her arm into his.

"Mother, Father, you remember Miss Kingston."

"Yes, I remember her," Lord Rotherham said. "I'm not so old as you might wish, Aston. Good morning, Miss Kingston."

"Good morning, my lord, my lady," Samantha said, determined to be as well-mannered as he was not.

The marchioness of Rotherham dipped her head in acknowledgement. Her smile was polite, but not warm, and Samantha detected curiosity with a hint of judgment in her gaze. Samantha wasn't sure what to think of Lord Aston's mother yet. She had been mostly silent during their meeting at the opera, and it seemed she planned to continue in the same vein now.

"I knew your grandfather," Lord Rotherham said. "He was a good man. Excellent shot. No sense about horseflesh, but he took care of his land and managed his affairs well."

"Yes, he was a good man," Samantha said when it seemed a response was required of her.

"You come of good stock," Lord Rotherham continued. "However, even good families can be brought down by a bad seed, and there are some rumors flying about that raise the question of your respectability."

"Father!"

Lord Aston glared at his father, stepping forward as though to shield Samantha.

"It is a valid concern," Lord Rotherham said. "If you are truly intending to bring this girl into our family, it is one we must consider carefully."

If Samantha had been courting Lord Aston in earnest, she might have been upset by his father's statement. As it was, she was more concerned for Lord Aston than for herself. He looked ready to come to blows with his father.

"I did not realize you listened to gossip, Father," Lord Aston said. "Surely the Rotherhams are above such petty nonsense."

"Ordinarily, yes, but when it concerns our family's reputation, I take an interest. The attention you have paid Miss Kingston may have caused some people to temporarily forget that she lived with an unmarried man while unmarried herself, but it won't be forgotten forever."

While people had been speculating about her relationship with Wyatt for months within her hearing, something about Lord Rotherham's bald statement, stripped of any nuance, emboldened her to respond in kind.

"You're right, it won't," she said, noting with satisfaction Lord Rotherham's startled reaction as she spoke up. "But, while I agree with you that a bad seed can damage an ordinary family's reputation, I'm surprised that you think a family of your rank and distinction, who came over with the conqueror, couldn't overcome such a comparatively minor scandal."

Lord Aston's posture relaxed, and he grinned at her. "Touché, Miss Kingston."

"If you are thinking to use our family to save your name..." Lord Rotherham began.

"And what if she is?" Lord Aston said. "I dare say it's been done before. If I don't mind, why should you?"

Lord Rotherham's face purpled, and he opened his mouth to

respond, but Lord Aston cut him off.

"We've held you up long enough, Miss Kingston," he said. He took her hand and raised it to his lips. Winking, he pressed a brief kiss to it before adding, "I hope you enjoy the rest of the Exhibition. Good day."

He released her arm and moved to take his mother's. Lady Rotherham looked between the two of them with a frown, then dipped her head again to Samantha.

"Good day, my lady," Samantha said, "My lords."

Lord Rotherham sent his son a look that promised the conversation would continue once she was out of earshot, then he bid her good day as well. As Samantha watched them go, she wondered if Lord Aston regretted asking her to pretend to court him. Rather than encouraging his father to give him peace regarding his marriage prospects, it seemed to have had the opposite effect.

Samantha began to look for Madge and Lord Bradwell in earnest then, skipping past several promising exhibits and speeding through the foreign picture gallery. As she walked past an enormous paddle wheel in the machinery department, she felt a hand on her elbow and turned in surprise to see Wyatt.

"Wyatt!" she said with a mixture of joy and relief.

"I can't believe I found you," he said, smiling and looking around them. "There must be thousands of people here."

"I know. I've lost Madge and Lord Bradwell, and I'm beginning to despair of ever finding them again."

"May I offer my assistance?"

He held out his arm, and she took it.

"Thank you," she said. "Are you here on your own, or have you also been separated from your party?"

"I was meant to come with my friend Carstairs, but he was late meeting me, and by the time I gave him up and came on my own, I'd missed the opening ceremonies."

"You didn't miss much," Samantha assured him. "It's the exhibits themselves everyone has come to see, not the speeches or even the queen's cousin."

"Is that who represented her?"

"Yes, the Duke of Cambridge. Mr. Panzer will be disappointed. He was certain it would be the Prince of Wales."

They had reached the end of the room and begun to walk up the other side. A man examining a placard looked up as they were about to pass him and his eyes lit with recognition.

"Mr. Wyatt!" the man said with every appearance of delight. "I thought that was you. It's good to see you again."

He took Wyatt's hand and shook it enthusiastically.

"It's good to see you, too, Mr. Leclerc. May I introduce you to my friend? Miss Kingston, this is Mr. Leclerc. Mr. Leclerc, Miss Kingston."

"It's a pleasure to meet you," Samantha said.

"The pleasure is all mine," he replied.

She watched him with renewed interest as he and Wyatt exchanged pleasantries. So, this was the inventor whose blueprint Mr. Ponsonby had stolen. For some reason, she had pictured him as a mousy, balding man, perhaps because he had lacked the fortitude to address the problem himself. She had also imagined him perpetually cast down. The man before her, however, stood straight and tall. Far from being bald, he had a full head of long dark hair, tied back from his face as had been the fashion a century before. He was also full of energy, speaking quickly, with his hands moving along with his words.

"Are you certain it's a good idea for you to be here?" Wyatt asked. "Doesn't Ponsonby have a display in the machinery department?"

Mr. Leclerc's smile dropped by a degree.

"He does. He's even put the part he stole from me in it. That's why I'm here. I know you said he's probably figured out what I did, but what if he has? What he did was much worse, and I have proof. Unless you have a viable plan to get me what I'm owed, I'm going to confront him about it."

Samantha could tell that Wyatt wanted to argue but wasn't sure how. He had told her he'd been more concerned about Skinny Jim than the problem with Mr. Ponsonby lately, so she wouldn't be surprised if he didn't have a plan and felt guilty about it.

"You said your invention is here, did you not?" she said, hoping to distract Mr. Leclerc while Wyatt formulated a response. "Can we see it?"

"Yes, of course," Mr. Leclerc said with a return of some of his former spark.

He led them down the row to a machine that appeared to have been designed for use in a cotton mill. Directing their attention to one of the giant, slowly rotating metal wheels, he pointed to a small apparatus beside it.

"It's just there," he said. "It's a safety measure—prevents the wheel from running backwards and causing a snarl, leading to the machine shutting down."

Wyatt and Samantha nodded, though she at least wasn't sure she was even looking at the right bit of metal.

Mr. Leclerc laughed. "I know, it's not the most exciting piece of equipment."

"It doesn't have to be," Wyatt said diplomatically. "Safety is important."

"True, but even I can't muster up much enthusiasm for it. It pays my bills, though, or it will, once I get Ponsonby to see reason, and I can sell it to other cotton manufacturers. That will allow me to pursue my passion project."

"What's that?" Samantha asked.

"Have you heard of the phonautograph?"

As Wyatt shook his head, Samantha said, "I don't believe so.

Judging by the name, however, I assume it has to do with sound and writing?"

Mr. Leclerc smiled. "It does, indeed. It is a device that records sound waves onto paper."

"Did you invent it?" she asked.

"I did not, but I did build one from the original designs. I plan to..." He paused, seemed to consider for a moment and then asked, "Do you enjoy music, Miss Kingston?"

"Certainly. Playing and listening."

"Then you will understand the nuance of a performance. The way a musician can infuse a piece of himself into what he plays—a bit of his soul. No two musicians play a song the same way, even with the same notes."

"That is true."

Mr. Leclerc's head bobbed with excitement. "Yes. I have always thought it a shame that, while we can celebrate the genius of artists like Michaelangelo, Caravaggio, van Dyck, et cetera, by viewing their original brushstrokes, we cannot do the same for Mozart or Bach or Beethoven. We can replicate what they wrote through their sheet music, but we cannot appreciate the nuance of their performances. We cannot hear the music as they intended it. That is where my interest lies. I want to create a device that will allow us to play back what the phonautograph records. A phonautograph player, if you will."

Samantha found herself caught up in his enthusiasm. She had never thought about art and music in that way, but he was right. The possibility of recording music and listening to it whenever one desired sounded almost magical and yet, here they stood in a temple of progress. They were surrounded by proof that the possible could be made real.

"How do you get on?" she asked. "Have you made much progress?"

She thought she saw a moment of hesitation, but then his

smile grew.

"Not as much as I would like, but that is because I have been hampered by unrelated difficulties. I must split my time between my passion and the work that pays my bills. I had a patron at one point, but he was unable to continue supporting me, and I've been on my own since then."

"It's a fascinating idea," Samantha said.

She thought of Mr. Spenser and his opinions on the importance of advancing industry. Surely art was just as important. Art brought joy. It inspired progress. Perhaps she could be a part of that. Still, she did not want to act precipitately.

"What do you think, Wyatt?" she asked.

"I think," he said carefully, "if it works, it has the potential to be significant, not to mention profitable."

She nodded, considering his words. It would be a risk, but not much of one. If the music player didn't work, all she would lose would be money, something she currently had far too much of, anyway. Also, it wasn't as though she had to decide this minute whether or not to patronize it.

"If you are willing to show me your research," she said to Mr. Leclerc. "I would like to discuss the possibility of patronage with you. I would love to support such a marriage of science and art."

"Do you mean..." His eyes grew round, and his face broke into a broad grin. "I had not even considered...yes, of course!"

"I am staying with Lord and Lady Bradwell in Grosvenor Square," Samantha said. "If you let me know when you might be available, we can arrange a time to meet so that you may show me your research."

"I look forward to it, Miss Kingston." He bowed, then turned to Wyatt. "As far as matters with Ponsonby go, I suppose I could wait a bit longer."

"Thank you," Wyatt said.

Mr. Leclerc took his leave of them, and they continued alone.

When Samantha turned to Wyatt, he was watching her with his oft-present enigmatic expression. She sighed.

"What?" he asked.

"I never know what you are thinking when you look like that. It is vexing."

"You could ask me."

"Would you tell me if I did?"

"I might. But then you might regret asking."

"Oh?"

He shrugged, a hint of a smirk on his lips.

"Very well. I am curious now. What were you thinking?"

He began to lead them down the gallery and was silent for long enough that she thought he wasn't going to answer. When he did speak, his voice was so quiet that she had to lean in to hear him as they rejoined the crowds.

"I was thinking that your eyes are even more beautiful when they are lit with passion. I was thinking that you are the most remarkable woman I know. And I was thinking that I would very much like to kiss you again."

"Oh."

It was possibly the most romantic thing anyone had said to her, and for a moment she simply appreciated the beauty of his words. Then she began to fret over her response. Should she have thanked him? Returned the compliment? Told him that she would, too, very much like him to kiss her? Did she want him to kiss her? She could feel her cheeks warm as the seconds dragged on. Wyatt seemed to sense her discomfort.

"I want to thank you for how you handled Mr. Leclerc," he said, mercifully changing the subject.

"It was nothing," Samantha said. "Besides, I am intrigued by his ideas about the phonautograph."

"Still, I'm glad you were able to change his mind. I don't think it's a good idea for him to confront Mr. Ponsonby. I doubt any good would come of it, and it might cause more problems for Mr. Leclerc. Ponsonby has already proved himself unscrupulous."

"What will you do?"

"I don't know that there's much I can do at this point. The other blueprints are gone, so we can't use them to prove a pattern. Even Leclerc's blueprint doesn't help him now that the invention is on display for all to see. Ponsonby could say Leclerc drew the blueprint after seeing the part at the Exhibition and was trying to claim credit."

"Oh, no," Samantha said. "I hadn't thought of that."

"The truth is that I've failed at every step of the way with this case," Wyatt said. "I should have taken all of the blueprints as soon as I found them. Barring that, I should have told Leclerc to go to the police as soon as he got his blueprint back. He might have been able to persuade them to get a warrant to search for the others before Ponsonby had the chance to hide them. And I should never have met with Leipzig merely to confirm my suspicions that Ponsonby was a thief. I got his hopes up for nothing."

"First of all," Samantha said, "it's much easier to judge from the end of something than from the beginning. You know things now that you didn't know then. Second, you were being careful, and I don't think you should chastise yourself for that."

"'He who hesitates is lost.'"

She frowned up at him.

"And sometimes he who hesitates stops himself from making a disastrous mistake. All I'm saying is that the answers weren't obvious, and you cannot dwell on what might have been unless you want to make yourself miserable. We've done that to ourselves enough with Skinny Jim and Charles and everything from last summer."

"True." Wyatt gave her a rueful smile. "Thank you."

"You're welcome."

They were quiet for a moment, though it wasn't an uncomfortable silence. Wyatt was the one to break it.

"Shall we look for Madge and Bradwell?" he asked.

"Yes," she said. "I've looked through most of the main galleries. Perhaps we could try the British picture gallery?"

"Where would that be?" Wyatt asked as they left the western annex.

"There are stairs at the southern entrance."

They moved at an unhurried pace, occasionally stopping to look at a display that arrested their attention in one of the foreign exhibitors' courts. The Russian "Golden Bible" bound in precious metals and studded with jewels drew Samantha's eye, as did the beautiful pianos in the Switzerland section. Wyatt stopped to study the anatomical representations of the human body in the Austrian court.

They had almost reached the southern stairs when Wyatt came to an abrupt stop, his face grim. Samantha followed his gaze and saw a couple approaching them. The man was Wyatt's brother, Tom, Lord Boxley. Samantha did not recognize the woman, but it was easy enough to guess who she was. At first, Samantha thought she must be quite old, for she had bundled herself in a profusion of shawls and appeared to lean on her son for support. Her eyes, however, so like her sons' in color, were sharp, and her skin too smooth to be as old as she portrayed herself.

"Mother," Wyatt said. "I did not expect to see you here today."

He spoke in clipped tones and Samantha, sensing his tension, put her free hand on his arm. He covered it with his hand and held tight.

"I did try to persuade her that it might be better to come on a day when a lighter crowd could be expected, but she was insistent," his brother said.

He looked strained and unhappy.

"Will you not introduce me to your friend, Theseus?" Wyatt's mother asked, her eyes fixed on Samantha.

She could not have been speaking to anyone but Wyatt. Yet, in the moment after Samantha realized that Theseus must be Wyatt's second name—the "T" in V.T. Wyatt—she wondered that even his mother did not address him by his given name. Wyatt's jaw tightened, and he did not release Samantha's hand, but after a moment he inclined his head.

"Mother, this is Miss Samantha Kingston. Miss Kingston, my mother, the dowager Lady Boxley."

"It is an honor to meet you, my lady," Samantha said.

"Ah, so you are Miss Kingston." Though her tone expressed surprise, it rang false as Wyatt's mother eyed Samantha with calculation. "I hear so much about you that I almost feel I know you, yet I had begun to wonder if we would ever meet."

"It is my understanding that you rarely leave Kent, my lady," Samantha said, wondering if Wyatt's brother had spoken about her or if the "so much" she had heard was simply the usual rumors. "I am not sure how we would have done so."

"Perhaps not in the normal course of things, but, with your reputation having become so entangled with our family name, I might have thought it natural that you would wish to meet with me, to explain your story to me in person, if nothing else."

Samantha's eyebrows rose at her audacity, which completely eclipsed that of Lord Aston's father.

"She does not owe you an explanation, Mother," Wyatt said.

"Does she not?" his mother asked. "Do I not have a right to know who it is who makes so free with my son's protection and why?"

She made it sound as though Samantha was Wyatt's mistress, and by her calculated expression, Samantha could tell it was intentional. Fury at the injustice of it, both to her and to Wyatt, tore through her and, though the question was clearly meant to be rhetorical, Samantha answered it. "I think that if you knew your son at all, you would not need to ask. You would trust his judgment. He might even have told you himself."

Wyatt squeezed her hand but what he meant by it, she couldn't be sure. His brother's eyebrows rose in surprise even as Lady Boxley's eyes narrowed.

"There is Lady Halifax, Mother," Wyatt's brother said abruptly. "She will wish to greet you."

"Yes, do not let us keep you," Wyatt said. "After you made the effort to come all the way to see the Exhibition, I would hate for you to miss a minute of it."

He gave a stiff bow.

"Good day, Lord Boxley," Samantha said. "Lady Boxley."

Wyatt hurried her away before either of them could reply.

"That was wonderful," he said when they were out of earshot at the top of the stairs. He laughed. "You were wonderful. I haven't seen my mother at a loss for words in years."

She grinned. "I'm glad. I wasn't sure if I had overstepped."

"You didn't. She was...well, she was as she usually is, which is to say, completely inappropriate and manipulative. You were entirely justified in your response. I wish more people called her out like that."

"So..." Samantha began, arcing an eyebrow at him. "Theseus?"

He winced.

"I hoped you hadn't noticed."

"How could I not? I've learned one of your great secrets."

"It's not such a secret to anyone who knows my mother. It's what she's always called me."

"She never called you by your Christian name? I thought Madge said she chose it."

"She did." Wyatt sighed. "She and my father were fighting, which in itself was not unusual. She wanted something—I'm not sure what—and he refused. That was rarer. He had told her when they married that she could name the children, and she thought if she threatened to name me something dreadful, he'd relent. He didn't. She held off until the last moment, hoping he'd change his mind, but he never did. I imagine she thought if she didn't go through with it, he wouldn't take her seriously the next time. Afterward, I think calling me by my Christian name reminded her of her failure, and she's pretended she always wanted to call me Theseus."

"She named you out of spite?" Samantha asked, appalled.

"She does a lot out of spite. My name was nothing special."

"Is that why you go by Wyatt?"

"Partly. I also despise both of the names she chose. I much prefer Wyatt to Theseus."

"Does your mother like Shakespeare? I remember your sister was called Helena."

Wyatt smiled. "Yes, she was. And yes, my mother loves Shakespeare. I wonder that she does not see more of herself in Lady Macbeth. Tom's second name is Hamnet, Shakespeare's son. And Helena's was Beatrice."

"What happened to Helena, if you don't mind my asking?"

"Cholera. She was thirteen."

He looked away.

"I'm sorry," she said. "I can see that you loved her very much."

"We all did." He cleared his throat. "It was impossible not to love her. Even Mother had some real affection for her. And she could make my father laugh. When she died...I sometimes think she was the only reason we were a family. After she was gone, it was as though we had all become untethered. We were never the same. Not that we were a happy family before. I suppose we just stopped pretending. There didn't seem to be a point anymore."

Samantha's heart ached for Wyatt. She squeezed his arm, wishing she could do more to comfort him.

"My father died a few years later, and then I finished school.

After my grand tour, I took up residence in London in a house an aunt had left me. I haven't been back to Kent for more than a month altogether since."

"How does your mother feel about that?"

They had been walking along the picture gallery for some minutes without looking at any of the pictures. Wyatt stopped in front of a collection of Turner's landscapes and turned to Samantha.

"I don't pay heed to anything my mother thinks or feels, and I hope you won't, either. If she's ever had an unselfish motive in her life, I've never seen it."

"What does your brother think?"

"About me or my mother?"

"Either, I suppose."

Wyatt shrugged. "I'm a disappointment to him and our mother is...a responsibility. I don't think he much likes her anymore, though there was a time when he thought she hung the moon. But Tom has always been driven by duty, so he will care for her as he does the estate."

Samantha pursed her lips and looked up at the painting before them, a lifelike picture of ships in a storm titled *Calais Pier*.

"Do you ever feel guilty that he has that responsibility for your mother?"

Wyatt didn't answer for several moments, and Samantha worried she had crossed a line.

"I suppose I ought to feel guilty but, no, I don't. I feel relief and, perhaps, if I am honest, a certain degree of satisfaction, knowing he must deal with her." His eyes searched hers. "Does that disappoint you?"

She could see that her opinion mattered to him, so she considered carefully before responding.

"I don't believe I can offer a judgment on your feelings, particularly as I hardly know your mother or your brother, but I appreciate that you were honest with me."

"Always."

He looked as though he wanted to say more, but they were interrupted by the appearance of Madge and Lord Bradwell.

"I see we need not have worried about you," Madge said dryly.

"I didn't mean to worry you," Samantha hastened to explain. "I ran into Wyatt after we were separated, and we've been looking for you."

Madge raised an eyebrow, but her lips formed a knowing smile. "Yes, I can see that."

"A temporary stop," Wyatt assured her. "We've been looking for some time, but we needed a rest."

"Naturally. Now that we're together again, have you seen the Foreign Picture Gallery?"

She led the way down the hall, talking as she went about the disappointment she and Lord Bradwell had felt in the design of the textile gallery. Wyatt and Samantha followed, catching only half the words because Madge kept looking around at the artwork as she spoke, her voice lost every time she turned away. Samantha couldn't help but smile and, when she caught Wyatt's eye and saw him doing the same, she had to press her lips together to keep from laughing.

ELEVEN

Two weeks passed with no word from Skinny Jim. He didn't even seem to be sending people to follow them anymore. At least, not with the frequency of before. Wyatt occasionally caught sight of the Irishman and once, the man who had spoken to them outside the ball, but they no longer followed him every time he left the house.

Madge heard back from the witnesses she had written to, including the curate, and discovered that, as Wyatt had suspected, Skinny Jim hadn't been bluffing. They had all been questioned and had confirmed Madge's lack of alibi. When she reported this to Samantha and Wyatt, they'd talked about what to do next. Madge thought it might still be possible to save face, even when they revealed that Samantha had lived as a beggar on the streets. It was all in how they told the story, she said, but she needed time to lay the groundwork and discover who might be their most useful allies.

In pursuit of this plan, Samantha and Madge, who had previously gone out no more than three nights a week—an amount Madge claimed already taxed the limits of her patience with Society—filled their calendars until they were engaged almost nightly and paying calls every afternoon. Bingo accompanied them to most events, as Madge's husband had gone home to Derbyshire immediately following the Exhibition opening. Wyatt tried not to be jealous of the time his friend spent with Samantha, but it was difficult. He felt as though he hardly saw her anymore and, when he did, she was too exhausted to talk long.

When, on a Friday in mid-May, the Irishman cornered Wyatt outside his club to deliver the long-awaited message from Skinny Jim, Wyatt was almost relieved. At least they would finally know what was wanted of them.

"It's been a long time," the Irishman said with his customary cheeky grin. "You don't look too well. You been taking care of yourself?"

"Just give me the message," Wyatt said.

The Irishman clicked his tongue. "Tetchy, aren't ya? Alright, here you go."

He handed Wyatt a small paper package—about the size of the one Kieran had taken from the house in Seven Dials.

"What?" Wyatt said, turning it over in his hands. "No summons for me to come to Blackfriars?"

"No need," the Irishman said. "It's a simple job. Just put this in the bedroom of Sir Anthony Guilford by next Friday. Somewhere he'll be sure to see it."

"That's all?" Wyatt asked with a heavy dose of skepticism. "Just put it in his room? What is it, an explosive of some sort?"

"Wouldn't that be fun?" the Irishman said with a laugh. "No, it's only a reminder. Take it out and check if you don't believe me."

Wyatt unwrapped the package. Though he hadn't really thought it was an explosive, he still felt the need for caution as he carefully peeled back the paper to reveal a circular medallion about the size of his palm. It was embossed with the image of a lion on one side and an eagle on the other.

"A reminder, eh?" Wyatt said. "How much does he owe?"

"This is why I like you, Wyatt," the Irishman said. "Always straight to the point."

"So I put this on his pillow and...what? Report back to the pub? Or do I ask around the city for you? That'll be tricky, as I've never caught your name."

"You won't need to look for me, Wyatt. I'll find you. I always do."

With a mock salute, the Irishman took a few steps backwards before spinning on his heel and disappearing into the crowd.

Wyatt had only a passing acquaintance with Sir Anthony. He knew he was a member of Parliament and a bit of a gambler. He hosted a weekly card game at his house. It seemed that he, like dozens of others, had made the misguided decision to borrow money from Skinny Jim and was now in the unfortunate position of being unable, or possibly unwilling, to pay him back. Skinny Jim wanted to use Wyatt's access to the homes of the wealthy and titled to scare Sir Anthony—to show him that he could get to him whenever and wherever he wanted. It was similar to the tactic he had used on Wyatt and Samantha and, while it was reprehensible, leaving the medallion wasn't criminal, and it didn't put anyone else in danger. Skinny Jim could have asked much worse of him and, if only to buy time for Madge and Samantha, Wyatt was inclined to do it.

For perhaps half a minute, Wyatt considered keeping his conversation with the Irishman to himself, at least until after he visited Sir Anthony. But, he had promised Samantha he would be honest with her, and he was determined to keep his promise. So, abandoning his plans to spend the evening in his club, he hailed a cab to take him to Madge's house.

*****

For the first time in weeks, Samantha was looking forward to an evening out. There would be no balls or dinner parties tonight. She wouldn't have to sit through hours of ill-disguised barbs from the town gossips or uncomfortable flirtations from fortune hunters. Tonight, she was going to the theatre with only Madge and Mr. Leclerc for company.

It was later than she had intended her meeting with the inventor to be. Madge's plans had eaten up most of her availability. Samantha had been relieved when Mr. Leclerc agreed to meet at the theatre, because she wasn't sure she could have managed to fit him in otherwise. She had high hopes for his research but, if he proved less capable than he was imaginative, she consoled herself that she would at least see a good show. *Our American Cousin* was a popular play.

While she waited for Madge to come down, Samantha sat in the drawing room, attempting to slog through *Great Expectations*, which had been published in book form a few months previously.

"Isn't that the same place you were when I last saw you reading?"

Wyatt's voice at her shoulder made Samantha jump and drop the book. She looked up to see his arm draped over the top of her wingback chair, the hint of a smile playing across his lips.

"Headley should have announced you," she said, holding a hand to her racing heart. "How did you come up so quietly?"

"I told him I didn't need to be announced." He let his arm drop to his side and came around the chair to stand before her. "I wanted to surprise you."

Samantha held out a hand and he pulled her to her feet. The momentum brought her swaying a little too close to him, and she took a quick step back. He let go of her hand.

"Well, you accomplished your goal," she said. "How long were you standing there?"

"Less than a minute. You'd have noticed me if you hadn't been so absorbed in your reading."

"Less absorbed than determined. Madge was right, it is not his best work, but I feel I ought to give it a fair chance."

Wyatt leaned down and picked up the book. He flipped it open to the marked page, which was about a quarter of the way through. "I'd say this was fair enough. He's a prolific writer. They can't all be good. And it's not as though he'll know you didn't read it."

"I suppose you're right." She took the book from him and tossed it onto the settee behind her. He uttered a surprised laugh. "Why are you here, Wyatt? Madge and I are preparing to go out."

"I won't hold you up," he said, "but I needed to tell you something. Skinny Jim sent a message."

She felt the blood drain from her face.

"He did? When? What did he say?"

"Just now. He sent my usual tail. He wants me this time, not you."

He was trying to reassure her, but she was far from reassured.

"You? What does he want you for?"

Wyatt wasn't anywhere near small enough to be a snakesman, and he wasn't the one who had signed himself up to work for Skinny Jim. He was, however, an expert in disguise and an experienced investigator with many skills a man of his background wouldn't normally have. She hadn't considered that Skinny Jim might try to exploit him like he had her, but she realized she should have.

"It's nothing to worry about," Wyatt said. "He wants me to give a warning to Sir Anthony Guilford—that's all."

"That's all?" Samantha repeated skeptically. "Just like all we were supposed to do in Seven Dials was steal back Skinny Jim's property?"

"It's not like that," Wyatt said. "I've been given a week, and I'm doing it on my own. There won't be anyone with me to change the mission."

Samantha closed her eyes and kneaded her temples.

"I'm going to do it," he said.

Her eyes flew open. "What?"

"Think about it," Wyatt said. "If I do this relatively simple job, it should buy us more time. We'll keep him happy, and it might be another two weeks or more before he gives us another job."

It was a valid point, but Samantha still didn't like the idea of him doing Skinny Jim's dirty work.

"Sir Anthony hosts a weekly card party on Tuesdays," Wyatt said. "I can get an invitation, and I won't even have to break into his house. It will be easy."

"I suppose so," Samantha said. "You should see what Madge says, though."

"I don't think she'll object. Not when it aids her plans."

"Very well. If you're sure. I'll tell her after we get back tonight."

At that moment, Madge strode into the room.

"Wyatt," she said with surprise and delight. "What brings you here? We were on our way out. Did Samantha tell you?"

"Yes, she did. I only stopped by to tell her something. I'll be on my way."

"Nonsense," Madge said cheerily. "You must come with us. Or did you have plans of your own?"

Wyatt looked at Samantha, a question in his gaze. Ignoring the way her heart sped up at the prospect of his company, she nodded.

"I'd be delighted," he said to Madge. "Where are we going?"

"The Haymarket," Madge said.

"*Our American Cousin?*"

"Have you seen it before?" Samantha asked.

"Yes, but I don't mind seeing it again. I enjoyed it."

"I hope I'm able to enjoy it. This evening is meant to be for business more than pleasure."

"Oh? What business?"

"I'm meeting with Mr. Leclerc."

"Did the first meeting go well then?"

Samantha smiled wryly. "This is the first meeting. Scheduling it proved difficult."

"He put up his own obstacles," Madge said, leading the way into the hall. "It wasn't only us."

"Is he coming to escort you or meeting you there?" Wyatt asked.

"He's meeting us there," Samantha said. "He says the theatre isn't far from his house and it wouldn't make sense to come out here only to retrace his steps."

"Apparently the inconvenience was so strong as to overcome his manners," Madge said.

"It makes sense," Samantha said, coming to his defense. "And it is a business meeting, not a social call."

When the carriage dropped them off in front of the Grecian portico of the Haymarket Theatre, Mr. Leclerc was waiting for them. His surprise at seeing Wyatt swiftly transformed to delight, and he spent most of the walk to the Bradwells' box talking to Wyatt, inquiring about his recent investigations. Samantha was left to walk behind the two with Madge. When Wyatt shot her an apologetic look, she shrugged and smiled. She didn't want him to feel guilty when Mr. Leclerc's inattention to her was not his fault.

She had expected the inventor would be as obsequious to her as her suitors since he wanted much the same thing. He was clearly not worried about whether she would agree to fund him. She wondered if she ought to take his dismissal of her as evidence of his confidence in the impressiveness of his work or of his assumption of her inability to perceive its flaws. She was inclined to think it was the latter.

Though Mr. Leclerc did sit beside Samantha in the front of

the box, they did not speak during the play, so she was able to watch it. The titular cousin was a caricature of a rustic American—brash, unrefined and unflinchingly honest. She enjoyed the play, though not as much as she might have had she not been aware, at all times, of the opera glasses trained her way.

She had always known that, for many, the purpose of attending the theatre was to see and be seen. Opera glasses were used more often to spy on people in the other boxes than to watch the play itself. Until this Season, however, Samantha had not been an object of much interest, and not many had bothered to spy on her and her aunt and uncle. Tonight, she could imagine what a show she was giving with this unknown man sitting beside her. The other playgoers must be beside themselves trying to identify him and his relationship to her. That thought made her smile.

During the intermission after the first act, while Wyatt went to get refreshments for Samantha and Madge, Mr. Leclerc did finally speak to Samantha, or rather, at her. He flipped through the papers he had brought with him so quickly that she barely had time to read them, and when she asked to look at a drawing again, he declined to show it to her, explaining that it was a technical drawing she would not understand, anyway.

It didn't help matters that they were frequently interrupted. Madge's sister-in-law, Lady Chesterton, stopped by with her daughter, Miss Fanshaw, and her daughter's friend, Miss Thorpe. After confirming Samantha's and Madge's attendance at her ball next month, she left without being introduced to Mr. Leclerc. Samantha was certain she considered him beneath her notice. Their next visitor, Mr. Lennon, did ask to be introduced, though it was clearly out of a fear that Mr. Leclerc might be a suitor of Samantha's. When he realized there was no threat to his suit, he left satisfied.

Eventually, sensing Samantha's frustration, Madge moved to block the doorway, forcing any further visitors to speak with her in the corridor, which allowed Samantha and Mr. Leclerc the opportunity to finish their discussion.

Overall, Samantha was disappointed with the interview. What little she had seen of his research left her with the impression that, though he had a revolutionary idea, he did not have a well-crafted plan of how to carry it out. She could easily admit that she was not a scientist and wouldn't have the first notion how to create sound from a drawing of a soundwave. Indeed, the very idea still seemed incredible. However, Mr. Leclerc's jumbled notes and drawings seemed less technical than aspirational, like the scribblings of a child imagining a fantasy world.

Mr. Leclerc did not seem discouraged by her diminishing enthusiasm, however. In fact, he seemed hardly to notice her response, so set was he on delivering the monologue he had prepared. When Wyatt returned and handed Samantha her drink, he shifted his attention to him and restarted his pitch. To Samantha's relief, the curtain went up then, and everyone's attention reverted to the stage.

The second act was even more entertaining than the first. Despite never having seen the play, Samantha had heard of Lord Dundreary, the imbecilic nobleman character who appeared in the second act. His side whiskers, which were long and bushy and stuck out of the sides of his face like handles, had been copied, in jest, by some of the more rackety young men in Society. They called them "dundrearies." The actor playing Lord Dundreary possessed excellent comedic timing and had the whole theatre laughing uproariously, Samantha included. His way of misspeaking aphorisms was one of the highlights of the play.

"That was quite good," Madge said when the final curtain had fallen. "What was it that American called Mrs. Mountchessington? A sock something?"

"A sockdologizing old man-trap," Wyatt supplied.

Madge chuckled. "I shall have to remember that. I know a few sockdologizing old man-traps myself."

"Thank you for joining us," Samantha said to Mr. Leclerc, determined to remain polite despite her frustration with him.

"To be sure, to be sure," Mr. Leclerc said, nodding. "It is an excellent play." He tapped the folder under his arm. "I look forward to discussing our next steps with regards to my invention."

Samantha hummed in response. She had decided against telling him that evening that she would not be patronizing him. She thought a letter might be the best way to convey her refusal. After all, considering the flow of their recent conversation, he wasn't likely to listen to her, anyway.

"You've worked with Inspector Whicher before, haven't you?" Mr. Leclerc said suddenly, turning to Wyatt.

Samantha almost rolled her eyes. He was her invited guest, and yet she felt like a fifth wheel.

"In a manner of speaking," Wyatt said guardedly. "Why do you ask?"

"I wondered if I might involve the police after all," Mr. Leclerc said. "Perhaps with someone like the inspector on my side, Mr. Ponsonby would be more inclined to listen."

Samantha and Wyatt exchanged glances. Samantha knew Wyatt was thinking that, after they dragged him to Blackfriars in the middle of the night, Inspector Whicher was unlikely to be in the mood to help Wyatt with anything for a while.

"Speak to Whicher if you like," Wyatt said, "but don't be surprised if he's unable to assist you right away. He's quite busy at the moment and may not be able or inclined to help with a case of fraud."

"Of course," Mr. Leclerc said, snapping his fingers. "The robbery and stabbing in Soho. Begging your pardon," he added, with a slight bow to Samantha and Madge.

"I think we can manage to hear the word 'stabbing' without

being overset," Madge said dryly.

"As you say," said Mr. Leclerc. "I suppose it was a murder of a sort. They haven't caught the culprit then?"

"I think if they had," Wyatt said, "it would have been reported immediately."

"True, true," Mr. Leclerc said. "I just thought, considering that you worked with the inspector last summer, you might have some information not generally known."

"I may have worked *with* him," Wyatt said, "but I do not work *for* him and as such am hardly likely to be the recipient of sensitive information, nor would I share it if I were."

Samantha could see the tension in Wyatt's jaw as he spoke. She understood his frustration. Mr. Leclerc was presuming a lot on a thin acquaintance. She looped her arm through Wyatt's. He looked down at her in surprise, but she felt him relax as she squeezed his arm. As she turned back to Mr. Leclerc, she saw Madge watching them with a knowing smile.

"I beg your pardon," Mr. Leclerc said, holding up his hands. "My mistake. I had hoped you were well-enough acquainted to garner me an introduction. He might be more likely to help me if he knew you and I are friends."

"I didn't realize you were," Samantha said with a polite smile. "I was under the impression that Mr. Wyatt helped you at the request of your mutual friend Mr. Canard."

"That's true," Wyatt said, shooting her a grateful look. "George is a good friend to have, isn't he, Mr. Leclerc? And it was good to see you again tonight. I'm glad you and Miss Kingston were able to talk. Now, however, I had better see these ladies home. Have a good evening."

Mr. Leclerc shook Wyatt's proffered hand with a subdued air and bowed to Samantha and Madge.

"Did you learn what you hoped to?" Madge asked Samantha as they stood under the portico waiting for their carriage to be brought round.

"Sadly, no," Samantha said. "It's a shame because I was quite excited at the idea of patronizing a great invention."

"There will be other inventors," Madge said. "One hopes the next might be a bit less loquacious."

*****

It hadn't been too difficult to wrangle an invitation to Sir Anthony's card party on Tuesday. Carstairs was a great friend of his and was more than willing to bring Wyatt along, though he found the whole situation amusing.

"I can still hardly believe it," he said as they walked down the lane to Sir Anthony's Kensington townhome. "Wyatt, at a card party. You know I haven't seen you play since Cambridge. I thought you'd given it up."

It was true. Though Wyatt had some skill at cards, he had never enjoyed "playing deep," risking large amounts on games that were often as dependent on luck as on skill. The aunt who had gifted him her house on her death had been generous in her Will, but he didn't have near the resources of some of his peers, nor their recklessness.

"I'm as surprised as you are to find myself here," he said.

They were let in by the butler and led upstairs. Taking careful note of his surroundings, Wyatt surmised that the house was laid out similarly to his own. The sound of voices grew as they approached the drawing room, coming to a crescendo as the door was opened and they entered. Through a haze of cigar smoke, Wyatt could see close to thirty men seated around half a dozen round, wooden tables that lay scattered throughout the green-carpeted room.

Sir Anthony sat at the table nearest the door, a cigar poking out from beneath his bristle brush mustache. When he saw Carstairs, he brightened and motioned him over.

"We've a good crowd tonight," he said. "There are a few tables of brag over there. Bentley's got a three-stakes game going if you want to join. Or you can come in on faro. I've got the bank." He frowned at Wyatt. "Didn't think I'd ever see you here, Wyatt. You're welcome, of course, but you should know we play deep."

"Told him so myself," said Carstairs. "Never managed to dissuade Wyatt from whatever he wanted to do, though, and he would insist on it."

"I appreciate your hospitality, Sir Anthony," Wyatt said. "I may watch for a few hands."

"Only a few," Sir Anthony said sternly. "We don't hold with peepers here. Players only."

Wyatt nodded and followed Carstairs to a table at the far end where a group of three were playing at brag. Once they'd finished the hand, Carstairs asked to be dealt in. Wyatt watched for a minute, then casually wandered by a couple of other tables before checking that Sir Anthony's attention was on his own game and stepping quietly out the door.

Outside, Wyatt hesitated. He couldn't very well stop a maid and ask to be shown to Sir Anthony's bedchamber. However, based on his own home, he figured he could guess within one or two which door was his host's. Moving swiftly but silently up the stairs, Wyatt reached the second floor without incident.

The corridor was quiet. Thick rugs helped to hide his footsteps as he checked the first room on his left. It was empty—not only of people, but of furniture. Though it was dark, by the light of the hall lamps, Wyatt could see discolored shapes in the wallpaper that seemed to indicate paintings or looking glasses that had recently been removed. The next room was similarly bereft of furnishings, though a pile of linens lay stacked in one corner and a couple of trunks in another.

On his third try, Wyatt was certain he had found Sir Anthony's room. He was, by now, unsurprised to find it somewhat lacking. The bedcurtains had been removed from the handsome four-poster bed, giving it a strangely skeletal appearance. The walls were bare.

A sound from the corridor sent Wyatt scrambling beneath the bed. He pulled his arm under just as the door opened. Small-booted feet stepped efficiently across the room. Wyatt twisted his neck and saw the back of a white cap as a maid passed by, carrying an armful of clean linens. She opened the wardrobe, and he could hear her shifting the contents around before closing it again. When she reached the threshold of the door, she paused and turned back. Wyatt lay still, holding his breath, but her manner was unsuspicious and, a moment later, she left the room.

Releasing his breath, Wyatt crawled out from under the bed and stood up. He caught sight of his reflection in the looking glass above the ablutions bowl and bit back a curse. His formerly black evening kit was grey with dust. The maid was clearly not a thorough cleaner. For several minutes he could scarcely afford, Wyatt did all he could to remove the dust. He shrugged out of his jacket and shook it out, but the dust clung to his trousers. Crossing to the wardrobe, he searched within it until he found a clothes brush, with which he attacked his clothes with vigor. When he had done the best he could, he closed the wardrobe and reached into his inner jacket pocket for the medallion the Irishman had given him. Setting it on one of the pillows, he hurried to the door. Just as he reached it, the knob turned in his hand and the door opened inward. Wyatt didn't have time to hide and so was forced to come face-to-face with his host.

"What do you think you're doing?" Sir Anthony growled.

Wyatt's brain sifted through half a dozen possible excuses, but he knew it was a lost cause. He'd been caught, and there would be no talking his way out of it. After all, what possible explanation could he give for being in his host's bedchamber during a card party?

"I said," Sir Anthony repeated through gritted teeth, "what do you think you're doing?"

Releasing the doorknob, Wyatt stepped back and gestured for him to enter. Sir Anthony's brows rose, and Wyatt almost laughed at what he knew must appear to his host as the most brazen audacity—inviting the man into his own room.

"If you really want to know, you may as well come in," Wyatt said. "I don't think it's a conversation you'll want to have overheard."

With evident reluctance, Sir Anthony stepped inside. Wyatt shut the door behind him and pointed to the bed. Sir Anthony raised an eyebrow, but turned to look. His gaze fixated on the medallion lying on the pillow, and Wyatt watched as his face drained of all color.

"How did you..." he sputtered. "Do you...did you...?"

"I wasn't given specifics," Wyatt said. "You may rest easy on that account. I was only told it was a reminder."

Sir Anthony turned to him, his eyes wide. Wyatt detected a hint of fear behind them. "How long have you—"

"I don't work for him," Wyatt hastened to assure him. "At least, not until recently and, I hope, not for much longer. I'm sure you of all people must understand how persuasive he can be."

Sir Anthony's face relaxed a few degrees. "Yes, I do. Of course, I do."

"Whatever it is you owe him, I'd suggest you find a way to pay it soon. I've heard he's not averse to killing if he thinks there's no chance of repayment."

"What do you think I've been trying to do?" Sir Anthony asked. He gestured expressively to the empty walls. "I've sold almost everything of value. The drawing room and the dining room are the only furnished ones in the house apart from this one, and that's just so I can keep up appearances for the games."

"Faro isn't paying out?"

"Not nearly enough. I spend half the takings on food and drink for the next evening."

"Why did you borrow from someone like him in the first place?"

Sir Anthony shrugged. "He offered what seemed a reasonable rate, and I couldn't afford to be choosy. This private club isn't my first business venture, and I've lost some faith with my other investors. I thought I could pay him back easily. They say the house always wins, so I figured I couldn't lose."

Wyatt couldn't believe the gullibility of some people. He let out a derisive snort.

"Don't look at me like that," Sir Anthony said. "How was I to know it wouldn't pan out?"

"How indeed," Wyatt said dryly. "I'm going to go. I've passed on the message, and I need to let him know I did it. It's in your hands now."

"You don't want to stay and try your luck at the tables?"

Wyatt shook his head. "I don't think you want me to do that."

TWELVE

Three days after his encounter with Sir Anthony, Wyatt was in the library of the United University Club, having fallen asleep in an armchair by the fire, when he was shaken gently awake.

"Sorry to bother you, sir," Alfred, one of the club waiters, said, "but there's a gentleman here to see you."

Blinking, Wyatt yawned and sat up. Alfred stepped back, holding himself stiffly. He was new to the position and unusually young—in his early twenties. He had a tendency to compensate for his youth and inexperience by acting overly formal.

"No need to apologize, Alfred. Did he give a name?"

"Inspector Whicher, sir."

Now fully awake, Wyatt got to his feet and was about to head for the door when a cough from Alfred stopped him.

"Yes?" he prompted.

"I was told, if that gentleman were to return, to remind you that guests are not permitted anywhere but the dining room."

Wyatt's eyebrows rose. "Are they still on about that? It was one time. We sat for five minutes at most."

"The club rules are rather strict on these points, sir," Alfred said apologetically.

"I know, I know. I'm sorry they saddled you with the task of reminding me."

"It is the privilege of the club leadership to delegate less pleasant tasks."

"Am I that unpleasant to deal with?" Wyatt asked mildly.

"No one likes to be reminded of the rules, sir."

"I suppose not. Thank you, Alfred."

Inspector Whicher stood in the front hall of the club, fingering the brim of his hat and ignoring the haughty looks of the doorman. When he saw Wyatt, he strode forward.

"Will you be offended if I tell you that I feel a sense of dread whenever I see you?" Wyatt asked, only half in jest.

"It's a common enough sentiment, Mr. Wyatt. Might I have a few minutes of your time?"

"Of course, but it might be better if we go for a walk. I've been reminded that guests are only permitted in the dining room, and I doubt you have the time for overpriced fish."

After Wyatt had collected his hat and cane, they set off down the Pall Mall.

"I'm surprised to see you," he said. "After our conversation in Blackfriars, I assumed you were angry with me."

"I am angry," Whicher said, "but I'm not here for a social call. I've come to ask you about your connection to Mr. Theodore Spenser."

"The man who was killed in the robbery?" Wyatt asked, his sense of foreboding increasing.

"The same."

"I don't have one. At least, not directly. He was a friend of Miss Kingston's."

"Did you never meet the man?"

"Not that I recall."

"Did Miss Kingston discuss him with you or you with him?"

"I don't know if she discussed me with him, but she and I

talked about him once or twice before his death. More afterwards. Why all the questions? What have you learned?"

Whicher drew him aside as a gentleman strolled past them.

"We had been acting under the assumption that the attack was a robbery," he said. "The victim's wallet and watch chain were missing when constables arrived on the scene, minutes after the body was discovered. However, we found both items in a pawn shop and were able to trace the man who sold them. He's well known to us—a drunk and an opportunist, but not a killer. Nor does he match the description of the man witnesses saw in the aftermath of the attack. He claims he came upon the body moments before the constables arrived, after the victim was already dead."

"Do you believe him?"

"I do."

Wyatt had been hoping, for Samantha's sake, that Mr. Spenser's death was an unfortunate accident, the result of the panicked actions of a desperate thief. Tragic, yes, but nothing more. If it was murder, that meant a murderer was on the loose, and he might be one of Samantha's new acquaintances.

"If you don't think it was a robbery, I assume you're considering it murder," Wyatt said. "Do you have any idea why, or who the killer might be?"

"We are treating it as a murder investigation, yes, but we do not have any suspects as yet. We don't have a lot to go on—just witness descriptions of the man in the brown checked suit walking away and a small brass button that was found near the body. We did, however, learn that Mr. Spenser's home had been burgled around the time he was murdered."

"Around? You don't know more specifically?"

Whicher shook his head. "According to his staff, he didn't allow anyone into his study, even to clean it. It was some days after his death before they entered the room. When they realized that it had been ransacked, they reported it, but they had no way of knowing when the burglary had occurred."

"What was stolen?"

"Impossible to tell," Whicher said. "No one could confirm what were the usual contents of the room. It's taken us a long time to comb through it all. There was money in the desk, though, so it seems that wasn't the motive."

They were separated by a large group of people walking in the opposite direction. When they had pushed their way through the crowd and reunited on the other side, Wyatt searched Whicher's impassive face.

"Why are you telling me this?" he asked.

"I found this." Whicher reached into his pocket and pulled out a card. He flicked it around to show Wyatt his own name and address on the face of it—his card. Wyatt stared at it, unsure what to think. "It was on the floor near the door along with a pile of papers I believe were dropped by the thieves on their way out. There were a handful of legal documents related to Spenser's charitable work, a blueprint of some sort and a couple of personal letters."

"Did you say a blueprint?" Wyatt interrupted.

"Yes," Whicher said slowly. "Why? What does that mean to you?"

"What was it for? A building or a piece of machinery?"

"Machinery, I believe. Do you know why Mr. Spenser had it?"

"I have no idea, but it might be relevant. Could I see it?"

"It's at the Yard if you want to come by."

Wyatt nodded, his mind a whirl. Was it possible Mr. Spenser was involved with Ponsonby? Samantha hadn't mentioned that he was an inventor, but it may have been a hobby of his.

"Do you know why he had your card?" Whicher asked.

"I don't know that, either," Wyatt said. "I didn't give it to him. I can ask Miss Kingston if she did, though I can't imagine why she would have. She could have introduced us if he wanted to meet me."

"Do you have any connection to his charitable work?" Whicher asked. "Might your card have been placed with those documents?"

"None, apart from what Miss Kingston was doing with him."

"What was that?"

"She and Mr. Spenser were planning to create an asylum for fallen women in Hammersmith." He hesitated, then added. "You should probably know, one of Skinny Jim's men followed them to the house they were considering purchasing. Miss Kingston saw him before he disappeared."

The inspector looked grave.

"For what it's worth," Wyatt said, "he claims not to have killed him, and I believe him."

"Who claims?" Whicher asked sharply. "Skinny Jim? Is that why you were in Blackfriars last month?"

So much for the inspector not wanting to know what they'd been doing. Wyatt wished he hadn't brought it up.

"He told Miss Kingston to come see him," Wyatt said. "We weren't going to go, but then Spenser was killed, and we thought it might have been a message aimed at her."

Inspector Whicher's eyebrows flew up, then drew down into angry daggers. He opened and closed his mouth three times, pursing his lips tight before taking a breath and speaking.

"So, you sent for me in case...what? He killed you, too?"

"I didn't think that was likely, but—"

"Why? Did you learn nothing from what happened to Charles Prescott? And the witnesses to his death?"

"He'd been trying to get Miss Kingston to meet with him for some time," Wyatt said. "He could have killed us any time he liked if he really wanted to. I sent for you in case of some other kind of trouble."

Whicher worked his jaw. "Why did he want to meet with her?"

The truth would be out soon enough. Wyatt scanned their surroundings. The street was crowded, but no one was following them close enough to hear. Still, he lowered his voice as he said, "He met Miss Kingston when she was in hiding, and he'd figured out who she was. He threatened to tell the world what she'd really been up to if she didn't come back to work for him."

He watched Whicher for his reaction and was surprised to see resignation on the inspector's face.

"I was afraid it was something like that," Whicher said.

Wyatt waited for him to continue, but he didn't.

"Is that all you have to say?" Wyatt asked.

"Yes. You work for Skinny Jim now. I have to watch my words."

"Whoa," Wyatt said, holding up his hands, palm out. "I don't work for him."

"He has leverage on you. If he wants insight into one of my cases, he'll make sure you give it to him."

"I would never do that," Wyatt said, annoyed and even a little hurt that Whicher would think it of him. "I've done a couple of things that were questionable, but just to buy us time until we can destroy his leverage."

Whicher pursed his lips again. "If you do that, you'd better plan to leave town. He won't take it well."

"I know."

The words were heavy on Wyatt's tongue. He knew he and Samantha were navigating dangerous waters. Whicher stopped walking and looked at him appraisingly.

"I'll meet you at the Yard in an hour," he said. "I want you to look at the blueprint."

Realizing that Whicher had decided to trust him in spite of his reservations meant more to Wyatt than he would have expected.

When Wyatt entered Whicher's office an hour later after stopping off at home, he found the inspector standing over his desk, laying out a small stack of papers one at a time so that they were all visible.

"Does any of this look familiar?" he asked.

Wyatt scanned the legal documents and the letters without much expectation. "None of these do. Where is the blueprint?"

Clearing a space, Whicher unrolled a thin sheaf of paper, using a whiskey decanter and glasses to hold down the edges. Wyatt leaned forward and examined it. He knew little about the inner workings of machinery, but the shape was distinctive and the name, familiar. Mr. Spenser might not be an inventor after all, but, in possessing this particular blueprint, he was still connected to Ponsonby.

Wyatt straightened and pulled the folder he'd brought with him from under his arm. Flipping it open, he thumbed through the papers until he found the one with Franz Leipzig's name at the top.

"Durand is even better than I gave him credit for," he said, laying the drawing down beside the blueprint. "Or perhaps my memory is."

It wasn't a perfect replica, of course, but the drawing looked enough like the blueprint that it was clear they were a match.

"What is this?" Whicher asked. He looked from Durand's drawing to the blueprint and back. "Why do you have this?"

Briefly, Wyatt explained how he had come to be involved with Mr. Leclerc and the man's quest to receive credit from Ponsonby for his work. He went on to tell, keeping the details as vague as possible, how he had discovered other blueprints besides Leclerc's and had his valet draw them from his description.

"Are you saying that this blueprint was in Mr. Ponsonby's possession when you saw it last? You are certain?"

"As certain as I can be. I didn't memorize every detail, but you'll agree the drawings are quite similar."

"They are, yes."

"I don't know how Mr. Spenser came to be in possession of it. It was well hidden in Mr. Ponsonby's house, and I can't see why he would have given it to someone else."

Whicher picked up the drawing and examined it. "Did Miss Kingston know you...*liberated* the blueprint for Mr. Leclerc?" he asked.

"Yes," Wyatt said, electing not to go into the part she had played in helping him to do so.

"Did she discuss it with Mr. Spenser?"

"I have no idea, but I don't know why she would have."

Whicher nodded thoughtfully. "If she did, or if he found out through some other means, perhaps when he came into the possession of one of the blueprints himself, he intended to discuss it with you. That may have been why he had your card." He nodded to the folder in Wyatt's hands. "May I borrow those?"

Wyatt handed it over. "I only remembered one of the other inventors' names. I wasn't able to track him down, but I did speak to Mr. Leipzig."

"This Mr. Leipzig?" Whicher asked, pointing to the blueprint.

"Yes. His story was similar to Leclerc's. He hadn't pursued the matter because he didn't have the resources, but he was very interested in retrieving his property. He asked me to let him know if I found anything."

Whicher hummed. "In light of the connection to Mr. Spenser's death, I'd prefer it if you didn't contact him yet. I'll pass on the information myself when I interview him."

"I understand. Will you be speaking with Mr. Ponsonby?"

Whicher began to gather up the rest of the papers. "More than likely, though not until I have some more information." He stopped what he was doing and gave Wyatt a stern look. "There is nothing to be gained by confronting him before that. He may or may not have been involved in Mr. Spenser's death, but if he was, I'd rather not tip my hand."

"I hope you aren't implying that I would be so foolish as to compromise your investigation," Wyatt said, bristling.

"I am less concerned about Mr. Wyatt than I am about Mr. Signet," Whicher said dryly.

He was referring to a persona Wyatt had invented to interview a witness to a robbery the summer before. Whicher had confronted Wyatt about the incident at the time, and Wyatt had refused to confirm that he was Mr. Signet, mostly out of stubborn pride. He couldn't defend himself now without admitting to the charade and it irked him, particularly as he thought he saw the ghost of a smile flicker across Whicher's lips.

"You can leave the folder at my club when you're done with it," he said instead. "I'll see myself out."

*****

The Royal Horticultural Gardens, though not officially part of the Great Exhibition, had been laid out the year before in anticipation of the crowds that would flock to the city. The exhibition building bordered the gardens on one side and, as Samantha walked along the canal, breathing in the scent of fresh grass and flowering trees, she thought the building didn't look nearly so unprepossessing as she had first judged it. As for the gardens themselves, they were beautiful, palatial in size and, particularly with the sky such an unusually clear blue, within them one could almost imagine oneself transported far from London.

Beside Samantha, Mrs. Heywood walked unhurriedly, swinging her parasol in one hand. She had invited Samantha for tea not long after Mr. Spenser's funeral, and they had gotten along surprisingly well. Samantha had tried to return the invitation, but they had been unable to find a day that worked for both of them until today.

"Did you hear that?" Mrs. Heywood said, craning her neck to

look behind them. "I think I heard a violin being tuned. Can you see the bandstand?"

Samantha followed her gaze, but the large gazebo-like structure was too far away for her to be able to distinguish the people milling in and around it.

"I didn't hear anything," she said, "but I'm sure you're right."

"I hope so," Mrs. Heywood said. "We've got lovely weather and a beautiful view. Music would be just the thing to make the day perfect."

"Indeed."

Samantha was more than a little distracted, as she had been ever since Wyatt told her about his conversation with Inspector Whicher. She could not conceive how Mr. Spenser had acquired Wyatt's card or why he had it. She was fairly certain she had mentioned Wyatt to Mr. Spenser once or twice, but merely in passing. Their conversations had been too few and too focused for idle chatter.

Then there was his possession of Mr. Leipzig's blueprint, which she and Wyatt had last seen hidden away in Mr. Ponsonby's study. How could Mr. Spenser possibly have obtained it? And why? She and Wyatt had speculated about whether he'd had the other blueprints as well. After all, his home had been burgled and his study ransacked. Mr. Leipzig's blueprint had been found on the floor by the door. It might conceivably have been in a pile with the others, dropped in a hasty retreat.

"Miss Kingston?"

Mrs. Heywood had stopped walking and was watching her with concern.

"Forgive me," Samantha said, shaking her head a little to clear the fog. "I'm afraid I was woolgathering. Did you say something?"

"Just that the peelers came 'round yesterday to ask me about Mr. Spenser. I thought you'd want to know that they're still investigating, seeing as how you thought he might have been murdered."

"The police asked you about Mr. Spenser?" Samantha asked, incredulous to find the conversation so relevant to her musings. "Why?"

"Well, it's my opinion that they're just trying to look like they're doing something. The papers keep scaring people into thinking they're about to be strangled to death on every corner, and no one's got sense enough to point out it's only been one garrotting and one stabbing and nothing since. Course, it doesn't help that now they're saying Mr. Spenser was probably garrotted 'fore he was stabbed and the peelers covered it up to prevent panic."

Samantha was well aware of the growing panic in the city. She'd even heard of some men attempting to fashion anti-garrotting collars, though she wasn't sure if that was true or the invention of the cartoonists.

"But what reason did they give for coming to speak with you?" Samantha asked. "Are they talking to all of his friends? Why?"

"No, nothing like that," Mrs. Heywood said airily. "They were searching his home for some reason and found a letter I sent him, so they asked me about it."

Wyatt had mentioned that a handful of personal letters were among the things Inspector Whicher had described to him.

"Why would they do that?" Samantha asked.

Mrs. Heywood looked sideways at Samantha, then sighed. "I don't suppose it matters now he's dead, but Mr. Spenser and I had an...arrangement. I wasn't lying when I told you I didn't know him particularly well, because it had only been about six months and we didn't talk much, but I did know him in the biblical sense. The letter they asked me about was to arrange an...I suppose the polite word is assignation."

"I see."

Samantha kept her expression carefully neutral. She was not

ignorant of such matters, but she was not used to hearing them discussed so frankly.

"I did care for my husband, Miss Kingston," Mrs. Heywood said. "He was sweet, and he loved me dearly. He spoiled me and was happy to indulge me, but I'm not such a fool as to think I could be so lucky twice. I won't marry again. What Mr. Spenser and I had was purely practical, for both of us, and so I told the peelers when they were rude enough to ask."

Though Samantha may not have approved of Mrs. Heywood's morals, she could understand her desire to remain unmarried. It was a frightening thing as a woman to put one's life in the hands of a man.

"I am glad they're investigating his death, though, even if it is only for show," Mrs. Heywood said. "Do you still think he was murdered?"

"I do." Samantha was almost tempted to tell her why she thought so, but refrained.

"I still can't think of anyone who would want to murder him," Mrs. Heywood said. "Unless he had some questionable past dealings no one knew about, though that seems unlikely. The man was practically a saint. It was a bit annoying, to tell you the truth."

They dodged out of the way of a family with excitable children, and Mrs. Heywood linked her arm with Samantha's.

"That's the trouble with speculating about these things, though," she said. "Because, of course, one can't help but wonder if he really was the person we all thought he was, or if he was hiding something. And suddenly the pure-white Mr. Spenser becomes very grey at the edges."

Samantha declined to point out that he had been hiding his relationship with Mrs. Heywood. Instead, she said, "I'm sure he'd be the first to say he wasn't as pure as people liked to paint him. No one could be. But it doesn't follow that he was a villain."

"No, that's true."

They had come to a small, hedged garden. Ahead of them, a stone sundial took up the center of the space. It showed half past four. Samantha would need to leave soon if she was to get ready for the opera she was attending with Eden that night.

Suddenly, a small form barreled into her legs, and she looked down to see a tiny blond head bury itself in her skirts. A muffled shriek that sounded like it might be "Miss Kingston!" came from the region of her knees.

"William Edmund Atherton!"

Eden strode towards them, her expression stern and fixed on the boy now grinning up at Samantha with what she feared might be strawberry jam spread across his lips and now, no doubt, her skirts.

"Good afternoon, William," Samantha said, giving the boy what she hoped was a warm smile.

Samantha had little experience with young children, and her first meeting with Eden's four-year-old son had been uncomfortable, but his sweetness and cheerful demeanor had endeared him to her. She doubted she would enjoy the company of a different child, but she had developed a certain fondness for William.

"Hello, Samantha," Eden said, flashing her a brief smile. "Mrs. Heywood. It's good to see you again. If you'll excuse me."

She took her son by the arm and knelt down in front of him.

"What do you think I'm going to say to you?" she asked.

William tapped a finger to his chin and said, "Er...I think zero things?"

Samantha had to turn away to hide her smile. She looked down to see that there was, indeed, a streak of jam, bright red against the black and white checked fabric of her skirt.

Eden sounded as though she was having to force herself to sound stern. "William Atherton, you know very well that you are not to run ahead."

"Yes, Mother."

"Nor are you to leave the table when your hands and face are unclean."

"But it wasn't a table," William argued. "It was a fountain."

Eden gave him a stern look, and he hung his head.

"Now, apologize to Miss Kingston for covering her in jam."

William turned to Samantha, his cherubic grin back in place.

"I beg your pardon, Miss Kingston."

"Thank you, William. You are forgiven."

Eden rose to her feet and held out a hand to her son. Then she turned her attention back to Samantha and Mrs. Heywood.

"Mrs. Heywood," she said, "may I present my son? William, this is Mrs. Heywood, a new friend of your mama's and Miss Kingston's."

Mrs. Heywood bent down and shook William's hand.

"A pleasure to meet you, young man."

"You sound like my nanny," William said. "Are you a nanny?"

Eden flushed scarlet and tried to hush her son, but Mrs. Heywood laughed.

"I'm not a nanny," she said. "I don't think I've ever even met one before. Are they nice?"

"Oh, yes," said William. "Well, sometimes. Sometimes they're cross and call one a naughty boy."

"Perhaps I wouldn't like to meet one, then. I don't think I'd like being called a naughty boy."

William giggled.

"I should get him home," Eden said. "I'll see you this evening for the opera, Samantha. Good day, Mrs. Heywood."

"I like her," Mrs. Heywood said when Eden and her son had disappeared into the crowd.

"She's a good friend," Samantha said. "I haven't had many in my life, so I feel fortunate to have found her."

"Well, I hope you may consider me one of the few," Mrs. Heywood said. "I like you too. Though, even if you'd rather not be friends, I hope you'll agree to a business partnership. I think you and Mr. Spenser had a good idea, and it would be a shame to see it fall by the wayside."

"I would be honored to call you a friend," Samantha said, surprised, but touched by the overture. "With regards to a partnership, I appreciate the offer, but I don't wish to burden you."

"Oh, pish. I'd have offered from the beginning if I'd thought of it, but Mr. Spenser always was the more forward-thinking."

"In that case, thank you. I would be happy to work with you."

"I should let you know, I've never done anything quite like this before. My main interests have always been the arts, of course, and veterans' affairs, for my late husband. He was a soldier, you see, before he became a banker and made his fortune. However, I'm a hard worker and I know how to organize. And I care about helping those women, which is half the battle, I think."

"That is important," Samantha agreed. "When Mr. Spenser and I talked about Urania Cottage, I thought it was a shame that it closed down."

"It was a shame," Mrs. Heywood said. "Though, I always thought the cottage was a bit of a vanity project for Mr. Dickens. Not that there weren't women who benefited from the program, but he did like to be the hero. Then, when he found another, more enjoyable, way to stroke his vanity, it fell by the wayside."

"What do you mean?"

Mrs. Heywood shook her head. "I won't be a gossip. What I will say is this: for however much I disapprove of Mr. Dickens' abandonment of his project, no one can deny that he put in the work when it mattered to him, and it was a lot of work. We have a lot of work ahead of us."

"Good work," Samantha said, "and worthwhile."

"Oh, by all means, but still, a lot."

In the carriage on the way back to Madge's house, Samantha wondered if she had made the right decision in agreeing to partner with Mrs. Heywood. It wasn't her new friend's usefulness or dedication she doubted, but her own. The problem of Skinny Jim overshadowed everything about her life at the moment and she had no idea how it would resolve. Should she really be making plans for a future that was so uncertain?

THIRTEEN

There was nothing quite like the Derby. Even Samantha, who had been anxiously awaiting the next message from Skinny Jim, could not help but feel her spirits lift as she followed Madge and her husband out onto the upper balcony of the grandstand. The very air hummed with energy. The babble of talk and laughter around her floated above the general roar of tens of thousands of spectators. She could see them as she gazed out at the racecourse below. They surrounded the track inside and out, crammed into every available space. Above her, she could hear the sound of feet stomping along the stands, and below and to each side, hundreds, if not thousands, of people found their seats.

The Derby was one of those unique events in which rich and poor alike participated, though in their separate arenas. The wealthy owned the horses, and the poor rode them. There was some enjoyment for all in watching the race itself, but it was the spectacle that appealed to most. That and the betting.

Alice would be down below somewhere, along with most of the Bradwells' staff. Samantha had advanced her pay so that she would have money for the sweet vendors and entertainments available in the striped tents at the center of the field. Annie was there, too, and, though Samantha knew the threat to her safety was largely gone now that Skinny Jim had other ways to control her and Wyatt, she still worried about Annie. Peter had promised to look out for her, which was some reassurance, if not enough. It would be easy to get lost in those crowds.

Pulling out a pair of opera glasses, Samantha trained them on the crowd. Though she hated the practice of people-watching at the theatre, when the focus ought to be on the play, she had no objection to it in general, and the Derby was the perfect place for it. She scanned the grandstands below her, but people moved too much for easy observation, forcing her to refocus her glasses so often that she began to feel seasick, so she soon moved her attention to the area around the track.

"See anyone you know?"

Wyatt's voice tickled her ear as he leaned in to be heard over the noise.

"No, but I found a man juggling beer bottles, which is much more entertaining."

"Can I see?"

She handed the glasses to Wyatt and pointed to the spot she had been watching.

"I don't see it," he muttered, squinting through the lenses.

"Here." She took them back, found the man and pulled her head out of the way. "Now look."

Wyatt's leg nudged her skirts as he stepped closer and leaned down to peer through the glasses. As he reached his hand up to steady them, his fingers brushed hers. Even though they both wore gloves, she could feel tingles run up her arm.

"What are you looking at?"

Lord Aston's bright, cheerful voice startled Samantha so much that she jumped and knocked the opera glasses into Wyatt's face.

"Ow!"

Wyatt stood up and rubbed his eyes where the glasses had hit him.

"Oh, no!" she said. "Forgive me."

Lord Aston snickered.

"Miss Kingston claimed she saw a juggler somewhere down there," Wyatt said. "She was attempting to show me when you startled her, and she nearly gave me a black eye."

"I am sorry," Samantha said with a wince.

"Think nothing of it," said Wyatt. "It wasn't your fault."

"You could go down there and see the juggler for yourself," Lord Aston said. "The race doesn't start for another half hour."

"Have you been down on the field?" Samantha asked. In the handful of times she'd been to the Derby, she'd never been anywhere but the grandstands. It was a shame, really, because the field seemed so much more exciting.

"Naturally," Lord Aston said. "How else do you think I came by this?"

He produced a package of roasted nuts from his pocket and handed her one before popping another in his mouth.

"Will you take me?"

Lord Aston coughed and thumped his chest. "Take you? Down to the field?"

"Yes, you and Wyatt. I'd love to see it."

"It's not...it's a bit rough, Miss Kingston," Lord Aston said, with a glance at Wyatt. "And there are unsavory characters there, you know. I thought you were meant to be careful about."

"I will be careful. I'll have two stalwart companions by my side, ready to defend me if called upon. But I doubt the need will arise. We are at a temporary détente with Skinny Jim, or did Wyatt not tell you?"

"I told him," Wyatt said. "Though I don't feel the détente is something we can wholly rely on. He could change his mind at any moment. Not to mention, we're still awaiting his next task."

"We may as well give him the chance to give it to us when

we're together," Samantha said.

"It's notorious for criminal activity, is the Derby," Lord Aston said. "Heaps of pickpockets about."

"Then I will leave my reticule with Madge," Samantha said.

Wyatt still looked unconvinced, but he said, reluctantly, "As you wish."

She told Madge her plans, handing over her reticule, and they took their leave of the Bradwells, exiting the balcony via the stairs to the ground level. To preserve the appearance of their courtship, Lord Aston took Samantha's hand, and Wyatt trailed behind them as they made their way across the track to the central field.

It was chaotic. Carriages were parked along the edges of the field. Their occupants were crammed into the seats or, in the case of the closed carriages, piled on the roof, all the better to see the horses when they came thundering by. Families sat about the lawn with picnic baskets open before them, indulging in cold sandwiches and fresh fruit. Groups of men huddled together around tiny, spindly-legged tables, placing bets on the outcome of three-card tricks and thimble-rigging.

Samantha and her companions were drawn along with the crowd, people pressing in on all sides, until they reached the wide thoroughfare where the private tents had been set up. There, the crowd thinned, and Samantha loosened her hold on Lord Aston's arm as she looked around eagerly.

"Where do you want to go?" Wyatt asked, taking her other arm.

"Let's see the acrobats," she said, nodding in the direction of a father-and-son tumbling pair.

For the next ten minutes, they wandered the field, watching the performances of various street acrobats, jugglers, and magicians. Lord Aston wanted to stop to watch a man in a mustard-colored jacket doing something on one of the tiny, spindly-legged tables, but Wyatt dragged them away. He bought Samantha a flower from a gypsy girl and presented it to her with an exaggerated flourish that had her giggling.

It was as they walked past the Reform Club's private tent that Samantha noticed something that stopped her short. Or, it would have, if not for the two men on either side of her who continued on, pulling her with them.

"What is it?" Wyatt asked, when she tugged on his arm.

"Isn't that Mr. Ponsonby?" she said, jerking her head behind them to where a lanky man with grey hair seemed to be arguing with another, rougher-looking man.

Wyatt looked over his shoulder with a frown. "Yes, I think it is."

As they watched, both men disappeared between the tents.

"Mr. Ponsonby?" Lord Aston said. "Is that the one with the blueprints?"

"Yes," said Wyatt.

"Did you see whom he was talking to?" Samantha asked. "I could be wrong, but it looked like one of Skinny Jim's men—one of the ones who used to follow me."

"I can't tell," Wyatt said, craning his neck. "Wait here. I'll be right back."

He released Samantha's arm. Samantha watched him double back and look down the aisle between two tents. He returned seconds later.

"I think you're right," he said. "I'm going to follow them. This could be important. You go on with Bingo. I'll meet you both back in the grandstands. Be careful."

"You, too," Samantha said.

"Good luck," said Lord Aston.

She would have liked to go with Wyatt, but she knew that two people were more likely to be noticed than one. Besides, Wyatt knew what he was doing, and she trusted he would tell her what he had overheard when he returned. That thought gave her pause, and she took a moment to reconsider. Did she trust him to tell her? Six months ago, she wouldn't have, but slowly, as he had promised he would, he had rebuilt her trust in him. He hadn't hidden the truth from her even when he could have easily, as when Skinny Jim had ordered him to give a message to Sir Anthony. He had also not objected to her accompanying him to Blackfriars, going so far as to allow her to be the one to speak with Skinny Jim.

She trusted him, and that was more than she had expected after so short a time. But did she trust him enough to marry him? Of that, she was less sure.

Samantha and Lord Aston came upon a cluster of people surrounding a pair of acrobats. The smaller of the two was balancing upside down on the hands of his partner. As they watched, he settled his head gently on his partner's and slowly removed his hands until he was supported solely by his head. Applause broke out. Samantha and Lord Aston joined in.

Then, a shout pierced through the applause. Necks craned, trying to determine the source. A large man in a grey jacket and hat stood on the other side of the crowd. He seemed to be struggling with something. A woman in front of her moved, and Samantha was able to see the small, ragged boy who stood at the man's feet, squirming and wriggling, trying to pull his hand from the man's strong grip.

"He tried to take me watch!" the man said.

There was a rustling as the other spectators patted their pockets and reached into their bags.

"My wallet's gone!" shouted one man.

"I've lost my handkerchief!" shouted another.

Chaos erupted as, all around Samantha, the crowd surged forward, intent on demanding their possessions back from the captive boy. Samantha was bumped and jolted from behind and beside. Then came a shriek as the boy apparently broke free and half a dozen people tried to grab him, tripping over one another in the process.

At some point, Samantha's arm was wrenched from Lord Aston's. Then, she was knocked to the ground as someone shoved past her. Her fingers were nearly crushed by a boot, and she scooted back quickly to avoid being trampled. As she scrambled to her feet, she looked for Lord Aston, but in the sea of top hats and bonnets, she couldn't distinguish anyone.

Samantha stood near the tents for several minutes, anxiously twisting the fabric of her skirt as she searched, hoping he might appear. She felt more vulnerable than she had in a long time, standing in the midst of strangers. Skinny Jim wasn't the only man of ill intent in London and, though she had no doubt that most of the people milling around her were simply out for a day of entertainment, she could not help reading suspicion and malice into the glances cast her way.

When Lord Aston did not appear and her nerves had begun to fray, Samantha decided her best course would be to return to the grandstands. It was where Wyatt expected her to go and where Lord Aston would eventually return, as long as nothing terrible had befallen him. Having a plan helped calm Samantha's anxious thoughts. Shaking the dust from her skirts, she set off down the thoroughfare, keeping the tall, metal structure in sight. She passed groups of revelers as she went. A party had set up a picnic on the grass. She recognized a few of the gentlemen and hurried past. Then, as she reached the end of a row of tents, she saw Mr. Ramsey.

He didn't see her at first, and she hoped she might pass unnoticed, but he looked up, and she saw the light of recognition in his eyes. He tipped his hat, and she nodded stiffly. Then he seemed to notice her lack of escort, and his smile grew.

"Why Miss Kingston, what a surprise to see you here," he said, coming to stand before her and blocking her way forward. "I would have expected you to be up on the balcony."

"I was," she said. She tried to smile back. After all, he didn't know that she knew about the bet he'd made to steal a kiss from her. It might be best to pretend ignorance. However, she could feel that her smile was strained. "I'm on my way back, as it happens."

"Is Lord Aston not with you?" Mr. Ramsey asked. "Or Mr. Wyatt? Lord Bradwell?"

He could see that they weren't. His disingenuous questions irked her, and irritation momentarily eclipsed her anxiety over Lord Aston's whereabouts and her own situation.

"Lord Aston is with me, yes," she said. "He was momentarily delayed, but I expect he'll be here soon."

"Allow me to wait with you, then. A beautiful lady such as yourself shouldn't go about unescorted."

"How kind," Samantha managed to choke out, though she knew he was anything but. "It is unnecessary, however. I wouldn't wish to keep you from your amusements."

"No chance of that," he said, and held out an arm.

The implication in his tone that she was one of his amusements made her stomach churn.

"Oh! There he is." Samantha pretended to see Lord Aston over Mr. Ramsey's shoulder. She waved. "I'll go join him. Thank you, Mr. Ramsey."

With a quick dip of her head, she hurried away. When she reached the striped tents, she circled behind them and ducked into the back of the last one. She hoped if she waited a few minutes, Mr. Ramsey would have moved on, and she could continue in peace.

The tent was empty of people, though it contained a few wooden benches and a box filled with what looked like temperance pamphlets. Samantha sank onto one of the wooden benches. A moment later, the sound of the fabric shifting behind her made her turn, and her heart leapt to her throat as she saw Mr. Ramsey parting the tent flap, a wolfish grin on his face.

"Why, Miss Kingston, where is Lord Aston?"

*****

Wyatt followed Ponsonby and Skinny Jim's man for several yards, unable to hear what they were saying until they came to a stop beside a pile of crates stacked behind one of the tents. Wyatt ducked behind a large barrel and strained his ears.

"...can't bend over every time he tells me to," Ponsonby was saying. "How does he expect me to make money for him when he keeps taking what I have? I can only do so much with these dwindling resources."

"That's not his problem," the other man growled.

"It's going to be. He can pressure me all he likes, but it doesn't change facts. I can't make something from nothing."

"I'd suggest you try harder. Otherwise, he'll be forced to call in the full debt."

When Skinny Jim's man stomped away, Ponsonby swore loudly and brought his fist down on the pile of crates. Then he went back the way he'd come. Wyatt circled around behind the barrel before standing straight. He watched Ponsonby stride away into the crowd.

It sounded as though Ponsonby was another of those fools, like Sir Anthony and Charles Prescott, who struck a deal with Skinny Jim in exchange for a loan without fully considering the consequences. If that were so, he wasn't stealing blueprints out of greed only, but also out of desperation. Wyatt realized then that Mr. Leclerc's hope of being compensated for his invention was a forlorn one. Ponsonby didn't have the money to spare.

Another thought, no less pleasant than the first, struck Wyatt. It wasn't only legal prosecution Ponsonby faced if his theft became known, but also loss of income and retribution from Skinny Jim.

Wyatt still had no idea how Spenser had ended up with one of the blueprints, but if he had known it was stolen and had confronted Ponsonby about it, possibly threatening exposure, Ponsonby had a strong motive to kill him.

The race would be starting soon. Wyatt knew he needed to hurry if he was going to be able to watch it from the grandstands with the others. He lengthened his stride, dodging around half-drunken revelers and street performers. Then he saw something that made his blood run cold. Bingo was hurrying towards him, looking harassed, and there was no Samantha at his side.

"Where is she?" Wyatt asked as soon as Bingo was within earshot.

"I don't know." Bingo removed his hat and wiped sweat from his forehead. "We were watching a performance and a pickpocket set everyone into a panic and I lost her."

"How could you lose her?" Wyatt asked, fear transforming into anger. "She was right beside you!"

"We were pulled apart by the crowd. I turned to look where she'd gone, and I couldn't see her anywhere. It took me some time to extricate myself, but I've been up and down this whole area twice, and I can't find hide nor hair of her."

He looked so upset that Wyatt swallowed his anger. "Where did you see her last?"

Bingo showed him where they had been separated. The entertainers were gone, and the crowd was sparse. Wyatt ran a hand through his hair as he spun around, his eyes searching everywhere.

"When she lost you," he said finally, "she'd have gone somewhere she knew we'd think to find her. I think she would have gone back to the grandstands. Have you looked there?"

"No. I only lost her ten minutes ago." Bingo squinted over at the grandstands. "Do you really think she's there?"

"If she is, she's safe, but I don't want to risk it if she isn't. You go to the grandstands—"

"No," Bingo said. "Like you said, if she's there, she's safe. If she isn't, I'll be more help here. It's not as though I can let you know to stop looking if I do find her over there. The race is about to start. The track will be closed off."

"Very well. Let's head in that direction, though. Keep a look out."

Wyatt's heart thumped hard in his chest as he half walked, half ran, his head swiveling in every direction, hoping for a glimpse of the lilac dress Samantha had been wearing. The logical part of his mind considered that he might be overreacting. After all, they were following Skinny Jim's plan, and the chances of him deviating from it were low as long as it continued to benefit him. Still, Samantha had a tendency to attract trouble. He could vividly recall the way he'd felt watching Charles Prescott hold a gun to her head, or the fear he'd experienced when she pulled up in a carriage bleeding from the head after being abducted right off the street. Then, there was the time she'd been knocked cold while investigating the abbey on the Bradwell estate. And the time she got a black eye from a street fight. Even the logical part of his mind had to concede that he had reason to worry.

In a matter of minutes, Wyatt and Bingo had gone the length of the inner oval of the track. Wyatt stopped and looked around. Beside him, Bingo did the same. They were surrounded by people, but there wasn't a lilac dress in sight.

"Isn't that Hawkins?" Bingo asked. "What's he doing there?"

Wyatt followed his pointing finger to the front of the Temperance Society's tent. Its flaps were closed, but a man stood at the front. It looked as though he were peering through a small gap in the fabric, his knees slightly bent.

With a sense of foreboding, driven by the knowledge that Hawkins was the man with whom Ramsey had made the bet about Samantha, Wyatt approached him, Bingo close on his heels.

The man turned as he heard them come near. It was Mr. Hawkins. His beady eyes were unmistakable. He paled as he recognized them and, without a word to either, he dropped the tent flap and ran.

"I've got him," Bingo said, giving chase.

When Wyatt ducked into the tent, he saw Samantha, backed into one of the wooden tent poles with Ramsey looming over her. She looked small and vulnerable, dwarfed by Ramsey's broad, muscular frame. The look on her face, however, was determined, and as Wyatt dropped the tent flap, she balled her hand into a fist and punched Ramsey hard in the nose. He let out a grunt as his head snapped back, but his recovery was swift. He seized Samantha's wrist and twisted it behind her back, pinning her against the pole. Wyatt ran forward and grabbed him by the shoulder, yanking him back before slamming his fist into the man's jaw.

"Wyatt!" Samantha gasped. Shock seemed to dissolve into relief as she stared at him, open-mouthed.

Ramsey released Samantha and staggered back.

"What the—" he began, but Wyatt swung his fist again, this time connecting with the man's temple. Ramsey collapsed in a heap.

With no more thought for her attacker, Wyatt turned his full attention to Samantha. She stood against the tent pole, her face pale, her hair in disarray. The relief of a moment ago had dissipated and she looked...lost. Moved by instinct rather than conscious thought, Wyatt stepped forward and wrapped his arms around her. She melted into him, burying her face in his chest. Her arms came around him, and he rested his head atop hers.

In that moment, everything felt right, and he lost all sense of time, content just to feel her in his arms. How long they stood like that, Wyatt didn't know. At one point, he heard an increase in the noise outside, and he suspected the race might have started, but he put it out of his mind. He kept expecting Samantha to end the embrace and step away, but she didn't. She stayed where she was and, though Wyatt tried to focus on his reasons for holding her and the comfort he hoped he was giving her, he was more aware of her body against his with every passing moment.

Eventually, she shifted and tilted her head up to meet his eyes. He couldn't read her expression, so he was shocked when she reached up and brushed her lips against his. For a moment, he stood frozen, then he slid his hand behind her head and drew her closer as he returned the kiss.

It was achingly slow and sweet, like something out of a dream. Wyatt was afraid it might actually be a dream, and he was determined to savor every moment. He deepened the kiss, tangling his hand in her hair as her arms tightened around him.

Eventually, though far sooner than Wyatt would have liked, Samantha pulled back. She tilted her head up to look at him, her lips swollen and her expression gratifyingly dazed. She raised a hand to his cheek, and he leaned into her touch.

"Thank you," she said in a voice so soft it was almost a whisper. Then, a little stronger, she added, "I don't know how you found me, but I'm glad you did. I don't know what would have happened if you hadn't—"

"Don't think about it," he cut in. He could see the distress in her eyes, and he hated it. "I found you, and that's all that matters."

"Yes, it is, isn't it?"

She looked somehow more distressed at these words and her eyes searched his with what seemed to be rising consternation.

"Wyatt, I...I think...I don't know..."

"What is it?" Wyatt asked, brushing his knuckles over her cheek. "What's wrong, dearest?"

The endearment had slipped out, and he immediately wished he could recall it when he saw her reaction. Her face crumpled, and she tugged out of his hold, pressing a hand to her mouth as she choked back a sob.

"I'm sorry," he said. "I didn't mean to say..."

She shook her head vehemently and held out a hand to forestall him.

"No, no," she said. "Don't apologize. I just...you *were* there for me. You always are and I...I don't know. I want to...but I don't know..." Hope warred with caution as Wyatt watched her take a shuddering breath, then bring her eyes to his. "I'm scared, Wyatt. I've been alone for most of my life. I've had to rely on myself. I don't...I can't..."

Wyatt's chest was tight. He wanted to ease her fears, but he knew he had to tread carefully. It felt as though the future he hoped for them hung by the thinnest of threads as he considered his words.

"I know," he said. Gently, he brushed a hand over her face and cupped her chin. "Your strength and your courage are part of why I love you. You've persevered through extraordinary circumstances, and I have no doubt that you will continue to do so, with or without me. You don't need my help, but I'm offering it just the same. Let me help you shoulder the burden. Let me walk beside you."

Her tears flowed freely now. Wyatt brushed them away with the pad of his thumb.

"Don't answer now," he said. "I don't want you to speak in haste. The last thing I want is for you to feel beholden to me or to manufacture feelings to ease your conscience on my behalf. If you do not think...if you cannot love me, I will survive. I won't pretend it won't be difficult, but I don't want you to concern yourself with me. I only tell you this to assure you that I am and always will be your servant."

He brought her hand to his lips and pressed a kiss to it. She had accused him of having an enigmatic expression but, watching her now, he had no idea what she was thinking. Did she believe him? Did she trust him? He had offered her his heart and, while he meant it when he told her not to answer him yet, he wished she would give him some indication of where her feelings might be leading her.

As he lowered his hand, the cheering outside rose in volume.

"What was that?" he asked.

"I think the race may have ended," she said faintly.

"In which case, Madge and Bradwell will be concerned about your absence. I should return you to them." He held out his arm and she took his elbow in her gloved hand, her movements automatic.

They didn't speak as they moved through the surging crowd towards the grandstands. In truth, they had little opportunity, as they were pushed first one way and then another. Bingo met them on their way to the balcony and explained that he had ensured Hawkins would keep his mouth shut about what he had seen. Wyatt thanked him, and Bingo insisted no thanks were needed—it had been a pleasure.

Once they had reached the Bradwells, Wyatt apologized for their absence, taking the blame, and made his exit before anything further could be said. It was a retreat, and he knew it, but his emotions were too near the surface for him to speak any further with Samantha. Nor did he wish her to respond in haste. It was better for them both that he give her time to think.

FOURTEEN

At Lady Chesterton's ball the next evening, Samantha felt like one of the automata she had seen at the Great Exhibition. Wound up and released, she moved automatically from conversation to conversation and dance to dance, responding when it was required but giving no thought to what she did and hardly any to what she said. Her mind was in turmoil, as it had been from the moment Wyatt pulled Mr. Ramsey from her and knocked him to the ground.

Of the moments that had preceded her rescue, she preferred not to think at all. If her thoughts did drift back that far, she yanked them forward before she could feel anything more than a sick twisting in her stomach. However, dwelling on Wyatt's actions did not afford her much more peace. His arrival had been so unexpected, yet the relief that flooded her on seeing him had not been prompted only by gratitude.

She had been alone in her defense, a state to which she had become accustomed over the years. Then he had appeared, and it was as though a piece of her she had not known to be broken was suddenly whole, as though she had been waiting for him and only him to arrive. It was at once incomprehensible and fitting, wonderful and terrifying.

When he had embraced her, the fear induced by Mr. Ramsey's attack had vanished, and when she looked into his eyes, she wanted nothing more than to kiss him—to let her feelings flow through her in a way she could not express in words. Then he had said those words, "I found you, and that's all that matters." She knew he meant them to comfort her, to take her mind off Mr. Ramsey, but instead they had sent her into a panic because, in that moment, she realized they were true. She didn't care about anything else, only that he had found her, and that she was with him. Her heart was no longer just within her—he held a part of it. The armor she had spent years building around it was gone, and if he crushed it, even unintentionally, she would be devastated.

He expected an answer from her. For the second time, he had offered himself to her, and this time, she knew him to be sincere. Still, she hesitated. Though she deplored her own cowardice, she was not certain she could overcome it.

So, having no more idea of what to say to Wyatt than she'd had the day before, she avoided him. It was not hard; he didn't seek her out. When she caught him watching her, he looked away, sending cracks through her fragile heart.

The ball was a terrific crush. There were so many people in attendance that several hours had passed before Samantha discovered Eden was there.

"It's so good to see you," Eden said, giving Samantha a quick kiss on the cheek. "It seems an age since we last talked."

"It does," Samantha agreed, pulling herself from her stupor and forcing herself to focus on her friend. "I didn't know you would be here tonight."

"I almost didn't come. I was so tired after taking little William to the Exhibition again this afternoon. We've been three times now."

"Have you? You should tell me if you go again. I would love to go with you two."

"If he had his way, we would go every afternoon," Eden laughed. "I, however, will need a respite. I will let you know when I have the stamina to go again." She sobered. "Are you well? You look pale."

Samantha could well imagine that she did after a night spent tossing and turning, fighting off memories of Mr. Ramsey's crushing grip and, when those abated, Wyatt's gentle touch.

"I didn't sleep well last night," she said.

"I'm sorry. Are you ill?"

"No. I had a lot on my mind."

"Ah. Is it still unresolved—whatever kept you awake?"

Samantha nodded and was about to explain further when she spotted a short, greying man making his way towards them.

"Oh, no," she said. "It is Mr. Panzer. Quick, perhaps if we...oh, never mind. He's seen me looking."

A moment later, Mr. Panzer was beside them.

"Lady Stuart-Lane, Miss Kingston," he said pompously. "You are looking well this evening. I came this way hoping I might be so fortunate as to catch you before your dance card had filled up, Miss Kingston."

He gazed at her expectantly.

"I'm afraid," she said with a frown of false disappointment, "that I do not mean to dance anymore this evening, though I thank you for your kind offer."

Mr. Panzer deflated slightly but rallied enough to wish her well before departing.

"If I could find whoever it was that said ladies have the power of refusal, I'd hit him," Samantha said, frowning after him. "What power is it when to refuse to dance with any man means we must sit out the rest of the evening? Why must we be denied the pleasure of dancing with the men we like simply to avoid slighting the men we most certainly do not?"

"That is one reason why I haven't been to London for the

Season since my Edmund passed," Eden said. "Not that I receive as many offers as you do, but I think we all face the same dilemma. When Edmund was alive, he was my shield. I told him whom I did not want to dance with, and he was so good at giving just the right sort of look to scare them off whenever they tried to solicit my hand."

"I'm sorry he's gone," Samantha said. She had often wondered about Eden's late husband but had been afraid to broach the subject. She knew Eden missed him, and she hated to intrude on her grief.

"He was the best partner," Eden said wistfully. "I have often found myself unconsciously turning to him since coming back to London, particularly when I see something that would have amused him. I had almost become used to his absence at home. Here, it is as though it is fresh once more."

"I think I understand what you mean," Samantha said. "I have not been back to my grandfather's estate since his passing, but I imagine if I did, I would expect to see him at every corner, or sitting in his favorite chair."

Eden nodded sadly. "That is the trouble, I think. I haven't seen London without Edmund."

"How did you meet?"

"At a ball." Eden smiled at the memory. "It was nothing very unusual. We danced. I thought him handsome and charming. He came to call on me the next day, and we went for a drive. He told me about his home by the sea. It sounded so romantic. He laughed a lot. I loved his laugh. I wish...I wish I could remember it, but it is hard to remember sounds, isn't it?"

She was silent for a moment. Samantha waited for her to continue, not wishing to interrupt her remembrances.

"When we married, Edmund brought me to his family home in Cornwall. I fell in love with the sea and even more so with him. I have never believed in soulmates—I think we can build meaningful connections with many people—but in Edmund I found my other half. The Bible says, 'The two shall become one,' and I believe that we did. I miss him dearly."

"I am sorry," Samantha said again. "I truly am."

"Thank you." Eden drew a shaky breath. "It is hard knowing that William will never know his father, and that his memories of him will be few. Edmund was an excellent father. I often worry whether I am sufficient in his place. I am now mother and father. I see to his education; I manage the estate that will one day be his."

Samantha reached out and squeezed Eden's hand. "You are an excellent mother and, one day, William will be thankful for all you have done."

Eden gave her a watery smile. "I hope so." She sniffed and looked up, blinking rapidly. Then she laughed. "I should never have mentioned Edmund. I can never do so without weeping, and this is certainly not the place for that."

"May I ask," Samantha began hesitantly, "how did you know...how were you able to trust Edmund?"

Eden gave her a knowing look. Samantha hadn't told her about Wyatt's proposal until after Eden returned to Cornwall that winter. Writing it in a letter had been less daunting than telling her in person, especially while she was still sorting through her own thoughts on the matter. Eden had been understanding, neither condemning her for refusing him nor pressuring her to change her mind. They hadn't ever spoken of it, but Samantha was certain that Eden had watched her interactions with Wyatt since their return to London and understood far more than she let on.

"It is a frightening prospect, is it not?" Eden asked. "To put one's faith in another person? To bind one's hopes to someone who has the power to crush them?"

Samantha nodded, comforted by Eden's words which so perfectly matched her own thoughts.

"It is faith, in the end," Eden said. "I had faith in Edmund as he did in me."

Samantha must have looked skeptical, because Eden continued.

"I do not speak of blind faith. Faith isn't baseless. It requires evidence. I knew the type of man Edmund was. He showed me every day by his actions." She looked out on the dancers. "We can never know the future, but there is much we can predict. We can be fairly certain that Lady Penelope will say something outrageous tonight that will set all the chaperones talking because that is her habit. We can also suppose that Miss Milton will be as miserable a wife as she is a debutante because she chooses to view life through a clouded lens. And we can foresee ruin in Mr. Tavistock's future because he is an unrepentant gambler." She turned to Samantha and regarded her intently. "There is much we can predict about the future if we know a person's character. What we can't predict is how long we will have with them. I thought I had a lifetime to spend by Edmund's side."

Unable to think of a response, Samantha could only nod. Eden seemed to understand. She remained where she was, her eyes on the dancers as she gave Samantha the opportunity to think about what she had said.

Samantha had been trying so hard to control her life, her future. Yet, what Eden said was true. She couldn't affect every outcome. Even should she choose not to marry, she couldn't guarantee her future happiness. She might lose her friends, her fortune, her health. Nature and mortality were not predictable and, yet, people could be. She had feared, for a time, that she had lost her intuition, but Wyatt had helped her to see she hadn't.

She didn't even need intuition with Wyatt. She knew him. Over the past nine months, and especially the past four, she had come to know the bad and the good of him. He could be stubborn and proud, but he could be humble, too, willing to change his mind if well persuaded. And, while his tendency to direct those around him was frustrating, he had shown he was not intractable. He was loyal, generous, and clever. He challenged her at every turn, and she enjoyed sparring with him. She found that she valued his opinion over anyone else's. His habit of running his hands through his hair when he was agitated was endearing, and she loved the half smile he gave her when he teased her. She loved his laugh, too. In fact, she loved...him. And suddenly, the thought of losing him, of not spending every day by his side, was more frightening to her than the knowledge that he held her heart in his hands.

"I have to talk to Wyatt," Samantha said, buzzing from her sudden revelation.

Eden beamed. "I hoped you might."

She took Samantha's hands in hers and squeezed them.

"You know," she said, the corner of her lips turning up in an arch smile. "I think I am ready to return home. Would you like to accompany me? If you will let Madge know you are leaving with me, I'll see if Mr. Wyatt can escort us."

Samantha found Madge on the far side of the dance floor in conversation with Lady Chesterton.

"The flowers are exquisite." Madge seemed to be assuring her sister-in-law, who was shifting from side to side, looking anxiously about the room. "The music is excellent and the whole event is an absolute crush, so there is no reason to harangue me with your apprehensions. I can barely move without tripping over someone or other, which I abhor but should make you incandescent with joy. Ah!" Her eyes sparkled as they lit on Samantha. "Ask Miss Kingston, and I am sure she will tell you the same."

"It is a beautiful ball," Samantha said automatically.

Lady Chesterton appeared somewhat mollified, whether from Madge's words alone or their combination with Samantha's, and she excused herself to check on the food.

"What has happened?" Madge asked, looking Samantha up and down. "You look happy, or near to it. Considering the cloud that has hung about you since yesterday, this is a consummation devoutly to be wished."

A twinge of guilt temporarily distracted Samantha from her purpose. Madge had asked her what was wrong the moment they returned home the day before, but she had rebuffed her, not ready to speak of it.

"I've come to tell you I'm leaving," she said.

"Without me, I suppose."

"Yes," Samantha said with a wince. "I will be taking Eden's carriage. I can't explain now, but I will tomorrow."

"I look forward to it," Madge said blandly. Then, as though to soften her words, she smiled. "I trust you to know your own mind, my dear. You are not beholden to me, and no explanation is owed. Besides, I cannot leave now, however much I may wish it, without seriously offending Constance, which, in spite of everything, I am loath to do."

"Thank you for understanding," Samantha said. "Owed or not, I will give you an explanation."

She squeezed Madge's hand and hurried off to collect her shawl. A moment later, she was outside. Wyatt was there, standing beside Eden in front of Eden's carriage. Samantha's heart flipped at the sight of him, but she forced herself to remain calm as she walked down the front steps to join him.

"Are you alright?" Wyatt asked. "Lady Stuart-Lane said you needed to go home. Are you ill?"

"I'm not ill," she said, though her voice was unsteady.

"She will be cold, however, if you stand out here much longer," Eden said, ushering Samantha and Wyatt towards the carriage.

After helping Samantha inside, Wyatt held out a hand for Eden, but she shook her head.

"I've decided I'd rather walk," she said, taking a step back.

For a moment, Samantha was confused, then Eden gave her a

reassuring smile and she realized this had been her friend's plan all along.

Wyatt's brow furrowed. "You want to walk? Why?"

"I don't live far," Eden said. "And it's such a lovely night."

Samantha bit back a smile.

"You just said Samantha would be cold standing outside for more than a minute," Wyatt said.

"I'll take Matthew." Eden ignored him as she waved her footman over. "You two take my carriage. I will see you tomorrow, Samantha."

"Goodbye, Eden," Samantha said.

"My lady, wouldn't you—" Wyatt began, but Eden cut him off.

"Do not concern yourself with me, Mr. Wyatt. I will be well enough. Come along, Matthew."

She waved to Samantha and walked briskly away, her footman hurrying to catch up.

"What was that?" Wyatt asked, staring after her.

"She's just trying to help," Samantha said. Her amusement at Eden's antics faded, replaced by a heightened nervousness now that the moment had arrived. "Are you coming?"

He climbed into the carriage and shut the door.

"Help with what?" he asked. He tapped the ceiling, signaling for the driver to be off.

"I told her I needed to talk to you," Samantha said, twisting the fringe of her shawl. "So, she found a way to make that happen."

"Talk about what?" Wyatt asked, his expression guarded.

She took a deep breath and let it out slowly, settling her hands in her lap. It wasn't that she was worried about his response, but she wanted to say the right words, especially after he had been so patient with her.

"I've come to a realization, and I wanted to tell you. I needed to tell you. Not only because it concerns you, but because you are the first person I want to tell when I have good news. Or bad news. Especially bad news. Because you listen and you care and, in your arms, I feel safe."

The pure, unadulterated hope in his eyes brought tears to her own.

"I want you to walk beside me," she said.

Wyatt crossed to her side of the carriage and took her face in his hands.

"You're certain?" he asked.

She nodded, smiling through the tears.

"Completely," she said. "I love you. I love you, Wyatt."

A smile lit his eyes with a joy that echoed her own. Then he kissed her. When their lips met, the sparks she felt every time they touched ignited as they had before. Wyatt's mouth moved over hers with a hunger that fed her own. One kiss became two, then three, then countless more. His hands pressed her to him, caressed her face and tangled in her hair. She was completely lost to anything but the feeling of him. If only they had no need for air, she would have gone on kissing him forever, at home in his arms.

He pulled away first, breathing heavily. She looked up at him through half closed eyes and tried to bring his face back to hers, but he shook his head.

"Wait," he said. "I think the carriage has stopped."

Sure enough, when Samantha shook herself from her daze, she realized they were no longer rattling over cobblestones, but quite stationary. She glanced out the window and saw the front door to Madge's house opening and Headley stepping out onto the stoop, clearly confused that no one was exiting the carriage.

"Oh," she said. She looked up at Wyatt and saw the corner of his mouth curve up in a half-smile.

"Much as I hate to stop now," he said. "I don't think that

shocking Headley is the best idea."

"True," Samantha said regretfully. She slid her arms down from around Wyatt's neck. He caught one of her hands and brought it to his lips.

"Though, perhaps not the worst idea."

He began to kiss her fingers slowly, one at a time. She almost allowed herself to give into the sensation, but the sight of the butler coming down the path sent her into a panic. Wyatt may not care, but she did not relish the embarrassment of being caught in a compromising position by Madge's stoic retainer.

"He's coming to the door," she said, snatching her hand away.

Wyatt laughed softly, but moved back. A moment later, the door opened, and Headley gazed at them in surprise.

"Miss Kingston," he said. "Mr. Wyatt. Where is her ladyship? And why are you in Lady Stuart-Lane's carriage? Without Lady Stuart-Lane?"

The humor of their situation hit Samantha, and she burst into a fit of uncontrollable giggles.

"I was asked to escort Miss Kingston home, Headley." Wyatt climbed out of the carriage and turned to hold out a hand for Samantha. "Lady Bradwell will return later."

"I see," Headley said. "Will Lady Stuart-Lane's carriage be taking you home, or shall I call for one of her ladyship's?"

"I don't wish to be a bother," Wyatt said. "I know the coachman is with Madge. I'll take Lady Stuart-Lane's carriage."

"Good night, then, sir," Headley said, standing stubbornly beside Samantha like a protective guard dog.

"Good night," Wyatt said. Then, to Samantha, "I'll be back in the morning. At the first opportunity."

She nodded, but as he started to walk away, she called out, "Wait!"

He stopped and turned back, watching her expectantly, but she had nothing to say. She just hadn't wanted him to leave, not yet. He grinned in a way that made her think he understood.

"I love you," she said.

The grin softened to a smile, and he said, "Say it again."

"I love you, Wyatt," she said. "So much."

Then, heedless of Headley's presence, he pulled her to him and kissed her hard on the mouth. It was briefer than she would have liked. She didn't think she would ever have enough of him. When he broke away, they were both smiling.

"I'd ask you now," he said, "but I want to do it properly this time."

Her heart sped up and her smile broadened. "I think I can wait."

"I'll see you tomorrow, then. You too, Headley," he added, with a wink at the butler.

Samantha turned to see Headley struggling to maintain his stoic demeanor as a hint of a smile threatened the corners of his mouth.

"Good evening, Mr. Wyatt," he said.

"I think I'll go to bed," Samantha said as the carriage pulled away. She hoped it was dark enough that the butler couldn't see the blush creeping up her cheeks. "When Lady Bradwell returns, please tell her I will see her in the morning."

FIFTEEN

When Wyatt woke the next morning, he could not at first recall why he felt so happy. Then, he remembered the carriage ride with Samantha and her final words to him, and he grinned.

"You are in a good mood this morning, *monsieur*," Durand said when he entered a few minutes later.

Wyatt flicked shaving soap from his razor into the washbasin. "I am. Remember that ring I asked you to put somewhere safe? Do you think you could bring it out for me?"

Glancing into the mirror as he slid the razor down his cheek, Wyatt saw Durand grin. "Yes, sir. And might I offer my congratulations?"

"Readily. Thank you, Durand. I'll be leaving directly after I've breakfasted, so bring the ring to me downstairs."

"Very good, sir."

Wyatt had just sat down for breakfast when Mrs. Hexam bustled into the room.

"That man of yours," she said huffily, setting the post down by his plate. "Got airs, he has."

Wyatt chuckled as he lifted a slice of toast from the rack.

"What has he done that's upset you so?"

"Dropping hints that something big's gonna happen and getting Jenny all in a tizzy trying to winkle it out of him. I told him to stop it, and he winked at me. Winked, I tell you."

"Ah." Wyatt hadn't considered that Durand would be so indiscreet. Though, he supposed the engagement wouldn't be a secret much longer, and no doubt Durand relished the opportunity to remind the others of his unique position in the household. Wyatt supposed this was what he got for employing such an unconventional valet

"I wouldn't presume to tell you what to do with your manservant," Mrs. Hexam continued, "but I know this is his first position as a valet, and it seems to me that he might benefit from some reinforcement of the rules. I told him, whatever may have been the practice in his last place, we do not gossip about the family in this house."

"And I appreciate your discretion, Mrs. H." Then, because he was not above taking a cue from his valet, he decided to tease her, adding, with banality, "No doubt my wife will as well."

"Your wife?" Mrs. Hexam looked momentarily bewildered, then she gasped. "Your wife! You are to be married?" She clapped her hands together in delight and then, before he could stop her, grabbed his face and kissed him on both cheeks. "Oh, I'm all of a tizzy. Married. I never thought I'd see the day. My little boy, all grown up." She reached into her apron for a handkerchief and dabbed at her eyes.

Though somewhat taken aback by her sudden show of affection—she hadn't kissed him since he was a boy—Wyatt was not displeased. When she lowered her handkerchief, he half stood from his chair and leaned over to bestow a fond kiss on her cheek. She clucked her tongue and swatted him away, but he could see she was pleased.

"It will mean some changes around here," he said, resuming his seat. "My wife is likely to be more exacting than I am about standards."

"Thank heavens for that. At least someone will appreciate all the work I do." She sniffed and shoved the handkerchief back into her pocket. "And I'm not worried. Miss Kingston seems like a fair mistress. It is Miss Kingston, is it not?"

Wyatt laughed. "I can't hide anything from you, can I?"

"I would have to be blind to miss what was right in front of me. The way you two look at each other, I'd've expected an announcement long before now."

"You may tell Jenny and relieve her of her curiosity," Wyatt said. "Mrs. Plummet, too, of course."

Mrs. Hexam nodded and left the room muttering to herself. "A real lady at last. We'll be needing kitchen help if we're to start hosting, and we should be able to finally get rid of those awful curtains in the parlor..."

Chuckling to himself, Wyatt bit into his toast and shifted through the pile of newspapers until he spotted *The London Inquirer*. He often found George's newspaper more entertaining to read than the others, if less factual, and that morning he didn't want to read anything that would dampen his good mood.

He should have known better. One of the first articles on the front page was headed in bold by the words *MP Garrotted in Pall Mall*.

> *Returning from a late-night sitting of the House of Commons, Sir Anthony Guilford, member of Parliament for Blackburn, was walking through Pall Mall when he was set upon by two men. According to eyewitnesses, one of the men grabbed him around the throat from behind while the other stole his pocket watch. The arrival of a patrolling constable scattered the assailants, and Sir Anthony narrowly escaped the fate of the late philanthropist Mr. Theodore Spenser, who readers may remember was killed during a robbery at the end of April.*

The attacks on Sir Anthony and Mr. Spenser, both prominent men of the city, are the latest in the alarming upward trend in violent crime that plagues London. Fears that—

Wyatt stopped reading. He could guess how the article would continue. Concern for the victims would be set aside to make way for fearmongering and politics. He pulled out the *Times* and quickly found a similar article near the top of the page. *The Observer* had it, too.

Rubbing a hand over his face, Wyatt blew out a breath. It was only two weeks since he'd seen Sir Anthony in his home and delivered Skinny Jim's warning. While it was possible that the two events were unrelated and that Sir Anthony was the victim of a random robbery, the coincidence was too strong. If he were a betting man, Wyatt would put very good odds on Skinny Jim's involvement. Sir Anthony must not have paid him. Wyatt guessed he ought to be glad Skinny Jim had not asked him to do the deed, though he supposed the man knew there were limitations to what Wyatt would do, even under blackmail. It was a stark reminder, however, of how important it was for him and Samantha to get out from under the man's brutal thumb.

The chime of the clock reminded Wyatt of his purpose that morning. He shoveled a few last bites of egg into his mouth, took a swig of coffee and stood up. After a moment's hesitation, he picked up *The London Inquirer* and took it to his study, where he dropped it onto his desk to examine more closely later.

Wyatt arrived at Madge's to find the ladies finishing breakfast. Madge sat at the far end of the table, buttering her toast as she read the newspaper. Samantha stood by the buffet, spooning porridge onto her plate. He watched her for a moment, appreciating the way the morning sunlight danced over her hair. She turned, and their eyes met. He could feel himself grinning and was gratified to see her flush with pleasure.

"Good morning," he said.

Madge looked up in surprise. Her gaze landed on him and her brows rose as she took in his besotted grin. When her eyes flicked to Samantha, her expression morphed into a satisfied smirk.

"Thank heavens," she said, throwing her head back and raising her hands to the sky as though filled with immense relief. "At last. Have you settled on a date yet?"

Samantha let out a surprised laugh.

"I believe it's customary to ask the woman to marry you before you choose a date for the wedding," Wyatt said.

"You haven't asked her yet? What are you waiting for?"

"I suppose I'm waiting for you to quit the room."

Samantha's smile widened, and Madge pretended to look shocked. "Of all the cheek. Commanding me in my own home?"

"Acquit me." He splayed his hands. "I didn't command, merely answered your question."

"Hmm. As it happens, I was finished eating."

She rose to her feet, folded up the newspaper and tucked it under her arm. As she passed Samantha, she squeezed her shoulder. When she reached Wyatt, she said, "I am happy for you, my boy. When you are ready, I'll be in the morning room. We have a lot to discuss."

The door closed behind Madge, and Wyatt turned to Samantha, feeling suddenly nervous. He wanted to get it right. They both deserved a better memory than his disastrous first proposal.

"I won't say 'no' this time," Samantha said, setting down her plate, which she'd been holding since he walked in. She laughed nervously as her fingers traced the back of the chair in front of her. "I thought perhaps I should get that out of the way before you begin."

Though he had known as much, he was still glad to hear her

say it.

"You had good reason to say no before," he said. "I didn't think it at the time, but I understand now."

"It does seem silly that we should both be so anxious when we know what you'll say and what I'll say."

"I hope you don't know what I plan to say," he said, the corners of his mouth twitching with amusement. "Otherwise, I wasted a lot of time last night thinking it up when I could have been sleeping."

"You did?" Her eyes lit as she smiled.

"Well," he said languidly, sauntering towards her. "It wasn't the only thing keeping me awake."

She blushed and bit her lip. "I confess, I didn't sleep much last night, either."

He reached out to brush a curl back from her face. "Did you know you have the most beautiful eyes? It was one of the first things I noticed about you."

"Before or after you kissed me?" she asked playfully, fingering the buttons of his waistcoat.

He groaned. "Am I never to live that down?"

"Never." She slid her hands up to his neck. "It's part of our story."

"I like that," he said. "Our story."

"Isn't there a question you're meant to ask me?"

"Right, yes." He cleared his throat and stepped back. Her hands slid down his waistcoat and he caught them in his own. "I did think of some things I wanted to say, but I didn't write them down. Usually, I don't need to—I have quite a good memory—but you have me distracted, and I can't recall them exactly."

"Shall I apologize for distracting you?"

He brought her hands to his lips and kissed them. "Never. I will just say what I can remember, and if it is less than it ought to be, know that there is more in my heart than my head can express."

"That is a very good start."

"You are generous." He cleared his throat again. "The day I met you—I suppose I should say for the second time—was the best day of my life. It didn't feel like it at the time. It certainly didn't feel like it after you dropped me gasping to the ground with that trick of yours and stole my pocketbook." She laughed. He continued more soberly, "But I don't think we know the best days for what they are in the moment. It's only when we look back that we see them. That day changed my life. It was the day I met the most fascinating, beautiful, intelligent, generous, stubborn and determined woman I have ever known, and I knew, within a month, that my life would be the poorer without her in it."

He sighed and looked up at the ceiling to gather his thoughts, before bringing his eyes back to hers. "But I was an idiot. I was so caught up in my own concerns and hesitations about marriage that I didn't even consider yours. I didn't think what marriage would mean for you or consider the drastic turn your life had taken and how it might have affected you. I've tried to show you over the past months that I have learned from my mistakes, but before I ask you for the honor—the absolute honor—of your hand, I want to assure you that I've considered your future as well as my own."

She watched him, eyes shining with unshed tears as he let go of one of her hands and reached into his jacket, drawing out a folded piece of paper. "I spoke with a lawyer about what legal options there might be to allow you to retain control over your fortune. I asked him to write it all down so you could look it over, but it seems that we should be able to set up a trust. Whatever sum you deem appropriate we can put into the trust, and it will be yours no matter what happens. I—"

But the rest of his words were cut off as she threw her arms around him and pressed her lips to his. Wyatt responded instantly, dropping the paper and wrapping his arms around her, drawing her close.

"Thank you," she said, pulling back to look him in the eye. Tears ran down her face, and he tasted salt on his tongue. "Thank you for understanding. Thank you for finding a way. Just...thank you."

"I love you, Samantha," he said. "And if you'll have me, I will spend every day showing you precisely how much. Will you marry me?"

"Yes," she said, and for a moment he forgot to breathe, overcome with joy at hearing the answer he had so long hoped for. Nodding and smiling through the tears, she said it again. "Yes, I will marry you."

He drew her back in for another kiss.

Sometime later, a little breathlessly, she said, "Madge is probably wondering what we're doing."

"Madge knows exactly what we're doing," he said, trailing kisses along her jaw. "It's why she left us alone, remember?"

She laughed. "Yes, but she may get it into her head soon that we've been alone too long, and I'd rather not have her walk in on us."

He sighed and straightened. "I suppose you're right."

"Wait." She held him to her. "Before we go, there is something I want to say to you: That day was the best day of my life, too, and not only because I got a whole sovereign off of you." He laughed. Then she grew serious, sliding her hand up to cup his face. "You are the most honorable man I know—a loyal, generous, and patient friend. It may have taken me longer to understand my love for you, but I promise you I love you now and I will choose to love you every day for the rest of our lives."

Swallowing a lump in his throat, Wyatt grabbed her hand and turned his face to press a kiss to it. With her other hand, she reached up and brushed back his hair.

"I thought you wanted to go see Madge," he said teasingly. "If you keep looking at me like that, we'll be in here all day."

"I think I would like that."

He groaned. "You can't say things like that to me. At least, not until we're married, which will be as soon as possible if you have a care for my sanity."

"This afternoon?"

Wyatt laughed with delight. "That may be sooner than possible, but I am happy we agree."

He kissed her one last time and led her to the door. They had just reached it when he realized he'd forgotten something important.

"Wait." He held her back. He reached into his jacket pocket and pulled out the ring Durand had given him before he left. Light from the window glinted off the facets of the hazel sapphire stone, highlighting the blue and green undertones blended within it.

Samantha's quick intake of breath and the widening of her eyes was all the indication he needed that he'd made the right choice.

"It's beautiful," she said in awed tones, holding out her hand as he slid the silver filigreed band onto her finger.

"I saw it in a shop in Bond Street last month. The gem reminded me of your eyes. I bought it in the hopes that I might need it one day."

She reached up and kissed his cheek. "It's perfect."

When they entered the morning room, Madge rose from her seat by the window where she had been writing and came to greet them.

"May I congratulate you now?" she asked, looking from one to the other.

Samantha nodded and Madge smiled, grasped her hands and leaned forward to kiss her on both cheeks.

"You, too, my boy," Madge said, motioning Wyatt closer. As he stepped forward, he considered ruefully that, between Madge and Mrs. Hexam, he was fast reaching his tolerance of impulsive affection.

When Madge had kissed him, she stepped back and surveyed them with satisfaction. "I always knew you would come together in the end. I will miss having you here, Samantha, dear, but I am pleased that you chose the best of my cousins so that we may always be connected."

"I will miss you, too, Madge," Samantha said, and Wyatt noticed a catch in her voice. "I cannot thank you enough for all you have done for me."

"It was a pleasure," Madge said. "*You* were a pleasure. I came originally as a favor to Wyatt, but I wouldn't have invited you home with me if I hadn't liked you, too. Now, time enough for sentiment and celebration later, we need to discuss what happens next."

"Do you mean the wedding?" Samantha asked.

"That, too," Madge said.

Madge resumed her seat in the chair by the table and gestured for them to sit as well. Samantha settled into the sofa. She looked up at Wyatt expectantly, and he gladly sat beside her.

"Are you talking about Skinny Jim?" he asked Madge.

"Yes," she said. "Your engagement is a fortunate turn of events where he is concerned."

"Do you mean because, once we're married, we can leave London together?" Samantha asked.

"Partly," Madge said. "But also because it will be so much neater a story to tell when we reveal the truth about last summer. Those people who have been certain in their own minds that the two of you did something untoward will be so occupied with self-righteous congratulations that the lies we told will be of secondary consideration. As for the rest, scandal is more easily forgiven when the rules of Society are followed. People feel easier in their minds when the couple caught in a compromising position are forced to marry—it is neater that way."

"I would never have married Wyatt just to appease Society," Samantha said.

Wyatt smiled at her indignant tone.

"I know you wouldn't have," he said. "Nor would I have wanted you to."

"Yes, yes," Madge said. "Very commendable, but immaterial. What matters most now is telling your story in the best way possible. I haven't been running myself ragged these past weeks dragging Samantha all over only to make her better known to the right people. I've also been dropping hints that there was more to the story of this last summer than we felt safe to tell at the time."

"Safe?" Samantha asked.

"Yes. Well, if we'd told everyone what you'd really been up to while you were on the streets, Skinny Jim would have realized who you were and might have sought retribution. After all, it was you who identified the men who worked for him and connected them to the murders of your aunt and uncle. If we make that the focus of our explanation, it should make the lies we told more understandable, if not more forgivable."

Wyatt considered this explanation to be stretching the truth somewhat on Madge's part. Samantha had been concerned about concealing her identity from the beginning, from both Skinny Jim and his associates, but that had not been Wyatt's motivation for bringing Madge in on their deception by pretending to have been chaperoning him and Samantha all summer. At the time, he hadn't known Samantha's true identity or that Skinny Jim had a connection to the murders of her aunt and uncle. By the time he figured it out, he had been more concerned with protecting her from Charles—the actual killer—and making sure that his selfish actions didn't ruin her future. A large part of that involved protecting her reputation—a delicate thing for a woman in their society.

It was true, however, that Skinny Jim was known to punish those who crossed him. He wasn't above killing a man who couldn't pay him the money he was owed, and he had a reputation for ruthlessness. If the Irishman and Skinny Jim's other messenger hadn't indicated that he wanted to speak with Samantha, Wyatt would have thought the attack on Annie as well as the attack they thought had been ordered on Mr. Spenser were punishments rather than messages. Wyatt considered that, if they had told the truth of Samantha's activities last summer, she may well have been in danger from Skinny Jim, as she would be soon.

"I don't know," Samantha said, wrinkling her nose. "It still sounds deceptive. Isn't the point of revealing the truth to stop deceiving people?"

"The point of revealing the truth," Madge said, "is to remove that awful man's ability to blackmail you for his own purposes. That it will also permit us to stop lying is a secondary, though by no means unimportant, benefit. However, you must not conflate honesty with transparency. We none of us lay our lives out bare for all to see. We all present a public face, whether consciously or unconsciously. I am talking about presenting you in the best light."

Samantha looked as though this explanation did not make her feel much better. Madge sighed.

"We will tell the truth," she said, "but we will focus on those aspects of it which will help people to remark on your good character and Wyatt's: your intrepidity, his honor. We will also point out to people how your experiences have influenced your desire to use your newfound wealth for charitable purposes, which will help to mitigate some of the resentment you face on that front. Finally, we will focus on how the *in no way dishonorable* bond you two formed grew into love. Your story has all the makings of a penny dreadful. This will work. Trust me."

"There's something else that might help," Wyatt said. "Did you read about the attack on Sir Anthony Guilford?"

"Sir Anthony was attacked?" Samantha asked. "How? When?"

"It was yesterday," Madge answered for him. "I was reading about it before Wyatt came over. He was garrotted. Nearly to death, if the papers are to be believed, though it seems a little overdramatic to be true."

"I think Skinny Jim ordered the attack," Wyatt said. "I think Sir Anthony didn't pay in time and, this was his punishment."

"It makes sense," Samantha said, a grim set to her mouth, "but how does that help us?"

"Ah," Madge said, her eyes lighting up. "I see where you are going with this, Wyatt, and it's a good idea. If we let people know that the attack on Sir Anthony was perpetrated by Skinny Jim, it will help them to see what a threat he continues to be and why you have reason to be wary."

"Precisely."

"I would have thought the murder of Charles would have been enough for that," Samantha said, "but this certainly can't hurt our cause."

"No, indeed," Madge said.

"I can foresee one difficulty with the plan you've laid out, though," Wyatt said. "If you are intending to make a point of our love story, how will you explain Aston?"

"What do you mean?" Madge asked.

"Oh, no." Samantha's eyes widened, and she put a hand over her mouth. "You're right. We've spent all this Season allowing people to believe that he and I are courting."

"That won't be a problem," Madge said with her usual confidence. "You haven't announced anything, have you? You've spent time together, yes, but it isn't as though you were betrothed. If you like, you can say he was helping you to keep the fortune hunters at bay while you courted Wyatt in secret, but I don't see that you need to say anything at all."

"We should still talk to him before we announce anything," Samantha said. "At least his parents will be pleased. They were less sanguine than he predicted at the prospect of having me as a daughter-in-law."

She gasped and turned to Wyatt.

"Your mother!" she said. "And your brother. What will they say?"

Wyatt realized then that he hadn't given even a thought to either of his disagreeable family members.

"I'll handle them," he assured her, though the idea filled him with distaste. "There's no need to worry about them now." Turning to Madge, he said, "I suppose you have a plan for how to begin?"

"Naturally. I will invite Mrs. Haviland and Lady Saunders for tea. Separately, of course. In strictest confidence, I will tell them about Samantha's circumstances and the fact that the man with the absurd name has found her, precipitating your speedy marriage and trip to the continent."

"Is that where we're going for our honeymoon?" Wyatt asked ironically. "You have thought of everything."

"It is the most sensible course. Did you not plan to go to the continent?"

Wyatt had, indeed, intended a trip to the continent, though he had planned to discuss it with Samantha first. He didn't respond to Madge's question, and she didn't seem to expect him to—continuing, rather, to explain her plan.

"You'll need to marry almost immediately. As soon as Skinny Jim realizes you have preempted him and destroyed his source of blackmail, you will be at risk for his wrath. I suggest we invite the gossips round tomorrow but keep them ignorant of the specifics regarding the wedding itself. If we plan a small, private wedding in our home to take place on Monday, that will give the gossips a day and a half to spread the news, and you can be safely away before anyone even knows you're married."

"Monday," Samantha said somewhat dazedly.

"Yes. I should be able to arrange everything by then."

"In two days?" Samantha asked.

"I've been prepared for your announcement for some time," Madge said. "I've done most of the work already."

"Have you?"

Samantha looked startled and, Wyatt thought, not best pleased at this revelation. Hoping to prevent an argument, he asked, "Why not wait until after we've left to tell the gossips?"

"Because I want Samantha to be there with me," Madge said. "Her presence will be of enormous help in convincing Mrs. Haviland to take our side. Also, starting the rumors before you leave will give you, Wyatt, the opportunity to confirm them among the men in your clubs. Emphasize our focus in doing so. Samantha's intrepidity and charitable works, your honor—"

"Skinny Jim's evil machinations and our penny dreadful love story," Wyatt finished. "My memory is not so poor that I have forgotten what you said not five minutes ago."

He hadn't meant to snap at her, but the enormity of what lay before them was starting to settle on him.

"You did ask for my help, my boy," Madge said, not appearing in the least bothered by his rudeness.

Seeming to rally herself with an effort, Samantha said, "We appreciate all you've done. It is a good plan. But, perhaps you might leave the arrangements of the honeymoon to us?"

"I have no desire to manage your life after marriage, my dear. By all means, do as you please. However, if it is not the continent you plan to visit, do tell me before I meet with the old gossips."

"We will," Wyatt said. "I apologize for my terseness. You have been extraordinarily gracious with your time, and we are forever in your debt."

"Very prettily done. You are forgiven. It is a trying time for anyone, arranging a marriage, and you have quite the added difficulties. Now, Samantha, if you had any plans these next few days, cancel them. I'll send out invitations to tea this morning, and we'll get started."

"Will you come for dinner tonight?" Samantha asked Wyatt. "I'll invite Eden, and you could invite Lord Aston. We can use it as an opportunity to let them know what's going on."

"What an excellent idea," Madge said. "We can consider it your engagement celebration. It's not quite the event I might have hoped for, but, under the circumstances, it will do." She got up and crossed the room to ring the bell. "I'll need to discuss the menu with Mrs. Meadows, then Samantha and I will commence with the wedding planning."

"I see that I am being dismissed," Wyatt said with some amusement.

"I wish you didn't have to go," Samantha said with a half-smile, laying her hand on his knee.

Wyatt's heart leapt, and he caught her other hand, pressing a kiss into her palm.

"I wish I could bring you with me," he said. "Now that we're together, even a few hours seems too long to be parted from you."

"I think I preferred it when you were not openly acknowledging your feelings," Madge said. "I am like to become unwell if I must listen to such trite dialogue as this between the two of you."

"All the more reason for you to speed our plans for matrimony," Wyatt said, unapologetically. "Now, if you will turn away, I would like to kiss my fiancé goodbye."

SIXTEEN

When Wyatt entered Boodles sometime later, it was to find most of the membership in the lounge in a state of some agitation.

"Broad daylight!" shouted Lord Perbright, stabbing a withered finger into the air. "The effrontery of it. The audacity!"

"Well, not quite broad daylight," Wyatt's friend, Lord Fenton, said reasonably. "It was gone six in the evening."

"This would never have happened if your government hadn't pushed so hard for prison reforms," Lord Henry Knox spat at the man seated beside him. "Prison reform. You went soft on them, and they've taken advantage. Giving out those yellow tickets of parole like they're sweets for children, filling our streets with criminals. What did you expect?"

"The prisons are overcrowded," Lord Fenton argued as Wyatt threaded his way through the seats to stand beside him. "And only non-violent offenders have the opportunity for release. If we didn't insist on prison as a punishment for every crime from petty thievery to solicitation, we wouldn't worry about running out of space for those who pose an actual threat to society."

"Every criminal is a threat to society," Lord Perbright insisted. "They threaten its very moral fiber!"

Wyatt was hard-pressed to restrain himself from uttering a

derisive snort at the hypocrisy of a man like Lord Perbright championing the moral fiber of society.

"How's your leg, my lord?" he asked instead.

Lord Perbright had developed a persistent numbness in his left leg after contracting syphilis as a result of his habit of visiting houses of ill-repute before and throughout his marriage. His lordship looked confused by what he saw as a non-sequitur, but Fenton caught Wyatt's eye and gave him an approving half-smile.

"Crime is on the rise," Lord Henry said, returning to his theme. "Has been for years. And what does this government do? Let the criminals off! Let them back on our streets to fill up the slums. They're spilling out all over. Can't walk for tripping over them. Little beggar brats—thieves, the lot of them."

"You seem to be conflating criminals with the poor," Lord Fenton said.

"There is no difference, as I see it. 'If a man will not work, neither shall he eat.'"

The willful ignorance of the statement ignited Wyatt's temper.

"Do you think they don't want to work?" he asked. "You think they are poor because they *choose* not to work?"

"Their physical poverty is a reflection of their moral and intellectual poverty," Lord Henry said callously.

"Their intellectual poverty, where it exists, is a reflection of their lack of opportunity," Wyatt said. "Though what excuse you might have, I cannot imagine."

Lord Henry's face grew red as the men around him guffawed. Wyatt regretted his words. Not that he didn't think Lord Henry deserved to be set straight, but he was supposed to be building bridges and smoothing the way for himself and Samantha, not agitating influential members of Society. It was not lost on him however, that, not only had the likely culprit of the recent garrotting never been imprisoned, but the reason he hadn't been was partly as a result of his relationships with men of influence—

men like the ones in this room.

"If you'll excuse me, gentlemen," Wyatt said.

He left and made his way to the library. It was always quiet at that time of day. When Wyatt entered, there were two men in chairs by the fire snoring softly, one with a newspaper spread across his lap which fluttered as he breathed out. At the far end of the room, basking in the warmth of a rare beam of sunlight, sat Bingo. The newspaper beside him lay forgotten as he stared idly out the window. As Wyatt approached, he looked up, and his contemplative expression morphed into his usual grin.

"Did you hear about Sir Anthony?" he asked by way of greeting.

"They're all talking about the incident downstairs," Wyatt said. "Though I can't say I've heard anyone express concern for his health. Do you know how he fares?"

"No idea. Never have liked him, personally. Not that I wish him ill, of course."

"He must be alive, at least. I'm sure we would have heard about it if he weren't."

"Is that what brought you here?" Bingo asked. "Hoping to hear word of Sir Anthony?"

"No, I came to see you, actually. I have some news."

"Good news or bad?"

"Some of both, I suppose, though mostly good."

"Tell me the good news, then."

"Samantha and I are to be married."

Bingo beamed and reached over to clap him on the shoulder. "Is that so? May I be the first to offer you warmest congratulations. Incidentally, am I the first?"

Wyatt grinned. "Apart from Madge, who was there when I went to propose, yes. I didn't so much tell her as she figured it out, though, so I suppose you are the first to be told."

"I will take that. It's only fitting, really, considering that Samantha and I are supposed to have been courting all this Season."

"Ah, yes." Wyatt winced. "I'm sorry about that."

"Don't be. It was always going to end at some point, and what better reason could there be? Incidentally, is it a secret? Or will you be announcing it soon?"

"In a way. Madge will be letting some of the old gossips know tomorrow."

"Why?"

"We've decided the only way to deal with Skinny Jim will be to take away the hold he has over us."

Bingo whistled. "Are you going to tell them everything? That she lived on the streets? That she worked for him?"

"Not everything, but most of it. You might get some questions. Answer or don't as you like, but I'd rather you didn't lie."

Bingo leaned back in his chair and fixed Wyatt with a penetrative stare.

"How do you feel about this?" he asked. "More to the point, how does your bride feel?"

Hearing Samantha referred to as his bride brought a smile to Wyatt's lips. Then, he considered Bingo's question, running a hand through his hair. "I think she's nervous, certainly overwhelmed. We both are. We're fairly certain we'll be in danger once he finds out what we've done. That's why we're leaving the city as soon as we marry."

"When will that be?"

"Monday, but we're not telling anyone that. It'll just be a small ceremony at Madge's. I need to get a special license today. I hope you'll stand up with me."

"I'd be honored to." Bingo placed a hand over his heart. "Have you told Tom?"

Wyatt grimaced. "No. I will, and soon, but I've been loath to ruin what has begun as a good day."

"And your mother?"

Wyatt sighed. "It's tempting to leave that happy task to Tom, but I probably should be the one to tell her, and before Madge tells the old gossips. I'd never hear the end of it if she found out about her son's engagement from Lady Saunders."

"In that case, I wish you luck."

"Thank you. Oh, and before I forget, you're invited to Madge's tonight for supper to toast the engagement. Lady Stuart-Lane has been invited as well, but I think she's the only other guest."

"I'll be there." Bingo shook his hand effusively. "Congratulations, Val. You deserve every happiness."

As Wyatt stood outside his family's London residence, he fought the urge to flee. It had been years since he had crossed the threshold—not since his aunt had left him her house and he'd moved out on his own. On the rare occasions when he visited his mother, it was at Boxley Abbey, their country seat, and when he and Tom met in the city, they did so at their clubs.

"Good day, Mr. Wyatt." Yardley, who had been butler of the town residence as long as Wyatt could remember, stepped back as he entered, then took his hat and cane. "Are you here to see her ladyship or his lordship?"

"Both, as it happens."

"Very good, sir. If you will take a seat in the drawing room, I will see if they are available."

Wyatt waved Yardley away when he attempted to escort him and made his own way to the drawing room. He almost didn't recognize it. Gone was the chinoiserie-patterned wallpaper that had been out of fashion even in his childhood. Instead, the walls were covered in a repeating pineapple motif that was reflected in carved details on the legs of tables and chairs and the bases of the lamps. In fact, the longer Wyatt looked, the more pineapples he seemed to find. It almost made him miss the old chinoiserie, which he had always hated.

"What are you doing here?"

Tom's tone was almost accusatory and so sharp that Wyatt jumped, hitting his head on the shelf of the bookcase he had been examining. Rubbing the sore spot, he composed his features before he turned to face his brother.

"Is Mother here?"

Tom stood in the doorway, one hand on the lintel as though expecting to leave as suddenly as he'd appeared.

"She's in her sitting room," he said. "Why are you here?"

"I have news. I thought you both should know."

A flicker of emotion passed across Tom's normally stoic countenance, but it was gone too quickly for Wyatt to read.

"Is this about Miss Kingston?" he asked. When Wyatt nodded, Tom released the lintel and walked slowly into the room. "Are you engaged?"

"Do you disapprove?"

"That depends on your reasons."

"My reasons are none of your concern."

Tom's lips thinned. "Naturally, not."

He came to a stop beside the fireplace, on the opposite side to Wyatt, and rested a hand on the mantle.

"I'm not marrying her for her money, if that is what troubles you," Wyatt said. "I'd marry her if she hadn't a cent to her name."

"You may come to wish she hadn't."

Wyatt could not imagine what he meant by that. Reluctantly giving into curiosity, he asked, "Why?"

"Mother," Tom said simply.

"Is that all?" Wyatt asked. "I can handle her."

Tom made a derisive noise in his throat.

"You think I can't?"

"I think you underestimate her," Tom said. He traced his fingers over the mantle. "She will think she has won, you know. She may not have liked Miss Kingston, but you know she wanted you to marry her to increase the family reserves and you, the obedient son at last, are acceding to her wishes."

"That is ridiculous," Wyatt scoffed. "She knows I would never —"

"You'd be surprised what she can think when she wants to. She'll be working on her next victory now."

"She can do as she likes. I won't be so easily swayed."

"What about your wife?"

Wyatt snorted. "If you knew her at all, you'd know she's even less likely than I am to bow to Mother's wishes."

"I hope so, for her sake. And yours."

For a moment, Wyatt thought Tom was going to say something else, but he shook his head and stepped away from the mantle.

"For what they're worth, I offer my congratulations."

"Do you?" Wyatt was skeptical. "I thought you opposed the match."

Tom shrugged. "I was concerned about the scandal, but I begin to think Mother was right. With all the fuss being made about these garrottings, Samantha's history is hardly sensational news anymore."

"About that," Wyatt said, feeling a twinge of guilt. "You might hear some rumors soon. About Miss Kingston. And me. A new version of the events of last summer."

"What sort of rumors?" Tom asked, his demeanor sharpening.

"Not what you're thinking," Wyatt said scornfully. "I didn't lie about that. Our relationship has been perfectly respectable.

However, it didn't start as early as we led people to believe. Samantha was on her own for a time—on the streets—and Madge and I lied to preserve her reputation."

"And you are revealing the truth now because..."

"Someone has been blackmailing us with the information, and the situation has become untenable."

Tom pinched the bridge of his nose and closed his eyes.

"How soon?" he asked.

"What?"

"How soon will I hear these rumors?"

"I believe Madge plans to invite Mrs. Haviland for tea tomorrow, so I should imagine by tomorrow evening."

Scrubbing a hand over his face, Tom nodded.

"The wedding is on Monday," Wyatt said.

Tom dropped his hand and stared at Wyatt, open-mouthed.

"It will be a small affair," Wyatt continued, "and we're not putting a notice in the paper until after the fact. We want to be away from the city when it becomes known."

"Because of the blackmailer?" Tom asked, with a return of his usual sangfroid.

"Yes."

With another nod, Tom said, "I'll tell Mother."

Wyatt was taken aback.

"You will?"

"She won't be happy to hear you lied to her, and she will hate that the wedding is being rushed. She's going to have a fit, and it'll be all the worse if you're there. I can handle her."

After wrestling with his conscience for a moment, Wyatt uttered the words he never thought he'd say to his brother.

"Thank you."

Tom blinked. Then he said, "I'm not doing it for you. I'm doing it for her. She might have a heart attack otherwise, and I'd never hear the end of it."

Before Wyatt could rescind his thanks, Tom cleared his throat and added, "You're welcome."

There followed an awkward pause. It was the least amount of animosity Wyatt had experienced with his brother in years, and he wasn't sure what to do with it.

"I should go," he said, when it was clear Tom was at just as much of a loss. "Madge is expecting me for dinner."

"Of course."

Tom rang for Yardley, who retrieved Wyatt's hat and cane. Wyatt bid his brother goodbye and left, shoving aside the unsettled feeling their strange détente had left him with—to be examined at another time or, more likely, never.

SEVENTEEN

The engagement dinner was an enjoyable interlude which Samantha wished could have lasted longer, knowing the whirlwind of activity that awaited her, some of it pleasant but much of it decidedly not. When she woke the next morning to the sound of the drapes being drawn back, she took a moment to steel herself before sitting up and stretching.

"Good morning, miss," Alice said cheerfully as she filled the washbasin with fresh water. "Her ladyship asked me to inform you that the dressmaker will be here in an hour for your fitting."

"So soon? Why did you not wake me earlier?"

"Her ladyship told me not to," Alice said. "She said you'd need all the sleep you could get."

Throwing off the covers, Samantha slid to the floor and padded over to the washbasin, where she splashed away the last vestiges of sleep. Then she sat at her vanity and began to brush out her hair, trying to ignore the knot of anxiety that had formed in her stomach.

It wasn't her upcoming marriage that concerned her. She had been only half joking when she suggested after Wyatt's proposal that they marry that afternoon. Having made up her mind to love him for the rest of her days, she was happy to begin those days as soon as possible. What she was less enthusiastic about, however, was the strategic revelation of the secret they had held for nearly a year which must needs be timed with their furtive nuptials and subsequent escape to the continent, all while they looked over their shoulders for Skinny Jim.

Seeking to distract herself, she addressed her maid.

"What do you think, Alice?" she asked.

Alice was laying out her morning dress and did not look up.

"About what, miss? The fitting?"

"No, about my...marriage."

The word felt strange on Samantha's tongue. Alice looked up at her in surprise.

"About your marriage?"

"Yes. It will be a change for you, too. You'll be coming with us on our honeymoon, and then we will move to Mr. Wyatt's house."

Alice came to join her at the vanity, taking the brush from her hand and beginning to plait Samantha's hair.

"I look forward to the opportunity to travel," she said. "As for living in Mr. Wyatt's house, it is no more significant to me than moving to your uncle's house or to Lady Bradwell's. It is a change, to be sure, but one that is to be expected."

"I see."

Samantha wasn't sure why this answer disappointed her. Perhaps because it was so empty of meaning. Her relationship with Alice was a strange one. At times, she felt they were almost friends and that she could tell her anything. They had been through so much together. Yet, she knew so little about Alice's own hopes and dreams. It was in moments like these when she felt the chasm of rank that separated them.

"Do you want to get married, Alice?"

Alice's hands stilled for a moment before she resumed twisting Samantha's hair into a knot.

"I suppose I might," she said, her tone cautious. "Someday."

"I'll miss you when you do. I don't suppose...is there a young man in your life now?"

Pinning the knot in place at the nape of Samantha's neck, Alice said, "No, miss. There's no need for you to worry on that score."

"I'm not worried," Samantha said. "If you had a young man, I'd be happy for you. I want you to be happy."

"Thank you, miss."

Alice went to retrieve the crinoline. Samantha stood up and stepped into the hoop. As Alice lifted it to her waist, she added, "I want you to be happy, too, miss."

Samantha smiled. "Thank you, Alice. I am."

The dressmaker turned out to be Madame Foussard, the woman who had made Samantha's and Madge's mourning clothes for the funeral of Prince Albert that winter. When Madame entered Samantha's room in a flurry of energy, she was followed by an assistant carrying a large box which, when opened, was revealed to contain a nearly completed wedding gown.

"What is that?" Samantha asked as the assistant lifted out the dress and laid it across the bed.

"It is your wedding gown, of course," Madame Foussard said.

"But I haven't chosen a gown yet."

"Oh, I had Madame start it weeks ago," Madge said, entering the room. "I knew that, by the time you two were ready, we would have very little time, and Madame does not like to be rushed."

Samantha opened her mouth to respond but found she lacked the words. When Madge told them the day before that she had been preparing for the wedding for some time, Samantha had been upset. Madge, of all people, had known her reservations about marriage. Samantha had tried to set aside her feelings in light of all that needed to be done, but now she found herself overwhelmed by resentment all over again.

Though she knew she would not have been able to order a new gown in two days, she had thought to alter an existing one. At least then, the choice would have been hers. That Madge had chosen her wedding dress for her was so presumptuous and, though she knew it had been done with the best of intentions, represented a complete disregard for Samantha's own wishes.

"Come, come," Madame Foussard said, clapping her hands. "I do not have all the time. You must try it on so I can make the final adjustments. You like it, no?"

Samantha looked down at the delicate layers of white organza fine as spiders' webs and flecked with gold that covered the silk gown.

"It's lovely," she assured Madame, with an attempt at enthusiasm.

It was lovely. She could hardly complain at such a beautiful dress and yet...

"I wish you had told me you were doing this, Madge," she said, injecting her tone with a sweetness to hide her frustration.

"Why? You know you would have told me not to do it," Madge said airily. "And then where would we be? Without a dress, for one."

"But I had no plans to marry when you ordered this dress," Samantha said, allowing Alice and Madame's assistant to help her undress.

"Yes, but I knew you would."

"How prophetic you were."

Madge sat on the edge of the bed and fixed Samantha with a penetrative stare.

"You are angry with me," she said, her tone as matter-of-fact as her statement.

"Not angry, precisely, but I confess I am not pleased to find that you acted without consulting me. Supposing I had chosen not to marry Wyatt?"

"Then Madame would have made it over for another bride. There is no need to concern yourself about that."

"I am not concerned about the dress, Madge. It is the sentiment behind it—that you would make a choice for me, assuming you knew best about my own life. I appreciate all you have done for me—I truly do—but—"

"But you are your own woman," Madge finished for her, with a nod of her head. "I understand. And I apologize."

Samantha gave her a wry look. "Do you?"

Madge returned the look. "I should not have interrupted you just then. It did rather undermine my apology. I beg your forgiveness. You are right. When you came to me, you were so broken down after all that awful business with Charles Prescott being shot that I suppose I became accustomed to taking care of you. But you know your own mind. In truth, you remind me of myself at times, and I do hate to have others speak for me, so I understand."

"Thank you."

"Now," Madge said, standing up again. "Hurry and finish dressing so I may see the full effect."

With Alice and Madame's help, Samantha was ready in minutes. Madge motioned for her to turn around, and she did a slow spin in the dress, marveling at the way the gold sparkled in the light from the window. When she stopped, Madge was smiling at her.

"Beautiful," she said. "I knew it would be, of course, but it is quite another thing to see you in it."

She stepped forward and took Samantha's hands in hers, then bent down to kiss her cheeks.

"You must allow me to fuss over you," she said. "I do not have a daughter. Samuel is years away from marrying, and if Linwood continues to demonstrate such poor taste in brides as he has, I have not much hope in that quarter. You may be my only chance to enjoy mothering a bride."

Samantha's heart warmed. She suspected that Madge's intentions were more selfless than she let on because, while it may or may not have been Madge's only chance to mother a bride, Samantha had never expected to be mothered at all.

"I would like that," she said.

Samantha soon discovered there was very little Madge had not already begun preparations for. The flower order was on standby, the music had been selected and a limited guest list drawn up. Invitations had been ordered and the menu for the wedding breakfast designed. Even with these early preparations, however, there was still so much to do that Samantha had no time to think about Sir Anthony or Skinny Jim or even Mr. Spenser, who had so long occupied her thoughts. Her distraction wasn't to last, however, as Lady Saunders arrived promptly at two that afternoon.

When Headley announced her, Lady Saunders flounced into the room with her maid trailing in her wake, carrying an armful of wriggling fur.

"My dear Lady Bradwell," she said between swift pecks to each of her hostess' cheeks. "It has been too long. Far too long. You remember Charlemagne?"

"How could I forget?" Madge said, eyeing the little dog with distaste.

"When I leave him behind, he pines, poor dear," Lady Saunders said, reaching out to stroke her pet.

"You remember Miss Kingston," Madge said, laying a hand on Samantha's arm.

Lady Saunders scrutinized Samantha with the same mixture of curiosity and wariness to which Samantha had become accustomed. "Of course. Good day, Miss Kingston." Then, in a sharper voice, she addressed her maid. "Let him down, Addie."

With an appearance of resigning herself to the inevitable, the maid lowered the furball to the lush carpet. Immediately, it began to run around, sniffing at the chair legs and biting at the carpet while yipping so loudly that Madge had to raise her voice to be heard as she offered Lady Saunders a chair. Before Samantha could take her own seat, the dog skittered over to her and began attacking her skirts with tiny paws that appeared from within the mass of fur.

"Just shift him aside," Lady Saunders said unconcernedly as she settled herself into a Queen Anne chair.

Samantha looked down at the dog and over at Madge, who gave her a sympathetic grimace. Reaching down, she tried to lift the dog, but his nails had caught on her skirts and they came up with him. Samantha looked pointedly at Lady Saunders, but she was unmoved.

"Such a playful boy," Lady Saunders clucked. "Are these your famous vanilla biscuits, Lady Bradwell? How thoughtful of you to remember how much I like them."

As Madge responded, Samantha gritted her teeth and shifted the dog under one arm, detaching his claws from her gown with some difficulty as he wiggled and yipped. Finally, holding him away from her dress, she handed him to Lady Saunders' maid who, after a glance at her mistress, blissfully unaware of the disturbance, took it.

With the dog safely handled, Samantha sat beside Madge. She endured half an hour of tedious conversation about the latest gossip related to various acquaintances, listening with half an ear as she waited for Madge to bring up the primary reason for the visit. In the end, it was Lady Saunders herself who provided the transition.

"So, she's gone off to the continent," she said, concluding a long story about the widowed Mrs. Banks. "No idea when she'll be back."

"Perhaps you will see her when you go," Madge said, turning to Samantha.

Samantha recognized this as her cue to bring the conversation around to its main purpose.

Lady Saunders turned beady eyes on her. "You're going abroad? When?"

"Within the week, I should think," Samantha said casually, as though the matter were of no great concern. "Though, I am not sure Mr. Wyatt has made any definite plans yet."

"Mr. Wyatt?" Lady Saunders was practically panting like the dog she had long forgotten.

"Yes." At Madge's nod, Samantha leaned forward. Lady Saunders mirrored her as Samantha lowered her voice. "This is in strictest confidence. We will be putting a notice in the *Times*, of course, but we would prefer not to announce it yet. Mr. Wyatt and I are to be married."

"Married?!"

"Oh, yes," Madge said, taking up the reins. "Lord Bradwell and I are so pleased for them. After all Samantha has been through, it is a comfort to know she has found such happiness."

"Do you have a date chosen for the wedding?" Lady Saunders asked Samantha.

"We do," Samantha said. "Though we are not prepared to share it as yet."

"It's a matter of safety, you see," Madge said.

"Safety?" Lady Saunders' eyebrows rose. "Whatever can you mean?"

Madge's sigh was a little too theatrical. It was clear she was enjoying herself.

"It is a long story," she said, "but in light of the recent rise in crime and knowing that Samantha has a particular enemy in a powerful criminal, we consider that she is in great danger."

Lady Saunders, who had already been on the edge of her seat, leaned farther forward. "I was not aware she had an enemy. A powerful criminal?"

"His name is Skinny Jim. Dreadful man. Samantha met him when she was hiding from the men who killed Sir Arthur and Lady Prescott. Unfortunately, for a variety of reasons, we felt it best to hide the truth of Samantha's activities at that time. One of those reasons being to protect her from this Skinny Jim. Sadly, our efforts have proved vain, and he has found her out. Hence, the hurried trip to the continent."

"I had no idea. How dreadful." Lady Saunders looked positively delighted. "How did you ever meet him, Miss Kingston?"

Samantha looked to Madge, who nodded. It was time to come clean with her story. She swallowed and looked into the eager face of Lady Saunders.

"To begin with, I suppose I should explain that I did not meet Mr. Wyatt the night of the murder of my aunt and uncle. In fact, it was more than a month after before we met."

She proceeded to explain what had happened with emphasis, as Madge had suggested, on her desperation to get home and clear her name and her fear that she could not trust anyone. When she spoke about the lodging house she had lived in with five other women, Samantha avoided detailed description, focusing, instead, on the empathy she had developed for those in need, and the way it had driven her to use her money to help where she could.

When she got to the part where she and Wyatt met ('No need to go into details as to how,' Madge had suggested), she explained that she hadn't known who he was or whether she could trust him with the truth any more than anyone else. He, not knowing she was a lady, had asked for her help with an investigation and, in assisting him, she had come in contact with Skinny Jim. Of course, being an honorable man, once Wyatt worked out who she was, he offered his protection and sent for Madge to preserve propriety.

Madge took up the tale then, describing her role as chaperone and her conviction, from almost the first moment of meeting Samantha, she said, that she and Wyatt would be perfect for one another. She then proceeded to tell her version of the progression of Samantha's and Wyatt's relationship which, while true in its particulars, was embellished with Madge's own opinions and left Samantha red with embarrassment by the end of it.

When Madge had finished speaking, it was a full minute before Lady Saunders had any response. In the silence, Samantha could hear the squeaking of the little dog in the corner, as he fought against his restraint.

"That is quite an extraordinary story," her ladyship said finally. "I am...I don't...well. Well, well." She cleared her throat. "You two must have a lot to do with a wedding to plan. I don't wish to keep you any longer. Addie! Get Charlemagne." She rose to her feet, and Madge and Samantha followed. "Thank you, Lady Bradwell, for your hospitality. Miss Kingston...I wish you a good day."

She left with slightly less aplomb than she had entered with. When the door shut behind her, Samantha exhaled.

"Well done, my dear," Madge said.

"Did she believe us, do you think?" Samantha asked.

"I think so," Madge said. "I suspect she is trying to decide how she ought to respond. I've no doubt she is shocked, but she will wait until she has told the story to at least half a dozen people and seen their reactions before she decides whether we are too scandalous to be borne or merely eccentric."

It was not a comforting thought.

"Never fear," Madge said. "Among the first people she will tell will be Mrs. Eastbourne, whom we have already converted to our side. You, with your excellent manners and deportment and me with my introductions to those ladies with whom she particularly wished to become acquainted. I think we may be safe to rely on her to soothe Lady Saunders' worries."

Samantha could feel a headache coming on. She rubbed her temples.

"Get some rest," Madge said kindly. "Mrs. Haviland won't be here for another hour."

Samantha returned to her room in a daze and sat on the edge of her bed, staring blindly out the window. One conversation down, one more to go, and then the truth would be out in the world. Only time would tell the result. She wanted to feel relieved but, knowing that they still had Skinny Jim to worry about, she wasn't. She kneaded her forehead as the headache deepened and lay back on her pillow. She assumed she would be unable to rest, too full of thoughts that chased themselves around her head, but within minutes, she was asleep.

*****

Wyatt had spent the morning at home, attempting to plan his honeymoon and handle the legal matters related to his marriage. He'd sent Durand on half a dozen errands and approved a list of items Mrs. Hexam considered necessary to make his home habitable for a lady. Despite the happy reason for the work, it was still mostly tedious. When a note from Inspector Whicher arrived by courier at half past noon, Wyatt was more than ready for the distraction.

Wyatt—
P gone missing. Be on the lookout. Have found evidence to connect him to death of S.
—Whicher

Wyatt re-read the note twice before the words fully registered. When they did, his first reaction was surprise, followed swiftly by confusion. Why would Ponsonby have disappeared? Had he known the police were closing in on him? Had he been warned? Possibly by Skinny Jim? Then it hit Wyatt. With all that had happened with Samantha after, he had completely forgotten the conversation he overheard between Ponsonby and Skinny Jim's man at the Derby. He'd never told Whicher about it, meaning Whicher was acting without a vital piece of the puzzle.

Propelled into action by a mixture of guilt and worry, Wyatt grabbed his hat and cane, shouted to Mrs. Hexam that he was going out and rushed to catch a cab.

Half an hour later, as Wyatt sat across the desk from Inspector Whicher, he was surprised to see the normally unflappable detective looking haggard. There were dark circles under his eyes, and he had at least two days' worth of stubble on his chin.

"The city is in a panic," Whicher said, digging through a pile of paper in front of him and nearly upsetting the next pile. "First, that old man was garrotted in Soho. No doubt it would have been forgotten except that the Spenser murder also took place in Soho. Now, with the attack on Sir Anthony, all the papers are saying we've got another garrotting crime wave on our hands, even though Spenser wasn't garrotted. *The Daily News* is calling London 'a lair of footpads and assassins by night'. We've had people in here every few minutes demanding to know what we're doing to stop it, and there are letters piling up in the corner from every Tom, Dick and Harry telling us how to do our jobs."

"That sounds awful," Wyatt said, immensely thankful he did not have to deal with the public en masse. "I'm sorry."

"Yes, well." Whicher seemed almost to deflate as the irritation left him. "It can't be helped."

"Do you know who was responsible for Sir Anthony's attack?" Wyatt asked.

"Oh, there were half a dozen witnesses, but no one can agree on what they saw. We know there were two men—one doing the strangling while the other stole his pocket watch. Otherwise, we've been told both were tall; one was tall and one short; both wore black; both wore brown; one had dark hair; both were fair. In other words, absolutely useless."

"If it helps at all, I think it was more than likely Skinny Jim behind it. I know for a fact that Sir Anthony owed him money and he was behind in his payments."

Inspector Whicher sighed. "I'm sure you're right, but it doesn't help much. I could take a guess at half a dozen men I'm fairly certain work for him and would be strong enough to do the garrotting, but there's no evidence to tie them to the crime, and I doubt I could get the witnesses to agree on one of them. It's worth a try, I suppose." He rubbed a hand over his face. "It won't make much of a difference to the public even if we are able to arrest the men. They're all convinced they'll be murdered in the streets, if not by those men, by others. The newspapers aren't helping. Ever since Spenser's murder, they've been digging up every theft and minor assault they can find and reporting it, stirring up a panic."

"Speaking of Spenser," Wyatt said. "He is the reason I wanted to talk to you. Well, Ponsonby, really."

"Ah, yes. Mr. Ponsonby. I've alerted the constable that patrols his street to watch for his return and sent constables to check on Mr. Leclerc and Mr. Leipzig, in case he goes to confront either of them about the blueprints. I wish I could post a round-the-clock guard, but that would be difficult at the best of times, and we're stretched too thin now."

"I saw Ponsonby at the Derby talking to one of Skinny Jim's men," Wyatt said. "From what I heard, it sounded as though Ponsonby is in debt to Skinny Jim."

Whicher lifted his eyes to the ceiling and groaned. "Of course he is. He and half the city, it seems. If you're right, it may have been Skinny Jim who alerted him we were coming to speak with him. Or perhaps it's Skinny Jim he's hiding from."

"What evidence did you find?" Wyatt asked.

"I was able to track down four more inventors whose blueprints he stole," Whicher said. "They are prepared to swear that he refused to return their property, and we've found at least one more of the inventions that he put into production, so we have him on theft. I'd prefer to get him for the murder if we can, though. We had a search warrant for his house. I hoped to surprise him and to see his reaction when I told him about the blueprints we found at Mr. Spenser's.

"When we arrived, his butler said the staff hadn't seen him in three days. He'd never been gone that long before without telling them where he was going. They were at a loss for what to do and happy for us to look around to see if we could discover clues to his whereabouts."

"Did you find any?"

"No, but we did find a blood-spattered, brown-checked suit shoved into a pot in the back of the garden shed. The jacket was missing a button exactly like the one we found beside Spenser's body."

Wyatt blinked. "That's...wow. Why didn't you lead with that information? That's incredible."

"It would be more so if we hadn't lost our main suspect," Whicher said. "We can't very well do much until we find him."

"Do you think Spenser was blackmailing him?" Wyatt asked. "Is that why he was killed?"

"Blackmailing or possibly just asking questions," Whicher said. "Though, what I still can't figure out is why Ponsonby did it the way he did. Killing Spenser in the street with witnesses nearby was risky. If he'd actually stolen from Spenser, I might have thought he intended it to look like a robbery gone wrong, with no one the wiser. If he could pull that off unseen, I might call it clever. Only, he didn't steal anything. He left Spenser's wallet, his pocket watch, everything."

"Maybe he was counting on someone else to do the stealing," Wyatt suggested, "so that he wouldn't have to worry about disposing of the goods."

"He'd have to hope a thief found the body before anyone else did. Not a completely unreasonable hope, as it turned out, but not a guarantee, either. It leaves too much to chance."

Whicher lifted the decanter that sat on the edge of his desk. He tilted it towards Wyatt in a mute offer then, when Wyatt shook his head, poured himself three fingers of whiskey.

"Do you think I might search Ponsonby's study?" Wyatt asked. "Having been there before, I might be able to tell if something stands out as unusual. I still don't understand how Spenser got ahold of the blueprints in the first place."

"Normally, I'd say no," Whicher said. He drained the glass and set it back down. "But, as I've told you, we're stretched thin, and I can't devote the resources I'd like. So, yes. You may as well. I'll take what help I can."

It wasn't quite a vote of confidence, but Wyatt took it as progress in their relationship.

"I'll let you know what I find out," he said.

*****

Mrs. Haviland had been gone an hour when Wyatt pulled up in front of Madge's house in a rented gig and offered to take Samantha on a drive. Madge seemed inclined to object, citing their long list of tasks before the wedding, but Samantha readily agreed, assuring Madge she would make up the time that evening.

"How did it go with the old gossips?" Wyatt asked when she had settled in beside him.

"Better than I expected," Samantha said. "Though I did worry we might have to call a doctor for Mrs. Haviland. She was nearly paralyzed with excitement."

"Did Lady Saunders bring that miserable dog?"

"Yes, and he fell instantly in love with my skirts. He would have shredded them to bits if I'd let him."

"With her ladyship's blessing, I'm sure."

"Oh, certainly." Samantha tucked her arm into his. "Now tell me, what's this about? I can't imagine you decided to take me on a drive on a whim, knowing how busy we are."

Wyatt reined in the horses as they came to a crossing. While they waited for the carriages in the other street to pass, he turned to her.

"Mr. Ponsonby has disappeared," he said.

Samantha gaped, but she remained silent as Wyatt explained what he and Inspector Whicher had discussed, including Mr. Ponsonby's connection with Skinny Jim.

"Do you think Mr. Ponsonby is hiding from Skinny Jim or the police?" Samantha asked. "Or do you think he's not hiding at all? Skinny Jim may have taken him."

The path cleared, and Wyatt urged the horses forward. The carriage wheels clattered on over the cobblestones. After he had negotiated the crossing, he said, "I have no idea, but I asked Whicher if I could look around Ponsonby's study to see if I could find any clues to his whereabouts."

"And he agreed?"

She was surprised. Inspector Whicher may have warmed to Wyatt after what she understood to be an initial animosity, but she found it hard to believe that he would willingly accept Wyatt's assistance in such a matter.

"He's overworked and undermanned," Wyatt said. "He gave me a key and his blessing."

She laughed. Then his full meaning became clear, and she said, "Wait, is that where we're going now? To Mr. Ponsonby's house?"

"I thought you might like to help. After all, you've also been there before."

Warmth filled her heart, both from excitement at the prospect of investigating with Wyatt and from appreciation of his gesture. He was showing her that nothing would change between them. He would still value her insight, and he wouldn't force her to stay home. She squeezed his arm and kissed him on the cheek. "Thank you."

He shifted the reins to one hand and put his arm around her, squeezing her shoulders and kissing the top of her head. She smiled and leaned into him, content in their new, open affection.

When they pulled up in front of Mr. Ponsonby's townhome, Samantha jumped down and looked around while Wyatt secured the horses. A young couple strolled down the opposite side of the street and a maid carried a basket into the house two doors down, but otherwise, the street was empty.

When Wyatt joined her, he slid his hand into hers and their fingers locked. It was an almost unconscious movement and Samantha marveled at how natural it felt in spite of its newness. Lifting his free hand, Wyatt rapped lightly on the door. They waited. No one answered. He tried again, knocking louder, but there was still no answer.

"Perhaps they aren't home," Samantha said, though she thought it unlikely. "I suppose the servants might have taken the day off with their master away, especially now they know the police are looking."

"No matter," Wyatt said. With his free hand, he reached into the pocket of his jacket and pulled out a large metal key, which he inserted into the lock. It turned easily and he opened the door, allowing her to precede him inside.

They were met by an eerie stillness in Mr. Ponsonby's front hall. Perhaps because she was remembering the bustle and noise of the concert the last time she had been there, the quiet seemed unnatural and left her with a feeling of unease. Her footsteps echoed across the smooth tile as she peered into the rooms on either side of the hall. They were empty of inhabitants. The curtains had been drawn tight, or perhaps had never been opened that day, making the whole house dark and uninviting. Samantha found herself thinking of ghost stories she had heard as a child. She repressed a shiver, then chided herself for falling prey to her imaginings.

"Ready?" Wyatt asked, a hand at her back.

She nodded, and they proceeded up the stairs. Mr. Ponsonby's study was on the first floor, the same as the drawing room, where the concert had been held.

"Oughtn't we to have encountered someone by now?" Samantha asked. "A housemaid or a footman?"

"Maybe you were right," Wyatt said, "and they've taken the day off. Or, with less work to do with Ponsonby not in residence, they may just be downstairs."

"Of course," Samantha said, trying to convince herself.

"In which case," Wyatt said, taking her hand and tugging her to him. "It would seem we're alone up here."

"It would seem so," she said. Suddenly, her fears seemed irrelevant.

His hands encircled her waist, and she wound hers around his neck, weaving her fingers into his thick, wavy hair.

"To be clear," Wyatt said, drawing her closer until there was no space between them, "I do want you to look at the study with me, but I won't pretend this wasn't on my mind when I suggested it."

"Indeed?" Samantha asked, raising an eyebrow. "What else was on your mind?"

The golden brown of Wyatt's eyes deepened as his grip on her waist tightened. He leaned down and spoke into her ear, his breath tickling her neck so that she shivered again, though for a very different reason.

"This," he said, placing a kiss behind her ear. She gasped and her eyes slid closed. "And this." He kissed her neck. "And this." He kissed her jaw. "And this." The corner of her mouth. She made an involuntary sound in her throat, and he responded with a low groan, gathering her in his arms and bringing his lips to hers with a fierceness that left her breathless. She reacted with enthusiasm, matching him kiss for kiss.

The sudden pain of a doorknob jabbing her in the back brought Samantha out of her blissful haze and she drew in a sharp breath.

"What's wrong?" Wyatt asked, pulling back and eyeing her with concern.

Samantha let go of his shoulder and reached behind her back to massage the injured area.

"The doorknob," she said.

"Are you alright?"

"Yes." She gave him an apologetic smile. "Perhaps we ought to stop?"

He sighed and ran a hand through his hair. "When are we getting married?"

She laughed. "Not soon enough. But we did come here for a reason. Another reason."

"I suppose we did."

Samantha stepped away from the door and Wyatt leaned forward and turned the knob. He pushed the door open, and she entered ahead of him.

Just as in the other rooms they had seen thus far, the drapes of Mr. Ponsonby's study were drawn shut. Unlike the rest of the house, however, the study was not dark. The gas lamps had been lit, and it was by their light that Samantha saw Mr. Ponsonby himself slumped over his desk, his head resting in a pool of blood.

EIGHTEEN

At Samantha's gasp, Wyatt, who had been shutting the door behind them, turned. When he saw Ponsonby's slumped form, he almost didn't believe his eyes. Ponsonby was missing, presumed to have either fled or been taken forcibly. The last place Wyatt would have expected to encounter him was in his own home.

"I don't suppose there's any chance..." Samantha trailed off, lowering her hands from her face.

"Wait here."

Wyatt strode across the room and stopped in front of the desk. A revolver lay in Ponsonby's limp left hand. Wyatt touched it gingerly and felt cool metal beneath his fingertips. He didn't know precisely how long it took a gun to cool completely after it had been fired, but he knew it was long enough to remove any chance that Ponsonby had not succumbed to his injuries. He had only to glance at the man's temple to know the chance had never been good. He had probably died instantly.

"He's dead," he called back to Samantha.

He heard the rustling of fabric as she came to join him.

"Why didn't anyone know he'd come back?" she asked in a soft voice. "Surely the staff would have sent word to Scotland Yard? Or do you think they are there now, and that's why we haven't heard them?"

Wyatt turned to her and saw that, despite her calm demeanor, her face was white.

"I don't think so," he said gently. "He's been dead for some time now. Time enough for them to have gone and returned."

"I can't believe we were...and he was in here, like that."

She covered her mouth, looking as though she might be sick. He had to admit it was unsettling to think of what had been beyond the door while they were taking advantage of their moment alone. But they hadn't known, and there was no point in dwelling on it now. He pulled her into his arms, and she rested her head on his chest.

"Don't think about it," he said. "Think about what we're going to do now. We need to get word to Inspector Whicher, but I don't think we should leave the body alone."

"I could see if any of the staff are in their quarters," Samantha said. "If so, we could send one of them to Inspector Whicher."

"I don't like the idea of you searching the house when we don't know who is or isn't here," Wyatt said.

"Well, I'd rather not stay with...him," she shuddered, "while you are gone for however long it takes to search the house. There isn't likely to be anyone here, anyway, or they'd have heard the shot and we wouldn't have found him alone."

She was probably right, but Wyatt still didn't like the idea of her wandering the dark house on her own.

"Take my gun with you," he said, pulling the pistol he always carried from his inner jacket pocket and handing it to her. "Just in case."

She nodded, a grim set to her features as she took the gun.

"I'll be back," she said.

"I'll be here."

With Samantha gone, Wyatt took the opportunity to inspect the room for anything that might be helpful in determining where

Ponsonby had been all this time and why he'd come back. He scanned the bookcases and the other furniture before returning to the desk.

At last, his eyes lit on a paper, partly covered by Ponsonby's slumped body and stained with blood. If he angled his head a certain way, he could just make out some of the words. It looked to be a letter—a suicide note—in which Ponsonby admitted to murdering Spenser and claimed his unwillingness to go through the shame of a trial. It wasn't the note that struck Wyatt most, however, but the blood upon it. He was no expert in death, but it seemed to him strange that blood would still be flowing from a corpse when it and the murder weapon had long grown cold. And yet, even as he watched, the red stain grew slowly across the paper, covering more of the words.

Wyatt had just noted this bizarre phenomenon when something else caught his attention. Movement. Out of the corner of his eye, he saw the heavy window drapery billow out at about the level of his knee before falling back into place. A sense of déjà vu settled over him, but this time, it wasn't Samantha hiding behind that curtain, ready to punch him in the nose. There was no doubt, however, that someone was there.

For a moment, he regretted not having his pistol, but on the chance that the person behind the curtain wasn't the only one in the house, he'd rather Samantha be armed than himself. Picking up a stone paperweight from the desk, he hefted it in his hand.

"I know you're in there," he said, "and I'm armed. Come out slowly with your hands where I can see them."

For a moment, nothing happened, and he experienced a flicker of doubt. Then, the curtain was pulled aside and Mr. Leclerc stepped out.

Wyatt almost dropped the paperweight. He gaped at the man who stood before him, hands raised with palms facing out, a pale set to his features.

"I'm sorry," Leclerc said, glancing at the corpse beside them. "I found him like this, and then I heard something hit the door and I panicked."

"What are you doing here?" Wyatt asked, at a complete loss to understand how Leclerc of all people was in Ponsonby's study. "How did you get in?"

"The butler let me in. I told him Inspector Whicher had sent me."

"But he didn't." Wyatt was at least certain of that.

Some color returned to Leclerc's cheeks. "No, he didn't. I—well, I suppose I had better tell you rather than have you think me here for some other reason—I came here to steal from Ponsonby." He grimaced as he lowered his arms in a placating gesture. "It sounds bad, I know, but the police constables said he'd run off, and I thought, if he were caught, his assets would be tied up with the courts, and if he were killed, they would be inherited by someone else. I wanted to get some of my own back. He owes me. Owed me."

"I can't let you take anything."

"I understand you don't want to be party to it," Leclerc said, "and I wouldn't wish you to go against your moral code, but could you not look the other way for a moment?"

Wyatt sighed. "You can't leave now. You discovered the body. The police will want to talk to you."

"I could just take a few things, stash them and come back. No one would have to know."

"I think it would be best if you stayed. I can't pretend not to notice you stealing from a dead man."

Leclerc closed his eyes and pinched the bridge of his nose. "Are you sure?"

"Yes."

With a speed Wyatt would not have imagined he possessed, Leclerc reached into his jacket and whipped out a revolver, cocking it and aiming it at Wyatt's chest in one fluid motion.

"That's a shame," he said. "You might have saved yourself if you had."

*****

It took only two wrong doors for Samantha to find the back stairs. As she descended these, she kept her ears open for signs of movement or voices drifting up from the kitchen, but all she heard was the echo of her steps. When she reached the bottom, she stopped and listened again. Silence. It was what she had expected, if not what she had hoped, but it was still disconcerting. Surely at least one of the servants ought to have been home to watch the house, even if the rest had taken the day off. Tiptoeing down the corridor, Samantha paused at the first doorway and looked in.

Discovering Mr. Ponsonby bleeding over his desk had been shock enough, but it was nothing compared to the sight that awaited her in the kitchen. Four people—two women and two men, all servants judging by their clothing—sat around the large wooden table, slumped forward, unmoving. On the floor beside them, a fifth person—a maid, by the looks of her—lay in a crumpled heap.

Samantha's hands flew to her mouth as she stifled a strangled cry. For several horrified moments, she thought she was witness to the scene of a mass murder. Then she noticed the rise and fall of the maid's chest and, sliding her gaze to the table, she could see that the others were breathing as well. Raising Wyatt's pistol and pointing it ahead of her, she stepped into the room, checking the corners for signs that anyone else was there. The room was empty. She sank to her knees, suddenly light-headed.

When she had regained her faculties, Samantha scooted over to the maid and attempted to rouse her. She would not wake, in spite of Samantha's best efforts. The same occurred when she shook those at the table. They appeared to be a footman, either a butler or a valet, and two upper female servants whom she assumed to be the housekeeper and the cook.

As Samantha stepped back from the footman, she noticed the half-drunk cups of coffee in front of each person. Not far from the maid, a cup had rolled under the table, leaving a trail of dark brown stain on the wooden floor. Had they been drugged? Had Mr. Ponsonby done it? Had he hoped to prevent anyone stopping him or calling the police to report his return? Or had someone else been involved?

Whatever the reason for their current state, Samantha was at a loss what to do about it, but it was clear that none of them would be able to run for Inspector Whicher anytime soon. Samantha decided she had better return to Wyatt so they could discuss what to do next.

As she reached the first floor, she heard a harsh male voice that was definitely not Wyatt's coming through the open door to the study. A trickle of fear ran down her spine, and she froze for a moment before stepping carefully forward, grateful for the thick rug that lined the hall, muffling her footsteps.

"I said, don't move!" the man snapped. His voice was familiar, but she could not quite place it. "I'd rather not shoot you right here, but I will if I have to."

"That would rather disrupt your suicide scene, wouldn't it?" Wyatt asked, his tone mild.

Fear spurred her forward, and she reached the door just as the man said, "Drop it."

Peering around the corner of the jamb, Samantha could see Wyatt, his eyes on the man who was striding around the desk to stand before him. She could not see the man. His back was to her. As she watched, Wyatt lowered his arm and dropped what looked like a paperweight to the floor. It landed on the dark wood with a thud.

"That is what you were doing, isn't it?" Wyatt asked. "I noticed the blood around Ponsonby's head is still flowing even though his body is cold. It's not his blood, is it?"

"Very clever," the man said. "Now, step over to the wall."

As Wyatt obeyed, Samantha pulled her head back and leaned against the doorframe, her heart in her throat. She closed her eyes and took a deep breath, then stepped out into the room, Wyatt's gun in her hand, and leveled it at the man before her.

"Drop the gun," she said, only a slight tremor in her voice.

The man turned his head, though his gun remained trained on Wyatt, and the click of metal as she thumbed the hammer of the pistol echoed in the sudden silence. Mr. Leclerc, for she had recognized him at last, glanced at her before returning his attention to Wyatt.

"I wondered when you would return," he said over his shoulder. "I thought you might have fainted."

"I said, drop the gun, Mr. Leclerc," Samantha said, her voice stronger despite her growing fear and confusion. She had no idea what the inventor was doing here nor how likely he was to shoot Wyatt.

"I'm afraid I can't do that," Mr. Leclerc said. "Your timing is quite poor, you know. If you'd been even half an hour later, I would have been gone and neither of you any the wiser. It would have been a very neat wrap to the whole affair. Mr. Wyatt might even have received another round of congratulations from the London press. As it is, I'll have to kill you both, which will mean more work than I anticipated today."

Bang!

In the split second after the shot, several things happened at once. Wyatt dove forward, Mr. Leclerc recoiled, and a second shot reverberated. Samantha stood rooted to the spot, her pulse racing as she lowered her hands and the still-smoking gun.

"You shot me!" Mr. Leclerc cried out, a mixture of shock and outrage on his face as he looked up at Samantha from the floor where Wyatt had pinned him.

"Are you alright?" Samantha asked Wyatt, her eyes searching his body for injuries.

"Yes," he said. "I think his shot was a reflex. I'd already moved out of the way. I expect we'll find a bullet in the wall over there. Excellent shot, by the way."

He grinned up at her, and she smiled faintly back, still shaken.

"Thank you."

"You shot me!" Mr. Leclerc repeated.

"In the leg," Wyatt said with a touch of impatience. He shifted so he could inspect Mr. Leclerc's calf, which was a mess of bright red blood. "It looks like a clean shot. It won't even be a long recovery. However, unless you'd like a matched pair, you'll do well to stay still. Samantha, you should reload. You'll find what you need in my right pocket."

Mr. Leclerc dropped his head down and closed his eyes, his breathing irregular.

"How did he get in here?" Samantha asked as she rummaged in Wyatt's jacket. Now that the imminent threat of danger had abated, she had the luxury to question the scene before her.

"He was hiding behind the curtain," Wyatt explained, lifting his elbow to make it easier for Samantha to access his pocket. "I think we interrupted him in the process of setting the room up to make it appear Ponsonby's death was a suicide. It might have worked if I hadn't noticed the curtain. And the blood."

"What do you mean?"

"Ponsonby and the gun were both cold, indicating he'd been dead a while, but the blood was still flowing. I'd guess he was killed elsewhere, and Leclerc added blood to make it look like it happened here. Animal blood, I'd imagine."

"Pig's blood," Mr. Leclerc said without opening his eyes.

"Why?" Samantha asked.

"It's easy to acquire in the right quantities."

"I meant—"

"I know what you meant."

He opened his eyes and narrowed them at Wyatt. Samantha hurriedly reloaded the pistol.

"Have you known where Ponsonby was all along?" Wyatt asked.

Mr. Leclerc snorted. "From the moment he disappeared. I was the one who wrote the note that led him to flee in the first place."

"Why?" Samantha asked.

Mr. Leclerc turned his head to look at her. Before he could speak, they were distracted by a banging and shouting from below and then a crash.

"Metropolitan Police!" a voice called out and Samantha realized the crash was the front door being forced open. "Is someone hurt? We heard gunfire!"

"We're up here!" she shouted towards the hall.

A moment later, a young constable ran into the room. He stopped short at the sight of the supine Mr. Leclerc, pinned beneath Wyatt while Samantha stood above them, holding a gun.

"What's all this?" he asked, holding up his truncheon and pointing it back and forth between Samantha and Wyatt, clearly unsure who was the perpetrator of the scene.

"Mr. Leclerc tried to kill us when we found him with Mr. Ponsonby's body," Wyatt said. "Go get Inspector Whicher, and be quick about it."

The constable did a double take as he finally noticed the body sprawled across the desk. His mouth dropped open.

"Now, man!" Wyatt urged.

Snapping his mouth shut, the constable nodded dumbly and backed out of the room. Soon, Samantha heard him sprinting through the front hall and out the door. She wondered wryly what the inspector would say when he realized Wyatt had summoned him again despite what they'd promised that night in Blackfriars.

"Do you intend for me to bleed out?" Mr. Leclerc asked. "Or will I be allowed some medical aid?"

"With what?" Wyatt asked. "Or did you bring bandages and medicine along with a body and a bag of blood?"

"You could use your shirt. Or mine, if you'd allow me space to remove it."

"Not likely."

"My petticoats, then," Samantha said.

"No," Wyatt objected.

"It's alright, Wyatt," she assured him. "He's right. We should tend to his wound."

"Thank you," Mr. Leclerc said. "I would hate to bleed all over Mr. Wyatt's fine coat."

Samantha handed the pistol to Wyatt, who used one hand to point it at Mr. Leclerc's back, while the other restrained his arms. She then searched the desk until she found a pair of shears. Using the desk as a blind, she lifted her skirts and cut a few swathes of fabric from her petticoats, trying not to look at the dead man feet from her. When she had finished, she returned to Mr. Leclerc and began to bind his wound.

"Why?" she asked again as she wound the fabric around his calf. "Why did you kill him?"

"He deserved it."

The hatred in his voice was palpable, and Samantha almost recoiled.

"Because he tricked you out of your invention?" Wyatt asked.

"He didn't trick me," Mr. Leclerc snapped. "He stole it."

"But you got it back," Samantha pointed out. "Wyatt got the blueprint for you. You could have gotten the money you were owed."

"I was owed a lot more than money," Mr. Leclerc scoffed.

"He took my genius, my hard work, and passed it off as his own. I couldn't let him get away with that."

"So, you killed him out of revenge?"

"I didn't just kill him." Samantha could hear the smile in his voice. "I terrified him. And, if you hadn't interrupted me, I would have humiliated him, too."

"What do you mean you terrified him?"

"Mr. Wyatt is the genius detective. Let him figure it out."

Samantha looked at Wyatt, who was frowning. Mr. Leclerc sighed.

"I'll paint you a picture," he said. "One day, Lucas Ponsonby wakes up, oddly enough, in the back garden of his own house. His head is splitting, and he can't remember how he got there. Then, as he comes to full consciousness, he realizes he can't remember much at all past lunch the previous day. As this is settling in his mind, he looks down at his clothes and discovers, to his horror, that they are covered in dark red stains, spattered across the trousers, but particularly on the jacket, which is also missing a button."

A jacket with a missing button. Hadn't Wyatt said a button was found near Mr. Spenser's body? And the witness mentioned in the newspaper had described a man running away from the alleyway with blood on his trousers. Mr. Leclerc said he had terrified Mr. Ponsonby before killing him. Terrified him by making him think he killed Mr. Spenser and might be caught? But the missing button hadn't been reported in the newspaper, which meant the only way Mr. Leclerc could have known about it would have been if he had been at the scene of the murder. She looked at Wyatt and saw her own dawning comprehension mirrored in his face.

"Ah," said Mr. Leclerc. "I see you understand."

"You killed Mr. Spenser," Samantha said, hardly able to speak the words. She felt sick. "And you tried to make Mr. Ponsonby take the blame."

"Yes," Mr. Leclerc said. "Though my plan hit a snag when the police thought it was a robbery gone wrong. Thankfully, Ponsonby was still convinced he'd done it. And the police got there in the end, with a little help."

"But why Spenser?" Wyatt asked, voicing the question foremost on Samantha's mind. "There's no way you could have known Spenser had found out about Ponsonby stealing the blueprints. Your blueprint wasn't among those Spenser got ahold of because you already had it back."

"Yes, you were quite helpful in that regard."

Wyatt frowned. "And why did you ask for my help getting yours back if you were planning to kill Ponsonby, anyway?"

"That wasn't really what I wanted your help with," Mr. Leclerc said. He was watching Wyatt with something approaching glee, and Samantha felt a sense of dread. "It was just the necessary first step."

"First step?"

"Oh, yes, Mr. Wyatt, I couldn't have done any of this without you." Mr. Leclerc grinned at Wyatt's befuddlement. "I needed a connection between Ponsonby and Spenser, and I needed someone, preferably someone with the ear of a police detective, to make that connection for the police."

"What do you mean, you needed a connection between them?" Wyatt asked. "They were connected. Spenser had one of Ponsonby's blueprints."

"And your card. I needed to make sure you were consulted so you could identify them."

Samantha stifled a gasp.

"You planted the blueprint in Spenser's house?" Wyatt said. "And you knew where Ponsonby kept them because...I told you."

Samantha's heart broke at the look of shock and regret in Wyatt's eyes.

"I see you aren't completely brainless," Mr. Leclerc said with contempt. "I never would have guessed after how easy it was to manipulate you. Mr. Wyatt, the hero, the clever Society detective. You couldn't pass up an opportunity to prove yourself, could you? All it took was a word in the ear of George Canard, and you were breaking into Ponsonby's office. I knew he kept the blueprints together and that you'd see the others when you found mine. I must admit, I overestimated your initiative there. I expected you to investigate him immediately, but you didn't. No matter. You remembered them, at least, when I planted them in Spenser's house with your card, so it still worked. I always plan for contingencies."

"But why Mr. Spenser?" Samantha asked, yanking the binding as hard as she could as she tied the final knot so that Mr. Leclerc grunted in pain. "You wanted Mr. Ponsonby to be blamed for a murder to explain his fake suicide, so you fabricated a connection between them to give him a motive. But why did you choose Mr. Spenser? He was a good, charitable man."

"If he had truly been a good man, he would not have stopped funding my recorded music player," Mr. Leclerc spat out. "He was so enamored of the speed of industrial progress that he refused to see that some things take time. The best things, the most important things, do."

"That's why you killed him? Because he stopped funding your research?"

"I gave him every opportunity. I practically begged him to reconsider, to recognize the importance of what I was doing, but he refused to hear me out. Said he had better uses for his money. I couldn't let that stand."

"But," Samantha began, appalled at what she was hearing, "I chose not to fund your research, and you didn't kill me. Or were you planning to?"

Mr. Leclerc scoffed. "Don't be absurd. The situations are completely different. Spenser *did* fund my research for a time, then stopped. You never began. If I killed everyone who rejected my proposal, my back garden would be overflowing with bodies. Not everyone has vision. But Spenser did, at one point. He saw the need for my invention, the genius of it, and he lost faith."

"Or perhaps he saw reason," Wyatt suggested.

Samantha tensed, expecting anger from Mr. Leclerc, but the smile he gave Wyatt was almost indulgent.

"I would not expect you to understand. You have no appreciation for the arts—no soul. You live in a world of black and white. Such a dull existence, I cannot but pity you."

"If I were you," Wyatt said, "I'd be much less concerned with others' souls than with my own."

"Unnecessary. I have no intention of dying anytime soon."

"Your intentions are irrelevant. You'll hang for your crimes."

"You think so?"

He raised a supercilious eyebrow, and the hint of a sneer played around his lips. Samantha looked over at Wyatt and saw his brow furrow, no doubt wondering the same thing she was. Did Mr. Leclerc know something they did not? Had he fabricated evidence that would exonerate him?

Taking advantage of their distraction, Mr. Leclerc suddenly twisted around, knocking Samantha back and wrenching his hands from Wyatt's. He wrapped long fingers around Wyatt's wrist, forcing the arm that held the gun upward towards the ceiling. Wyatt fought back, elbowing him in the face. Mr. Leclerc's head jerked back, but he did not release his grip.

"Get back!" Wyatt shouted, his eyes pleading with Samantha as he and Mr. Leclerc wrestled for control of the gun.

Samantha obeyed, scooting back with the intention of ducking behind the desk, but her fingers brushed metal and she looked down to see Mr. Leclerc's revolver where he had dropped it. She snatched it up and, with no time to check how many bullets it still held, raised it towards the struggling pair. Wyatt was on his back now, the arm with the gun stretched above him as Mr. Leclerc strained to reach it. Samantha's hands were shaking as she took aim, but then Wyatt shoved Mr. Leclerc off and he was back on top. She released the hammer and lowered the gun, afraid of hitting Wyatt.

The two men began to roll on the ground. Now Mr. Leclerc was on top, now Wyatt. Grunts and curses spewed forth in equal measure. Samantha's pulse was racing, her heart in her throat. She felt powerless to help and yet she felt she must do something. Wyatt was back on top, and he had pinned one of Mr. Leclerc's arms with his knee. The gun was trapped between them. She saw a look of triumph on Mr. Leclerc's face, then she heard a gunshot.

The ringing in her ears was louder and more insistent than before. It drowned out the sound of her breath's sharp intake and the clatter of the revolver as it slipped from her numb fingers to the wooden floor.

Wyatt's shock seemed frozen on his face. Samantha's heart skipped a beat. She felt as though she were moving through molasses as she rose to her knees and began to crawl towards him.

"Stay back!"

His arm shot out to hold her back, and he turned to face her. She could see streaks of blood on his left cheek and across his temple. His eyes were wide, and his chest heaved with fast, irregular breaths.

"Don't..." he began. She could hear him better now. The ringing had gone. His voice was shaking. "Don't come any closer. Please. I don't...you won't want..."

He pushed himself unsteadily to his feet and stepped over Mr. Leclerc. It was only then that her eyes dropped to the man who lay still, immobile on the floor. The ghost of his final grin remained, but the eye that she could see stared, unseeing, above him.

Samantha looked up at Wyatt in shock as he stepped in front of her, blocking her view.

"I thought you...but Mr. Leclerc..." she stuttered. "Are you hurt?"

Wyatt shook his head, and relief coursed through her. Then he held out a hand and pulled her up.

"What happened?" she asked, searching his face.

He ran a hand over his jaw. One of his fingers brushed the blood on his cheek. He flinched and dropped his hand.

"He kept trying to grab the gun," Wyatt said, his voice hollow, his gaze locked on some point behind her. "He had part of it, and I think he was trying to pull it free. My hand was under his, but he didn't realize...My finger was near the trigger. When he was twisting the gun, he squeezed my hand...His face. I don't want you to see his face."

Samantha wrapped her arms around his waist and held him tight. For a long time, he didn't move. Then his arms came around her and his fingers wound into her hair. That was how they still stood when Inspector Whicher arrived sometime later.

*****

By the time they had finished answering Whicher's questions and been released to go home, it was past nine o'clock. Wyatt supposed he ought to be hungry—they'd missed supper, after all—but he wasn't. He wasn't anything. He felt numb. He and Samantha didn't speak as they climbed into the hired gig. They were silent all the way to Madge's.

"I don't think I'll go in," Wyatt said when they reached Grosvenor Square. "I'm tired, and I'm sure you are as well."

She nodded, but when he brought the carriage to a stop in front of Madge's door, she didn't move.

"Wyatt," she said, and he tensed at her tone. It was too gentle, too understanding. But her next words surprised him.

"There's something I never told you about what happened after...after Charles died."

He turned to look at her, and she gave him a strained smile.

"In truth, it began before his death, after my aunt and uncle were killed, but his death made it worse."

Wyatt could see that it was costing her to speak. He reached over and took her hand. Her lips trembled as she continued.

"I began to have nightmares. Vivid nightmares. I still have them from time to time, though they are less frequent. I relive what I witnessed. It's as though I'm experiencing it all over again."

He'd been afraid something like that might happen. He'd tried so hard to prevent her from seeing Charles, but she'd fought against him.

"Stop it," she said.

"What?"

"You're scowling, and I'm sure you are chastising yourself for not keeping me from watching Charles die, but that was never your responsibility. Nor is it why I am telling you this." She sighed. "I struggled with sleep for those first few months after and, while Madge knew I wasn't sleeping, she didn't know why. I didn't want to tell her because I was afraid it made me look weak or childish or possibly even mad. I didn't tell you for the same reasons."

"Why are you telling me now?" he asked.

Samantha gave him a searching look.

"What happened back there" —she pointed in the direction they had come— "no one should experience."

"It was nothing," Wyatt said dismissively, hoping to forestall any further discussion.

"No, it wasn't. I know you want to protect me, and I thank you for stopping me from seeing what I couldn't unsee, but you saw it. You watched him die in a horrific way right in front of you. Whatever you are feeling right now—whatever you are pushing down so that I won't see it—it doesn't make you less of a man."

As he watched her eyes glisten in the moonlight, he marveled briefly how, for all she complained that he was inscrutable, she could read him so well.

"I tried to hide how I was feeling after Charles died," she said. "I thought I had to do it alone. But you don't. I'm here."

It was a beautiful sentiment, and he knew she meant it, but a lifetime of pushing back his emotions whenever they threatened his self-control could not be undone in a night.

"Thank you," he said.

She seemed to be waiting for him to say more and, when he didn't, a brief pang of disappointment flashed across her face before she smoothed her expression.

"Good night, Wyatt," she said.

"Samantha, wait," he said when she moved to get down from the carriage. It was an effort to force himself to speak up, but he hated that he'd hurt her, and he didn't want her to leave feeling as she did. She turned to look at him, and he steeled himself before saying, "I feel...tired. Exhausted, really. And a little like I might be sick."

Samantha sank back into her seat.

"I'm sorry," she said, resting a hand on his leg.

"I can't lay claim to any other feelings," Wyatt said, the words coming more easily. "I'd rather not try to call them up."

"I understand."

He realized then that she did understand, and that thought brought him comfort he hadn't known he needed. They sat in a silence of mutual contentment until Samantha shivered and drew her shawl tighter around her. The movement reminded Wyatt that they were sitting in a carriage outside Madge's, and it was getting late.

"You should go," he said.

"I know." She reached up and kissed him on the cheek. "Thank you. I know that wasn't easy."

"I love you."

"I love you, too."

He didn't think he would ever tire of saying it or, especially, of hearing her say it back.

NINETEEN

Walking down Pall Mall on his way to the United University Club on Sunday afternoon, Wyatt hardly noticed his surroundings. Images kept flashing before his eyes: Ponsonby lying in a pool of blood, the look on Leclerc's face as he whipped out his revolver, Samantha standing tall with a pistol pointed at Leclerc. Whenever a flash of Leclerc's lifeless, mangled face appeared, he forced it back down, but the effort was exhausting.

Wyatt was so preoccupied that he didn't notice George until he was right in front of him, his coat more rumpled than usual and dark circles lining his eyes. He seemed to check himself as Wyatt focused weary eyes on him, and the furrow between his brows deepened.

"You look like death," he said.

"You don't look so wonderful yourself," Wyatt replied.

"It's been a rough week."

"I can well imagine."

"I've had a tip from my friend in the Society pages," George said. "There was a rumor spreading at a ball last night that Miss Kingston's story—the one you offered me as an exclusive and which I printed in my paper—was a lie. They're saying she lied to hide her identity from Skinny Jim."

Wyatt had forgotten about Madge talking to the gossips in the midst of all that happened after. He was almost impressed at their quick work.

"Oh?" he said, not in a mood to be helpful.

"Is it true?" George snapped. "Did you make a complete fool out of me with that 'exclusive interview'?"

"That was not my intention," Wyatt said evenly. "Much of what she told you was true. We just altered certain facts to protect her."

"You lied to me!" George shouted. Several passersby stared at them, but George ignored them. "I don't care about your intentions. The fact is, you looked me in the face and lied to me."

"You said from the start you knew there was more to the story," Wyatt pointed out. "You even told me that if I wanted a favor, that was the price."

"Yes, but I didn't expect a complete rewrite!"

"I'm not going to apologize," Wyatt said. "If that's what you're looking for, you may as well leave. You and I both know you would sell me out in a heartbeat for a story. Our friendship has always been tenuous at best. And when have you ever cared about the truth, anyway? You embellish all the time. So, embellish. Make yourself the hero of the story for helping to protect Miss Kingston."

A smirk crept across George's face.

"Alright, you've got me," he said. "I may have already half-written just such a story. I only wanted an apology."

"How about I give you something better?" Wyatt said. "Information."

"I can live with that."

Wyatt looked around to make certain they could not be overheard, then said, "Inspector Whicher knows who killed Mr. Spenser."

George squinted and grimaced, shrugging his shoulders.

"That's good for him and the man's family, I suppose, but it's hardly going to interest people now after the attack on Sir Anthony. It's old news."

There was a sad sort of irony in George's lack of interest in the case, considering how intimately, if unwittingly, he had been involved. Wyatt wanted to take him to task for introducing him to Leclerc, but he didn't feel like explaining everything that had happened, particularly not to George.

"It's not just some robbery gone wrong," he said instead. "It's much more complicated than that. Think, two more bodies complicated."

George's eyes lit up. "Now that's intriguing."

"I won't say more," Wyatt said. "You can ferret out the rest."

"Yes, I can." George looked as though Christmas had come early as he bounced up and down on the balls of his feet. "Thank you. And, to prove to you that we really are friends, I'll tell you something, too."

He stopped bouncing and became serious. "This attack on Sir Anthony. It's aroused so much contention in just these few days that some MPs are calling for reinstitution of aggressive criminal justice measures—undoing the past few years of reforms. Harsher punishments, no parole, et cetera. A lot of dangerous people are unhappy about this, as you can imagine, and while they look for someone to blame, the finger points pretty solidly at Skinny Jim."

Glancing around, George lowered his voice. "It's well known in certain circles that Sir Anthony owed him money he couldn't repay. An attack like this is exactly the sort of thing Skinny Jim does when he wants to make a point. Only he went too far this time, attacking an MP in front of witnesses like that. No one is saying anything overtly. No one's got the guts yet. But, it's starting to sound to me like the beginnings of a mutiny."

Wyatt raised his eyebrows. "I didn't think anyone would dare. Or that anyone could. As far as I can tell, he's got friends in every level of the city."

"I'm not saying it will work," George said, "or even that it will definitely happen, but he's stirred up a lot of anger. I'd say if he's ever had a weak moment, it's now, and he's made plenty of enemies over the years along with those friends."

*****

Samantha had never been romantic. Before her inheritance, she'd seen marriage as a necessary and practical arrangement, and after, it had seemed unnecessary at best. Consequently, she had no childhood dreams or imaginings to hold up beside her experience. Monday was just another day. And yet, it wasn't.

As she stood before her vanity mirror in the white silk organza gown Madge had chosen with a crown of flowers in her dark hair, Madge's family diamonds gracing her neck, she was struck with a sense of unreality. It was her wedding day. She was getting married. Not to some staid, older man as she had always thought, with whom the best she could hope for was a comfortable, quiet future, but to Wyatt—kind, clever, handsome, wonderful Wyatt who loved her and whom she loved. She didn't know what their future held, but she knew there was no one else she wanted to discover it with.

Eden entered as Alice was placing the veil on Samantha's head.

"You look beautiful," she said, coming forward to embrace her. She stepped back, still holding Samantha's hands, and looked her over. "Are you ready?"

"I think so," Samantha said, feeling suddenly nervous.

"They're waiting downstairs," Eden said. "Madge sent me to fetch you. My uncle is waiting outside the door to escort you down."

Her uncle—Lord Bradwell—had intended to return to the country after the Derby, but Madge had persuaded him to remain for a few days. Once Samantha and Wyatt got engaged, he had agreed to stay through their wedding and even offered to walk Samantha down the aisle. She had accepted gratefully, not only because she had no remaining close male relatives to perform the honor, but also because she had come to view Madge and her husband as family.

"It's done, miss," Alice said, shaking out the veil so that it trailed elegantly behind Samantha.

Samantha turned to thank her and saw that Alice's eyes were glistening.

"You do look beautiful, miss," she said with a sniff.

"Thank you, Alice."

Then, heedless of how odd it might look to Eden, Samantha threw her arms around Alice. Though stiff at first, Alice relaxed enough to return the gesture, letting go quickly as Samantha pulled back.

Samantha felt a prickle in the corner of her eye and blinked back a tear as she smiled at Alice, then turned to follow Eden out the door.

The ceremony was a blur. What Samantha remembered most about it was her first sight of Wyatt when she entered the drawing room on Lord Bradwell's arm. His dark hair—unruly even at such an auspicious occasion—and golden-brown eyes filled her with a sense of calm. She had walked past the seated guests, visible only out of the corners of her eyes, with her gaze fixed on him, and when they stood together before the vicar and he smiled at her, she knew she was where she belonged.

Before she had quite registered what was happening, they were saying their vows, then they were proclaimed man and wife and Wyatt was kissing her.

It was only when they moved to the dining room for the wedding breakfast that Samantha was able to take note of their guests. Lord Aston was there, of course. Lord Bradwell's sister, Lady Chesterton, had been invited because Madge said she would never hear the end of it if she weren't. She had brought her daughter, Miss Fanshaw, and her daughter's friend, Miss Thorpe. Samantha had invited Mrs. Heywood, and she found it amusing to watch Lady Chesterton's look of horror as Mrs. Heywood spoke to her, her cockney accent more pronounced than usual.

As Wyatt's brother took a seat beside Lord Bradwell, Samantha realized that Wyatt's mother was notably absent.

"Is your mother ill?" Samantha asked Wyatt as they sat beside each other near the middle of the table.

"No," Wyatt said with a wry smile, "merely sulking. She refused to attend in protest."

"Why?" Samantha asked, perplexed. "I thought she wanted you to marry me for my fortune."

"Yes, but she wanted us to marry in front of all of Society at St. George's, Hanover Square."

"She must be so disappointed," Samantha said with a growing smile.

"I think she hoped her refusal to attend would make me rethink my plans," Wyatt said. "Instead, it gave me a reason to be glad of our need to marry discreetly."

His brow furrowed suddenly, and he leaned closer to Samantha, searching her face as he said, "Does it bother you that we weren't able to have a real wedding?"

"This is a real wedding," Samantha said, "or did I misunderstand when the vicar said 'man and wife'?"

His lips twitched. "You know what I mean. You deserved a big wedding with as many guests as you could want, all there to see you in your beautiful dress."

"Stop." Samantha put a hand on Wyatt's chest and looked him in the eyes so that he would see her sincerity as she said, "I had as many guests as I could want. A few more than I wanted, truth be told. And the only one I want to see me in my beautiful dress is you."

He reached down and cupped the side of her face, his eyes drinking her in. Then he leaned forward and captured her mouth with his. He didn't seem to have noticed that they were in a room full of people and, after a moment, neither did she.

"Miss Kingston!"

At Eden's son's familiar shriek, Samantha broke off the kiss and looked around, hoping to head him off before he plowed into her. She needn't have worried, however. Lord Aston was nearby and scooped the boy up seconds before his crumb-filled face reached her skirts. He winked at Wyatt, and Samantha blushed, knowing he had seen their kiss. Then, he addressed the boy.

"What's this?" he said, holding William at arm's length and looking him up and down. "Why, Miss King—Mrs. Wyatt, it appears a monkey has escaped from Regents Park and found its way to our gathering. I'll just deliver him back to the zoo, shall I?"

Suspended above the floor, William giggled as he kicked his legs and struggled to break free.

"I think I see the monkey's keeper," Samantha said as Eden came towards them, her expression apologetic.

"No!" William shrieked. "I'm not a monkey, I'm a boy!"

"A boy?" Lord Aston pretended shock. "Surely not!"

"He's a naughty boy, that's what he is," Eden said.

As she fixed a stern look on William, he stopped swinging his legs and looked sheepish. Then he swiped a sleeve across his face, smearing the crumbs and jam. Eden sighed. She held out her arms, and Lord Aston set William in them.

"Thank you, my lord," she said. Then she looked down at her son and added, "Thank the gentleman, William. He saved you from ruining Mrs. Wyatt's beautiful dress."

"Thank you, sir."

"My lord," Eden corrected.

"Thank you, my lord, sir."

Samantha could hear Wyatt laughing behind her, and she bit her lip to keep from joining him.

"You're welcome," Lord Aston said with a gravity that belied the laughter in his eyes.

"I'm a lord, too, you know," William said. "Lord Stuart-Lane."

"I did know that," Lord Aston said, smiling. "And, seeing that we are peers, if you'd like, you may call me Aston rather than 'my lord' and I could call you Stuart-Lane."

William's eyes lit up. Then he frowned.

"I don't mind calling you Aston," he said, "but could you call me William? The other name is too long."

"If you like, William."

William beamed and Eden mouthed "Thank you" to Lord Aston before carrying her son off to find a serviette.

"You may call me Aston as well," Lord Aston said, turning to Samantha. "Now that you've married the nearest thing I have to a brother" —he clapped Wyatt on the shoulder— "I consider us family."

Wyatt grunted and shoved his friend off, but he was smiling. A contented happiness filled Samantha.

"I would be honored," she said. "And you must call me Samantha."

Time continued to lurch forward in fits and spurts. One minute they were eating their first bites of poached egg; the next, their plates had been whisked away. One minute Lady Chesterton was exclaiming over the lace detail on Samantha's veil, and the next, Madge was announcing the bridal pair's imminent departure.

Samantha and Wyatt said farewell to their friends as Alice and Wyatt's valet, Durand, directed the packing of their trunks in the carriage that would take them to the train station. There were tears in her eyes as Samantha embraced Eden and William, Aston, Madge and even Lord Bradwell. Then she and Wyatt climbed into the carriage across from Durand and Alice, and they were off to the station.

Samantha still had no idea where they were going. Wyatt had offered to tell her, had even asked for her input, but she wanted it to be a surprise. They didn't talk much in the carriage. The presence of the servants made private discourse impossible, but Wyatt slid his hand into Samantha's after sitting down and didn't let go until just before they arrived at the station.

Durand collected their tickets while Alice found porters for the luggage. The station was crowded and noisy as ever, and Samantha held tight to Wyatt as they were jostled to and fro. Eventually, Durand and Alice departed for the second-class carriages, and Wyatt led Samantha to their private, first-class carriage.

When he shut the door behind them, there was silence for the first time that day.

"Finally," Wyatt said.

He took Samantha's hand and pulled her to him. She came willingly, her growing smile matching his. He wrapped his arms around her, holding her tight against him, and bent down to kiss her. She could feel his heartbeat quicken beneath her palm and she smiled against his lips.

"We're not alone," she said, as she pulled back. "Not yet. The conductor will be by soon for our tickets, and anyone could walk in."

"Let them."

He drew her back to him and kissed her with such passion that she forgot all her objections. Soon, pins were flying from her hair as he dragged his fingers through it until the style Alice had so carefully arranged was lost, and Samantha's curls tumbled around her shoulders.

There must have been a knock at the door, but they didn't hear it. Their first awareness of the conductor came when he cleared his throat beside them. They broke apart to see a short, balding man, face red with embarrassment, holding out a hand to check their tickets.

"I beg your pardon," Wyatt said as Samantha turned away and tried to gather what was left of her dignity. "I have them right here."

When the conductor had left, Wyatt began to laugh.

"It wasn't funny," Samantha said, stifling a grin. "That poor man. He could hardly look at me he was so embarrassed."

"Serves him right for interrupting us."

"It wasn't his fault. I told you he would be by soon."

Wyatt dropped onto the seat and leaned back, putting his hands behind his head. "Very well, it was my fault. Though I don't blame him for being scandalized by your appearance." He allowed his gaze to travel over her body in a way that brought a different sort of flush to her cheeks than the embarrassment of moments ago. "With your hair down like that, you are positively alluring, Mrs. Wyatt."

A thrill shot through her to hear that name on his lips.

"Is that so?" she asked archly.

Wyatt cast a glance at the door. When he returned his gaze to her, the smile on his face held a hint of mischief and something more that filled her with anticipation.

"I've just realized," he said. "There's a lock on the door."

TWENTY

Samantha yawned as she opened her eyes and stretched. Rolling onto her side, she smiled at the sleeping form beside her. Wyatt lay on his stomach with his arms up by his head, facing away from her. She watched the rhythmic rise and fall of his broad, muscular back for a minute, marveling at how the sight of him in her bed could be at once strange and familiar.

Careful not to wake him, Samantha sat up and shifted to the edge of the bed. Her fingers searched the thin netting that surrounded it until she found the division between panels. She created a small gap for herself and slipped out. As she crossed to the window, she heard the opening notes of the hauntingly beautiful *muezzin*. The call to prayer had been one of her first intimations that they were truly in a different part of the world when she heard it sung as they stepped off the boat in Cairo two weeks ago.

Of all the places they had visited in the two months since she and Wyatt had been married, Egypt was her favorite. From the towering pyramids of Giza to the intricately decorated pillars of the temple of Luxor to the sparkling waters of the Nile as seen from the deck of a dahabeeyah, she had loved it all.

Samantha wrapped her dressing gown, which she found

thrown across a chair, around her and opened the shutters. Their room in Shepherd's Hotel overlooked the terrace on which European guests took their tea, as well as the street beyond it. As it was dawn, the terrace was empty and the street relatively quiet, but Samantha knew it would soon teem with life.

A grunt of frustration drew her attention to the bed, and she saw Wyatt wrestling with the mosquito netting. She laughed and went to extricate him.

"You do this every morning," she said. "I would think you'd be used to it by now."

Free of the netting, which lay open between them, Wyatt grabbed her around the waist and pulled her onto his lap.

"Maybe I am," he said, leaning down and kissing her neck. "Maybe it's just an excuse to bring you back to bed."

Her heart skipped a beat at that, and she almost let him distract her, but after a moment, she pulled back. When he tried to kiss her again, she put a hand over his mouth.

"No," she said firmly, forcing her own mouth into a frown. "You promised. All of the dragomen say that climbing the pyramids is best done out of the heat of the day. We need to get ready if we're to get there in time."

Wyatt sighed as she removed her hand. "Very well. But..." He brightened. "Does that mean we'll be back here by midday?"

She laughed. "If you like."

"I do."

He kissed her again and might have derailed their plans if not for the knock at the door. Muttering under his breath, Wyatt got to his feet and went to find his dressing gown. Then he stepped through the connecting door to his room, but not before sending Samantha a final wink.

"Come in," Samantha said, and Alice entered.

Climbing the pyramids was not as simple as it sounded. For

one, the stones were too far apart to do so easily, particularly in skirts, so locals were hired to help the ladies and any unathletic gentlemen. One or two would stand on the stone above and pull, occasionally assisted by more men pushing from behind. Samantha and Wyatt, along with Durand and Alice, were assisted by a group of four men. They were friendly enough and clearly at ease as they chatted with one another in Arabic, but Samantha couldn't help feeling embarrassed at the need for assistance. She almost asked Ibrahim, their dragoman who served as both guide and translator, to apologize to the men, but she wasn't sure what for. For asking them to do their jobs? Or perhaps for being there at all—silly, foreign tourists that they were.

She sometimes wondered how the locals felt about all of the European travelers. Did they welcome the income they provided? Or did they resent their presence—forced on them by the French who had taken over governance of their land. Her fear that it might be the latter had begun to mar her enjoyment of Egypt, much as she otherwise appreciated its beauty.

When they had reached the highest point of the pyramid on which one could stand and Alice, the last to arrive, had been assisted to her feet and dusted her skirts, they all looked out at the view. For a moment, Samantha forgot to breathe. Her eyes widened as she tried to take in everything at once. All of Egypt lay before her, spreading out for miles in every direction. There was the half-buried statue of the sphinx. There, the Nile River, glittering in the sunlight. There, the bustling city of Cairo. And everywhere else was a sea of sand, stretching to meet the sky.

Wyatt wrapped his arms around her from behind, his chin coming to rest on her head. She leaned back against him and smiled as a surge of contentment washed over her. For the first time in her life, she felt at peace.

When they returned to Shepherd's, a telegram awaited them.

Wyatt thanked the *sufragi* who had given it to him and tucked it away as he led Samantha up to their rooms. When she suggested that she call Alice to help her change so they could get lunch, he insisted on being the one to help her and, with the distractions this help entailed, it was some time before they were ready to eat. By then, the telegram had been forgotten so that it wasn't until just before dinner that Wyatt remembered it.

Samantha was sitting before the mirror as Alice pinned up her hair while they discussed the street food they had sampled that afternoon. Wyatt had already dressed and was sitting on the edge of the bed while he waited for her. She saw him open the telegram. His eyes scanned it quickly, then widened. His face paled and he stared at it, frozen.

"What is it?" Samantha asked, dread gripping her. "What's wrong?"

Mutely, Wyatt handed her the paper.

TOM THROWN FROM HORSE STOP LIFE THREATENING INJURIES STOP COME HOME IMMEDIATELY STOP

Samantha looked up to see Wyatt watching her. He looked so lost, so vulnerable, that she felt her heart squeeze.

"Alice," she said, turning to her maid, "find Durand. We need tickets on the next ship home."

Days of travel by boat, train and carriage had taken their toll, and as the hired carriage from the station trundled over a rough patch of road, Samantha pressed her fingers to her temple against an oncoming headache. Beside her, Wyatt stared out the window. His normally clean-shaven face was shadowed with stubble, and his eyes were red from lack of sleep.

"How much farther, do you think?" Samantha asked.

"Ten minutes or so."

He lapsed back into silence. Samantha traced the back of his hand with her fingers.

"Do you see that?"

He was pointing out the window. Samantha leaned across him and could just see, through a break in the trees that lined the road, the edge of a pond. She nodded.

"Tom and I used to swim there every summer when we were younger. It was filthy and full of algae and other water plants, but it was the only water around. I almost drowned once when my feet got tangled in the plants that grew along the edge. Tom had to cut me free."

He stopped talking then, and she saw him swallow hard. Squeezing his hand, she leaned her head on his shoulder. He put his arm around her and kissed her head. They stayed like that until the trees on either side of the road began to thin.

"We're almost there," Wyatt said, sitting straighter and looking out the window again.

Samantha sat up and reached for her hat, which she had set on the seat opposite when they entered the carriage.

"You'll be able to see it better from this side," Wyatt said. "If you look now, you'll see..."

His voice trailed off. Concerned by his stricken expression, Samantha leaned forward to look out the window.

Boxley Abbey, Wyatt's family seat in Kent, was, like many buildings of its age, a pastiche of old and new. The grey and yellow stone of the 12th century abbey remained in places, primarily the chapel, but there were clear Tudor and Stuart additions as well. In other circumstances, Samantha might have been intrigued to see the place Wyatt had called home for so many years, but in that moment, the only detail that mattered was the heavy black cloth that draped the windows.

Samantha's heart sank. She looked at Wyatt and knew that he

had seen it, too. His face was pale, and there was a haunted look in his eyes, but he didn't speak to reference the black cloth or what they both knew it meant, so Samantha did not, either. Instead, she leaned against him, sliding her hand into his and squeezing it, showing him he was not alone.

The household staff had arranged themselves in two rows on either side of the front door. Footmen and maids alike wore black armbands. They stood to attention as Wyatt stepped out of the carriage and turned back to help Samantha. As she and Wyatt walked past them, they kept their eyes lowered, but she spied more than one furtive look sent their way.

No doubt they were curious. Wyatt had told her he'd hardly been to his family's country home since he left school. They must be wondering what sort of person he had become and, now that his brother had died without heirs, what sort of master he would be.

When they reached the head of the line, the butler bowed somberly to Wyatt and Samantha in turn, then said to Wyatt, in solemn tones, "Welcome home, Lord Boxley."

Author's Note

One thing I learned in researching for this book is that you can find very detailed records of sporting events, like the Oxford-Cambridge boat race and the Derby even as far back as the mid-19th century. Though I didn't use the information, I found a list of every horse in the Derby that year as well as the odds laid on each. The winner started, if I remember right, at 40 to 1, so I imagine the race must have been very exciting to watch, if Wyatt and Samantha hadn't been otherwise occupied. The boat race of 1862 really did play out the way I described, with a steamer called Citizen J cutting in front of the Cambridge boat partway through the race. I decided it would be fun to put Wyatt and his friends actually on the steamer just to add to their frustration.

Angela Burdett-Coutts was a real person. I first learned about her from a Terry Pratchett book, *Dodger*. It seems he included her because he wanted to bring awareness of this extraordinary woman to a modern audience. In my case, at least, mission accomplished! Miss Coutts inherited a vast fortune from her independently wealthy stepmother and spent her whole life advocating for those most downtrodden in Victorian society, including the poor, "fallen" women, children, and animals. She was also a great collector of art.

Miss Coutts' friend Mr. Crabb-Robinson was also a real person. He kept a diary for years which was later published and can be viewed online. It's a great first-hand source of information about the time. It was through his diary that I learned about Dr. Skey and Mrs. Brown, who both traveled with Miss Coutts.

One of my favorite paintings in The National Gallery is *The Execution of Lady Jane Grey* by Delaroche. I wanted so much to feature it in the scene where Samantha and Wyatt visit the gallery but, while it was painted in 1833, it wasn't acquired by the gallery until 1902. The reason I mention it here is mainly to plug The National Gallery's Instagram page, which was how I learned about that painting as well as *The Tailor*, which did appear in this book. If you are at all interested in art, you should give The National Gallery a follow. You will learn a lot.

The phonautograph mentioned by Leclerc was invented in 1857 as a way to record sound waves on paper. It was, however, unable to play them back, so its significance was largely eclipsed by Edison's phonograph when it came along twenty years later. Many of the recordings of the phonautograph were saved, however, and with modern technology, are now able to be played for the first time. If you search YouTube for phonautograph recordings, you can hear a very scratchy recording of a man singing *Au Clair de la Lune* in 1860.

Mid-nineteenth century Britain was a time of great change. Centuries-old practices were made obsolete by new technology, leading to a complete upheaval in both rural and urban life. Though there were drawbacks and plenty of predictions of doom, as the century wore on and people adjusted to the change, there was also a growing sense of optimism. The world had changed so much and so fast that suddenly anything seemed possible. The nineteenth century saw the birth of the women's suffrage movement, the growth of labor unions, the founding of both the Royal Society for the Prevention of Cruelty to Animals and what became the National Society for the Prevention of Cruelty to Children (both of which were co-founded by Angela Burdett-Coutts), and more. I touched on some of this in previous books, but this book, which takes place during The International Exhibition of 1862—an event designed to celebrate Britain's progress as a nation—seemed the perfect place to highlight some of these issues.

Thank you for reading *An Exhibition of Malice*! If you liked it, please consider posting a review. If you would like to read more of Samantha and Wyatt's story, join my newsletter at www.emilylfinch.com to be notified when the next book releases. You can also follow me on Facebook or on Instagram @writer_elf.

Made in the USA
Middletown, DE
10 October 2024